HELL'S GLEN

H.J. RUSSELL

For Willeen & Bill

'O wad some Power the giftie gie us
  To see oursels as ithers see us!'

— **ROBERT BURNS**

(What a powerful gift it would be to see ourselves as others see us)

WARNING

This story contains information about sexual assault and/or violence which may be distressing to some audiences, but is essential to the plot. Reader discretion is advised.

PROLOGUE

Kathryn

Kathryn was allowed to take the path leading to the loch but she was forbidden to walk through the woods after school. Her mother would be angry if she knew she'd risked it. If her mum was sober.

She picked her way over the icy path. Regular walkers in these woods, she and the dog knew the trail well.

"C'mon Frisky" she called, seeing how far behind the elderly sheepdog had fallen.

She felt a stab of sadness watching him hobble through the glassy ditches, his long coat streaked with mud. He'd never been an energetic dog, even as a puppy, but at ten he'd slowed and she felt guilty for having taken him the long route. She'd needed the solace of the woods and an escape from the atmosphere at home after another argument between her mum and Phil. Mum was blind drunk and he was yelling at her and, although this wasn't unusual, the slap was. Kathryn had frozen in the hallway and listened as the beating escalated. When she heard dull thuds followed by grunts from her mother, she'd fled with the dog. At thirteen, she felt powerless against her stepfather.

After an hour of trudging between Scots pines in freezing temperatures, she was regretting not having swapped her footwear for something better than ankle boots. The path beneath her feet was slippery and she'd already fallen once. She followed the trail that led onto the top of the ridge and, when she reached the summit, she looked down over the steep gorge below where the river gouged a scar through the Avon valley. The wind whipped her hair and obscured her view, and she pulled the collar of her jacket against the cold.

Frisky's yelp startled her. He'd tumbled several feet down the incline and was struggling to get back up. She backtracked gingerly along the rough path, sliding on sheets of ice between the troughs. As she neared the dog, she slipped and fell hard. She heard the crack before pain shot through her ankle. Screaming, she slid down the banking, grasping at bramble tendrils before coming to rest in a small thicket of rhododendron bushes. She tried to sit up but the pain in her foot was excruciating and she gasped. She lay on her side, clasping her ankle, and sobbed as Frisky paced and barked on the ridge above. When the pain ebbed to a throb and she'd caught her breath, she wiped her face with her sleeve and attempted to pull herself up the banking using the roots and branches. Blood poured between her lacerated fingers.

She heard Phil's voice before she spotted him next to the dog and she froze.

Oh, please God, no!

Her step-father peered around the wood and the gorge below then called to her that he was on his way. Frisky barked and snarled but he ignored him. Phil was tall and powerfully built, and he'd no trouble in reaching her in his walking boots. Her heart thumped in her chest as he crouched beside her. She caught a strong whiff of stale body odour and alcohol; his jeans were ripped and his unkempt hair was greasy. Casting beady eyes over her, his gaze settled on the exposed flesh of her thigh where her tights had torn. She shied away and tried to pull down her school skirt.

"Can you stand?" he asked, extending a hand.

Kathryn shook her head. "Think my ankle's broken."

Scrubbing a hand over his unshaven chin, he looked around the thicket and the incline above. He stood up and stared at her as she lay helpless at his feet. The shadows had lengthened but the chill she felt was from his leer. She shuffled away from him, grasping at the undergrowth, the fright and pain making her cry out.

He seized her by her good ankle and pulled her deeper into the thicket, and she clawed at the earth and branches.

And then she screamed.

GENESIS

"This is my comfort in my affliction, that your promise gives me life."

— PSALM 119:50

Kathryn

Ten years later - January, Scotland

Pulling up the hood of her jacket against the sleet, Kathryn walked to the train station for her daily commute. She called into the local corner-shop, disappointed to see Abdul wasn't serving. She liked Abdul; he always had a smile and a friendly word, and he placed her change on the counter. This guy was new and he'd a feral look about him that made her uneasy. It was something about the eyes, the way they roved over her, and his wolfish grin. It reminded her of … she brushed the thought aside with a shiver. The shop was empty and a prickle of awareness trickled down her spine as his gaze followed her. When he ducked beneath the counter and made a beeline for her, she fled.

Heart pounding in her chest, she sprinted to the train station. The platform was quiet, one of the reasons she always left early for work.

She hated packed trains, preferring to get up at half past five rather than face a crush of bodies.

Half an hour later, she arrived at the headquarters of the Alba Mutual Society in Glasgow. She lowered her hood as she walked through the marble foyer towards the lifts. A man in a dark wool coat loitered in front of the doors, and he nodded a greeting. Ignoring him, she pulled her hair over her face and stared at the floor. The doors opened and he stepped inside and turned, his finger on the hold button. She glanced around; there was no one else.

"You getting in?" he asked, throwing her a curious look.

Shaking her head, she stepped back and let the lift doors close. She took the stairs to the fifth floor, where she swiped her door card and entered Alba Mutual's office. She'd worked here for almost two years, first as a temp doing admin, and then as assistant to the Head of IT, Tod Grantham. During the pandemic, she'd preferred working from home to being in the office. She loathed Tod but he'd given her the opportunity to work as a trainee software developer after she'd begged him for the position. Having left school with no qualifications, this was her chance to get a foot on the career ladder. But only if she passed the probationary period.

Almost three months into the role, she was delivering high-quality work well ahead of schedule and George, her team leader, had already approved her probation. Tod hadn't, and he'd put a meeting in her calendar to discuss it. She dreaded the thought of being alone in a room with him, knowing of his reputation.

She went to the toilet and examined her reflection in the mirror, wondering what she'd done to attract the attention of the man in the shop. Although she'd no boyfriend, she wore a wedding ring on her left hand which had belonged to her mother, and its presence was usually enough to deter an advance. She wore no makeup or perfume and her oversized clothing concealed her slender figure. Maybe it was the hair? Pulling her light brown tresses in a curtain around her face, she considered cutting it short. But then she wouldn't be able to hide behind it. She yanked her baggy jumper over her hands and down over her hips. Nothing attractive here, she thought.

After making a mug of strong tea in the staff kitchen, she sat at her desk and switched on her computer. As it whirred to life, she checked the personal mail on her phone. Scotty had sent her a message.

[Scotty] *Hey Moniker, when you meeting with fuck-knuckle?*

Kathryn chuckled. Scotty was one of her online friends. She didn't know his real name, and he didn't know hers. Although they'd never met in person, she and Scotty had known each other for many years after he'd rocked up in a Star Trek chat room. An infamous 'flamer', he'd been thrown out of dozens of forums for his sneering tirades and fiery invective. She adored his humour and never took offence, knowing he did it for a laugh or, in Internet parlance, the 'lulz'.

She typed a reply.

[Moniker] *This afternoon when everyone's gone home. Eek!*

[Scotty] *F-king dungjack better offer you the job or we'll be coming for the balding, attention-seeking douche bag*

[Moniker] *Its not the job offer that worries me*

After sending Scotty a smiley face, she checked no one was around and then hacked into Alba's personnel files. When she'd started as a temp, she'd heard gossip about the sexual harassment claims made against Tod, and she knew of his extra-marital relationship with Jane in Human Resources. But so far he'd kept his nose clean and he'd been promoted up the ranks in IT where few women worked. Kathryn spotted a new entry in his file detailing an allegation from Sandra, his current assistant. In her early twenties, Sandra was quiet, single and pretty; exactly the type of woman he'd prey upon.

She closed the files as people began to arrive in the office. The morning passed quickly and she delivered her code, fully tested and ready for quality assurance. She took lunch at her desk and made a start on her next task. One of the perks of working in IT was a half day on a Friday, and George and her colleagues wished her a good weekend as they packed up and left. She glanced at her watch realising her meeting with Tod was in a few minutes. Resentful of being kept back on a Friday and eager not to be alone with him, she'd tried to move it to earlier but Tod had declined.

With her stomach feeling as though it was full of snakes, she walked slowly through the deserted floor towards his large corner office. Tod glanced up when she knocked and entered.

"Take a seat Miss Sinclair," he said getting up from behind his desk.

"It's Ms."

Tod's sartorial choices had yet to evolve beyond Top Man and his cheap blue suit hung limply on his skinny frame. She recalled one of the women remarking that there's wasn't much meat on those bones for his wife and mistress to get hold of. She also remembered her grandmother's words about how you could tell a man from his shoes; what would she have made of Tod's brown pointy brogues? Tod picked up a manilla folder from his desk, on top of which sat a row of scrabble letters in a wooden holder that spelt *The Boss*.

Before joining her at the table, he closed the venetian blinds on the window overlooking the IT floor. He pulled up a chair opposite her, leant back and laced his fingers behind his head. Kathryn drew back in her chair and tugged on the sleeves of her sweater as his eyes swept over her and settled on her chest. She curled her shoulders in around herself and glanced at him through her curtain of hair.

Sighing, he said "So MIZZ Sinclair, your probation period's up next Friday. How do you think you've performed?"

She swallowed and in a shaky voice replied, "Uhm, well, I've completed all my work within the deadlines, and George seems happy with it."

Unclasping his hands, he bent towards her and raised an eyebrow. "But it's not just about the work, is it?"

Frowning, she said, "Err, how do you mean? I've done everything asked of me."

He gave a dark chuckle and shook his head. "Not quite, my dear. You're not easy to get along with." He opened the folder and began to read, "Doesn't socialise, lacks self-confidence, not a team player."

She gawped at him. "No one's said anything to me."

"They're not likely to if they find you unapproachable." He fixed her with his gaze. "I can't approve your probation until you demonstrate that you can be a lot friendlier towards your colleagues." He bent closer, "So how about you start now?"

With horror she saw him lock the door, stand in front of her and begin to lower his zipper.

"Show me how friendly you can be," he said, his voice slurring. "Then I'll sign off your probation."

Her heart thumped in her chest and she gasped for air. Shaking, she tried to get up. He pushed her shoulders down and stood before her as he fumbled with his underwear. She twisted her head away and gripped the chair for support. Frozen, she couldn't breathe, couldn't scream.

There was a knock on the door and a woman's voice, "Tod, you in there?" The handle turned. Another knock.

Cursing under his breath, he zipped himself up and glowered at Kathryn. In a low voice, he said, "We'll continue this discussion next week."

With an expansive smile, he opened the door and greeted Jane from HR. Pretty and petite with short platinum hair, she glanced from one to the other and shot Tod a questioning look.

"Come in," said Tod. "We were just discussing Kathryn's career progression but we've finished now." Turning to Kathryn, he smiled. "Have a lovely weekend, Kathryn."

Trembling, she pushed past Jane and fled.

~

"Jesus, who's rattled your cage?" asked Chris as he stumbled backwards under the onslaught.

Kathryn and Chris were training at the dojo as they did most Friday afternoons. The hall was empty except for them, and he held a foam punching pad against his chest for her to kick. Chris was one of few friends she had outside of cyberspace. They'd met when she was fifteen after her grandmother had encouraged her to take up karate, and they'd risen through the belts together. Now as senior grades, they were putting in extra practice ahead of the imminent black belt grading.

Winding up for another roundhouse kick, she unleashed her back leg with a thud on the pad and a grunt from Chris.

"I'm furious at myself," she muttered.

He put down the pad. "What's up?"

They sat at the back of the hall and she explained what had happened with her boss, and why she couldn't report him to the HR department since he was sleeping with the manager. She told him how much she needed the job and why she couldn't just up and leave.

"Sleazy bastard," fumed Chris, "want me to have a quiet word with him?"

She shook her head. "I've been training for years and I bloody froze. Couldn't move. What use is training if I can't stand up for myself?"

He took a slug from his water bottle and regarded her. "If you hadn't been interrupted, you might have kicked him in the happy sacks." Seeing her unconvinced expression, he added "Don't be too hard on yourself, he's the one to blame."

She sent him a rueful smile.

After a pause he asked, "Want to come for a drink with me tonight?"

"Sorry, can't, I'm busy."

He sighed and gazed heavenwards. "You're busy every night … well, every night I ask you out. Say yes, just this once."

Chris had been asking her out for as long as she'd known him and she always refused. It wasn't that he was unattractive – the opposite in fact – but he was her only friend in the real world and she didn't want to ruin that. And he didn't want for girlfriends; he seemed to have an endless string of admirers who never lasted more than a few weeks. Each time he finished with one, he'd ask Kathryn out. Recently he'd become more persistent.

"I just want to be friends," she said.

Chris tossed his karate belt into his kit bag. "Exactly, we're friends and we get along, it's a good basis."

Kathryn picked at a thread on her karate suit. "Let's not spoil what we have."

She glanced up to meet his hurt blue gaze.

His voice dropped to a low whisper. "You know how I feel about you. But in all the years I've known you, you've never once had a boyfriend. Or a girlfriend. Just give me a chance." His eyes searched her face.

Tears brimmed in hers. "I'm sorry, it's not that I don't like you … I just can't give you what you want."

She grabbed her kit bag and hurried home.

The bungalow lay in darkness and Kathryn made a mental note to put some lights on a timer switch. Since her grandmother had died, she hated returning to a cold, empty house, and now the cat had disappeared, it was worse. She missed Psi's furry body winding itself around her ankles, even if it was just to remind her that he needed feeding.

After pouring herself a glass of wine, she searched the fridge for a ready-meal. As she waited on the microwave's ping, she thought about Chris. She was fond of him and he was the only male she felt comfortable alone with, but she did not want him as a boyfriend. She didn't want anyone, and the thought of being with a man in that way made her shudder.

Haphephobia, her counsellor called it, the fear of being touched, together with genophobia, the fear of sexual intercourse. Knowing the medical terms did nothing to lessen the panic, terror and dread associated with them. At her next therapy session with Rosemary, she needed to discuss how she'd frozen in fear in Tod's office, and her anxiety at the thought of dating Chris, a man she liked and trusted. Tonight, however, there was a more immediate matter to attend to.

Carrying her wine and a bowl of steaming pasta, she padded through to the spare room and switched on the computer. The bank of monitors flickered to life, illuminating the seventies-style room with its swirly carpet and flowery curtains in a pale glow. The computer hummed as she launched the 1024-bit encrypted messaging application she'd developed, and pinged Pandora and Scotty. They were both online and waiting.

Part of a wider community known in the cyber world as Grey Nemesis, they described themselves as ethical hackers. Unlike those known as 'black hats', who set out to exploit and destroy, and 'white hats' who never strayed beyond legal boundaries, they considered themselves 'grey-hat' hackers who fell somewhere in between. Targeting only unscrupulous companies and individuals, they dispensed cyber justice. Swiftly. They never used their skills to benefit personally or to profit, but they'd been known to divert considerable funds to charities and deserving victims.

[Moniker] *Has GL given us the green light?*

[Scotty] *Aye aye Captain, it all checks out. Informant's a cop. Says Hendry's a known kiddy fiddler who got off on a technicality. They need the bastard caught. Urgently*

The Grey Nemesis collective got its tip-offs from various sources including jaded police officers, lawyers, social workers and teachers. Their leader, known as Grey Lady or GL, decided whom and what to target.

[Pandora] *Hendry's taken the bait*

Pandora had previously sent a log of her communication with Robert Hendry over the course of a few weeks in an online chat room. She'd been pretending to be a man of a similar ilk who'd access to merchandise he thought might interest him. The messages between Hendry and Pandora were sickening as Hendry believed Pandora was offering him an opportunity to abuse 'his' seven-year-old nephew. The liaison was scheduled to take place this evening at a flat close to where Hendry lived, and he'd already completed an online payment for the agreed amount. Pandora had instructed him to bring Duct tape, tissues and lube.

As she ate, Kathryn checked that everything was set, then replied.

[Moniker] *Everything and everyone's in place. Let's bag a paedo*

[Pandora] *I've messaged Hendry and he's on his way to the property*

Kathryn launched a window displaying CCTV images for them all to see, and she began recording. A grainy picture appeared of a scruffy, balding man in his fifties shambling down the street carrying a plastic carrier bag.

[Scotty] *Is that the worthless bag of shit? Cannae see his face …*

[Moniker] *It's him, just wait …*

She watched as Hendry approached a block of modern flats and pushed the buzzer next to the communal entrance door. She tapped her keyboard and the image on-screen switched to the camera above the door, the frame now filled with Robert Hendry's face.

As Hendry entered, she flicked the feed to display internal camera footage of him ascending several flights of stairs to a flat on the top floor, ensuring the images blended seamlessly together, with the date and time appearing on the bottom right of the screen. She watched as Hendry glanced around nervously and knocked on the door.

[Pandora] *He thinks he's meeting me, Pete Burns*

[Scotty] *Pete Burns? Really? Stupid dickfrog*

Pandora sent him a smiley face. With a few more keystrokes, the camera angle changed to one inside the flat. Hendry entered and was greeted by a younger man who introduced himself as Pete. They could hear the audio clearly as the two men shook hands.

Pete said, "He's in the back room waiting. I've given him a sedative but you'd best gag him. Don't want the neighbours complaining."

Hendry asked, "Where you gonna be? Not staying to watch?"

"Nah, pub across the road. You've got an hour. Only what we agreed, mind. Did you remember to bring lube? I cannae return him to my sister damaged."

"Won't he talk?" said Hendry, taking a tube of lubricant from his bag.

"Not if he knows what's good for him."

Hendry produced a chocolate bar. "I got him a sweetie for after. I'm no a monster."

They watched as the two men chuckled.

[Moniker] *I feel sick…*

Pete indicated the back bedroom and then departed. Hendry stood in the hallway and scrubbed a hand over his face. After a long pause, he took a step towards the exit.

[Scotty] *FUUUCK! He's going to bail? We might not have enough to nail the slimy fucktard if he does…*

Kathryn held her breath as she observed Hendry dither, and she cursed when he put a hand on the front door handle to leave. Suddenly, Hendry spun on his heel and marched towards the bedroom. Smiling, she switched the camera image to there and the surprise awaiting him. Instead of a sedated boy, two men not much smaller than a house greeted Hendry. She punched her fist into the air as they collared him. Roughly.

She switched off the cameras and audio feed for two minutes, as agreed, to allow the two vigilantes to have a quiet word with Hendry.

[Scotty] *Got the evidence we need. Well done all!*

[Pandora] *Great knowing he'll no longer be preying on children*

[Moniker] *Want to scrub my skin with a wire brush and Dettol after that*

[Scotty] *Chat's going mental. GLs given us kudos!*

Kathryn bundled all the recordings and transcripts together and uploaded them to the vigilante group and their police contact, while Pandora sent Hendry's payment to a children's charity. Afterwards, she chatted online with her friends and asked what was next for Grey Nemesis.

[Scotty] *GL wants us to lie low for a bit. We're taking a lotta heat for Sherwood*

Sherwood was the last major hack Grey Nemesis had carried out, so named because it was, in true Robin Hood fashion, about robbing the rich to give to the poor. Months in planning, they'd targeted the coffers of numerous corporations across the globe who'd profiteered from the Covid-19 pandemic. Determined to punish their unscrupulous behaviour, the group had diverted millions of dollars to victims, their families and charities. As part of this, Moniker, Pandora and Scotty had carried out reconnaissance by hacking into information held by government institutions including the IRS and several other US agencies. In doing so, they'd kicked up a storm.

She asked Scotty what he'd planned for the weekend and she laughed when he revealed he was going to intercept his neighbour's Amazon drone delivery of a smart coffee machine so he never had to wait on a cappuccino again. Pandora revealed she'd a date on Saturday, and she'd already vetted him thoroughly online. Kathryn felt a pang of sadness at having turned down Chris, certain he'd hook up with another girl soon. When Scotty inquired about her own plans, she explained what'd happened with her boss. After a string of expletives from her cyberbuddies, Scotty made her laugh.

[Scotty] *So you blowing the boss next week?*

[Pandora] *Ugh. Just hack in, approve the probation and give yourself a pay rise while you're at it. Make it look like Tod and Jane signed it off.*

[Moniker] *I've another idea...*

[Scotty] *Cannae wait. Til then, live long and prosper!*

～

It was Thursday and Kathryn had spent the week in avoidance. Avoiding men. Avoiding Chris. Avoiding her boss. It was going well until another meeting with Tod appeared in her work calendar for Friday afternoon. She'd had a knot in her stomach since receiving the invite, and at the thought of what she was about to unleash.

She blamed Scotty. He'd given her the idea with all his talk of Amazon deliveries and smart gadgets. It never ceased to amaze her what you could purchase online, and what gadgets manufacturers thought a good idea to connect to the internet. As a hacker, she loved this wave of new 'Internet of Things' products and appliances, but coffee machines, she decided, were much too important to risk being infected with malware.

She'd purchased two of her chosen gadget: one, she sent to herself; the other, direct to Tod care of the office. Earlier that day, she'd stifled a gasp when she spotted Tracy from Reception delivering the Amazon box to Tod's office. He'd been in a board meeting and it had sat on his desk all afternoon untouched, but Tod's absence had also given Kathryn the opportunity to add another device to his office.

She'd left work early, and had gone straight home and logged on. After checking everything was ready, Kathryn launched a couple of apps and pinged Scotty and Pandora.

[Moniker] *On-screen is Tod's office. You got popcorn?*

[Scotty] *Aye, cannae wait to see what you've planned for the vulgar little maggot*

While they waited for Tod to appear, she showed her buddies video footage of Tod having rough sex in his office with his mistress, Jane from HR.

[Moniker] *You know I can't bear to watch this kinda stuff, but it shows what he's like*

After the clip ended, Scotty replied.

[Scotty] *Ugh, you should see his come face!*

[Moniker] *No thanks*

[Pandora] *Love how you used his own web cam*

[Moniker] *This video feed's new, installed the camera today*

They didn't have long to wait before Tod appeared and closed the door.

[Moniker] *Show time!*

The picture was clear and Kathryn watched as he opened the box Tracy had delivered and removed the gadget inside. Perplexed, he turned it over in his hand.

[Scotty] *Oh no, you didn't?*

[Moniker] *Oh yes, I did!*

[Pandora] *WTF! Is that for real?*

[Moniker] *Aye. Please cyber gods, make him use it*

Holding her breath, Kathryn watched as Tod locked his door, closed the blinds and inspected the gadget. With a bemused expression, he read the accompanying gift note.

[Pandora] *Who does he think it's from?*

[Moniker] *Mistress Jane*

She chuckled as she watched Tod read the instructions and undo his trousers.

[Scotty] *FFS the stupid assbutt is putting it on!*

Kathryn watched as Tod freed himself from his underwear and poked his privates into the chastity cage for men. With a few quick taps of her fingers, she communicated with the device and locked it firmly into place around his penis. She'd practised already with its twin using miniature courgettes of a similar size. She laughed aloud at the look of panic on his face as the ring clamped around his length. Wide-eyed, he grasped at the gadget and tugged on it, to no avail.

[Pandora] *OMG funniest thing EVER*

[Scotty] *Fan-fuckin-tastic!*

Swearing, Tod scanned the instructions and attempted to install the manufacturer's app on his smartphone. He was still grappling with it when there was a knock at his office door. Eyes bulging, and in a falsetto voice, he asked who it was. He admitted Jane and locked the door behind her. Bent double laughing, Kathryn watched the pair of them tug on the chastity cage while, panic-stricken, Tod bounced from foot to foot.

[Scotty] *LMAO. You going to release the whiny little choad?*

[Pandora] *NOT YET PLEASE, this is way too funny*

[Moniker] *Eventually…*

[Scotty] *Guess he'll approve your probation after you show him the footage?*

[Pandora] *AND A PAY RISE*

[Moniker] *That's the plan, and I'll make sure he never harasses another woman or I'll be showing this to his BOSS and his WIFE*

Kathryn squealed with laughter at the expression on Tod's face as Jane used one hand to brace his balls and the other to tug on the chastity cage.

[Scotty] *Doesn't she realise you cannae change the laws of physics?*

Kathryn's doorbell sounded and she ignored it as she continued to chat with her buddies and laugh at the comedy show on-screen. It rang more insistently, and she ignored that too. Other than Chris, she'd no friends and she wasn't expecting any callers at this time of night.

Then someone began thumping loudly on the front door. Sighing, she let her friends know she'd be back.

[Moniker] *Doorbell, brb…*

JOB

Kathryn

"Kathryn Sinclair?" asked the man on her doorstep.

She stared at him, unable to tear her eyes from the deep scar on the left side of his face. His expression alone sent a wave of dread through her, never mind the four accompanying uniformed police officers.

Peering through the gap between the door and the jamb, she swallowed hard. "Uhm, yes, what's this about?"

Flashing a warrant card, he said, "Detective Sergeant James Denton, Police Scotland, may I come in?"

Oh, dear God, no!

She backpedalled into the hallway as the officers entered. Denton and a woman officer led her into the living room where he explained that she was being detained under various sections of the Computer Misuse Act, which he listed.

Kathryn felt the room pitch beneath her feet as he cautioned her with, "You are not obliged to say anything but anything you do say…"

Barely able to comprehend what was happening, she slumped into a chair and stared at him. Fear prickled down her spine as he explained that he was from the cyber-crime division. There were no handcuffs or shouting, just polite questions. Kathryn mumbled answers which the woman wrote down, while she watched a stream of uniformed officers trample through her home carrying boxes and evidence bags.

Denton snooped round the room, picking up a leaflet on a feminist lecture she'd planned to attend at Glasgow University. Dressed in a navy suit and tie, it was his demeanour, rather than his attire, that left her in no doubt he was in charge. After casting a disapproving eye over her bookcase, he selected Simone de Beauvoir's *The Second Sex* and fixed her with the full force of his icy glare. With a snort of disdain, he tossed it onto the floor and loomed over her using every inch of his six-foot height. Pulse racing, she began to tremble. He opened his mouth to say something only to be interrupted by peals of laughter from the back of the house.

"Jamie, you've got to see this," shouted an officer.

With a parting glower at her, he disappeared, leaving Kathryn with the female officer. He reappeared soon after and Kathryn saw his lips twitch in amusement as he asked his colleague to escort Kathryn to the bedroom. Several officers were huddled around her screen peering at Tod pulling frantically at the chastity gadget while Jane punched her finger at a smartphone. Tod began screaming.

Denton fixed Kathryn with a cold blue stare. "Care to tell me what that's about?"

Kathryn bit her bottom lip, fixed her eyes on the floor and said nothing.

Denton picked up the chastity ring and courgette lying next to her keyboard and shook his head. The officers sniggered. "Can you control that thing?" he said, pointing to the gadget onscreen.

Knowing the truth would incriminate her, she shook her head.

Denton raised an eyebrow. "Really? The poor bastard will need an angle grinder to get that off."

More sniggering.

When she responded with a shrug, Denton shot her a withering look and growled, "Get her out of my sight."

Jamie

October the following year, Scotland

DS James Denton slid into a corner table in the Happy Union pub, while his boss, Superintendent Gillian Millar, bought the drinks. It was a weekday lunchtime and the Happy Onion, as the local constabulary had nicknamed it, was quiet. Unchanged in all the years Jamie and his colleagues had been regulars, it boasted a brown and beige swirly carpet in the lounge, sticky worn vinyl at the bar, and nicotine-stained walls which bore black and white photos of a Glasgow that no longer existed. Someone had attempted to add charm with fake beams and horse brasses which appeared incongruous next to the fruit machine and television screen permanently tuned to a sports channel.

Jamie had slept badly after drinking on his own the night before, not an unusual occurrence these days, and a headache pounded behind his temples. Gill slid a lager towards him.

"Well, it's not good news if you're buying me a pint," he muttered.

She offered him a rueful smile as she took the seat opposite. Denton liked Gill, she was a good boss and she'd been supportive after his mother had died of cancer the previous year, and later when he'd split with his partner.

"Thought it better to chat here than at the station. The panel made their decision. They're giving it to Dean."

Jamie blew out a hard breath and shot her an incredulous look. "Really, after I handed them Sinclair?"

She mouthed 'sorry'.

"Christ, it should have been in the bag. I mean, she's one of the biggest catches in the unit's history. What do I have to do?"

Darting a glance around the pub, she leaned forward and in a low voice said, "It came down to the psych report. Says you're still exhibiting signs of PTSD, you're drinking too much, and your personal life is in flux."

"For fuck's sake. I split with Emma almost a year ago and we were limping to the finish line way before then. And so what if I have the occasional drink or nightmare? Doesn't everyone?" Jamie took a gulp of lager. "Christ, I fuckin' hate shrinks almost as much as I hate hackers."

"It's not a 'never', just a 'not yet'," said Gill placatingly. "Do the counselling, curb the drinking, keep your nose clean and you'll make Inspector next time."

"Counselling?" gasped Jamie wide-eyed. "Are they fuckin' joking?"

"Just tick the boxes Jamie, play the game. You're a good officer on accelerated promotion. And you're only thirty-two; you've a promising career ahead of you. This is just a bump in the road."

He muttered, "The career's all I've bloody got. I never wanted to be part of the cyber unit but I handed them Sinclair and if I cannae get a promotion on the back of that, what motivation is there? No offence Gill, but I'd be as well putting in for a transfer and starting somewhere new."

Eying him over the rim of her glass, she said, "Funny you should say that because there's something else I wanted to talk to you about."

He gave her a questioning look. "I'm listening."

"Moore's been contacted by Counter Terrorism Command. Something about a joint operation with them and the Security Service. Your name came up."

Jason Moore was Gillian's boss and a member of the senior team responsible for deciding promotions.

Jamie couldn't imagine what they'd want, but Gill's words had aroused his curiosity. "My name? What do the spooks want with me, especially after that psych report?"

She shrugged. "I'm too far down the food chain to know, but there's a meeting in London next week. I guess you'll find out then."

"London? That big?"

Gill nodded. "Maybe the clean slate you need Jamie."

Raising his pint glass, he said, "Surely cannae be as dull as the cyber unit."

～

A week later, Jamie found himself in an office in Thames House in London, the headquarters of the United Kingdom's internal Security Service, commonly known as MI5.

Gathered around the glass and chrome conference table were half a dozen suits, all representatives from MI5 and SO15 Counter Terrorism Command. The two factions lined opposite sides of the table, like warring parties, with a psychologist positioned between them. The psychologist, who'd introduced herself as Pia, was the only woman amongst them, and Jamie sat opposite her at the other end of the table. His heart sank.

Julien Tomkins, a Lead Operations Officer from MI5, had just finished outlining a high-level brief with the aid of a Security Service-branded PowerPoint presentation stuffed full of business jargon. Jamie stifled a sigh; it wasn't the assignment he'd hoped for. Financial fraud made the work of Glasgow's cyber-crime unit sound like the vice squad. Even the offices were a disappointment, despite their enviable view. It was more corporate than he'd expected, like the headquarters of a bank.

They all stared at him.

"You want me to investigate tax fraud?" he asked blankly.

"Well, it's not as simple as that," said Julien folding his arms, "or we wouldn't be sat here."

Jamie had come across desk wankers like Julien often enough in his army career; privately-educated, frightfully plummy, and recruited straight from Oxbridge. He bristled at Julien's accent, associating it with upper-class twits fresh from Sandhurst who couldnae organise a piss-up in a polo club.

"Surely a job for Revenue and Customs?" said Jamie.

"Or the police," said Julien, shooting a pointed glance at the faction opposite.

"Definitely your remit Julien, given American involvement,"

snapped one of the SO15 suits.

Jamie felt like he was back in a war zone as he watched the parties shoot glares at one another. Julien looked furious, his professional veneer slipping for a moment.

Commander MacLeish from SO15 raised his hands to silence further sniping. In his late fifties, he'd a worn face that exuded authority and the others appeared to defer to him. He said, "There's a much bigger picture here, one that wasn't apparent until an informer made contact and Julien and his team began to dig."

Jamie exhaled a long breath. "Okay but why me?"

MacLeish smiled. "You're tailor-made son. Your background, training and experience make you the perfect fit to be convincing in the role. In any case, we don't have the time to teach the knowledge and skills to another officer with more undercover experience. You've already got them in spades, plus you're familiar with the details from a previous case. It's just whether you're up for it or not?"

Trying to inject some enthusiasm into his voice, Jamie replied, "I can do it but I'm a cop, not a forensic accountant."

"This isn't a regular fraud case and it's not without danger. We've already lost one informant under suspicious circumstances."

They all stared at him again.

Knowing it was either this or an ignominious return to the cyber unit, Jamie said, "Okay, so let me get this straight, you want me to pose as a manager at a Scottish country estate to infiltrate a bunch of Jesus freaks you suspect of tax fraud?"

Julien nodded. "Pretty much. There's just one small detail we haven't mentioned."

Jamie couldn't believe his fucking ears.

Kathryn

Kathryn and her solicitor Sarah sat in the holding cell adjacent to the main court room in Westminster Magistrates' Court in Central London. Window-less and sparsely furnished, the cell seemed to reflect the depressing nature of its purpose, and Kathryn knew she'd likely have to get used to similar conditions if not worse for many years to come.

After she'd been charged, Kathryn had been denied bail and put in prison. Locked up with drug addicts and women in need of psychiatric treatment, it'd been a living hell in which she'd constantly felt under threat of physical attack. During her incarceration she'd suffered acute episodes of depression and suicidal thoughts. Sarah had finally kicked up such a stink that Kathryn was released on bail, on condition she wore an electronic tag and did not access the internet. She'd returned home to Glasgow knowing it was only a temporary reprieve.

The charges against her for computer hacking and conspiring to attack various government institutions were multiple, here and in the United States. Along with the Met's e-crime division and the FBI, Jamie Denton and his team hadn't just thrown the book at her, they'd hurled the entire library. Months of legal wrangling and hearings followed. Her expenses ran into the tens of thousands and she knew she'd have to sell her grandmother's house to pay for them, and still there wouldn't be enough to cover the costs even with state aid.

Finally, the case bubbled up through the system to the highest court for a decision on whether Kathryn could be extradited to the United States to face charges for breaching the security of the IRS, and hacking into the US Federal Reserve to steal the personal information of users. Sarah had prewarned her that she was expected to lose today because, in light of the serious charges and evidence against her, the British government were powerless to prevent the extradition.

While Sarah read case notes, Kathryn sat opposite her, rocking back and forth in her chair as they awaited the decision. She glanced at the clock on the wall wondering why it was taking so long.

Sarah looked up and gave her an apologetic smile. "Don't lose heart Kathryn, even if we lose today, there's still a chance it'll be overturned on appeal."

Wringing her hands, Kathryn said, "It's unlikely, there are no grounds, you said so yourself."

"But the process will delay things for months, maybe even years."

Tears welled behind Kathryn's eyes. "Only to see me extradited to the US where I'll spend at least twenty years behind bars."

Sarah reached across the table and squeezed her hand. "I won't stop fighting for you, you know that."

Swallowing, Kathryn mouthed "thank you" as she fought back tears of despair.

There was a tap at the door and Kathryn jumped. A court official appeared and summoned Sarah, and Kathryn paced manically as she awaited her return. When her solicitor reappeared, Kathryn began to sob loudly.

Sarah put an arm around her. "Sorry, nothing yet, they're running late so it might be another hour. I need to go and talk to the other legal team but I won't be long." She squeezed Kathryn's shoulder again. "Stay strong." Sarah bundled up her papers and left quietly.

After she'd gone, Kathryn slumped in her chair and wept. Alone in the holding cell, the enormity of what was happening overwhelmed her, and she clutched her sides to prevent herself from coming apart. After a few minutes, there was a knock on the door and the court officer appeared again. He gave Kathryn a half smile. "You've a couple of visitors Miss Sinclair."

Wiping her eyes with the back of her hand, she glanced up to see DS James Denton looking every bit as pissed off as the day he'd arrested her. He was accompanied by another man in a well-tailored dark suit who thrust out his hand and introduced himself as Julien Tomkins.

Ignoring his hand, she sniffed, "What do you want?"

"I believe you know my colleague, DS Denton?"

She met Denton's steely gaze, remembering how it'd bored into her during many long, tortuous hours of questioning. She'd hoped never to see it again. "Come to gloat?" she asked.

Denton sneered, the scar puckering his lip into a snarl. Julien pulled up a seat across from her and she caught a strong whiff of aftershave. Arms folded, Denton remained standing, glowering at her.

Julien produced a pressed linen handkerchief from his top pocket and handed it to her. "Quite the opposite Miss Sinclair. We're here to offer you a deal."

Kathryn dabbed her eyes and gawped at him. "A deal?"

From a leather folio, Julien produced a copy of the Official Secrets

Act and asked her to sign it. He then spent the next ten minutes outlining what was required in return for dropping all charges against her. Dazed, she listened as he explained that they wanted her help to investigate a group suspected of large-scale international tax fraud. Kathryn struggled to take it all in as he described how, after training, she'd go undercover and use her cyber skills to gather the intelligence they needed.

After he finished, he leaned back in his chair and asked, "So, do we have a deal?"

She stared at him for a few moments. "So, let me get this straight, the British government will stop my extradition, waive my legal fees and arrange for all charges for computer misuse to be dropped ... in return for more computer misuse?"

Julien gave her a wry smile. "That's one way of summing it up."

Raising an incredulous eyebrow, she said. "And I just have to sing Kumbaya, and dig around in a few servers owned by a bunch of happy clappies?"

Denton snorted with derision.

Ignoring him, Julien said, "There's a little more to it than that, and I have to warn you that it's not without risk."

"What's the catch?" she asked, glancing nervously at Denton who glowered balefully at her.

Julien's lips curled in amusement. "Hmm, I wouldn't say there's a catch but we'll get into the details later."

Denton scowled at him.

After the two men left, Sarah popped back in to speak to Kathryn after having been informed about the latest development by the Crown's legal team. She held a copy of the agreement and scanned through it.

Sarah shook her head in disbelief. "I've never seen anything like it in all my years. I was prepared for months of wrangling in the appeal courts." Glancing at Kathryn, she asked, "You sure you want to do this?"

Kathryn grinned. "I don't want to go to jail so yes, I'll do it."

"Just so long as you know what you're getting into." She stabbed a finger at the agreement. "I don't like this one bit, Kathryn. You'll be at the mercy of whoever they appoint as the senior officer, and it pretty much says that if you don't complete the training and see the job through to their satisfaction, you'll be straight back here." Sarah's brow furrowed with concern as she continued reading. "There are no guarantees with this."

"So, it's take it or leave it?"

Sarah nodded. "They won't budge an inch either."

Kathryn blew out a long breath and reached for the paperwork. "You got a pen?"

Sarah left Kathryn alone again while she went to meet with the prosecution's legal team to draft a public statement about the delay in the decision to extradite. Kathryn ran a hand through her hair as she scanned a copy of the agreement she'd just signed, caught between elation at avoiding prison and terror at the thought of becoming a puppet of the security services. And why was bloody Denton involved? He was a cop and surely wasn't going to be a part of this operation. Was he? She simply didn't know as the details were deliberately being kept sketchy. Still, if it was just a case of hacking into a few servers, then surely it'd be a walk in the cyber park. Could she really be that lucky?

After a few minutes, Sarah reappeared accompanied by Julien and Denton.

Julien smiled. "I'd like you to come with us now Miss Sinclair."

Wide-eyed, she spluttered, "What? Now?"

"Yes now."

Kathryn's stomach dropped to the floor as the full enormity of what she'd just signed sank in. Sarah shook her hand and wished her luck before she departed. Kathryn could feel Denton's animosity towards her; he seemed to exude it from every pore.

Kathryn followed them through the court buildings along dark corridors and out into a cobbled alleyway. Julien led them to a café on a nearby side-street. Warm and welcoming, if somewhat shabby, a server appeared and they were ushered to a quiet booth at the rear. Kathryn slid into the banquette seating opposite the two men.

After they'd ordered coffees, she looked at Julien and said, "I still don't understand why you need me for this. Don't you have people who do this sort of thing?"

"Exactly," muttered Denton, shooting her an excoriating look.

Julien nodded and in a low voice said, "We do and they've been digging for months without success. On the surface the group are squeaky clean. Too clean, even for a religious organisation which is suspicious enough in itself, but we've intelligence that there's something else at play. We have to do this the old-fashioned way, from inside."

"I still don't see why you think I'm the person for the job. Not that I'm unhappy about my get-out-of-jail-free card."

"Fitz tells me he's never come across a more skilled cyber-criminal. And you've shown you've got the guts to pull this off."

Bristling at the term cyber-criminal, she asked, "Fitz?"

"One of our people 'who do this sort of thing'," said Julien forming air quotes with his fingers.

"So, how do you plan on getting me inside?"

Denton puffed out his annoyance and rolled his eyes.

Ignoring him, Julien said, "The group are based in a remote part of Scotland." He paused while their server brought the coffees. When he'd gone, Julien took a sip of his espresso and added, "As well as their religious activities, they run a sporting estate that produces extra income. They've advertised for an estate manager."

She gasped out, "I don't know the first thing about running a country estate."

Julien put down his coffee cup, "But Denton does and you'll pose as his wife."

Open-mouthed, she looked from one to the other, then turned her full glare on Julien. "Is this some kind of sick joke? Seriously, I've to pretend to be married to *him*?" She narrowed her eyes at Denton, who returned a stony glare.

Denton snapped, "Trust me sweetheart, I'm no any happier about this than you."

She swallowed hard and turned to Julien, "When you say married…"

Denton snarled, "Oh, don't flatter yourself Sinclair, I'd rather stick my dick in that chastity cage you used on your boss."

Sighing, Julien folded his arms and looked at them like they were recalcitrant children. In a voice laced with exasperation, he said, "Listen Sinclair, I stuck my neck out to get you that deal. Screw it up and you'll find yourself on the next plane across the pond. Get us the evidence we need and you'll go scot-free." He took another gulp of coffee, slammed the cup into its saucer and got up. Leaning over, he whispered, "You two better stop squabbling and sort this out before you set foot on that estate because, if you don't, you'll be putting more than just yourselves in danger."

As Julien stalked off towards the toilets, Kathryn and Denton swapped a glower.

She hissed, "Right now, a plane to America sounds very appealing."

He bit out, "I'll drop you at the airport."

Julien and Kathryn left Denton stewing in the café, while Julien accompanied her to King's Cross railway station. She could hardly believe she was going home and not back to prison. As they wove their way through crowds of passengers, he explained that a car would collect her the following morning from her home and take her to the airport. She'd travel with Denton to London where Julien would accompany them to a training facility in England.

"So soon?" she said.

"We've only a small window of opportunity before they start interviewing to fill the vacancy, there's no time to lose."

After walking her to her platform, Julien left her with instructions to stay clear of the internet and to pack plenty of clothes for the next few weeks. "Mainly casual and exercise, with maybe a dressy item." She felt a moment's relief that her wardrobe ought to be able to cope with that. As she boarded the train, he said, "Don't let me down Sinclair."

As the train pulled away, she wondered just what the hell she'd gotten herself into. Pulling out her smartphone and breaking the conditions of her bail for the first time, she began to search for information on DS James Denton. Loathe to dig deep given her precarious situation, she limited herself to publicly-available social media sources. Like many police officers, he didn't have a Facebook page, at least not under his real name, but she soon found him tagged on a page belonging to an Emma Wright. Kathryn scrolled through Emma's posts where she found dozens of photographs of her pictured along with her boyfriend, Jamie Denton.

Jamie had found his Miss Wright.

Jamie

Jamie felt like he'd been kicked in the balls. He couldnae believe what he'd just witnessed. Seeing her freed was bad enough but to then sit across from her while she enjoyed a coffee as though they were equal partners, well that was just taking the piss.

What the hell was Julien playing at? She ought to be in jail. It's where she belonged and he and his team had spent months proving it, only to have Julien stroll in with his sharp suit and Received Pronunciation and spring her. Where was the justice in that? She was a terrorist, no different to the animal rights nutters who blew up shops at night then claimed they never hurt anyone. And she was a cowardly one at that, hiding behind a false identity and a VPN while she wreaked havoc on society and individuals. Didn't she realise that large corporations employ people and that if they go under it's these people who lose their jobs.

But, to top it all, she was a fuckin' liability. She'd no training, no experience, and that scared him more than anything. One mistake and she could put him and others in danger. He knew how important it was to trust your partner; in the military, you entrusted them with your life and it'd be no different on an undercover operation. Yet, here he was expected to put his confidence in a woman he'd put behind bars. There'd be no trust on either side. What did she bring to the party? He may not know how to hack but he could shove a USB stick into a computer as well as the next person, so why did they need her at all? None of it made any bloody sense.

When he'd first been told of the plan, he'd argued that there must be plenty of female officers they could use, but Julien had said there were few operatives with the skills in MI5 of a suitable age who could pose as his wife. When he'd pointed out that it was dangerous and unethical to use a civilian in this way, Julien had simply shrugged and replied that time was short, they needed her skills and, in any case, they had her over a barrel.

Regardless, he didnae want to be in the same room as the devious wee manhater, never mind a relationship, albeit a fake one. Jesus, what a shit show. Sighing, he swallowed a last mouthful of cold coffee and stared out of the window at the rain. Sinclair was right about one thing; it was a sick joke. Still, he wanted this opportunity, even if this operation was a nightmare because it was a chance to get his floundering career back on track. To get a job with the intelligence services had been a dream but, coming from the wrong socio-economic background and lacking the right accent, he'd never thought it feasible. Until now.

What was the alternative? Return home to Gillian's team in the hope of convincing a bloody shrink he'd pulled himself together enough to make inspector next time? What was the point in even trying given that Kathryn Sinclair, the best collar of his career, had just escaped justice? Nope, there was a better alternative. He'd simply make sure she royally screwed up and was put back behind bars where she bloody well belonged.

First opportunity.

Kathryn

"Welcome to A Branch," said Julien as he pulled up the car outside the training facility. "You're now part of the most effective surveillance team in the world."

The first day wasn't at all what she'd expected. A taxi had taken her to the airport where Denton was waiting. Sitting together on the plane to London, they barely spoke, and the only interest he'd shown was when he'd thrown a contemptuous glare at the book she was reading, Florence Given's *Women Don't Owe You Pretty*.

On arrival at Heathrow, Julien had led them to a Range Rover, which was full of personal items and children's toys. The latest Samsung mobile phone lay on top of *The Telegraph* newspaper on the front seat. They'd driven thirty miles to a training facility near Amersham in Buckinghamshire where, he explained, they'd spend the next few weeks until they departed for Scotland. Kathryn was anxious at the thought of having to spend time here with bloody Denton, and he didn't look any happier at the prospect either.

The training facility consisted of several modern rectangular buildings set in acres of rolling countryside. Once inside, they were shown straight to a sterile classroom with desks and a large screen where Julien introduced them to Steve Morris, their trainer. In his mid-fifties and powerfully built, Morris had a whiff of military about him. They stowed their suitcases at the front and sat on opposite sides of the classroom, and Morris had made an immediate start, outlining what they'd be covering.

"Normally surveillance operators spend months in training," said Morris, "but we've so little time to prepare you, we're only doing the essentials. They'll be no advanced driving or foot surveillance." He glanced at Jamie and added, "You'll be familiar with a lot of it already."

Kathryn wondered what he meant as that didn't sound like standard police training. There were no survival skills, parkour, self-defence, or climbing either, and sadly no Q character dispensing spike umbrellas. Instead, Morris led mind-numbing, PowerPoint-fuelled sessions on MI5 policies and protocols. Had James Bond had to undertake diversity training?

After lunch and a soul-destroying presentation on expense procedures, Julien reappeared accompanied by an elegant older woman who introduced herself as Pia, a psychologist. She'd short blonde hair and vibrant blue eyes, and Kathryn thought she detected a hint of a Scandinavian accent. Kathryn noticed Denton bristle when she greeted him, and it was clear they'd met already. Another woman he had difficulty accepting?

Handing each of them a large brown envelope, Julien announced, "Your new identities. You'll need to know this information off pat by the end of the course; yours and your partner's. I suggest you start immediately."

Pia said, "To help you with this while you're here, you'll live together and immerse yourself in these identities. Only share information with each other based on what's in these packs so as not to get muddled. We can't have you calling each other Denton and Sinclair."

They scowled at her.

Pia asked Denton if she could have a word and they departed leaving Kathryn to sit through an agonising presentation about the Covert Human Intelligence Sources Bill. By the end, she wasn't sure if it was about ensuring agents kept within the law, or about protecting the public from them.

Jamie

Jamie cast his eye over Pia's office. Spacious, bathed in light and overlooking the picturesque grounds, it housed a desk, upholstered chairs set around a coffee table, and heavily-laden bookcases. Jamie sank into the seat opposite Pia, crossed his arms and sighed. His foot bounced and he pressed his knee to stop it.

Pia had a kindly face and insightful eyes which he was certain missed nothing. Smiling, she placed a manila folder on the coffee table and said, "I've read your psych report."

Jamie looked up at the ceiling and exhaled a loud breath. He met her eye. "Suppose you're now gonnae recommend they pull me off this job?"

She steepled her hands. "No, I saw the report before they asked you to do it."

He looked at her in surprise. "You don't agree with the evaluation?"

"What I think is that you and I have a lot of work to do. Starting now."

"I don't need counselling," he snapped, "there's nothing wrong with me. So what if I have bad dreams, doesn't everyone?"

Pia peered at him over the top of her spectacles in a schoolmarmish way. "Jamie, you're suffering from PTSD; if you refuse to work with me, I will recommend they remove you. Working undercover is stressful and you'll be on edge most of the time. You can't go into this situation without addressing the root of your trauma, but I need your cooperation."

Jamie locked his arms over his chest and glowered at her. "Sounds like I've nae choice."

"Have you heard of trauma-focused cognitive behavioural therapy?"

When he returned a blank stare, she continued, "Over the next few weeks, you'll learn ways to unwind and process the events that triggered the PTSD. But first we're going to talk about dealing with avoidance."

Touching his scar, he replied, "I'm not avoiding anything."

She raised an eyebrow and compressed her lips. "Do not try and put a brave face on or conceal information. I have all your notes from the police and army."

He sighed loudly. "Aye, whatever."

"And prepare yourself for the fact it may get worse before it gets better." She opened the folder. "So, tell me about your friend Matt."

Oh fuck, did she just go there?

Kathryn

By the time Jamie returned to the classroom, Kathryn's eyes had all but glazed over. Glancing up at him, she could have sworn he was upset and his eyes were red. And for once he didn't scowl at her.

Morris said, "you've probably had enough for today. We'll resume in the morning. And if you're good boys and girls, we'll have story time tomorrow."

Jamie rolled his eyes.

Morris showed them to the accommodation block at the opposite end of the campus, which offered an apartment with a number of sparse single rooms. It reminded Kathryn of student accommodation, with its shared kitchen, living room and bathroom, although they appeared to be the only occupants. Morris explained that the canteen served lunches during the day but they'd have to fend for themselves in the evening on their subsistence allowance, and he told them about a couple of decent local pubs that served food.

"Don't be late tomorrow," said Morris. With a cheery smile, he pulled the door of the apartment closed, leaving Kathryn alone with Denton. So far, they'd managed to ignore each other, and at lunch she'd avoided him by eating her sandwiches in the grounds.

Grabbing the handle of his suitcase, Denton cast her a side-ways look and mumbled, "Want to grab a bite at the pub later, make a start on the legends?"

Making eye contact for as long as she could tolerate, no more than a nano second, she replied, "Sure." It was the opposite to how she felt.

"Seven o'clock downstairs?" he suggested.

She nodded. He disappeared into his room and she wheeled her suitcase to the one furthest away. After finding it locked, she tried the next along only to find the only unlocked room was next to his. Cursing, she locked her door, flopped face down onto the bed and groaned at the thought of having dinner with bloody Denton. How the hell was she ever going to act the part of his wife for weeks, possibly even months? She couldn't believe she'd ended up in this situation; the idea was ridiculous. What the hell was Julien thinking? She and Denton couldn't stand each other. It was bad enough here but the thought of being alone with him in the back of bloody beyond made her scalp prickle.

Then, remembering the pictures she'd seen of a women's prison in the US, she sighed and headed for the shower.

∾

Just after seven, she found Denton downstairs loitering inside the foyer, and she took a moment for a good look at him before he spotted her. He was dressed in a light blue shirt and dark jeans, with a tweed jacket swung casually over broad shoulders. His raffish brown hair was swept back, accentuating high cheek bones and a sharp bladed jaw with designer-stubble. If it wasn't for the ugly scar, she'd concede he was handsome, and she wondered what'd happened to him. Even scarred, he was attractive when he wasn't scowling. It pissed her off and so it was with a mixture of confusion and dread that she greeted him.

She caught the fleeting look of approval he cast her before he readjusted his expression back to neutral. She'd washed her shoulder-length hair and tied it back from her face, and she wore black trousers with a loose, pink jumper. Realising it was probably the first time he'd seen her in anything other than joggies and baggy sweaters, or the androgenous suit she'd worn to court, she was both irritated and bewildered by his reaction.

His phone rang and after checking the screen he flashed his fingers to indicate he'd be five minutes. Answering the call, he exited the doors saying, "How's ma best girl?"

Kathryn cringed out an "Ugh" as she plopped onto the sofa; she hated it when men referred to grown women as girls.

She watched him pace outside, laughing as he talked to his girlfriend. Dressed as he was and with his dazzling smile and perfect white teeth, he was unrecognisable as the policeman who'd collared her.

He finished the call and entered the lobby. Catching her pinched expression, he said, "What's wrong?"

She pulled on her coat. "Nothing."

He held open the door.

"I can get my own door," she snapped.

"Christ, I'm only being polite Sinclair. Can we at least try to be civil to one another? Anyway, what's wrong with opening a door for a lady?"

Bristling, she sent him a glare. "For your information Denton, adult females are referred to as women, not ladies or best girls."

He looked at her and laughed, his eyes twinkling with mischief. "For your information Sinclair, I was talking to my five-year-old niece who's been my 'best girl' since she was born."

Kathryn squirmed and felt a flush creep across her cheeks. "Uhm, sorry, didn't realise."

He cocked an eyebrow, "So, if you've quite finished your feminist rant, shall we go get dinner?" He extended a palm in the direction of town, flashed her a cheeky grin, and said, "After you my dear."

Cutting him a filthy look, she brushed past him.

He chuckled as he fell into step beside her. "I'll be sure to file that away under 'things that annoy Kathryn'." With a loud sigh, he added, "I've a feeling it'll be a large case file."

Gritting her teeth, she ignored him as they walked in silence towards the heart of the village where Morris's top recommendation, The Royal Oak, beckoned. Their breath plumed in the cold air and Kathryn pulled the collar of her coat against the chill. Denton shot her an impish grin as he held open the door to the pub with a flourish.

"Suppose you think that's funny?" she muttered pushing past him.

"Get used to it baby." He emphasised 'baby'.

She glowered at him and he laughed. Bloody laughed.

They chose a quiet corner table close to the open fire. Red embers glowed in the grate and the smell of woodsmoke filled the air. She spent an unusually long time studying the menu, conscious of the heavy silence between them. After the waiter appeared and took their order, Denton filled the lull by asking if she'd brought her pack. Glad to have something to focus on, she retrieved it from her handbag and pulled out the summary sheet.

"So, what do I call you?" he asked, his eyes sparkling with amusement.

"Kathryn Campbell. Maiden name MacDonald. What about you?"

She noticed he hadn't brought his pack, but he recited, "James Campbell, Jamie for short."

"How apt. Didn't the Campbells murder the MacDonalds at Glencoe?"

Jamie chuckled, "Aye, no doubt someone's idea of a joke. At least we're keeping our first names, less chance of slipping up under pressure."

"Let's just hope it doesn't end in murder."

Jamie narrowed his eyes. "Listen, I know neither of us chose this but we're gonnae have to make the best of a bad situation. So how about a truce … starting from now?"

She hissed, "Easy for you to say Denton, you weren't the one facing jail in a country you've never set foot in."

He blew out a hard breath and through gritted teeth said, "First it's Campbell, forget you ever heard Denton, and second I was doing the job I'm paid to do. What's your excuse?"

Their waiter appeared and Kathryn seethed in silence as he opened a bottle of red wine and poured two glasses. When he'd gone, she said, "Unlike you, I was dispensing fair justice."

"Really? By trapping a bloke's dick in a chastity cage?"

Taking a gulp of wine and a deep breath, she fought to remain calm, then explained about her predatory boss. She told him how Tod had behaved towards her, and how he'd treated other women in his employ.

When she'd finished, Jamie shook his head. "What a bastard." Topping up their glasses, he said, "It was bloody funny though, and all anybody in the station talked about for weeks. Where d'you get the idea?"

She told him about the Internet of Things. "There's been this explosion in gadgets which can be connected up so they can be controlled remotely. The adult sex toy industry has mushroomed in recent years. Trouble is, at the low end of the market manufacturers take security shortcuts which make it easy to hack into these devices."

Jamie seemed fascinated. She told him about a sex toy for women which included a camera that let the user share long distance images with her partner, but the device was also hardcoded to send the pictures secretly to another IP address.

Raising an incredulous eyebrow, he said, "So, some random pervert can watch her too?"

She nodded. "And maybe blackmail her."

Their starters arrived and as they ate, he flouted Pia's rules and asked about Sherwood and the Grey Nemesis cyberattack on the big pharmaceutical and biotech companies.

"You're not recording this, are you?", she asked.

Raising his palms, he produced his phone from his jacket pocket. "Nope, check if you want."

She did.

He leant in closer and chuckled, "Cannae believe I just handed my phone to a cyber-criminal."

Smirking, she replied, "What makes you think I haven't already hacked it?"

As they ate, she told him about Grey Nemesis and why they'd targeted particular firms that had profiteered from the Covid-19 pandemic and avoided paying millions of dollars in tax. She described similar cyberattacks on Big Tobacco, and Jamie listened as she explained that her grandmother had died of lung cancer, and how badly she'd suffered towards the end. With a few clicks, she said, they'd brought down websites which they'd deface with a message from Grey Nemesis. She also told him about their joint operations with the paedophile hunters and how they'd removed Robert Hendry from the streets.

"And you've never benefited financially?"

She shook her head. "We keep some funds to buy kit, and I make a small income from bug bounty programs when I report issues to companies, but nothing other than that. Despite what you think of me, I'm not a black hat. I only use my skills for the common good and I never profit personally. None of us do."

Jamie awarded her with an approving look. "You're different from what I expected Mrs Campbell."

Flashing him a rare smile, she thought 'so are you', but stayed silent. After a pause, she said, "Can I ask you something, but I'll understand if you can't tell me?"

"Sure, what?"

"How did you catch me? I've been over and over it but I can't figure out what gave me away? I'm always careful never to leave a trail."

Jamie wiped his mouth on his napkin and looked at her. "You don't know?"

She shook her head.

"One of your buddies ratted on you."

"NO!" She felt like she'd been punched in the stomach. "I don't believe you."

He offered her a rueful smile. "It's true."

At a loss for words for a few moments and dreading the reply, she whispered, "Who?"

"The one you call Pandora."

She gasped, "But I've known her for years."

"Aye, she caved under interrogation and handed you and Scotty to the Feds to save her own skin."

"Did Scotty talk?"

"Nope, disappeared without trace, hasnae been seen or heard of since."

She sat in silence for a while as she struggled to take in this news. Although shocked to the core at Pandora's betrayal, at least it explained how so much evidence had been amassed against her to secure a conviction, and that it wasn't the result of a mistake on her part. The only error she'd made was trusting someone other than herself, and she sure as hell wouldn't be doing that again.

Jamie settled the bill and they walked back to the training facility in a very different mood from the one in which they'd arrived, parting on amicable terms. The change had been undoubtedly helped by the good food and wine they'd enjoyed but Kathryn had found their conversation interesting.

Although tired, she lay on her bed unable to sleep as she replayed the evening over in her mind. She felt Pandora's betrayal like a physical pain, one that twisted in her gut. Years of online messaging and shared cyber missions had fooled her into thinking she was a friend whom she could trust. She'd never considered the possibility that a fellow hacker could have provided the wealth of evidence the authorities had gathered against her. Yet Pandora had deceived her and Scotty, with full knowledge of the likely consequences for them. Now she felt foolish for thinking there'd been any depth to a friendship which was clearly as shallow and fleeting as the ether over which they'd corresponded.

She also realised she much preferred Jamie Campbell to James Denton, and she was pleasantly surprised at just how different he was from the officer who'd arrested her all those months ago. She hadn't felt threatened by him this evening, nor had she detected any hostility. If anything, he'd been quite charming and she'd enjoyed his company. And he'd teased her.

For the first time, she felt a glimmer of hope.

~

Jamie

Jamie paced up and down his bedroom a few feet away from Kathryn in the adjacent room. Although still rattled by his session with Pia and what she'd dredged up, that wasn't what occupied his mind. It was Kathryn. She was the most intriguing woman he'd ever met.

Prior to this evening, he'd formed a picture of her as just another devious wee hacker, hellbent on wreaking chaos and destruction in the most cowardly way: from afar. But she wasn't like that; she'd scruples. Lots of them. She preferred to work a low paid job for a sleazeball boss, rather than use her skills to reap financial rewards. Jamie had enjoyed her company and listening to how passionately she'd talked of punishing corrupt individuals and organisations. Really, although they used different methods, their aims weren't so different.

He also thought about what Julien had said earlier. After his meeting with Pia, Julien had taken him aside and, in no uncertain terms, told him to cut Kathryn some slack. He acknowledged that no one was happy with the situation, least of all him, but he expected Jamie to put aside his feelings for the sake of the job, adding "she's not what you think, otherwise she wouldn't be here." Julien was right and that irritated him.

But it was more than that.

Jesus, of all the women to find attractive!

It was a natural beauty too, unadorned by makeup and fancy

clothes. Although she tried to hide her figure, she was tall, slender and curvaceous with legs that seemed to go on forever. He'd nearly choked when she walked into reception earlier; she looked like a different lassie. And her lustrous hair; he'd spent the evening wanting to untie it and run his fingers through it. Christ, he hadn't had sex for ages and, since splitting with his long-term girlfriend Emma, it'd been a series of unfulfilling one-night stands since. He let out a pained groan of frustration.

Kathryn hadn't once mentioned a partner and he knew from her file there'd been no mention of one although she wore a wedding ring. Christ what was he thinking? She was a colleague and a criminal one; he couldn't go there. Could he? As if she'd look at him twice, with his scar; he repulsed women.

He groaned again. Maybe a wank might help?

~

Kathryn

Next morning, Kathryn padded along the corridor to the shared kitchen and made tea. Dressed in pyjamas and a terry robe, her hair was still wet from the shower.

Jamie appeared fresh from a run, wearing a black T-shirt and shorts. As he kicked off his running shoes, she offered him tea but he said he preferred coffee to kickstart the day. As he rummaged through the cupboards for a suitable mug, Kathryn found her eyes were drawn to his sculpted physique. His shirt was damp and it clung to a powerful chest outlining the hard musculature beneath. He'd bulky upper arms that strained against the fabric, and powerful taut thighs.

He made his coffee and sat at the table beside her and she caught the intoxicating scent of fresh sweat mingled with his masculine shampoo. There were beads of perspiration on his brow and his hair was wet. He flicked it back and stared at her, and she struggled to process the sudden raft of confusing and unfamiliar feelings. Pulse racing, she rose and busied herself with washing her mug.

"Any idea what Morris meant by story time?" she asked.

"There's a briefing this afternoon. We'll find out then what they've planned for us."

With a nod, she returned to her room and let out a long breath.

"Meet Marcus and Ruth Colquhoun," said Julien.

The screen in the classroom showed an image of a smartly-dressed couple in their early fifties. Both wore tweed jackets and each held a black working cocker spaniel in their arms. Marcus was tall and handsome with salt and pepper-coloured hair, and Kathryn thought he looked like a model. Ruth by comparison was short and dumpy with a head too large for her body, and she grinned at the camera through a mop of mousey-brown curls and a row of peg teeth.

"What a munter!" exclaimed Morris. "How'd he end up married to her?"

Jamie laughed at Morris's comment and at the expression of outrage on Kathryn's face.

"She's wealthy," said Julien, "which might explain it, but I'll come on to that."

Kathryn threw them a look of disdain, "You're appalling, all of you."

Julien explained that the Colquhouns headed a small religious community based on the remote Knoydart Peninsula on the west coast of Scotland. Consisting of about two hundred members, he described their brand of Christianity as "Old Testament with tourism."

Knoydart, he said, was still a wilderness and accessible only by boat or a two-day hike over the mountains. He clicked and an impressive baronial home appeared, surrounded by numerous white cottages and farm buildings, all set amongst breath-taking scenery. Marcus had established the community about ten years ago and, in addition to their charitable works, ran a country estate of around twenty thousand acres, the income from which supplemented the group's coffers.

The picture changed to a small church. "They call themselves the Ehrlich Society," said Julien, "they're a conservative group that adhere to a traditional lifestyle, preach family values and believe divorce and subsequent remarriage to be wrong. Surprisingly though, they permit alcohol and contraception."

Kathryn asked, "Err, when you say traditional lifestyle?"

Julien offered her a tight smile, "They believe the man is head of the household and wives should submit to their husbands."

Kathryn gasped out, "You've got to be kidding!"

Jamie threw his head back and laughed, and she cut him a hard glare.

Ignoring them, Julien continued, "They run educational, vaccination and birth control programmes in the developing world, and train lay preachers whom they send across the globe." An article about their work in Africa appeared featuring a photograph of smiling children, a team of nurses and a pastor, entitled 'Ehrlich Society delivers hope after community decimated by COVID variant'. They operate as a charity and, as far as religious organisations go, other than old-fashioned ideas about men and women's roles, they're fairly main stream."

"Except for being up to their necks in fraud," remarked Jamie.

"And being misogynistic," muttered Kathryn.

The screen changed and she recognised a familiar face.

Julien looked across at Kathryn. "As you know, Elijah Hart is the billionaire owner of Hart Biotech and a vocal environmentalist. Ruth Colquhoun is Elijah's sister. Elijah and Ruth grew up in Tallahassee in Florida, where their father was a preacher in a sect not dissimilar to the Ehrlich Society. Before marrying Marcus, Ruth was an epidemiologist at Hart Biotech, known for her work on the control of SARS. The company are based in Florida..." Julien glanced at Kathryn and cleared his throat, "Of course, you're both familiar with the company after you ... err ... hacked it. Anyway, the point is they've come to the attention of our friends across the pond because Hart Biotech appear to be funnelling millions of dollars through the Ehrlich Society."

Jamie puffed out his annoyance. "I still don't understand why you need us to go undercover to investigate financial fraud?"

"Because we believe that to be just the tip of the iceberg."

A photograph appeared of a middle-aged woman lying dead in a pool of blood, her throat cut. Kathryn gasped and her hand shot to her mouth.

"Beth Melton was a senior scientist at Hart Biotech and an FBI informant. She claimed to have information about the company's more clandestine operations and their connection to the Ehrlich Society. She arranged to meet her handler with evidence she'd uncovered which proved that people's lives were in danger, but she was murdered before the meeting." Julien allowed them all to study the photograph of the dead woman. The background gave nothing away but the cause of her death was all too clear. "That's why the job is not without risk." Julien's brow furrowed as he looked from Jamie to Kathryn and she felt icicles drop down her spine.

"Which is presumably why the Yanks agreed to drop the charges against Kathryn?" said Jamie.

Julien nodded, "And why we're under considerable pressure to get a quick result. They want Elijah Hart."

Together with Jamie, Kathryn spent several days learning about the corporate structures, officers and operations of Hart Biotech, and the work of the Ehrlich Society. Much of the information on Hart Biotech was familiar to her after the Grey Nemesis attack on the company and her subsequent arrest for the part she'd played in it.

The company had made millions of dollars during the pandemic after patenting a method to store vaccines for long periods without the need for refrigeration. Beth Melton had been instrumental in developing this technology which greatly facilitated the supply and distribution of vaccines across the globe, and was particularly important throughout the poverty-stricken developing world.

Although Hart Biotech had played a key role in tackling the pandemic, they'd fallen foul of the US government and press because they'd not only profiteered but had controversially funnelled vaccines to various conservative Christian groups including the Ehrlich Society. The company was privately owned and Elijah Hart was estimated to be worth over $100 billion dollars. Kathryn reminded them that the company had hardly paid a dime in tax despite making money hand over fist, which was why Grey Nemesis targeted them. They learned that Elijah Hart was also a vocal climate change lobbyist and spent millions of dollars sponsoring birth control programmes in Africa and Asia.

Less was known, however, about the Ehrlich Society and its members other than Ruth and Marcus Colquhoun.

"We've had a first look at your targets, the Colquhouns," said Julien, "but we can't exactly send in a regular surveillance team." Passing them each a thick file, he said, "Marcus has two unmarried sons, Duncan and Angus who are in their mid-late twenties and live as part of the community. For Marcus and Ruth, theirs was a second marriage following the death of their spouses, both of whom had succumbed to Covid-19 around the same time. Because neither had divorced, they were permitted to remarry within the church."

Julien then filled in more background: Ruth had faced further tragedy in early 2020 when she lost her young son to leukaemia, and then her mother-in-law in a freak domestic gas accident. At the time, Ruth and her family had been living in London where she was completing her PhD thesis at Imperial College, and she'd published a number of academic papers on the spread of Covid-19. Later that year, Marcus and Ruth met at an online climate change convention hosted by Elijah Hart and had married soon after. As a major shareholder in Hart Biotech, she'd brought massive investment into the Ehrlich community.

Marcus had established the community after the family left the Isle of Lewis following a girl's disappearance. Julien showed them a copy of an old police report that mentioned Marcus's youngest son Angus had been questioned in connection with it.

Jamie asked, "Was she ever found?"

Julien shook his head. "No trace."

Kathryn and Jamie learned that life in the community was built around the family, although they'd many single members. Mothers were not permitted to work outside the home, while women without children could work provided it was within traditional roles. Kathryn asked what constituted a traditional role, and Julien listed childcare, housekeeping and office work. When she'd asked where in the bible it decreed that typing was women's work, Jamie had laughed.

Julien explained that the community had a reserved attitude to the use of technology. Families did not watch television, own smartphones, or use the Internet within the home, but technology was permitted for the purposes of running a business and members could own and drive cars. Julien glanced nervously at Kathryn when he explained she could only use a phone or laptop secretly as women were not permitted these items.

Julien showed them the advert for the position of Estate Manager which made it clear the community sought a married couple. Candidates were not required to be baptised into the faith, but were expected to be sympathetic to the beliefs and aims of the community, and to live and work as part it.

Jamie said, "You mentioned a contact within the Society."

Julien nodded and passed them a letter which had been sent to the headquarters of Police Scotland by a member of the community called Jean Douglas. Written a few weeks ago and posted in Mallaig, she'd asked to speak personally to an officer other than the local bobby 'on a matter of utmost concern'. Because the letter contained the Ehrlich Society's address, it had found its way into Julien's inbox.

Julien explained he had sent a retired police officer posing as an electrician carrying out routine safety checks to talk to Jean. She was in her sixties and lived on her own, and it had been almost impossible for the officer to speak to her in private as they'd been watched by one of Marcus's sons for the entire time. The officer knew she was frightened and something was seriously off, but he had managed to relay to Jean that someone would be in touch about her concerns.

Julien said, "She knows to expect you and we'll get a picture of you to her. The cover story is she knew your parents, Jamie, but hasn't seen you since you were a boy."

When not in the classroom, Kathryn and Jamie walked the grounds discussing their new identities and fake past lives. Jamie revealed his character's background was similar to his own, having grown up on a sporting estate, and then joining the army. Kathryn wished her background had been more like Miss MacDonald's, but didn't share this.

"Explains your accent," said Kathryn, "it's a blend of east and west coast."

Jamie chuckled, "Aye, I was a teuchter 'til I went to school in Glasgow."

They enjoyed firing questions at each other and became quite competitive. To Kathryn's annoyance, Jamie seemed to have perfect recall. So far, she'd failed to catch him out. After forgetting Miss MacDonald's astrological sign, she'd returned to the classroom to find a newspaper on her desk open at the horoscopes with Taurus circled, and Jamie grinning at her.

Today, they met Declan Fitzpatrick, or Fitz as he was known, who'd given a session on MI5's cyber tactics; it was the closest they'd come to meeting 'Q' if such a character existed outside of James Bond movies. As a senior cybersecurity officer, there was little he didn't know about hacking and cyber-crime. Fitz explained that the Colquhouns were, what was known in the trade as 'clean skins'.

"Other than official information like passports and tax returns," he said, "we know little about them. And the fact they live in the back of beyond and eschew technology means we've been unable to discover much about them or members of the community." Turning to Kathryn, he said, "We can see the computers they use to run the business but if there are others, and I suspect there are, they're not connected to the internet. You're going to need physical access."

Fitz also explained that targets are given code names comprising of two words. This was designed to aid communication, and prevent others not involved in the operation knowing the person's identity.

Kathryn said, "Oh, don't tell me! GREY SQUIRREL and RED FOX? I thought that was just in the movies."

Fitz laughed, "No, it's true but the words are chosen at random."

It was clear that Fitz was slightly in awe of Kathryn; something which, to her amusement, appeared to irritate Jamie. After a lengthy discussion between herself and Fitz about the challenges of compromising smartphones, Jamie announced his head was completely banjoed and he'd left the meeting early.

That evening, Kathryn and Jamie returned to the Royal Oak, where they polished off a bottle of wine with their meal. After a couple of glasses, Jamie seemed to be in a better mood.

He regarded her and said, "You okay? You seem anxious."

"I'm rattled knowing I'll need to get physical access to machines. I've never done anything like that before. It's one thing to hack something remotely, it's quite another to break and enter."

Jamie nodded, "You're not doing this on your own. I'll be there to help you."

She sent him a grateful smile.

He asked, "Seriously, did you understand what Fitz was on about?"

"I guess we talk the same language. Thought you worked on the cyber unit?"

"Aye as a detective, but we'd tech staff on the team." Jamie looked down at his hands, as if needing a pause before saying, "Mind if I ask why you were working as a trainee developer? I thought with your skills and knowledge, you'd have been heading up a cybersecurity department."

She explained that after leaving school with no qualifications, it'd been almost impossible to get a foot in the door in IT without a degree. She said, "I was studying part-time for one, and the job at Alba was my ticket out of low-paid temp work."

Jamie gave her a rueful smile. "And now you're having dinner with the person who wrecked that dream."

She shrugged. "To be fair, I think I wrecked that myself."

He ordered another bottle of wine and although he'd the lion's share, she felt light-headed on the walk back. In the apartment, Jamie suggested a nightcap and he produced another bottle of red wine. He poured them each a large glass and they sat at the breakfast bar chatting.

"How you feeling about things?" he asked. "This is a big change for you."

She met his gaze. "More positive than at the start of the week. I don't think it'll be easy though, especially if Fitz has got nowhere. What about you?"

He thought for a while then said, "I don't think they expect us to succeed. They're just paying lip service so they can say to the Yanks they've got people on it."

She stared at him. "Really?"

"Why else would they put us on it? I mean, no offence or anything but I'm a burnt-out cop and you're a convicted criminal. We're not exactly their finest. And Julien certainly didn't want his team involved; that was clear from the off."

"Do you think they're telling us the full story?"

"Doubt it. There's got to be something else going on … I mean why else would the spooks be involved?"

She pressed her lips together and sat up straight, "Well in that case, we'll just have to succeed and prove them wrong. In fact, my liberty depends on it."

He nodded, "To success." He clinked his glass against hers.

As the wine flowed, he became loquacious and, against Pia's advice, told her about his family. His face lit up when he talked about his niece and he showed her photographs of her with his sister and her husband. He explained his mother had died of cancer, and his father had taken his own life, which was one of the reasons he'd joined the army. When she asked why he'd left the army, he twisted on the bar stool towards her.

"My best mate was killed by friendly fire from a drone operator. He died in my arms." He touched his scar, "That's how I got this. I'd a hard time dealing with his death. Got a medical discharge."

In a quiet voice she said, "I'm really sorry Jamie."

"I prefer an enemy I can see. Maybe that's why I hate hackers."

"Because we're a step removed?"

Jamie's lips parted and his eyes locked onto hers. She felt a blush spread to her neck. He was very close.

Nodding, he slurred, "But I don't hate you." He gazed at her. "You're very different to what I expected Mrs Campbell."

She suddenly felt shy. "You're different too, Mr Campbell."

The heat in his gaze stopped her breath and her heart thudded in her chest; she wondered if he could hear it too. He leaned in closer, so near she could smell him; a heady mixture of wine, aftershave and musky maleness. Slowly, he reached out and cupped the side of her face. Transfixed by his aquamarine eyes, her breath hitched and she fought hard against the urge to flinch at his touch. Leaning in, he guided her mouth to his, his lips just brushing hers.

Panic-stricken, she lurched back and slapped him across the face. Hard, the crack of it reverberated around the kitchen. Rubbing his cheek, Jamie shot her an incredulous look as she fled to her room.

She locked her door and leant against it, battling to get her breathing under control. Unable to believe what'd just happened, she felt dizzy and her legs were like jelly. Trembling, she slid to the floor, clutched her knees to her chest and wept.

There was a soft tap on the door and Jamie said, "Kathryn. I'm sorry. Can we talk please?"

Despite his persistence, she ignored him until he finally gave up.

Next morning, Kathryn avoided him at breakfast and made her own way to the classroom. She'd slept badly and her red swollen eyes were ringed with dark circles. Morris was already there and, when Jamie arrived, he gave both of them a curious glance. When Jamie sat next to her, she ignored him.

He said in a low voice, "I'm sorry. It was unprofessional of me, but we need to talk."

Averting her gaze, she hissed, "I've nothing to say to you."

During the morning session, they blanked each other and the atmosphere grew so thick it was almost palpable, so it was no surprise to Kathryn when Pia asked to speak to her in her office.

Without preamble, she asked, "What's happened between you and Jamie?"

Kathryn shrugged. "Nothing. Just a misunderstanding."

Pia pursed her lips and regarded her. "It's not nothing and if we don't sort it out, the entire operation will be in jeopardy. I need to know."

Kathryn explained what had happened and how she'd reacted.

Pia asked lots of questions about how she'd felt after Jamie had tried to kiss her, then she said, "I can understand why you were upset, but what you're describing is a classic anxiety attack. Have you experienced this before?"

She admitted she had on several occasions and she described the situations in which it had happened, all of them triggered by a male advance. Pia listened and passed her a box of tissues when she began to cry.

"I can't help it," explained Kathryn, "it's not Jamie's fault and he didn't do anything wrong."

"Well, he did as there are strict rules forbidding relationships between colleagues, and he also misread the signals."

"We both had a lot to drink."

There was a long pause before Pia asked, "I've read your file and I know the circumstances surrounding your mother's death, but did your stepfather attack you as well?"

Kathryn began to cry.

"Anything you tell me is confidential," urged Pia passing her a tissue.

Through her sobs, Kathryn told her how her stepfather had sexually abused her from the age of nine until she was fourteen, when he'd strangled her mother. Afterwards, she'd gone to live with her grandmother. She told her about the counselling and how she'd begun to make progress up until the point she was arrested. When Pia asked if she'd ever been in a sexual relationship as an adult, Kathryn shook her head.

"I knew about your mother's tragic death, but not this. If I had, I'd never have allowed them to place you in this situation."

Kathryn blew her nose and looked at her beseechingly. "Oh God, don't take me off this job. I have to do it; if I don't, I'll be put back in jail." When Pia said nothing, she begged, "Please, I'll do whatever it takes." Great sobs wracked her frame, "Without this opportunity, I'll have no life."

Pia exhaled a long breath and regarded her. "Kathryn, I understand that but the stress of an undercover operation may be too much. It's not just your welfare I need to consider, it's Jamie's safety and the others involved in this operation. There's more than your mental health at stake here. People could die."

Wide-eyed, Kathryn gasped, "So, is that it, I'm finished?"

Pia offered her a half smile. "I need to give it some thought. I'll let you know when I've made my decision."

JAMES

"For I know the plans I have for you ... plans to prosper you and not to harm you, plans to give you hope and a future."

— *JEREMIAH 29:11*

Jamie

Jamie glanced at the clock. Kathryn had been with Pia for over an hour and he was beginning to worry about what they were discussing. If Kathryn told her about his stupid actions the previous evening, that'd be the end and he'd be on the next flight home. He really needed to curb his drinking, but self-medicating was the only way he could escape from his thoughts, and the nightmares and flashbacks were getting worse. He stifled a groan at the prospect of having to return to the cyber unit and face his colleagues; it was bad enough to be passed over for promotion, but to return in disgrace would be unbearable. And although this job might prove to be a dull financial one, it was a foot in the door at MI5 and a good career opportunity. He looked at the clock again.

Kathryn returned visibly upset and obviously still determined to ignore him. Jamie's gut knotted. When Morris announced he was "not happy" and suggested they took a half hour break, Jamie attempted to talk to her but she blanked him and left the room.

Cursing, Jamie went in search of Pia. Her office door was ajar and, as he approached, he overheard her on the phone.

"Julien, what's the point in me being part of this team when no one listens to a word I say? You couldn't have picked a less suitable pair."

Jamie halted as he was about to knock, and Pia spotted him. She told Julien she'd call him back, beckoned him in and invited him to take a seat.

She said, "Kathryn told me what happened."

Jamie paced the room and stabbed a hand through his hair. "It's entirely my fault. We were getting on really well, or so I thought, and we'd had a lot to drink. I just overstepped the mark."

"What were you thinking Jamie? You know the rules. You can't have a relationship with a fellow officer, and certainly not a junior one in your charge."

"I know, and it'll never happen again."

"But Jamie, there's more to this than either of us knew, and it's serious enough that I can't allow Kathryn to continue."

He gasped, "Pia, you cannae pull the plug. This is entirely my doing; she's done nothing wrong."

"I can and I have to. Even if Kathryn muddles her way through the interview, the stress of spending weeks undercover might tip her over the edge and pull you over with her."

He perched opposite her. "Pia, she'll go back to prison. Don't do this to her."

"Jamie there are lives at stake. One wrong move could result in catastrophe. You know that."

"I'm willing to take the risk and I'll do whatever it takes to help her if it means she can continue. Please Pia."

She rubbed her temples and groaned. After what seemed like an interminably long time, she looked at him and said, "I shouldn't be telling you this but you witnessed her panic attack. It's not something I can treat overnight."

"You don't need to. We just need to fool folk into thinking she's my wife."

"In a week? You do realise you've an interview with the Colquhouns soon?"

He blew out a breath. "Please Pia, I cannae throw her to the wolves. Just tell me what I need to do. You'll have my full cooperation from now on."

Pia went to the bookshelves and began selecting various text books which she fanned out on the coffee table in front of him.

She said, "I can't share what the issue is without breaking patient confidentiality, and I'm in serious danger of crossing professional boundaries doing this."

Jamie scanned titles on childhood sexual abuse, rape and incest.

"Fuck!" he exclaimed. Holding his head in his hands, he met Pia's gaze and they swapped a look. "I'd no idea."

"None of us did, but you need to be fully aware of what we're up against. What we're asking you to do could be dangerous for both you and Kathryn."

Jamie got up and paced again. "We have to help her, especially…" he indicated the books. "If we don't then she's being punished again for what happened to her. Please Pia, I'll take really good care of her."

Pia sighed. "Fine, you have one chance. But if there's another incident or if at any point I think she's a danger to herself, you or this operation, I will pull the plug."

"Thank you. I'll take full responsibility. Just tell me what I need to do."

"This won't be easy for either of you, Kathryn especially."

"I understand."

"I'm also concerned that you're forming an attachment, Jamie. You're going to have to maintain a strict professional and emotional distance while you're living together. Are you sure you can handle that?"

"Yes, absolutely. There'll be no repeat of last night."

He hoped his face didn't betray the fact he wasn't quite so sure.

~

Over lunch, Pia arranged for them to have a restorative meeting in her office. The two of them sat at the coffee table, and Jamie noticed that the text books had been returned to the bookshelf. Kathryn avoided his gaze and picked at her sandwich.

He flashed her a contrite smile. "I'm sorry. I was a dick."

She met his eye and with a brief shake of her head said, "You are a dick, but I overreacted."

"It's no excuse but I'd too much to drink. It won't happen again. You have my word."

She whispered. "But it has to. We've got to pretend to be husband and wife."

He fixed her with a cool blue stare. "And we will pretend Kathryn, your liberty depends on it." Placing his palms on his knees, he added, "I didn't mean to frighten you. I don't know what happened to you, Pia wouldn't say, but I'm not stupid. And I need you to know I'll never force you to do anything you're not comfortable with. I want to help you but you'll have to trust me. For both our sakes."

Looking at him through wet lashes, she mouthed, "Thank you."

Smiling, he said, "Now finish your sandwich and come a walk with me Mrs Campbell."

Kathryn

Pia called Kathryn to her office after lunch, and Kathryn explained that she and Jamie had cleared up the misunderstanding and were determined to make the project succeed. She thanked Pia for letting her stay.

Pia peered at her over the top of her glasses. "You're only here because Jamie fought hard to keep you. You've him to thank."

Kathryn's mouth fell open and she blinked.

Pia steepled her hands. "You and I have a lot of hard work to do in a very short time. It won't be easy because I'm going to ask you to revisit some painful memories and step well out of your comfort zone. I need you to reach the point where you can tolerate physical contact with Jamie. Most communication is non-verbal so it matters less what you say; it's how you are with each other."

"How do I get to that point quickly enough?"

"Have you heard of exposure therapy?" When Kathryn shook her head, Pia explained it was a form of Cognitive Behaviour Therapy for reducing anxiety responses where the person is gradually exposed to a feared situation and learns to become less sensitive over time. She said, "It's particularly effective for phobias so by the time you arrive in Knoydart, we'll have you behaving like newlyweds."

Wide-eyed, Kathryn said, "Uhm, okay."

Pia regarded her and asked how she felt about holding Jamie's hand later.

Kathryn felt a bead of sweat trickle down her spine. "I'm willing to try."

"Good." Pia sat back in her chair. "But first I want you to tell me about Moniker, and how you feel when you become her."

Kathryn considered her answer for a few moments. "Powerful. I'm more comfortable in cyberspace than I've ever been in the physical world. I know how it works and what to expect and I have friends. I can achieve anything I put my mind to."

"Anything else?"

"I feel safe. Or at least I did before I was arrested."

"I think we can use this. I want you to be more like Moniker in the real world."

"You mean fake it til I make it?"

Fixing her with her blue gaze, she said, "No Kathryn, I want you to fake it until you become it."

Pia left Kathryn with that thought while she went to fetch Jamie. Kathryn slumped back in the chair and sighed, unable to believe it was Jamie who'd fought her corner, especially after she'd rejected him. She'd assumed he'd have been delighted to see her in jail since he'd made it clear that's where he thought she belonged. So, to learn that Jamie Denton was the one pleading her case to keep her from prison was nothing short of a miracle.

What had changed his mind? Although she knew they'd been getting along well, was that enough of a reason or was there something else? Did he like her in a different way? Surely not. From her internet stalking, she knew he was in a relationship. But even if he wasn't, why would a smart, successful man like Jamie, who probably could have any woman he wanted, be interested in her?

At that moment Jamie appeared and flashed her one of his amazing smiles which made her heart leap. She smiled back as she reappraised him, feeling more confused than ever.

Pia asked them to pull their chairs closer together, then she said, "Kathryn, I'd like you to take Jamie's hand."

Kathryn swallowed hard and looked at his hand as if she'd been asked to hold his penis. Tentatively, she reached out and grasped his fingers. Her heart thrummed in her ribcage and she began to perspire. The contact felt alien and she could feel the gorge rising in her throat. Jamie smiled encouragingly.

"Excellent. Hold it for as long as you can," said Pia.

She managed a minute before feelings of panic overwhelmed her.

Pia smiled approvingly. "Well done, that was a really good start. Now, during the afternoon break, I'd like you two to go for a walk and hold hands for as long as you can. Then, from now on, each time you go anywhere, I want you holding hands. You'll find you can do it for longer each time."

She nodded apprehensively.

Smiling, Pia added, "Then, we'll have Jamie put his arm around you."

Kathryn felt a baffling mixture of excitement and nausea.

Next morning, Julien confirmed what Pia had said; the Campbells had been offered an interview with the Colquhouns during the following week in Glasgow. Julien was nervous because it was happening far quicker than anticipated and, with it being on home turf, there was the added risk of bumping into people they knew.

Fitz came to the rescue after intercepting email correspondence between the Colquhouns in which Marcus had sent Ruth a shortlist of candidates and sample interview questions. They were planning on seeing four couples and Julien was concerned because one couple appeared to have more experience than the Campbells.

"What if they offer it to this other lot?" asked Jamie.

Fitz chuckled, "They won't. I've already spoofed the Colquhoun's email address and cancelled their interview. And if the Colquhouns offer it to someone else, we'll soon make sure they retract it after they see the references, criminal records check and credit history I'll supply." Grinning, he added, "Sometimes, I really love my job."

After spending several days practising their undercover personas and their responses based on the Colquhouns' interview questions, Pia asked to speak to Kathryn in her office. They'd been meeting regularly, and today they were celebrating a major milestone after she and Jamie had held each other around the waist for over a minute. Kathryn had been surprised at how relaxed she'd felt and she'd have tolerated it longer had Pia not called a halt. She'd even leant her head against Jamie's chest.

"You're making really good progress Kathryn but we don't have long until the interview so we need to take it up a level."

"Uhm, when you say take it up a level?"

Pia smiled. "When you're in Glasgow, I'd like you to share a room."

Two days before the interview Morris announced that, if they were good boys and girls, they'd get to play dress-up. Kathryn asked what he meant and he explained that a team was coming to alter their appearance and take photographs.

Jamie added, "You've been on the front of too many newspapers because of the court case."

"I was wearing a beanie and sunglasses," she protested, "I doubt anyone'll recognise me."

Kathryn ran her fingers through her locks and wondered what they'd planned. She couldn't remember the last time she'd had her hair cut properly; she'd always trimmed her own fringe and split ends.

"Maybe they'll give you a short, back and sandpapered," he teased.

She replied, "Maybe they'll turn you ginger."

He scowled and she laughed.

Morris explained that they'd be issued with a passport, driving licence and bank cards under their new identities, along with other supporting material. Fitz would also insert fake records into the official bureaucracy, including tax returns and speeding fines in case anyone checked. In the past, he explained, spies assumed the identity of a dead child; however, apart from this being morally questionable, they'd had cases of cover being blown when death records had been unearthed.

"Are they likely to check that thoroughly?" asked Kathryn suddenly feeling anxious.

Morris replied, "Never ever underestimate your target."

Jamie

Back in the apartment, Jamie knew he was in trouble. Stretched out on the bed, he replayed the day's events in his head, conscious that she was just feet away in the next room.

The afternoon had been spent with a team of hairdressers, barbers and beauticians who'd dyed, cut, shaved and plucked them. After highlighting and cutting his hair, they'd shaved off his short beard. He disliked the clean-shaven look as his scar was more visible. He barely recognised himself, but his transformation was nothing compared to Kathryn's. Long blonde locks cascaded over her shoulders, cut to reveal her high cheekbones and arched eyebrows. She could have graced the cover of *Vogue*; she'd taken his breath away. Surprisingly, she'd been furious when the team had told her how they planned to alter her appearance and she'd railed against it. In the end Pia had to intervene and a compromise was reached with a darker shade of blonde, less makeup and the assurance she could still tie back her hair.

Morris had not been joking about playing dress up. In different outfits, they'd posed for passport, holiday, and wedding photographs and Kathryn had been nothing short of vituperative when she'd seen the clothes she'd to wear, prompting another intervention from Pia. But it was the beach scenes Jamie would remember, even if they were against the backdrop of a green screen. Kathryn's bikini hid nothing and neither had his shorts; he just hoped the bulge wasn't visible in the pictures. As he and Kathryn held each other for the benefit of the camera, Pia had sent him a wry smile. That woman missed nothing.

Later, each sporting a gold wedding band and in new clothes, they'd gone for dinner at the Royal Oak. They'd walked in with their arms around each other's waists, and Jamie had noticed every male head in the pub turn. He enjoyed having Mrs Campbell on his arm. She was very beautiful but, for him, the most attractive thing about her was that she'd absolutely no idea.

It wasn't just her beauty that enthralled him. She was different to any woman he'd known. He could talk to her, and intelligence shone behind her striking grey eyes to the extent he felt slightly intimidated. He chuckled at her besting of Fitz during their cybersecurity discussions, and Fitz appeared to be as intrigued by her as he was, and Jamie had felt a stab of jealousy which surprised him.

He'd had a few relationships, even a long-term one with Emma, but none of his girlfriends had affected him like this; in comparison, they'd been lacking any substance. This, whatever the hell this was, felt very different. He longed to hold her, run his hands through that hair, kiss those lips, lick... Jamie groaned in frustration. It wasn't going to happen. It couldnae happen. In any case, she struggled just to let him embrace her, and they'd yet to work up to a perfunctory kiss, never mind anything remotely passionate. He shuddered at the thought of what had happened to make her this way. It saddened him and he wanted to hurt whoever was responsible. Badly.

Cursing, he recalled how he'd misread the signals that evening when he'd kissed her. Or had he? There was something between them. A spark. He saw it in her eyes. She was not without feelings but these appeared to war within her, along with her demons. Could Pia help her? Could he? And in time? If they somehow muddled through the interview, they could be in Knoydart in a matter of weeks. And if they didn't, what then? He couldnae bear the thought of her in a prison cell. She didn't deserve to be there. She didn't deserve any sort of punishment. He wanted to wrap his arms around her, hold her tight and keep her safe.

Christ, he was in so much trouble.

Kathryn

Their interview with the Colquhouns was due to take place the following afternoon and, since the forecast was for snow, Julien thought it prudent for the team to fly up to Glasgow the day before. Jamie and Kathryn had travelled ahead of the others, in case they encountered the Colquhouns or anyone connected to the Ehrlich Society, and they arrived at a hotel in a quiet part of the city.

Pia explained that, as a reward for all their hard work and to help them relax before the interview, they could enjoy an afternoon off before the team reconvened. After checking in as Mr and Mrs Campbell, they lugged their overnight bags up to their spacious ensuite room. Opulently decorated, it boasted a sitting area in a bay-fronted window and a stunning view over Glasgow University's gothic buildings. And an enormous queen-size bed.

Jamie whistled his approval. Kathryn swallowed hard.

Catching her expression, he said, "I'll sleep on the sofa." Then, picking up the welcome pack from the coffee table, he asked, "What d'you want to do this afternoon?" A sheet of paper floated from the pack and he picked it up. Chuckling, he said, "Ah, looks like Pia's taken care of it." He passed her the sheet.

Reading it, she asked, "Err, what's a *Couple's Mineral Body Bliss*?"

"We're having a full body massage together."

Panic rising, she stammered, "Uhm, I've never…"

Smiling, he reached for her hand. "Relax Kathryn, it'll be a female masseuse and you'll enjoy it. Anyway, it's not til later. Fancy a swim?"

She nodded, but the action was at odds with how she felt.

Jamie was already in the pool when she appeared and she noticed the sweep of his gaze as she stepped into the warm water. She swam over to him, keeping her piled up hair out of the water. They hugged the sides of the pool and grinned at one another. Except for a young family splashing in the hot tub, they'd the place to themselves.

"You swim like a girl," he teased.

"That's because I am one, in case you hadn't noticed."

"Oh, I've noticed" he chuckled, fixing her with eyes the same colour as the water.

She felt herself blush under the intensity of his stare.

"Race you," he said, kicking off.

Launching herself into the water, she followed him but he was too fast for her hair-out-the-water breaststroke.

"What took you so long?" he said when she sidled up next to him.

"You cheated by giving yourself a head start."

"I'm going to buy you one of those floral swimming caps."

She flicked water at him. When he threatened to reciprocate, she squealed that she didn't want her hair wet which made him laugh even more, and he said he'd add it to his 'things that annoy Kathryn' case file. On the count of three, they repeated the race but he was too quick and he grinned at her with boyish delight.

"You're not competitive at all Mr Campbell," she panted, her voice laced with sarcasm.

"Not in the least Mrs Campbell."

After a few more breadths and a lot more teasing, he suggested a dip in the hot tub which the family had vacated. As he exited the pool she tried not to focus on his broad chest with its sharply defined pectorals, and the ripples of a six-pack that tapered to a narrow waist. Sleek and muscled like a sculpture, he exuded male beauty and power. They stretched out next to each other beneath the bubbles on the Jacuzzi's moulded plastic seats. She felt the press of his thigh against hers and she closed her eyes and tried to make sense of these unfamiliar feelings.

"What you thinking?" he asked.

Startled, she opened her eyes to find him scrutinizing her. He was very close. "Hmm, just about all of this. I could never have imagined this a few weeks ago. Especially with you."

He laughed. "Aye, me neither, it's bizarre." They gazed at one another.

She broke the silence. "You any idea how long we're likely to be in Knoydart? I mean if we get the job?"

Jamie looked out of the bank of windows into the middle distance, then back at her. "Depends how quickly we find what we need." He paused and regarded her. "It takes time to win a target's trust so, unless we get lucky, it's likely to be months rather than weeks."

She bit her bottom lip. "Uhm, okay."

He took her hand, interlocking their fingers. "It'll be easier once we're there. It's fear of the unknown at the moment, but you won't be on your own Kathryn, I'll be with you the whole time and I promise I'll take care of you." He squeezed her hand. She squeezed back and returned a wan smile, feeling completely out of her depth.

He rose and helped her up. "C'mon, time for a massage Mrs Campbell."

He only released her hand when they parted for the changing rooms. After she'd dried and dressed in her underwear and the hotel's white fluffy robe and slippers, she found him sitting in the spa's reception flicking through a magazine. She took a moment to appraise him before he noticed her. With his wet hair and a robe that did little to hide his physique, she realised he was the most handsome man she'd ever seen, even with the scar. And she wasn't the only one to notice; the woman across from him was staring at him. Surprised at the spike of jealousy she felt, Kathryn cut the woman a hard glare as she sat next to him. When she reached for his hand, his face lit up in a smile that set her alight.

They heard their names called and he placed his hand at the base of her spine sending tingles up her as they followed their two fresh-faced therapists to a small room. She felt a frisson of excitement at his touch, realising for the first time how welcome it felt, and she slipped an arm around his waist. Grinning in delight, he pulled her to him. I can do this, she thought.

The women left them to undress and get settled. Slipping from her robe, she couldn't fail to notice the appreciative look he cast her before tearing his eyes away. Face-down, she burrowed beneath the warm scented towels and let out a long sigh of satisfaction. The dimly lit room smelled of lavender, and tranquil music played through a speaker in the corner. Jamie made a similar sound to hers as he stretched out his long limbs and relaxed. Chin resting on the back of his hands, he grinned over at her, his eyes twinkling, and they swapped a smile.

The massage felt incredible and she could feel the tension of the last few weeks melt beneath her therapist's soothing touch. The women seemed to move silently, the only sounds the soft music and the occasional slurp of lotion before hands caressed her. Her head swam with the sensations and she didn't want it to end. Pia, she realised, was very clever; she would never have chosen to do this. At the end of the session, the therapists left them to dress and slipped silently away.

Kathryn felt like she was floating.

Jamie

Jamie had enjoyed spending the afternoon with Kathryn and she'd seemed happy and relaxed, and he hoped that was not all about to change. As they finished dinner in a quiet corner of the hotel restaurant, his phone buzzed. After reading the screen, he said, "Back to reality. The others are here."

Taking her hand, he led her through the busy restaurant towards the foyer, conscious of the looks she drew from other men. Mrs Campbell was strikingly beautiful and he felt a surge of pride being with her. When the maitre d' cast a lingering glance over her and wished them a pleasant evening, Jamie found himself slipping a possessive arm around her waist. She'd grown accustomed to his touch and he smiled at the fact she no longer flinched and, on occasion, even willingly sought his hand.

Julien opened the door to his room wearing a shirt without the top button done; the most casual Jamie had ever seen him. "Do come in, Mr and Mrs Campbell," he said, "I trust you've both had a lovely afternoon."

Kathryn smiled. "I've had a wonderful day, thank you."

Pia and Fitz joined in with their laughter. Pia sat in a wingback chair in the bay window and Fitz lounged on the bed, surrounded by an array of wires and equipment. The room was smaller than theirs and felt cramped.

"Nice work for some," mumbled Fitz, "we've had to rough it in here with room service." He took a bite from a cheeseburger.

Pia asked if Kathryn had enjoyed the massage.

Fitz gasped. "Massage! Oh, that's just not fair."

Chuckling, Kathryn said, "It was heaven."

Pia rewarded her with a smile and a wink at Jamie, who said to Fitz, "The three-course dinner was lovely too."

Fitz muttered something rude and took a slug from a bottle of beer.

"Right," announced Julien, "Holiday's over. Let's get down to business."

They spent the rest of the evening rehearsing for the interview with Julien and Pia role-playing the part of the Colquhouns, while Fitz hovered around fiddling with cameras and listening devices.

By the time they'd finished, both Kathryn and Jamie were looking a lot less relaxed.

Kathryn

Kathryn snuggled under the duvet and watched Jamie over its top. He'd emerged from the bathroom wearing only pyjama bottoms and, once again, she marvelled at his honed physique.

Wide-eyed, she watched as he approached the bed. He smiled at her as he took a pillow and threw it onto the sofa. After retrieving a blanket from the top of the wardrobe, he wished her good night and curled up underneath it.

She switched off the bedside lamp and lay awake staring at the ceiling feeling a mixture of relief and wanting something more. But what? It took her a while to succumb into sleep and when she did, her dreams were filled with Jamie.

She woke to the sound of him screaming.

Sitting bolt upright, she flicked on the light. It took her a moment to orient herself until she saw Jamie thrashing around on the couch and shrieking in terror. She leapt out of bed, approached him and called his name. When he continued to flail his limbs, she called his name again and placed a hand on his shoulder. He twisted around and glared at her, eyes wild and nostrils flaring. Frightened, she stepped back and shouted his name which finally seemed to wake him. She crouched down beside him and he reached out for her. He was drenched in sweat and he clung to her.

"Sorry," he rasped after gradually releasing her, "I should've warned you that might happen."

She sat back on her haunches, took his hands in hers and looked at him. "What were you dreaming about?"

He sucked in a breath and shook his head.

"Please tell me Jamie."

He paused for a moment then whispered, "Matt, my buddy, the day he was killed."

"Do you have the nightmares often?"

"Aye, most nights, always the same one. It's like a freeze-frame image of me holding him as he dies."

"C'mon," she said, tugging him to his feet. "Lie beside me."

He looked at her apprehensively. "I'm okay here, honestly."

"Jamie, the bed's huge and you need your rest before tomorrow."

Grabbing his pillow, he climbed in beside her. They lay on their backs and she took his hand over the duvet, their arms forming a barrier between them. Jamie fell asleep quickly, but it took her far longer, her thoughts full of how tortured each of them was in their own way.

To her surprise, she awoke in his arms. To her greater surprise, she didn't flinch or pull away. She gently disentangled herself so as not to wake him and padded towards the bathroom. She sensed something had changed, something had shifted.

Then she remembered what the day held in store.

~

After a late breakfast, they joined the others in Julien's room and Fitz fitted their clothing and Kathryn's bag with tiny cameras and listening devices.

After testing them, Fitz announced, "We're good. We have eyes and ears."

Kathryn's gut clenched and she excused herself to the bathroom; her second visit in as many minutes.

Pia handed her a camomile tea when she re-emerged. "Just let Jamie do most of the talking." She took her hand and whispered, "Remember, fake it til you become it."

Kathryn bit her lip and nodded. She'd rarely felt so far out her comfort zone. She reached out for what she knew, where she felt in control: "Are we any nearer finding out what it is these Ehrlich people are up to? What it is I'm to hack into?"

Julien shook his head. "We need to get you and Jamie to Knoydart so you can meet up with Jean and find out what it is that has disturbed her. That's when you can do your thing."

It wasn't the reassurance she needed but Kathryn took heart from the reminder that she had an important part to play.

When it was time, Julien bundled them into the back of a black cab and wished them luck. "Relax, we've got everything covered" he said, slamming the door.

Kathryn hoped he was right.

"Ready Mrs Campbell?" asked Jamie taking her hand.

Stood in the foyer of the Royal Scotsman hotel, Kathryn's heart pounded and she felt sick. Spotting her expression, Jamie whispered, "Hey, take a deep breath and relax. I've got you."

When she nodded, he guided her past reception and into the noisy bar restaurant. Her legs felt wobbly and she had to concentrate on not slipping in her low heels. It was packed full of long tables of office Christmas parties and, judging by the state of some of them, they'd been drinking for a while. She recognized the Colquhouns waving at them from a table in the far corner. Kathryn's pulse raced and she felt light-headed. Jamie squeezed her hand.

Marcus stood and thrust out a hand to Jamie. Over six foot tall and powerfully built, he made his wife look tiny by comparison.

Jamie shook it, saying, "Pleased to meet you Mr Colquhoun," pronouncing it properly as 'Colhoon'.

Marcus chuckled, "Full marks for getting the name right." He then pressed a strong hand into Kathryn's and she had to concentrate on not flinching at the power of his grip.

Ruth offered her a gentle hand shake and a warm smile. 'You-all come and sit here,' she said, indicating they should take a seat opposite. "You'll get used to the accent, it's a mixture of Scotland and Florida. I call myself a 'Tallahassee lassie'." Kathryn didn't know enough about American accents to be able to identify Ruth's but it certainly sounded Southern. She was reminded of one of her favourite childhood cartoons, Deputy Dawg.

"I'm so sorry about the noise," said Marcus in a soft Highlands and Islands accent. "We forgot it was Christmas party season."

A loud cheer went up behind them as a nearby table exchanged Secret Santa gifts. They turned to see a young lad darting round his colleagues waving a rubber dildo. Eyes crinkling with humour, Ruth exclaimed, "Oh lordy, lordy!"

After ordering coffees, the Colquhouns got down to business. Jamie kept hold of Kathryn's hand as they chatted about the responsibilities of running a profitable sporting estate, and Marcus explained their income also came from farming, fishing and forestry. They discussed the logistics of organising deer stalking and shooting parties, salmon and trout fishing, property maintenance, and staff management. Jamie answered their questions confidently and smoothly, citing his Yorkshire experiences, and the Colquhouns appeared impressed.

The conversation then turned to the Ehrlich religious beliefs, which Marcus summed up as conservatively Christian mingled with environmentally radical. He described himself as an "eco-theologian" who was passionate about caring for God's creation. Jamie explained that one of the reasons he'd decided to leave his current employment was that, much to his dismay, the new owners of the estate on which he worked had abandoned their sustainability pledge.

Ruth chatted to Kathryn about how she'd be expected to work part-time helping with housekeeping in the holiday cottages, and Kathryn produced her prepared answers. Beneath the table, Jamie clasped her hand reassuringly.

The hubbub around them increased to the extent it was difficult to hear above the raucous laughter and screeching. The lad with the dildo approached their table, and Kathryn looked up in horror as he dangled a sprig of mistletoe above their heads.

"Excuse me young man," snapped Marcus, "we're in the middle of a business meeting."

Ruth placed a steadying hand on his arm and said, "Oh it's fine honey, it's just a little ol' fun."

Spurred on by Ruth and his drunken colleagues, the swaying lad waved the mistletoe more insistently, slurring, "Aye, c'mon mate, it's Christmas, give the lassie a wee kiss."

Kathryn's heart pounded and she felt faint. Panic mounting, she battled to remain in control as the Colquhouns looked at her. Jamie clasped her hand tighter and fixed her with a cool blue gaze. Focusing on his eyes, she squeezed his fingers in reply. Eyes locked on her, he leant in slowly and placed a gentle kiss on her mouth. Her breath caught as his lips brushed hers, and she thought her heart would burst through her chest wall. Instead of flinching, though, she pressed her mouth to his and let the kiss linger. As laughing and clapping erupted around them, Jamie's eyes widened in surprise and they exchanged a smile as they broke apart. He clutched her hand firmly in both of his.

Ruth clapped like an excited schoolgirl, "Oh lordy, you're such a cute couple."

After badgering the Colquhouns to kiss, the young lad staggered back to his table and they all chuckled.

Marcus and Ruth exchanged a brief look, then Marcus turned to Jamie. "If we were to offer you the position, how soon would you be able to start? The advert stated the new year but, ideally, we'd like the new manager in place before Christmas."

Before Jamie could reply, Ruth asked, "How do you feel about that Mrs Campbell?"

Kathryn glanced at Jamie, dropped her gaze and said, "I'll let my husband decide."

The Colquhouns smiled approvingly.

Marcus wound up the interview and he and Ruth followed the Campbells back towards reception. Jamie took a firm grip of Kathryn's hand as he steered her past the noisy revellers. Relieved their ordeal was almost over, Kathryn failed to spot the danger until it was too late, and she let out a gasp of surprise as her training partner Chris stepped into their path.

"Hey Kathryn, I thought it was you," said Chris sweeping his eyes over her and Jamie and their clasped hands. Chris wore a ridiculous paper hat at a jaunty angle. "You look different."

Eyes bulging, Kathryn stammered out a greeting as Jamie retained a steady grip of her.

"Aren't you going to introduce me?" asked Chris shooting a questioning look at Jamie.

Kathryn was speechless. Jamie thrust his hand out and introduced himself as Kathryn's husband. The Colquhouns observed with interest.

Chris shot Kathryn a look of surprise and blurted, "I didn't realise you'd got married."

"It's a recent thing," said Jamie smiling.

Kathryn said nothing. Then a squeeze on her hand snapped her from her stupor and she mumbled, "Sorry, it's just been such a while since I saw you." Worried her knees were about to buckle, she clung to Jamie.

Undeterred, Chris said, "What happened in court? I didn't realise you were out…"

Jamie interrupted, "Yes, that's a recent thing too. Anyway, it was very nice to meet you Chris but if you'll excuse us, we're in a bit of a rush. Perhaps catch up another time?" He tugged Kathryn towards reception as Chris stared at them.

In reception, Marcus shot them a questioning look.

"Car accident," said Jamie. "Kathryn was in hospital for a bit but she's fine now. Drunk driver, ended up in court." Putting his arm around her waist, he pulled Kathryn to his side and added, "Still upsetting for her to talk about."

Grateful for his support, she hung onto him as the Colquhouns offered their sympathies and thanked them for coming. After shaking hands and saying goodbye, Jamie led her outside and around the corner. Swapping a look of relief, they exhaled a long breath which misted in the cold air. He wrapped her in his arms and held her, and she burrowed into his chest and released a torrent of tears.

He chuckled, "Well done Mrs Campbell, I think we pulled it off."

~

"I aged ten years watching that", yelled Julien as they entered the hotel room. "Who the hell was he?"

"Chris," mumbled Kathryn slumping into a chair. Fitz passed her a beer as she explained how she knew him.

"Smoothly done Jamie," acknowledged Julien with something akin to respect.

Jamie perched on the end of the bed and took a long slug of his beer. "Think we got away with it. But what were the chances?" He shook his head indulgently as he glanced at Kathryn.

"You were both brilliant," said Pia beaming at them.

Fitz tapped on his laptop, "I'm just creating some fake news stories about your car accident. In case anyone starts checking."

They all laughed, the tension finally easing.

But all Kathryn could think about was that kiss.

~

After a debriefing, they'd all taken an evening flight and returned to the training facility.

Next morning, Kathryn met with Pia and they discussed her martial arts training and the physical contact aspects of it. Kathryn reasoned that, because she'd known Chris since they were kids, she'd felt none of the anxiety that gripped her when a male she didn't know touched her.

"Hmm, interesting", said Pia, "it's situational as well as gender-specific. I think we can use this."

Kathryn didn't have long to wait to find out what Pia had planned. After lunch, Pia arranged for her and Jamie to train together in the facility's gym supervised by Paul, the resident PT instructor and self-defence coach. After Paul had put them through their paces, Kathryn was surprised to learn that Jamie also had some martial arts training under his belt, and as a boy he'd learned Taijutsu then later, in the military, Krav Maga.

"Bloody hell," gasped Jamie, "I think I preferred the demure wee wife."

Kathryn scowled at him and wound up to unleash another roundhouse kick into the pad he held. Jamie grunted as she followed up with another one into it.

"Aye, you've got a good kick on you," acknowledged Paul as he observed Kathryn. "But most fights go to the ground so, starting tomorrow, I'm going to show you techniques to deal with those situations."

Kathryn noticed the conspiratorial look Jamie and Paul swapped.

Next day, after a session about communicating with their handler who they were yet to meet, they returned to the gymnasium, accompanied by Pia who observed from the side. Paul explained that he was going to show them techniques from the Japanese art of Jiu-Jitsu.

He asked Jamie to help him demonstrate a series of holds for an opponent on the ground. Pinning Jamie to the mat on his back, Paul made the transitions from scarf hold to cross body and reverse scarf hold look fluid and seamless. He also introduced locks and holds to subdue an opponent, making Jamie tap out as he applied them. Kathryn chuckled until Paul got up and announced it was her turn. Telling Jamie to remain where he was, Paul coached her through recreating the flow of the movements.

Beginning with scarf hold, she lay with her back pressing against Jamie's side and slipped her arm under his neck. She used her legs to brace herself against him, and Paul showed her how to press down with her shoulder on the side of Jamie's face and pin him to the ground; a technique he called "the shoulder of justice." Jamie tapped the mat and she grinned in triumph. It felt very intimate.

Next, he talked her through shifting her weight into the cross body and reverse scarf hold positions, while introducing some filthy locks and holds which made Jamie wince and tap. She was enjoying herself until Paul asked them to swap round.

Kathryn gulped as Jamie put her in scarf hold. His weight felt suffocating. Panic rose and she tapped immediately. Jamie released her and sprang to his feet.

Stepping onto the mat, Pia said, "Deep breaths Kathryn. You say when you're ready to try again."

After a few minutes, she nodded and lay back down. Jamie repeated the hold slowly, keeping his eyes fixed on her. As he wound his arm around her neck, he whispered, "I'll release as soon as you tap, I promise."

Reassured, she nodded. Jamie applied his shoulder, pinning her face onto the mat. She lasted a few seconds before tapping and he released her.

"Excellent," said Pia. "Let's finish there and resume tomorrow."

Kathryn exhaled a long breath, making Jamie chuckle.

The next couple of days were spent in a similar pattern, classroom learning followed by practising groundwork at lunchtime while Pia observed. Everyone was nervous while they awaited a decision from the Colquhouns about the interview, especially Kathryn.

Today, Paul announced he was adding a new technique to deal with an attacker who's on top. Paul lay on his back, and asked Jamie to straddle him. Facing him, Jamie knelt down with knees either side of Paul's torso. He told Jamie to aim controlled punches at his head and body which he covered and defended using arms and elbows.

"Order the chaos," said Paul.

Kathryn watched as Paul shuffled up beneath Jamie, then bucked so hard Jamie fell forwards. Paul immediately hooked Jamie's arm, hugged it to him, and arched his back. Twisting his body, and in one fluid movement, Paul flipped him over to gain the dominant upright position, then rained down controlled blows onto his head and body.

Kathryn watched as Paul demonstrated the technique again, and she was caught between wanting to learn it, and knowing how alarmed she'd feel in such a vulnerable position.

Pia approached her and in a low voice said, "Think about the coping strategies we talked about. Don't fight the anxiety; accept it as part of you and control it. You can tap out whenever you want."

Kathryn nodded, determined to try. Paul began by having her on top, and she tried to dispel unpleasant thoughts as she straddled Jamie. The wicked grin he shot her didn't help but it did make her laugh.

"Behave yourself Mr Campbell," she said, "or I really will hit you."

"I'm trying to."

She began to rain down blows which Jamie defended. She gasped as he suddenly grabbed, bucked and flipped her over. He immediately leapt off and helped her up before she had time to panic. They repeated it several times.

"Want to swap?" asked Paul.

She looked at Jamie uncertainly.

"C'mon Kathryn, you can do it and I'll move as soon as you tap."

She lay on her back and Jamie straddled her. An image flashed through her mind and she gasped, the sudden crushing sense of panic pinning her to the ground more effectively than his weight. Startled, he jumped off looking every bit as alarmed. Kathryn's heart raced and she began to tremble.

Pia approached her. "Deep breaths. Embrace the fear, it's not your enemy and it does not control you."

Concentrating on Pia's soothing voice and words, she steadied her breathing as Jamie looked on, worry lining his brow.

"Want to finish there for today?" asked Pia.

She shook her head. "No, again."

They repeated the technique with Pia crouched at her side, coaxing her through it. She lasted a few seconds. On the third attempt, with

Paul's instruction, she wriggled up beneath Jamie which alleviated some of the anxiety.

"Excellent. You've done really well so let's stop there," said Pia smiling.

Jamie helped her up and in a low voice said, "that was really brave."

She smiled. His words made it worth it.

Julien popped his head round the door and called to them, "Congratulations Mr and Mrs Campbell. You got the job."

Kathryn's stomach hit the floor.

They'd very little time left before they were due to depart for Knoydart. The day before they were due to leave, final preparations were being made and they were given a series of forms to complete and sign. Some were minor logistical considerations, such as home insurance and caretaking for while they were away, but the ones concerning life assurance and a will brought home the enormity of the situation. But the task they were most dreading was to come in the afternoon when they knew they'd be interviewed by MI5 interrogation officers whose job it was to test their identities.

Jamie warned her, "They'll intimidate the hell out of you and put you under pressure to try and trip you up. If you don't know the answer, make something up that's as close to the truth as possible so you can repeat it."

Jamie was called first and she wished him luck. The afternoon dragged and, knowing she could be summoned at any moment, she couldn't focus on anything. Finally, Morris appeared and said she'd to make her way to room 101.

"Are you having a laugh?" she asked.

Morris gave her a half-smile and reminded her to stay calm.

Kathryn wished she had Jamie with her, took a deep steadying breath, then knocked and entered. The room was stark and windowless, with a white table and three plastic chairs, two of them occupied by men in dark suits. They looked at ease, slumped back with their hands laced behind their heads. The older suit sat up and invited her to sit, and she pulled the chair away a few inches and perched nervously on the edge. Swallowing, she looked from one to the other; they stared back at her with blank faces.

Biting her bottom lip, she clasped her hands tightly together as she glanced from one to the other. There was a horrible screech of chair on vinyl as the younger suit got up and began to pace behind her. The older man leaned towards her with a menacing grin.

"What's your name?"

Kathryn spent the next two hours being interrogated as they took it in turns, one to question her while the other paced. They used their physical advantage to loom over her as they quizzed her, and not just on the facts contained in her ID pack.

"What qualifications did you get at school and what were the grades?"

That one was easy. Nothing. But several times she'd to think on her feet and, remembering Jamie's advice to stick as close to the truth as possible, she spouted answers. Later, they produced some of the same questions and she managed to repeat her original answers.

When they finally dismissed her, exhausted, she pitched out of the room and slid down the wall of the corridor. The double doors at the far end opened and Jamie appeared grinning. "Looks like someone's in need of a drink," he said. Chuckling, he helped her up, put his arm around her waist and led her out into the grounds. She was glad of his support as she gulped in mouthfuls of fresh air.

"You okay?"

She nodded. "That was … that was…"

He laughed. "I know, it was something else. I found it bad enough and I've used the same techniques on suspects." He pulled her in for a hug and his lips brushed the top of her head. "C'mon, let's get a drink and I promise not to ask you any questions."

She laughed into his chest, enjoying the comfort, warmth and smell of him.

They returned to a pub that Jamie had nicknamed the Flying Tumbler and he bought them both a Rusty Nail cocktail, a potent mixture of whisky and Drambuie. As they sipped them, they chatted about the gruelling interrogation they had undergone, and she felt the anxiety of the last few days melt away along with the ice in her drink. They had another, and the amber nectar went straight to her head.

Before leaving, she popped to the ladies' loo which was situated along a narrow corridor beside the bar. Two lads in their early twenties in workers' overalls leant against the wall. As she walked past them, they leered at her and one gave a low wolf-whistle. She lingered in the loo hoping they'd go but they were still loitering as she headed back to the bar. As she approached, the taller of the two stepped forward and blocked her path.

She glanced up at him and said, "Excuse me please."

He didn't budge as his eyes raked over her and settled on her chest. Pulse racing, she shifted to his left. He blocked her path again. "Hey, what's your hurry sweetie, come and talk to me."

She glowered. "Get out of my way." There were only the three of them in the corridor and fear prickled the nape of her neck.

"That's not very polite, I was only being friendly." He shifted so she had to step back against the wall to avoid him. His associate moved to her other side, trapping her. The tall guy was so close she could smell the alcohol and cigarettes on his breath.

She pushed him away, "Leave me alone!"

He lunged for her and grabbed her wrist, and she twisted it before he could close his grip.

"Don't touch me!" she shouted. Her heart thumped in her chest and she felt dizzy. *Don't freeze. Don't freeze.*

He hooked her arm and pulled her towards him, "You need to learn some manners honey!"

Kathryn spun on her heel, grabbed his shoulder and drove her knee up into his groin. Grunting, he doubled over and dropped to his knees, clutching his balls. Raising her hands, she braced for the next blow as his mate launched himself at her, his face a picture of raw fury.

"GET YOUR FUCKING HANDS OFF HER" roared Jamie, grabbing him by the neck and shoving him.

He fell backwards, arms flailing, a look of shock on his face. Jamie manoeuvred Kathryn behind him, shielding her. The man swung a punch. Jamie raised his arm to block it and smacked him hard in the face, then followed it with a hard fist into his side. His knees buckled and he crumpled to the floor with a heavy thud and a hiss of air.

"You need to learn to treat women with respect," snarled Jamie. Then he turned to her, "You okay?"

She stared open-mouthed at him and at the two figures groaning on the floor. Placing a gentle hand on the base of her spine, he guided her back through the bar and then outside. Pulse still racing, she felt a confusing mixture of relief that she hadn't frozen in terror and gratitude for Jamie's help. They'd bloody well deserved what they got and there'd been a measure of satisfaction in dealing with them.

"I don't know whether to thank you or have a go at you," she said.

He gave her a half-smile. "Violence is rarely the answer but sometimes it's the only answer. And it pisses me off when scum like that think it's okay to harass a woman."

"I'm glad you were there." She added, smiling, "You're pretty impressive Mr Campbell."

His eyes sparkled at her compliment. "So are you. And no one messes with my wife, Mrs Campbell."

Ignoring the protests of the feminist voice inside her head, she realised how good those words felt.

Next morning, they were sat in the classroom recapping the Regulation of Investigatory Powers Act when Julien entered. With a deferential nod, Morris switched off the projector and left the room. Julien pulled up a seat and looked from one to the other.

"It's all happening pretty fast, you'll be in Knoydart soon," he said.

Kathryn's gut clenched at the thought of leaving the relative safety of the training environment.

"I'm going to be straight with you both. I'm under pressure to get a result and bring this to a rapid conclusion. No one wants to see this drag on, and I don't have the budget and resources in any case."

Jamie said, "When you say rapid, just how quick are we talking?"

"Couple of months tops."

Jamie blew out a breath. "That's no time at all for a job like this."

Kathryn swallowed, "And if we don't, what happens to me then?"

With an apologetic smile, he said, "If it was up to me and you performed your duties well, you'd be able to put all this behind you." He paused then said, "But it's not up to me." As he made to go, he added "It's only fair you understand the situation, but I've every confidence in both of you."

After he left, they exchanged a worried look. Remembering her solicitor's words, Kathryn wondered if Jamie was right and they were being set up for a fall, and the intention had always been to return her to prison. She felt tears prick her eyes.

Jamie reached for her hand, "We can do this Kathryn, it's not impossible, and I'll do whatever it takes to help you."

Before her tears had the chance to engulf her, the two MI5 officers who'd interrogated them entered. The older officer smiled and offered Kathryn and Jamie each a handshake, introducing himself as Keith. Kathryn found his sudden change in demeanour almost as unnerving as what he'd put her through the day before. He introduced his younger colleague, Gary.

Keith said, "I wanted to congratulate you both in person. I've interviewed far more experienced field officers who didn't perform half as well, especially you Jamie." He turned to Kathryn, his eyes crinkling with amusement. "I'm afraid you'll be seeing a lot more of me Mrs Campbell as I'll be your handler while you're a UC." Catching her bemused expression, he added, "undercover operator. My job will be to look after you and act as your main point of contact. I'll be nearby in Mallaig for the duration so I'm on-hand in case of any emergency. We'll have the backing of Julien's team in London too, of course."

Gary and Keith pulled up seats next to them and Keith said, "Before you leave for Knoydart, I need to read aloud the instructions for UC officers, and remind you that you're only there to observe and gather pre-emptive intelligence which you will pass to your handler." Turning to Jamie, he said, "You're not there to actively investigate and gather evidence, nor are you there to make an arrest, so I'll need you to surrender your warrant card."

It was beginning to seem very real and Kathryn's stomach knotted with dread. After Keith read out the instructions verbatim, a lengthy discussion followed to ensure they understood the task and the limits of their powers. Keith provided them each with a mobile phone containing his contact details explaining the phones were encrypted but he and Fitz would be able to track them, and access all of their emails, texts and messages. He also supplied Jamie with a satellite phone so they wouldn't be dependent upon a poor phone signal.

Gary said to Jamie, "Before you go, you'll also be equipped with a rifle."

Kathryn exclaimed, "A gun?"

"An estate manager would be expected to have his own weapon, it's not because we think you'll need it to defend yourself. You wouldn't be going if that were the case."

Gary then produced a portable wooden carry case and handed it to Kathryn. "A gift from Fitz."

Laying it on the desk, she opened it to reveal a professional-looking artists' set containing pencils, crayons, paints and a sketchpad. She threw Gary a curious look.

"You need something to hide your kit in. Lift the bottom tray."

Beneath the pencils lay a sleek silver laptop. She took it out and switched it on.

"Password's in your phone. There's space to hide your phone too as ... err ... I understand women are not allowed technology where you're going." Gary's lips twitched in amusement.

With a pinched expression, she said, "I haven't sketched since I was at school."

"Suggest you start watching Bob Ross on YouTube then," said Keith.

After entering the password, she tapped a few keys and whistled at the result. The laptop was state-of-the-art.

Keith made his scary face. "Also encrypted, and no need to remind you we can keep an eye on you, so no moonlighting."

"Who, *moi*?" she said, putting a hand to her chest which made even Keith laugh.

"The operation is called 'Lucifer' and your primary targets have been assigned a code name." Keith looked at Kathryn, a smile playing on his lips. "Normally code names are random but, since there's nothing normal about this operation, we thought we'd make an exception just for you. Marcus and Ruth Colquhoun have been given the names RED FOX and GREY SQUIRREL respectively."

Kathryn and Jamie shook their heads and chuckled.

Jamie asked, "And Elijah Hart, does he have one?"

Nodding, Keith said, "BALD EAGLE."

Finally, Keith reminded them of the need to memorise the telephone number for the MI5 Operations Centre. "They'll answer with 'Hello, can I help you?' to give nothing away about the organisation or who you're speaking to. You must always give your call sign at the start of any communication with me or Base."

Jamie cocked an eyebrow. "Go on, what's my call sign? Bet some jokers had a laugh."

"Your call sign is UCO Culloden," then turning to Kathryn, he said, "And yours is UCO Glencoe."

Jamie and Kathryn swapped a glance. She hoped it wasn't an omen of things to come.

RUTH

Kathryn

"Welcome to Glen Hourn. It's Gaelic for Hell's Valley but we don't put that in the marketing brochures", chuckled Ruth Colquhoun as she sped along the road north towards Loch Hourn.

The Land Rover Defender lurched over the uneven track and Kathryn clung to the seat in front for support. Travelling light, she and Jamie had taken the West Highland Railway to Mallaig and then a boat to Inverie in the south of the Knoydart Peninsula where Ruth had met them. As they drove north, single track roads gave way to rough trails that cut through some of the most breath-taking scenery Kathryn had ever encountered. Although cold, it was sunny. The surrounding mountains were snow-clad, the lower slopes sweeping down to sheep-studded fields.

"That horse-shoe shaped mountain is Ladhar Bheinn, it's the largest," Ruth waved her arm to point it out.

"It's beautiful" said Kathryn "and so unspoilt."

Ruth caught her eye in the rear-view mirror. "It's also wild and unforgiving. You're seeing it on a good day but many hillwalkers have died on these mountains, especially at this time of year. The Ministry of Defence wanted to buy the land to train squaddies. You can see why."

"Who owns it now?" asked Jamie.

"The John Muir Trust, they're a conservation charity who're sympathetic to our beliefs about the environment."

Ruth pulled the Defender around a corner and Hourn House came into view. A spectacular 17th century baronial mansion with turreted grey slate roof, white roughcast walls and stone-framed windows, its classical French architecture lent it an enchanted feel. It was pretty as a box of shortbread.

"Wow!" exclaimed Jamie and Kathryn in unison.

"Yes, it's really something" agreed Ruth, "I feel blessed to live here."

Various buildings were dotted around Hourn House, including a modern one next to the church which Ruth said was their community hall. On the periphery, near the tree-line, stood a contemporary oak barn with enormous glass windows.

"That belongs to Duncan, Marcus's eldest. He prefers the modern style. Even his car's the latest design, you'll not catch him in one of these old rust buckets," said Ruth as she followed the single-track past Hourn House towards a huddle of cottages bordering the loch. Pulling up outside the furthest of these, she cut the engine. "And this is Whitsun Cottage, your new home."

Like the others, the cottage had freshly-painted, white roughcast walls and two dormer windows set into a slate roof. A small garden with an overgrown gravel path dotted with planters surrounded it, and Kathryn imagined it'd be pleasant in the summer months.

With a reassuring smile, Jamie took Kathryn's hand and helped her from the Land Rover, and they followed Ruth into the cottage.

"No one locks their doors around here," remarked Ruth.

A small vestibule led to a sitting room on the right. Kathryn took it all in: greige walls, white coving, mink carpet, plaid-upholstered chairs and tasteful furnishings. A small fireplace with a wood-burner, already lit, gave it a cosy cottage feel. To the left of the vestibule was another room currently used as an office. A narrow kitchen ran the length of the back, fitted with grey shaker-style units, a shiny black Aga range cooker, and a large pantry cupboard. Outside the kitchen stood a lean-to woodshed stacked high with logs which Ruth explained also housed the generator. A steep, narrow staircase led up to a double bedroom and modern bathroom with both a bath and a shower.

Jamie whistled his approval as he strode through the cottage, while Kathryn remarked on how beautifully decorated it was. It was a far cry from her grandmother's dated bungalow.

"I'm glad you like my taste" said Ruth, "I'm slowly working my way round all the cottages but this is my favourite one."

After Jamie had fetched their bags from the car, Ruth said she'd leave them to get settled, adding, "The van with the rest of your things should be here later this afternoon. We're having a wee soirée in the community hall at seven to welcome you. There'll be food but I've left essentials in the cupboard in case ya'll are hungry. There's a shop at the back of the community hall and we make regular trips to the local village. I'll give you a proper tour tomorrow."

Kathryn asked how far the village was.

"About ten miles," said Ruth. Making her way out, she pointed, "Jean's cottage is over on the opposite side, last one on the right. She's so looking forward to meeting you. Says she's not seen you since you were a wee laddie, Jamie."

Ruth's Scottish dialect spoken in her Southern accent sounded odd to Kathryn's ears. After reminding them to keep the wood burner fed since a snow storm was forecast to be on the way, Ruth sped back to Hourn House.

"What d'ya'll think?" asked Jamie mimicking Ruth's drawl.

Kathryn popped more logs into the wood burner and chuckled, "It's a beautiful place and the cottage is lovely."

Jamie carried their bags upstairs and Kathryn followed him. A large metal bedstead dominated the room. There were bedside nightstands with muted lamps and plaid-upholstered bucket chairs. Wardrobes were built into the eaves and a pine chest of drawers stood against one wall. She gulped when she realised this was the only bedroom in the cottage, there was no sofa, and they'd have to share a bed.

"I'm going to pop over and say hello to Jean. Want to come?" asked Jamie.

She tore her eyes away from the bed. "Thanks, but I'll unpack and meet her this evening."

He took her hand and fixed her with his gaze. "Don't worry Kathryn, it'll be fine."

Looking at the bed again, she wondered if it would.

Jamie

As Jamie strolled towards Jean's cottage, his mind was on Kathryn. She'd looked so lost that he'd wanted to put his arms around her and comfort her, but he'd held back in case it spooked her. And seeing her expression at the sight of the only bed saddened him. He'd give his right arm to spend a night with her, so sleeping next to her without touching was going to be torture. Although they'd shared a bed in the hotel, he wondered how he'd cope long-term. And what if he had a night terror and accidentally hurt her?

He spotted a woman emerge from Jean's cottage that he recognised from the photograph Julien had shown him. In her sixties, with long silver hair, she wore a wax jacket, long corduroy skirt and Hunter wellingtons. A small black and white collie lurked at her heels and as she waved and approached, the dog bared its teeth and growled at him.

"You must be Jamie" she said with a warm smile. "Ignore Meg, she doesn't like men." Hugging him, she whispered in his ear, "Say nothing. Follow me."

She led him onto a rough path that ran behind the cottage and up into the foothills. Meg followed them, eyeing Jamie warily. A few metres from the cottage, Jean stopped and turned to him. Glancing around nervously, she said in low voice, "Thank goodness you're here, but I have to tell you right away you'll be watched closely. There are more bugs in your cottage than in East Africa. Whatever you do, don't utter a word about who you really are and why you're here."

Surprised, he said, "In *Whitsun Cottage*?"

"More like *Wits End Cottage*. Looks lovely but there's no central heating and the old generator's flaky." Glancing around again, she whispered, "Jamie, you can't trust anyone here."

He exhaled a breath and rubbed the back of his neck. "Okay, thanks for the warning, I'll let Kathryn know." Spotting the worry lines on Jean's brow, he asked, "Are you alright?"

She nodded. "I can't talk now, I'm due over at the house, but I'll have something for you tomorrow. I'm being watched but the party tonight will give me the chance to get what I'm after from the office. I've also kept a journal. Pop over tomorrow and I'll tell you everything." Her eyes darted towards Hourn House. "There's Ruth, I'd better go."

"Don't take any chances Jean, that's why we're here."

"If what I think is true, I'll have no peace until I tell someone. I couldn't live with myself otherwise."

"When are you planning to leave?"

"The twenty-third. Meg and I are off to my sister's in Sussex. I can't wait to put this behind me, I hate this place."

"Do they know you're going?"

"No. And I won't be the first to do a midnight flit. Your predecessors did the same."

Jamie gave her a quizzical look. "I thought the Pattersons moved to an estate in the Borders?"

"Aye that's what I heard, but we'd got close and Karen told me they were just upping sticks and going. Swore me to secrecy." Jean cast a nervous eye over the valley. "It really is Hell's Glen."

Looking around at the picture-perfect scenery, Jamie wondered what had made her so anxious that she could hate such a wonderous place.

～

Kathryn

Kathryn glanced up at Jamie's arrival. She was feeding more wood into the stove and as she closed the door, she said, "Did you talk to Jean? Did she say..."

Crouching beside her, he cupped her face and smothered her words with a kiss. Squealing, her hands flew to his chest to push him away but he held her tight and whispered in her ear, "Don't say a word." He pulled back and she stared at him wide-eyed, but let herself be tugged outside and into the woodshed.

Breaking from his grip, she thumped his shoulder. "What the hell do you think you're doing?", she hissed.

He raised his hands in surrender and whispered, "Sorry, but I had to stop you saying anything. The cottage is bugged. We can't talk inside and there might be cameras. I'll do a sweep but I can't remove them all, not without raising suspicion."

She stared at him. "Seriously? We're being listened to?"

He nodded. "Maybe watched too. Jean told me. I'll make sure there are no cameras in the bedroom, or bugs in the bathroom but I'll need to leave the rest."

She gawped in horror. This was not what she'd expected. And it was only day one.

"Is Jean alright?" she asked.

"Says she is but she looked really frightened. The good news is she's kept a journal which she'll give us tomorrow. With any luck, it'll be job done."

She put a hand over her mouth. After a pause, she said, "Uhm, sorry for thumping you."

"Sorry for kissing you."

They gazed at one another for a long time.

His lips twitched in amusement then, with a mischievous grin, he said, "Actually, that's a lie, I'm not sorry at all."

He walked away chuckling.

∼

The snow had arrived by the time Kathryn and Jamie went over to the community hall. It was warm and packed with people who'd braved the weather to welcome them. Every head turned as Jamie and Kathryn stepped into the main hall, hand-in-hand. Spotting them, Ruth swooped over to greet them and take their coats. When she began making introductions, Jamie kept his grip on her as they shook hands with a host of members and their families.

Marcus appeared and greeted them, apologising for not being there to welcome them earlier. He was flanked by a bear of a man who towered above him and Jamie. Kathryn reckoned he must be at least six and a half feet tall and, with his wild red hair and powerful build, he looked like a Highlander of yore. Marcus introduced him as Angus MacLean, his youngest son and head of the maintenance department. When Angus thrust out an enormous meaty hand, she fought down her panic and shook it. Jamie reassuringly tightened his grip on her.

"And let me introduce you to Angus's brother Duncan" said Marcus scanning the room.

Although Duncan was slightly shorter and older, he and Angus could have been twins and Duncan extended a warm smile and equally large paw for Kathryn to shake. Marcus explained that, as well as helping with maintenance, his elder son was their ghillie and spent most of his time in the summer months looking after guests who came to hunt and fish on the estate.

Marcus said, "We'll take you shooting as soon as the weather permits, it'll be a chance to show you some of the estate."

Duncan's eyes twinkled as he regarded Kathryn. "It'll be my pleasure to show you round."

Jean appeared and gave Kathryn a kiss on the cheek. "I'm so pleased to finally meet you," she said, beaming. "It's wonderful to have you both here."

Ruth handed each of them a glass of fizz and Marcus raised a toast to their newest arrivals. The hall reverberated with a shout of "Slainte" as glasses were drained.

"We'll crack open the whisky later when the ladies have gone to bed," chuckled Marcus.

Ruth tutted. "Jamie won't want to leave Kathryn alone on her first night."

Marcus shot a teasing look at Jamie. "Aye right enough, you'll be wanting to keep her warm."

Ruth slapped her husband's wrist playfully and they all laughed.

Jamie snaked his arm around Kathryn's waist and pulled her to him. "Can't have her catching a chill."

This was met with more laughter and Duncan's ears reddened. Remembering the double bed awaiting, Kathryn swallowed hard.

A large buffet had been prepared and they tucked in as they chatted. Kathryn knew she'd have forgotten most people's names by the morning but she made an effort at small talk, grateful that she and Jamie had practised their backstories so carefully. Being the only woman in trousers, she felt doubly conspicuous, especially since the others looked as though they made their own clothes.

Marcus introduced them to a couple of the young estate hands, Finlay and Cameron, who were keen to meet their new boss. Finlay was tall and powerfully built with a mop of dark hair, in contrast to the slighter and lighter Cameron.

Finlay regarded Jamie warily, staring at his scar, before asking, "What happened to your face?"

After an awkward few moments, Jamie fixed him with a hard stare and replied, "IED. Iraq."

Kathryn clasped his hand tightly and he shot her a brief smile. After giving Finlay a withering look, Marcus steered the conversation to a discussion of the work the lads were involved in. Ruth appeared and shepherded Kathryn away to meet her good friend Dr Vondell and his wife Myrtle. They were an older couple and Ruth explained that as well as being their resident GP, Dr Vondell was instrumental in the Society's vaccination program in the developing world.

As the evening progressed, Jamie stayed by Kathryn's side and every so often he'd give her hand a reassuring squeeze. It was their secret method of communication, and a way for him to check in with her. She liked the feel of his hand around hers and she was surprised at how accustomed she'd become to his touch. She couldn't get that kiss out of her mind either. Her initial reaction had been to lash out but afterwards, it was all she could think about.

Jamie seemed at ease as he talked of the estate in Yorkshire where he'd worked until recently; the lies slipped effortlessly from his tongue. Kathryn wondered what sort of partner he was to Emma, the girl she'd discovered pictures of during her internet stalking. Did he lie to her? Did she know he was here with her? She felt a sudden stab of jealousy at the thought of Emma and this surprised her. She really needed to stop this line of thinking and she brushed her thoughts of Jamie aside.

She cast her eye over the room looking for Jean but there was no sign of her. She watched as Angus laughed and joked with Cameron, who seemed to find whatever the enormous man was saying incredibly amusing. A heated discussion between Ruth and Duncan caught her attention. Standing outside the main hall in the corridor leading to the rear, they were in the throes of a hushed altercation. Ruth looked furious and she was gesticulating wildly at Duncan, who threw up his hands and stalked off. Kathryn watched as Ruth rearranged her expression before re-joining the party as the perfect hostess.

Marcus wandered over to them and said, "We'll be needing your help tomorrow Jamie, it's falling heavy out there and the road's already blocked."

"Want me to take a look now?"

Dismissing the suggestion with a wave of his hand, he cast a salacious glance in Kathryn's direction. "It'll wait til tomorrow. I wouldn't dream of denying your wife of your presence tonight."

Kathryn bristled but tried not to show it.

Jamie pulled her towards his side. "In that case, I think we'll turn in. It's been a long day and it sounds like I'll have an early start."

Marcus slapped Jamies's back and guffawed. After thanking the Colquhouns, and with a farewell wave to the others, they pulled on their jackets and stepped into a blizzard. The force of the wind took their breath away as they battled to remain on their feet through the white-out. Stumbling through the door of the cottage and brushing snow from their clothes, they laughed with relief.

"I'm glad you've a good sense of direction," said Kathryn shaking snow from her hair. "I'd never have found my way back."

Jamie grinned at her, then cursed when he realised that the electricity was off and the fire in the stove had gone out. He grabbed a torch and pulled up the collar of his jacket. "I'll get the generator going again. You go to bed."

Kathryn's gut gave a lurch. Using a small torch, she picked her way upstairs, and changed into her pyjamas in the bathroom, noting the surfaces were full of unfamiliar men's products such as shaving cream and razors. It was so cold that ferns of ice had formed on the inside of the windows.

Taking one of the extra pillows from the wardrobe, she placed it in the middle of the mattress to form a barrier between them. Then, keeping her socks and cardigan on, she climbed into bed and shivered. She could hear Jamie banging and cursing downstairs, and he appeared twenty minutes later holding a hurricane lamp, muttering that the generator was on the blink. She peered at him over the top of the duvet and blankets. He placed the lamp on the chest of drawers, and it cast a warm glow over the room. And then he began to strip.

Wide-eyed, she watched as he pulled his sweater over his head, loosened his trousers and unzipped them. She felt a frisson of excitement as he peeled them off, and she tore her eyes from the bulge in his boxer shorts. After removing his shirt, he placed his clothes in a neat pile on the chair next to the bed. His side. Cursing at the cold, he pulled on a T-shirt and climbed in beside her. The mattress sagged, rolling them together into the middle. Apologising quietly, they moved apart and she turned her back to him, teeth chittering, while Jamie shuffled to the opposite side. They lay in silence for a few minutes, then he turned towards her, his warm breath at her neck. Her whole body stiffened and her heart thumped.

In a low whisper, he asked, "Want me to sleep on the floor?"

Twisting to face him, she whispered, "You'll freeze to death, and you can't sleep downstairs if we're being watched."

He chuckled, "We might've had a fight."

"And it would've been all your fault."

Grinning, he said, "Okay, night baby," as he turned away.

Smiling at the use of what had become his pet name for her, she lay awake conscious of Jamie's sleeping frame mere inches from her own, feeling a confusing mixture of emotions she couldn't unravel. After half an hour, certain he was asleep, she turned slowly and drank in the sight of his slumbering form in the dim glow. She feasted her eyes on his high chiselled cheekbones, the thick eyelashes fanning over them, and his soft flawless lips, remembering the feel of them earlier. Leaning in, she listened to his gentle breathing, then inched closer until she felt his breath on her face.

Touching her lips to his cheek, she whispered, "Night Jamie. Then, with a contented smile, she settled to sleep.

She awoke in his arms.

Blinking in the cold grey light, she took a moment to orient herself. They'd rolled into the centre of the mattress and Jamie was spooning her, his arm flung across her shoulder. The extra pillow lay on the floor. But the strangest thing of all was that she felt no fear, no panic, no alarm. Relishing this wondrous new sensation, she remained perfectly still, feigning sleep until he finally woke, disentangled himself and rose.

∾

Jamie

Scrubbing a hand over his face, he looked at himself in the bathroom mirror and supressed a groan at the painful erection tenting his boxer shorts. He'd awoken with her in his arms and it had felt wonderful. He'd lain awake enjoying her warmth, the softness of her skin, the vanilla scent of her hair, and the feel of her bottom against his hip. But more amazing was what'd happened last night before he'd fallen asleep. She'd kissed him and whispered "night Jamie" and it had taken every ounce of his self-control to feign sleep and not reach for her. His heart soared at the memory and it confirmed what he'd hoped; she did have feelings for him and he hadn't imagined it. This changed everything, yet it changed nothing.

Now, though, he knew there was a chance, even if it was a slim one.

She'd made enormous progress in recent weeks in letting him touch her, and sometimes she'd even reach for him willingly. But last night and this morning, this was unprecedented. He couldn't act on this, could he? He wanted her, but was loath to scare her off. If he overstepped the mark, it'd be back to square one, and if he didn't act on it, they'd be stuck at this stage forever. He knew what he needed to do and he chuckled at the irony; he needed to court his wife.

There was no hot water so he made do with a cold shower which helped cool his ardour. After dressing, he brewed coffee and, after another unsuccessful look at the generator, he resolved to get it fixed. He made her a mug of tea and crept up to the bedroom and placed it on the nightstand. She opened her eyes, stretched and smiled at him. Even with tousled bed hair, she was beautiful, and she surprised him by reaching out a hand towards him.

"Mmph, thanks for the tea. You been awake long?"

He sat beside her, keeping her hand in his. "There's no hot water, I'll ask Angus to take a look."

They gazed at one another, then Jamie broke the silence, "I'd better go."

"Good luck for your first day Mr Campbell."

Grinning at her, he whispered, "See you later Mrs Campbell."

He rose and reluctantly let go of her hand. Yes, he thought, I definitely haven't misread the signals.

Jamie made his way over to the main office in Hourn House with his thoughts full of Kathryn and a skip in his step. By the time he'd trudged through the snow, he'd reminded himself of the real reason they were there and he hoped Jean would deliver the goods. The Estate Manager's office was at the front of the house and he found the boss waiting for him along with his two black cocker spaniels.

Marcus greeted him. "I don't normally pitch up this early but I couldn't sleep what with the storm. There's always work to do after weather like that."

Coffee in hand, they made an immediate start and Marcus

explained where everything was on the computer, and about the different projects they had planned over the coming months. Mid-morning, as they pored over a spreadsheet, Finlay the estate hand, ran into the office.

"You need to come. We've found a body on the moor."

Marcus sprang to his feet. "Who is it Finlay?"

"I think it's Jean. Her dog's going mental, that's how I found her."

Marcus phoned Angus and they grabbed their coats and bundled into the Defender with Finlay who pointed the way. As they drove, Finlay explained he'd been checking on the sheep brought down onto the lower ground before the storm and he'd spotted Meg out on the moor barking. The dog wouldn't let him near what she was guarding but he realised it was a body. Marcus drove as close to the spot as he could, and they abandoned the Land Rover and went on foot. Finlay asked to stay in the vehicle saying he wasn't feeling well. He was pale and Jamie thought he looked in shock, and he passed him a rug to keep warm.

Angus and Duncan appeared shortly afterwards having followed their tracks. Jamie spotted Meg in the distance, pacing frantically and barking next to a mound in the snow. As they approached, the dog snarled fiercely at them. Angus managed to chase her off, and Jamie had to stop himself from saying they shouldn't disturb the scene. Beneath the pile of snow, a small grey hand protruded. Jamie noticed there was nothing under the nails and no obvious defence wounds.

"I'll take a look," said Marcus. He crouched down and wiped snow off to reveal Jean's face. "Aye it's her alright. What in heaven's name was she doing out here?"

"Probably looking for that bloody dog," muttered Angus.

"Vicious bastard," said Duncan aiming a kick at Meg, who narrowly avoided it.

Marcus stood and looked around squinting in the glare. "We can't leave her here."

"Shouldn't we wait until the police get here?" asked Jamie.

"Road's blocked," said Duncan, "might be days til they can get through and by then the wildlife will have had her."

"We'll take her back to the house," said Angus. "I'll get the tarp."

As he trudged towards the vehicles, Jamie took a closer look around the scene. Other than Marcus's footprints and Meg's pawprints, the snow was pristine. He walked around the body in a clockwise direction, leaving a wide perimeter. There were no other prints or drag marks visible. Taking his phone from his pocket, he recorded the location's coordinates and the time, then he began to take photographs of the area and body from different angles.

When Marcus threw him a curious look, he said, "It's for the police." Jamie knew this death would be investigated by the Procurator Fiscal who'd request a post-mortem and an examination of the locus.

"Good idea," agreed Marcus.

Duncan looked less convinced. Jamie estimated nine inches of snow had fallen overnight and since the body appeared to be covered in approximately that, she'd been laying there all night. Following Marcus's tracks, Jamie approached the body and brushed away snow to reveal more of Jean. She lay face down with her right hand stretched out in front of her.

Meg approached and snarled and he shooed her away as he continued to move snow and photograph the scene. She was still wearing the long skirt and top she'd worn to the party last night but no jacket. There were no folds or rolls in her clothing to indicate she'd been dragged, and there were no obvious signs of trauma on the body.

Duncan loitered behind Jamie. "Must have frozen to death. It was minus ten last night."

Jamie crouched down and peered at her mouth but couldn't see any signs of blood or vomit.

"Looks like you've done this before," said Duncan.

Jamie glanced up at him. "When you lose an animal it's useful to know if it was the result of disease, an accident or a predator."

Duncan gave a curt nod and went to help Angus who'd appeared carrying a tarpaulin and a length of rope. Jamie helped them lift Jean's stiff body onto the tarp and wrap her in it. He took more photographs but couldn't see any sign of injury on her or evidence of a struggle. While the others were busy with the body, he felt the ground where she'd lain; it was cold to the touch but with only a light dusting of compacted snow.

Marcus sidled over to him. "What d'you reckon Columbo?"

Jamie got to his feet. "I'm no expert but it looks like hypothermia. Judging by the amount of snow on her, she's been here all night. Like Angus said, she probably came looking for the dog and lost her way in the white-out. Poor Jean."

Marcus nodded. "Yes, it's such a pity, and she was so happy at having you and Kathryn here."

"I didn't see her when we left last night, did she leave early?"

"Not sure, we left shortly after you and I don't remember seeing her either."

Angus and Duncan lifted Jean between them and they slowly made their way back to the vehicles. Jamie and Finlay helped them place her into the back of Duncan's pickup.

"We'll take her to the cellar," said Marcus, "she'll be safe there until the police get here."

Jamie whistled for the dog, hoping she'd come but she ran off whining, then he joined Finlay and Marcus in the Land Rover and they returned to Hourn House. No one spoke until they'd parked at the back of the building. Marcus dismissed Finlay for the day and the lad sloped off.

Duncan and Angus lifted the body out of the vehicle and followed Marcus through the back entrance and along a corridor. Marcus unlocked a door on the right which opened to reveal a flight of stone steps leading down to the cellar. Holding one end of the body, Duncan descended backwards with Angus supporting the other. Marcus flicked a switch to illuminate a cavernous stone basement with an arched stone ceiling. Along the two long walls stood well-stocked wooden wine racks, while the back wall housed three enormous industrial stainless-steel fridges. A long oak refectory table stood in the centre of the room.

"We'll put her there," said Marcus indicating the table.

"Certainly cold enough" said Jamie, shivering.

After they'd placed the body on the table, they ascended and

Marcus locked the cellar door. Then he led them through to a large kitchen and put the kettle on the Aga.

"I'll call the police" said Marcus heading for the office, "I'll tell them there's no rush, the road will be closed for a while."

Sitting around the large farmhouse table, they cut a sorry sight. Angus made mugs of tea and Duncan produced biscuits from a cupboard.

Jamie asked, "Any idea what time Jean left the party? I didn't see her go."

Duncan shrugged and Angus mumbled he'd no idea. Reluctant to push, Jamie sipped his tea and waited for Marcus to return. When he reappeared, he confirmed it'd be a while before the road was clear and the police could reach them.

"Grim business" said Marcus, "and not the best start for you either Jamie. Best take the rest of the day off, be with Kathryn."

"I'm fine to continue."

"I insist," said Marcus, his expression leaving no room for negotiation. "We'll gather everyone together this evening and see you then."

Jamie finished his tea, washed up his cup, then left, noticing the conspiratorial look Duncan and Angus swapped.

As he trudged home, he considered where Jean's death left their investigation. The timing was suspicious, immediately following on his and Kathryn's arrival, with Jean about to provide them with a journal and some evidence from the office. Without this information, it could take them months to uncover the truth, time they didn't have. Yet, so far as he'd been able to check, there was nothing about her death that suggested she'd died from anything other than hypothermia. Would a post mortem examination reveal anything else? Had Jean said anything before she died that may have compromised him and Kathryn, or was this the beginning of the paranoia Pia had warned them about that haunted undercover operators?

Sighing, he thought, 'and this is only the start'.

Kathryn

Kathryn had spent the morning unpacking their possessions which had arrived the previous afternoon. It felt like Christmas as she'd never seen most of this stuff before. She placed their framed wedding photograph in the living room and a snap of them in front of the Eiffel Tower in the kitchen. As she stood back to admire her display, she jumped as Ruth bustled into the cottage unannounced, holding a tray of freshly-baked biscuits.

"Just checking how y'all are," she said placing the tray on the kitchen table and casting her eye around the room.

Kathryn thanked her, making a mental note to lock the door in future since Ruth didn't seem the type to respect boundaries. Ruth inquired if she'd slept okay and asked if they wanted a firmer mattress, the offer of which Kathryn declined emphatically.

After Ruth left, she examined the contents of the kitchen cupboards and compiled a shopping list. With only a rough idea of what Jamie liked based on them eating-out together, she planned a menu for the next few days, concerned her cooking skills wouldn't be up to the job. She eyed the Aga nervously.

Then she decided her menu needed purchases to be made. She grabbed her bag, pulled on coat and boots and made her way over to the shop. Glen Hourn looked spectacular, the thick blanket of snow giving the place a magical feel. After collecting what she needed from her list, and chatting with the assistant, she bought a packet of biscuits and dog treats and went in search of Jean's cottage. The door was ajar and there was no sign of either Jean or the dog, which Jamie had described as a "sleekit wee bastard." Circling the cottage, she peered in the windows and called Jean's name, noting the trail of large footsteps in the snow. She popped her head inside the front door and shouted, to no reply.

She left the biscuits and dog treats just inside, pulled the door shut and headed back towards Whitsun cottage. Glancing up, she saw Jamie coming from the direction of Hourn House. She waved and when he spotted her, he broke into a jog. She could tell from his expression that something was wrong.

"What's happened?" she asked, placing down her shopping bags.

He grabbed her shoulders. "Jean's dead. One of the lads found her out on the moor this morning frozen to death. I've just been out there."

Clutching a hand to her chest, Kathryn listened as he told her what had happened.

"D'you think it was an accident?"

Jamie glanced around before replying, "The timing's bloody suspicious. She left the party early to get us information from the office. I was going to meet her today to find out what's going on and get her journal."

"D'you think there might be something in her cottage?"

"I'm going to look."

She pulled him back. "I'm coming with you."

"No, it could be dangerous. I don't want you anywhere near this."

"Jamie, like it or not, we're in this together and I'm going with you."

Nodding a reluctant acceptance, he picked up the shopping bags and they walked to Jean's cottage.

"I can carry a bag, I'm not weak and feeble despite what this lot will have you think."

"I know you're not. It's called chivalry Mrs Campbell, get used to it."

As they approached Jean's cottage, she told him about the argument she'd witnessed at the party between Ruth and Duncan. Meg ran up and started barking at them. Jamie explained that the dog had refused to come to him earlier. He placed the bags on the doorstep and called to Meg but she snarled at him then ran off.

"I was just here and I left treats for her inside," said Kathryn. Spotting the door ajar, she paused, "Jamie, someone's been here in the last few minutes. When I left, I closed the door."

"Stay here," he said.

He went inside and when she followed him, he grimaced at her. While he strode through the cottage peering into every room, Kathryn looked around the living room. After checking upstairs, he announced the place was empty.

"Someone's been searching in here," she said pointing to papers strewn across the floor beneath a writing bureau.

They began to rifle through the drawers and cupboards in the living room and kitchen.

She whispered, "What are we looking for?"

"A journal. Stuff from the office. I'm guessing a USB stick or paperwork."

She watched Jamie search in places it wouldn't have occurred to her to look, including inside jam jars and behind furniture units. He stuck his hand up the chimney and foraged inside the stove heater. As she rummaged through the papers in the bureau, Jamie hunted upstairs. After finding only invoices, she discovered him going through the laundry basket in the bathroom.

"Find anything?" she asked.

In a low voice, he said, "Only this." He passed her an old newspaper cutting about the disappearance of schoolgirl Mhairi MacLean on the Isle of Lewis, which Angus had been questioned about. "Surely that's not what she intended to give us. It's public knowledge. There must be something else, so unless she was stopped before she got it or it's on the body, then it's been taken." He stuffed the laundry back into the basket and finished his search of the bathroom.

"I'll check the pantry," she said.

As she made her way downstairs, she heard the crunch of footsteps on the path outside. She cracked open the front door to find Angus standing there with a rifle.

He aimed it and she screamed.

Jamie

Jamie heard the scream and the sound of a shot. Leaping down the stairs, he wrenched open the door to find her trying to wrestle a gun from Angus's grip.

"What the fuck's going on?" yelled Jamie as he grabbed the barrel of the rifle and pointed it heavenwards.

"Your wife's what's going on," bellowed Angus, attempting to prise the gun from both their hands.

Kathryn shouted, "He tried to shoot Meg." Beating at Angus with her fist, she yelled, "How could you?"

"Whoa, whoa, whoa," said Jamie positioning himself between the two of them, one hand still on the gun, "No one's shooting anything."

"The dog's feral, we can't have it running loose," snarled Angus, aiming his words at Kathryn. Then he turned to Jamie, "and you need to get your woman under control."

Kathryn tried to pummel him again. "You shoot that dog and you'll see what out of control is."

"We'll take the dog Angus," said Jamie calmly.

They stopped and stared at him.

Jamie said, "We came here to fetch her."

Huffing out his annoyance, Angus lowered the weapon and stared at Jamie. "You're crazy if you think you can keep Meg as a pet."

Jamie fixed him with a glare. "If my missus wants her as a pet, then she can have her as a pet."

Their eyes locked like horns, then Angus shook his head and muttered something about it being his funeral before he stalked off with the rifle slung over his shoulder. Jamie slipped his arm around Kathryn's waist as they watched him go.

Wrapping her arm around him, she gazed up at him and said, "Thank you."

He smiled and murmured, "Guess we'd better catch the dug."

After much coaxing, a bag of dog treats and a bowl of mince placed inside the kitchen door, Meg was persuaded back to Whitsun cottage. Jamie fashioned a dog bed from one of their packing cartons and lined it with an old jumper, while Kathryn found a bowl for water. Once Meg was settled near the Aga, they grinned at each other.

Kathryn said, "That mince was supposed to be for our dinner."

"It went to a good cause." He crouched to stroke Meg and she bared her teeth at him. Laughing, he said, "Maybe I should've let Angus shoot her."

"I can't believe he'd do such a thing. To a dog."

Jamie pulled a face to remind her they were likely being watched and listened to. "Their ways are just different, there's no sentiment with animals."

He fetched the basket for wood and, taking the hint, she offered to help him and followed him out to the woodshed.

"Sorry," she said, "I forget we can't talk freely."

He reached for her hand. "I need to search the body. There might be something on her."

When she insisted on going with him, he refused.

Pulling away, she put her hands on her hips and gave him a stern look. "Jamie, we're in this together. I'm not letting you do this on your own."

He shook his head. "It's too dangerous, I don't want you involved."

"And if you get caught? What then? If they catch us and shoot us, I'd much rather be shot with you."

He chuckled.

"What's so funny?"

He said on a laugh, "That's the most romantic thing anyone's ever said to me."

She joined in with his laughter, and they gazed at one another. Tentatively, she reached a hand towards him. Taking it, he wrapped his arms around her and she nuzzled into his chest.

Raising her head, she looked up at him. Taking a chance, he dipped his head and made to touch his lips to hers. There was an "Ahem" and he looked to find Duncan standing in the doorway, a toolbox in hand. They sprang apart.

"I've come to look at the generator," Duncan muttered, looking at his feet.

When Kathryn reached for Jamie's arm, he gave her a questioning look.

"Remember the wood," she said as she passed Duncan on her way to the kitchen.

He suppressed a sigh. Christ, they'd been so close to kissing, and a proper kiss at that, not one to support their cover story or smother her words. Anticipation had produced painful throbbing in his underwear.

After offering Duncan a coffee, he left him checking the generator and joined Kathryn in the kitchen. He found her in a Mexican standoff with the Aga and they exchanged a smile. More painful throbbing.

"You look baffled," he said. "Have you ever used one of these before?"

She shook her head. "Where are the controls?"

He explained how the Aga ran constantly on and it was a case of judging the heat rather than adjusting it. "This is a two-oven Aga. The top one," he opened its door, "is for baking and roasting. The one beneath is for simmering and slow cooking." He raised the top covers. "You use these plates to start the cooking process, then transfer pots to the ovens rather than letting their heat dissipate in the kitchen." He examined the oven more closely. "There's a hot water tank so once Duncan's fixed everything, we should be alright."

"You seem to be quite an expert," said Kathryn, looking at the notes she had been taking.

"I grew up in a house with a similar four-oven monster as the only source of heating and hot water. An Aga's the heart of a home."

He took Duncan out a mug of coffee, then Jamie returned to the kitchen where he found Kathryn making sandwiches for lunch.

After eating, he heard voices in the woodshed and went out to check on how Duncan was getting on. As he approached, he overheard Angus muttering, "his woman needs to learn her place."

When Jamie stepped into the woodshed, Angus's large ears reddened and he looked away.

Indicating the generator, Duncan said, "Needs a new part. I've a spare ready but it'll take me a couple of hours to fix."

Angus cleared his throat. "Err ... there'll be a meeting about Jean's death in the community hall at seven." Then, turning to his brother, he said, "I'm on the snowplough if you need me." With a brief nod at Jamie, he departed.

Jamie left Duncan fixing the generator and went to find Kathryn. She was upstairs in the bedroom and he asked if she fancied a walk. After wrapping up warm, they left Meg to sleep and headed towards the loch.

When they were far enough away from the cottage, he turned to her. "Angus and Duncan are busy and I just spotted Marcus and Ruth heading off in the Land Rover. It's an opportunity to get the key to the cellar from Duncan's house."

"How will you get in?"

"I'm hoping it's true and no one locks their doors."

"But it's a modern house with new locks. Haven't Angus or Marcus got a key?"

"I don't know but Duncan definitely has one and I'll recognize the keyring."

"If you can't get in, I've another idea but I'll need my art case from the cottage." His expression must have betrayed his reluctance and she added, "Remember, we're in it together … and if that means getting shot together, then so be it."

Laughing, he wrapped his arms around her and pulled her into his chest. "Oh God, Mrs Campbell, what am I going to do with you?"

"Stop trying to wrap me in cotton wool," she mumbled into his jacket.

Knowing that his every instinct was to do exactly that, he chuckled, "I heard Angus say to Duncan that you needed to learn your place."

She pulled away. "Pigs! I'll show them my place alright; it's called cyberspace."

He smiled. Christ, she was attractive when she was pissed off. And slightly scary.

"C'mon Mrs Campbell, let's go do what we're here for."

Kathryn

Kathryn's stomach gave a lurch at the thought of finally doing something dangerous and covert. So far, it had all been training and planning, but none of it had prepared her for how she would actually feel when the time came for action. Adrenaline pumped through her veins, her mouth was dry and she felt a trickle of cold sweat run down her spine. *Fake it until you become it.*

She grabbed her art case from beneath the bed and found Jamie in the woodshed talking with Duncan. He was telling him that they were going on a walk so Kathryn could sketch. Duncan nodded without comment.

Jamie took Kathryn's hand and together they walked towards Duncan's house, greeting any people they met on the way.

Set well back from the other cottages at the start of the tree line, Duncan's barn offered a good view over the valley below. Jamie suggested she "kept an edgy", as he called the task of keeping lookout. As he went off to investigate, Kathryn perched on a tree stump, pulled out her laptop and phone and went to work.

Jamie reappeared cursing. "I couldnae have picked a worse house. It's got CCTV, an alarm, and the locks are integrated electronic ones."

Taking her smartphone, she grinned at him and pressed a button. As the garage door began to roll up, she sniggered, "You couldn't have picked a better house."

Jamie's jaw dropped. "How the hell did you do that?"

"Hacked his fancy connected car. Garage code's stored in its infotainment system."

Casting an eye towards the shiny pickup truck parked outside, Jamie laughed. "But what about the alarm and CCTV?"

She said, "The idiot's stored his alarm code in the infotainment system too, so I've disabled it and unlocked the doors. If you get me the DVR details, I'll delete the camera footage."

"The what?"

"The Digital Video Recorder, Mr Campbell."

With boyish delight, he leant down and kissed her cheek. "You're bloody brilliant Mrs Campbell."

He ran off into the garage. While she waited for him, she began to sketch the view. She hadn't drawn since she was in high school and she found it remarkably calming under the circumstances. Jamie returned dangling a key attached to a keyring that featured a picture of a topless woman. He also had a laptop tucked under his arm which he handed to her.

After bypassing the password screen and quickly transferring the contents of Duncan's hard drive onto her own machine, she asked if he'd found the DVR. He showed her a photograph he'd taken on his phone of the box and its serial number. Using her laptop, she connected to the system and began the process of deleting the camera footage. As her fingers flew over the keyboard and the screen displayed rolling images of computer code and video footage, he peered over her shoulder and asked what she was doing.

"I found a one-time passcode on a web site that's allowed me to bypass the authentication on the DVR. I've replaced the CCTV footage with images from the webcam in the panda enclosure at Edinburgh zoo."

Jamie's mouth fell open, then he looked annoyed. "Kathryn, you cannae do that, he'll know it's us if you…"

She turned her screen to show him a baby panda and in an infantile voice said, "Ooh look how cute it is."

He narrowed his eyes at her while she squealed with laughter. "You're winding me up, aren't you?"

Her body shook with laughter as she nodded. "Tempting as it was, I've just deleted images for the time we were here so Duncan will be none the wiser."

He waved a finger at her and chuckled, "I'll get back at you for that."

"Bring it on Mr Campbell," she said.

Jamie returned to the house, replaced the laptop, then came back and joined her on the tree stump.

She tapped her phone and the garage door closed. After a few more taps, she announced, "That'll show him." The pickup truck beeped and its lights flashed once.

"Oh God, what have you done now?"

Feigning contrition, she smiled sweetly and batted her eyelashes. "Oops, I'm terribly sorry officer but I appear to have accidentally switched on the heated seats, fans and aircon." Then grinning menacingly, she said, "And once the battery's drained, that bastard ain't going anywhere."

Jamie scream-laughed.

～

The gathering was a solemn affair compared to the previous evening, and Kathryn found it hard to believe it was only the day before that they'd stood here in the community hall chatting to Jean. Several of the men approached Jamie and shook his hand after hearing he'd helped move her body, and many women wept.

Once everyone had assembled, Marcus stood on the stage and raised his hands like a preacher. The room fell silent. In a clear, confident voice, he explained what had happened and how Jean was now safely in their keeping, pending the arrival of the police. He acknowledged the role played by Finlay, Angus, Duncan and Jamie, and many heads turned to nod in their direction.

"I understand how shocked and saddened you must feel at our dear sister's death. Jean was a kind and generous soul and we were blessed to have her here. I know how much she enjoyed being part of our community and how much you will all miss her. Now let us pray."

Kathryn bowed her head and, as Marcus led them in prayer, she thought of Jean's words to Jamie about this being Hell's Glen.

After the prayer, Marcus recited various biblical quotes. "The bible tells us 'The days of our years are three score and ten'. Man that is born of a woman, hath but a short time to live, and is full of misery. He cometh up, and is cut down, like a flower; he fleeth as it were a shadow, and never continueth in one stay.' May the Lord, mighty God, bless and keep you forever Jean and grant you peace. Amen"

He then announced refreshments and the mood lifted. Ruth and some of the women appeared with trays laden with finger food, and Angus and Duncan wheeled in a trolley of drinks. Kathryn and Jamie mingled for a while chatting to people about Jean.

After half an hour, he gave her an almost imperceptible nod. She excused herself from the conversation saying she needed some air, and Jamie offered to accompany her. They snuck out of the hall and hurried to the back of Hourn House. The backdoor was unlocked and he led her along the corridor and unlocked the door leading to the cellar. Her heart was thumping in her chest and she shivered against the cold, regretting not bringing her jacket. He flicked on the light and she gasped at the sight of the tarpaulin on the table.

Jamie slipped on latex gloves and wasted no time in untying the rope and unwrapping the body. Tears welled in Kathryn's eyes at the sight of Jean's frail form as he quickly frisked her clothing. He missed nothing, even searching seams, underwear and boots. Glancing over at Kathryn, he shook his head.

"Nothing," he said as he rearranged her clothing.

As Jamie wrapped the tarpaulin around her again and bound it with the rope, Kathryn examined the wine racks and the fridge/freezers at the far end. The right and left-hand ones were stocked with labelled bags of venison and fish, and bottles of champagne, but the middle door was locked and she noticed it had a keypad on the front. She noted details of the make and model as it wasn't one she recognized.

Jamie placed a hand on top of the re-wrapped figure and said, "Forgive me Jean."

He stuffed the gloves in his pocket and led Kathryn out, leaving the cellar key in the door.

"Shouldn't we return it?" she whispered.

"No, it's less risk if they assume Duncan left it there. And I've an imprint of it."

They jogged back to the community hall and, as they hurried along the side of the building, they overheard Marcus shout "Anyone seen the Campbells?"

Jamie and Kathryn stopped in their tracks and swapped a wide-eyed look. As footsteps crunched near, Jamie spun Kathryn around, pressed her to the wall and kissed her. Pinned against the building and held firmly in his grip, she couldn't move as his mouth covered hers. Her first instinct was to fight and she flailed her arms. He tightened his grip and coaxed her lips apart, and she let out a whimper as she melted in his arms. A laugh startled them and they broke apart to find Marcus and Ruth grinning at them. Kathryn felt her face flush and she looked at her feet.

Chuckling, Jamie put an arm around her shoulder and said, "Were you looking for us? Kathryn needed some air."

"Were you giving her mouth to mouth?" laughed Marcus.

Ruth smiled, "Y'all are just so adorable."

Grinning, Marcus clapped Jamie across the back and they made their way back inside. Kathryn's heart thumped against her chest wall; not as a result of their daring stunt, but because of that kiss.

Jamie

When people began to disperse, Jamie and Kathryn trudged back through the snow to their cottage. Examining the body had been a grim task, but there was a sense of euphoria at having gotten away with it.

Realising she was anxious, he tugged her into the woodshed, saying, "We need to talk before we go inside." Gazing at her, he said, "Are you okay? I know that couldn't have been easy."

Close to tears, she nodded, "It wasn't, but I'm worried we didn't get the information we needed from Jean. If we can't find it, Lord only knows how long it'll take to find out what's going on here, not to mention the danger we could be in."

Trying to reassure her, he said, "There's no evidence she was murdered, even if the timing's suspicious. Try not to fret, it's early days."

"It's time we don't have though."

As she made to go inside, he pulled her back, uncertain whether to voice the other thing on his mind, the kiss they'd shared. She hadn't just tolerated it, she'd responded. And he wanted to kiss her again. And again. Certain now that there really was something between them, he wanted to know for sure how she felt. "There's something else I want to say."

"If it's about the kiss, I know why you did it, you don't need to apologise."

"I wasn't going to. I'm not sorry at all, even if I did break my promise it'd never happen again." He searched her face for a reaction.

She pulled away and glared at him. "Don't toy with me Jamie. This isn't real, none of it is, and we aren't a couple. Don't forget your real girlfriend is waiting for you back home."

Astounded at her words, he said, "What makes you think that?"

In a voice laced with sarcasm, she asked "Does the name Emma ring a bell?"

"You hacked my phone?"

Her eyes blazed. "I haven't touched your bloody phone, but you're splashed all over her Facebook page. Did you really think I wouldn't poke around your digital life?"

"Christ Kathryn, if you want to know something, you just have to ask."

Pointing to his chest, she hissed, "So you don't deny it! This is just a bit of fun for you, a distraction, someone to keep you warm while you're here, then discard when you're done?"

She shoved past him and disappeared into the kitchen.

Cursing, Jamie followed her, determined to put the record straight. Finding her crouched next to Meg, he said in a low voice, "Kathryn, can we talk please?"

"I need to take Meg out. Have we any rope?"

Thinking a walk the perfect opportunity to continue this discussion, because there was no way he was getting a wink of sleep tonight with things as they were, he hoisted up his jacket and began to unbuckle his belt. Wide-eyed, Kathryn covered her mouth with her hands, slunk from him and cowered in the corner. Meg leapt from her box and began barking at him.

Belt half way out the loops on his trousers, Jamie froze realising she'd turned a deathly ashen colour reminiscent of Jean's body. "Kathryn, what's wrong?"

Her eyes shot to his belt and she made a gasping sound, and he could tell she was having a panic attack.

"Oh God no, it's only to use as a lead for Meg." He slowly removed the belt, placed it on the counter, and extended his palms. "I'm sorry if I frightened you."

She burst into tears. Gingerly, he approached her, arms outstretched. She clung to him and sobbed into his chest. Nuzzling her hair, he whispered, "I'd never hurt you." Feeling a tenderness towards her that astonished him, he held her until she stopped trembling and her breathing returned to normal. Wiping away her tears with his thumbs, he said, "Shall we take our dog for a walk Mrs Campbell?"

When she nodded, he passed her the belt. "You'd better put it on her."

Kathryn felt the fur on Meg's neck and found she was wearing a roll collar. After looping the belt around it, she coaxed the reluctant dog out into the snow. Meg squatted immediately and peed, then pulled on the lead to get back inside.

Chuckling, Jamie said, "No Meg, we're going walkies so I can talk to Mrs Campbell."

Taking her hand, he tugged her and the dog away from the cottage and down towards the loch. The inky black water reflected a bright waxing moon.

He stopped at the water's edge and turned to her. "Emma's an ex. We finished over a year ago. There's no one else. Only you."

"But I'm not real Jamie, none of this is. I know Jamie Campbell, I don't know you."

He fixed her with his gaze. "You do know me. What you see is what you get Kathryn. And this … whatever this is between us … is real, at least it is to me."

"How can I trust anything you say? You're good at this Jamie, I've seen you in action, lies roll off your tongue."

Jamie shook his head, "I've never once lied to you."

She allowed a silence to grow before responding. "Trust isn't something that comes easily to me and for that to happen I would need to get to know the real Jamie."

"You will, warts and all. And I want to get to know the real Kathryn. The thing I've realised, the thing that's surprised me most is … you and I, we're not so different."

"Except I'm completely fucked up."

He laughed mirthlessly. "We're both completely fucked up, just in different ways. All I'm asking is you lower your guard and let me in." He reached for her hand. "I'm sorry if I scared you, but I need you to know I'd never do anything to hurt you Kathryn."

Tears welled in her eyes and he pulled her into his arms and held her. As he looked out over the still water of the loch, he wondered just what the fuck someone had done to her to make her think he'd beat her with a belt.

∿

Kathryn

Back in the cottage, Kathryn crouched to unloop the belt from Meg's collar.

"Err, Jamie", she said.

As he leaned down to look at the identity tube attached to the collar she held, Meg bared her teeth at him and growled. Kathryn calmed the dog and unscrewed the bottom of the barrel and removed a roll of paper. Jamie positioned himself to conceal what she was doing from the hidden camera. She unfurled the slip to reveal Meg's details printed on one side, and a scrawled message on the other: *St. Januarius*

Jamie pulled a face. "Uhm, I forgot the kindling."

Taking his cue, she followed him to the woodshed and they examined the slip in more detail.

"What the hell does that mean?" she asked.

"Damned if I know, but it's the only thing we've got."

He pulled his phone from his back pocket and searched, and she leaned in so she could read the results, aware of just how close he was. She could smell his aftershave mingled with his natural scent, and it was intoxicating.

According to Wikipedia, St. Januarius was the patron saint of Naples and, three times a year, the faithful gather in the cathedral to witness the liquefaction of what is claimed to be a sample of his blood kept in a sealed glass ampoule.

They swapped a bemused look. God he was so close and as he scrolled, she focussed on the lips that had kissed her just hours before, noting the V on the top one and the lush bottom lip. She remembered the press of his mouth on hers, the taste of him, the strength of his body as he pinned her to the wall. Butterflies fluttered inside her and she felt a tingling sensation. There.

He turned to her and her breath caught as he scanned her face slowly from eyes to mouth then back to eyes. For a second, she thought he was going to kiss her but, instead, he moved away and returned his phone to his pocket.

She felt a stab of disappointment. "Uhm, when are we checking in with Keith?"

"Sunday afternoon. Thought we could take Meg on a long walk." Regarding her expression, he reached for her hand. "Hey, what's wrong?"

Trapped in his gaze once more and with the feel of his hand in hers, the tingling became a throbbing pulse. "It's just been a long day."

He inclined his head. "Is that all? Talk to me Kathryn."

She sighed. "I will Jamie but I need time. There's stuff I need to tell you and once I do, you'll finally understand why we can never be a real couple."

Pulling her hand out of his grip, she walked away.

Jamie

Jamie felt like he'd just been punched in the gut.

They'd shared a moment and it had taken every ounce of willpower not to gather her in his arms and kiss her. Hard. Thinking about it made him stiffen. Hard. Raking a hand through his hair, he cursed. He couldnae go back into the cottage in this state; she'd freak. How the hell was he going to lie mere inches from her again and get any sleep when all he wanted to do was … He pushed the thought aside. Never going to happen.

And, if this wasn't bad enough, they still had the other problem he hadn't mentioned to her. Although there were no cameras upstairs, he'd found a listening device concealed in an air vent in the bedroom wall. He planned to install a jammer but didn't have one with him, and he didn't know how long it'd take for Keith to get hold of one. In the meantime, he could use a radio to muffle the sound but, until he sourced such a thing, his worry was one of them would talk in their sleep. It was every UCs worst nightmare and he'd heard stories of cover being blown as a result. And, given he was prone to regular night terrors, he was concerned. He'd been exhausted last night and had slept well but tonight, between worries over sleep talking and his yearning to touch Kathryn, he wasn't expecting to get a wink.

Ardour finally quelled, he went back inside to find her in the bedroom in her flannel pyjamas propped up on the pillows surfing her phone. He eased in beside her, hoping her proximity wouldn't fire him up again. She turned the phone towards him and peered at the screen which displayed floorplans. She scribbled on the artist's sketchpad. *Found plans for Hourn House. The cellar's much longer so what's behind fridge/freezers?!*

Jamie took the pencil and scrawled, *Need to get inside!* Thinking about what he'd just written made his lower regions twitch.

She nodded as she sent a quick text message to Keith. Ripping the sheet from the pad, she scrunched it up.

He took it from her. "I'm going downstairs, want anything?"

"No thanks." Smiling, she put her phone back into the artist's case and snuggled under the duvet. Turning her back to him, she said, "Night Jamie."

"Night Kathryn."

Resisting the temptation to lean over and kiss her, he returned downstairs. After burning the paper in the stove, he downed a glass of water.

Padding towards the bathroom he thought, I'd give my right arm to get inside her.

MARK

"For whatever things were written before were written for our learning, that we through the patience and comfort of the Scriptures might have hope."

— *ROMANS 15:4*

Kathryn

Again, she awoke encased in Jamie's arms despite her best attempts at distancing from him with the pillow she'd placed between them. Instead of balking though, she lay still and wallowed in the contact. His arm was draped over her waist and she could feel his thigh pressed against the back of hers. She'd never shared a bed with anyone ... not intentionally ... and it felt new and exciting. Thinking about their discussion at the loch and the fact he was single, she smiled. What was this relationship between them that he'd said was real? Was the stress of their situation playing tricks on their mind and blurring fiction with reality? Maybe Pia's advice to 'fake it til you become it' was what was happening.

Jamie stirred. Suddenly, feeling him hard against her bottom, she froze but, judging from his steady breathing against her neck, she didn't think he was awake and she relaxed. Through their clothing, she felt his erection brush against her. Her pulse raced as she inhaled his musky scent and she dared to imagine how it might feel to make love. Stoking her fantasy, she inched back against him. At the contact, desire flared through her and she heard blood thunder in her ears.

Jamie shifted away a little and she exhaled slowly. She sensed he was awake but he seemed in no rush to get up either. After ten minutes, he brushed his lips against her hair and extricated himself. She must have dozed off because when she opened her eyes, he was fully dressed holding a mug of tea. Placing it on the nightstand, he perched beside her and smiled.

Eyes glinting with mischief he said, "It's bloody freezing. I want to crawl back in beside you."

"Mmph, why don't you?"

Pushing a stray lock behind her ear, he growled, "Don't tempt me woman."

As they locked eyes, she swallowed hard, caught between enjoying their flirting, and fear at what it might lead to.

He gave her a crooked smile. "See you at lunchtime."

Jamie

Pulling his collar up against the driving rain, Jamie squelched through the slush towards Hourn House, his thoughts full of Kathryn. The snow was melting and it was treacherous underfoot. It had taken every ounce of willpower to disentangle himself from her this morning. Jesus, he'd have given his eye teeth to have made love to her after he'd woken to find her in his arms, and his mouth full of her hair, thanks to their saggy mattress. Caught somewhere between sleep and waking, he'd begun to dream about having sex with her and he'd roused with a painful hard-on. He'd lain still so as not to wake her, conscious he was a mere bawhair away from being inside her; the thought only making him stiffer. Then she'd pressed against him and … Christ, he'd been that close… He groaned out his frustration.

He needed to focus. With Jean's death and without the benefit of the information she'd gathered, he knew they were up against the clock. The office was empty and it gave him the chance to take a closer look for listening devices and cameras. They were usually easy to find and he'd plenty of experience in spotting them so he quickly identified the pinhole camera in the bookcase. He crouched as if reading the spines of books and examined it; it was angled to provide a good view of his desk and computer screen.

Marcus appeared with his spaniels, coffee in hand and, after offering him one, he led him through to a small kitchenette and told him to help himself. As Jamie heaped a spoonful of coffee into a mug, Marcus said, "Angus tells me you've started a family."

Jamie chuckled, "Aye, Meg's settling in nicely. She'll be good company for Kathryn."

"Dogs are like women. They need a firm master."

Jamie glanced at him, trying to determine if he was joking or not. Definitely not he decided, and he swallowed back the words he wanted to say. He was almost grateful when Angus appeared to inform them the police had arrived.

Marcus muttered, "That was quick."

The rest of the morning was taken up talking to Police Sergeant Buchanan about Jean's death. Jamie, Marcus, Duncan, and Angus were interviewed separately. There was no sign of Finlay and Marcus explained that he was out on the estate and couldn't be contacted.

When Jamie went to show Buchanan the photographs he'd collected from the scene, he noted the panda-themed wallpaper that had suddenly appeared on his phone, and he knew he'd have to think up new and imaginative ways to wind up his wife.

He was surprised at the questions the sergeant didn't ask; the policeman seemed to have made his mind up that this was an accidental death. After statements had been taken, Buchanan asked to be driven to where the body had been discovered, and Duncan offered to take them, only to appear shortly afterwards to apologise because he was unable to start his pickup.

Jamie said. "Aye, they don't make cars like they used to. Want me to drive?"

Duncan sneered. "Have you ever driven a Defender?"

"Aye, once or twice."

They all bundled into the grey Land Rover which Marcus had allocated for Jamie's use. It was still full of the previous owner's empty coffee cups and sweet wrappers and Jamie resolved to give it a thorough clean. Although he'd not driven one in a while, he'd no trouble in manoeuvring it over the rough track to where they'd parked the previous day, and Marcus remarked on his skilful driving, much to Duncan's annoyance.

At the scene, Buchanan made cursory notes and took more photographs which he explained were for the Procurator Fiscal.

Marcus said, "Sad as this is, I don't understand the need for an investigation. It's obvious she's gone looking for the dog and become disoriented in the blizzard."

Buchanan nodded, "I daresay you're right but I have to follow procedure. They'll want a post-mortem."

Marcus fumed, "That's an outrage. Jean should remain with us, we were her family, she should be buried next to the church."

"I don't make the rules Marcus," said Buchanan.

When they returned to the big house, the coroner's van had arrived and Buchanan disappeared into the cellar with Marcus to supervise the moving of Jean's body. Jamie made another coffee and returned to the office, pondering on why Marcus seemed so against an investigation into Jean's death. What was he afraid they'd find?

Then, glancing at the clock, he calculated how long it'd be until he saw Kathryn.

~

Kathryn

She and Jamie had lunch in the cottage. She'd made sandwiches again after her attempt at macaroni cheese on the Aga failed. Meg was licking the charred pot when he returned, much to his amusement and Kathryn's irritation.

"Colquhouns have invited us on a shoot tomorrow", he said.

"What's getting shot?"

"There's an injured stag needs taking care of."

"Strange idea of care giving."

Taking a bite of cheese sandwich, he shot her a warning glance. "What are your plans for this afternoon?"

"Meg and I are going a walk. Hazel in the shop found me a dog lead."

Jamie looked at Meg who still had her head in the pot. Grinning, he said, "Meg's enjoying her lunch."

She narrowed her eyes at him. "Just as well you didn't marry me for my culinary skills."

Eyes dancing with mirth, he chuckled, "Aye, just as well."

"I've also been invited to my first ever meeting of the Christian Wives Group. We're going to learn the five habits of a godly housewife."

Jamie's face crinkled with amusement. "Is one of them cooking?"

She threw a dish cloth at him and they laughed.

"Where did you and Jamie meet?"

Kathryn was glad of the hours she and Jamie had put into rehearsing their backstories since the wives had pumped her for information prior to the meeting; they were almost as bad as Gary and Keith. Despite this, she found the group welcoming and she'd received more compliments in the last ten minutes than she had in her lifetime. Martha, one of the older members, remarked on what a handsome couple she and Jamie were. Kathryn smiled and twirled her wedding band absentmindedly.

A middle-aged woman in a dowdy brown dress and headscarf called the room to order. Stood at the front of the hall, she introduced herself as Rebecca. Kathryn took a seat next to Hazel whom she recognized from the shop. Petite with long dark hair, she was of a similar age to herself and had been especially friendly and helpful since she and Jamie had arrived. She offered Kathryn a warm smile that reached her eyes.

After the room had settled, Rebecca switched on the overhead projector. A list of topics appeared and Kathryn read through them: bible study and prayer, godly thinking and conduct, practical homemaking skills, understanding marital obligations, and submitting to your husband and God. Kathryn prayed they weren't discussing the last item for fear she'd be unable to keep her opinions to herself.

Rebecca welcomed Kathryn to the group and explained they were part way through their syllabus about growing in faith and thriving in marriage, and over the next few weeks, they'd be covering practical homemaking skills including cooking, baking, cleaning, and sewing. Rebecca said she looked forward to Kathryn's input as the wives were always keen to learn new recipes and techniques. Kathryn smiled, wondering whether preparing a 'pierce and ding' microwave meal counted or not.

"Let's start by baking something easy," announced Rebecca.

There was applause and Rebecca produced a sheaf of recipes from which they could choose. Kathryn glanced through the selection and asked Hazel which was the simplest.

Hazel regarded her, "I take it you don't bake?"

Kathryn chuckled. "Nope, I'm a virgin."

Hazel laughed and, after flicking through the sheets, she suggested brownies.

Rebecca led the group through to the kitchens at the rear of the community hall where she'd set out the ingredients. Kathryn and Hazel teamed up at a station and chatted as they weighed, measured and mixed. Hazel explained she was married to Simon who was an ordained Free Church of Scotland minister, and that they'd joined the community five years ago. Simon and Angus had grown up together on the Isle of Lewis, where Simon's father had been a Wee Free lay preacher.

When Kathryn asked what the Wee Free was, Hazel said it was the nickname given to the Free Presbyterian Church of Scotland. She explained they were a conservative Christian church that didn't celebrate Christmas or Easter, and observed the Sabbath when nothing was permitted except worship, Bible study and eating.

"Goodness" exclaimed Kathryn, "must have been tough as a teenager. Why don't they celebrate Christmas and Easter?"

"Neither are mentioned in the bible. And yes it was strict so, after Simon and I married, we decided to seek something a little more modern. Here we do celebrate Christmas and Easter, we only worship on Sunday mornings, and music and dancing aren't considered wicked."

"Why's dancing wicked?"

Hazel laughed. "Well, I remember one preacher describing it as 'doing standing up what you'd like to be doing lying down'. And God help you if you were found wearing denim which was said to be the devil's material because it made men and women the same."

Fascinated, Kathryn asked about the Wee Free's attitude towards women.

Hazel shrugged. "Not unlike here really. The church is led by men, and wives promise to obey their husbands. Women and girls must cover their heads in church, grow their hair long and aren't allowed to wear trousers or makeup. There was a lot of talk about the fires of hell and eternal damnation."

"So, you prefer it here?"

"Definitely, although Simon and Marcus clash regularly about the direction the church is going in. Simon's keen for us to modernise, especially when it comes to women and girls." Hazel leaned in and whispered conspiratorially, "There aren't enough single women for the men. After the older girls go to high school on the mainland, lots leave. It's hard to find women who want to join."

Kathryn nodded, afraid to say anything in case she gave offence.

"You must find our ways a bit old-fashioned."

Choosing her words carefully, Kathryn said, "I believe it's a case of personal choice, as long as you're free to make a choice." She wondered how many of the women who grew up in these types of communities were aware of the options on offer outside, although it sounded like many of the older girls were voting with their feet.

"Did you vow to obey Jamie?" asked Hazel.

"I vowed to love, honour and cherish. I don't buy into the idea a woman must obey her husband. It sounds like a rule a man dreamt up, then proclaimed was the word of God."

Hazel laughed.

Kathryn glanced down in horror as smoke belched from the oven. "Oh no" she yelled, "talk about the fires of hell."

When she opened the door, the kitchen was consumed by acrid fumes and the smoke alarm sounded. Laughing, Hazel opened the windows and doors, and wafted a dishcloth at the alarm until it fell silent. Pulling a face, Kathryn reached into the oven with gloves and retrieved the burnt offering.

Hazel hooted, "Yeah! You've baked blackies."

Walking Meg and feeding the log-burning stove gave Kathryn and Jamie ample opportunity to chat freely so, after dinner that evening, Kathryn followed him out to the woodshed and watched as he filled the log basket. He didn't seem to feel the cold and he'd rolled up the sleeves of his shirt. She couldn't tear her eyes away from the tightly-roped muscles of his forearms.

She'd told him about the Christian Wives meeting and how Simon was risking the wrath of Marcus in trying to drag the Ehrlich Society into the 19th century, and he chuckled about her failed attempt at baking. After telling her about Marcus's resistance to an investigation into Jean's death, he explained he'd taken a closer look at the outside of Hourn House and spotted large aircon vents on the roof, but no aircon in the house itself.

"I need access to their files and accounts" said Kathryn, "I want to see the equipment they've bought and the work they've had done over the last few years. It might give a clue to what's in the cellar. With any luck it's the servers we've been looking for."

"I can't use my PC, there's a camera in the office. Want me to copy files onto a stick?"

She shook her head. "No, if they've half a clue, the system will detect a USB insertion, and your search might flag a warning. I'll need to check for countermeasures and determine what sticks if any are permitted."

"Care to say that in English please?"

She grinned. "Don't stick anything into your machine or search for files Mr Campbell."

Jamie exhaled a long breath. "What can I do?"

"If you can get a hold of one of their USBs, I may be able to brute force it.

Shaking his head, he muttered, "You speak a different version of the English language to me."

She chuckled. "I either need physical access to those computers or a way to connect to them."

"Leave it with me, I've an idea how to get you into the office."

She shivered. "Shall we go back in? I'm freezing."

He stood and looked at her uncertainly.

"What is it?" she asked.

He rubbed the back of his neck and looked at the floor as if needing a pause before saying, "Uhm, you know how we're supposed to be newlyweds?"

She arched a brow. "Err … yes … are you blushing?"

He laughed and shook his head.

"You are blushing. I've never seen you blush Mr Campbell."

Jamie grabbed his mop of hair and chuckled. "Jesus" he muttered. "Okay, I'm just going to come right out and say this." Lifting the axe, he added "I'd better put this out your reach first," as he placed it behind the woodpile.

"That bad?"

He paused as if choosing his words carefully. "If they're listening in, they'll know we don't make love."

She opened her mouth, then closed it again.

"Relax, I'm not suggesting we have sex … although if you absolutely insist on it, Mrs Campbell, I'll consider it." He grinned at her mischievously, but when she returned a scowl, he added, "they just need to think we are."

She remained speechless.

"All I'm saying is we should jiggle the bed a bit, make some noise … know what I mean?"

She raised an amused eyebrow. "Jiggle?"

His lips tugged into a smile. "Aye, jiggling."

"For how long?"

He guffawed, "All night long baby."

She thumped his shoulder which made him laugh more. "Don't make fun of me Jamie."

His expression turned serious. "I'm not." He paused and fixed her with his gaze. "Mind if I ask you something personal?"

"What?"

"Have you ever been in a relationship? You used to wear a wedding ring."

She crossed her arms over her chest and looked away. "It belonged to my mother. It was a useful deterrent. Suppose you think I'm some sort of freak?"

"Course not." He blew out a breath which plumed in the air. "I think someone hurt you really badly, and it makes me sad that a smart, beautiful woman like you has had that part of her life stolen."

She swallowed down the lump in her throat and her eyes filled with tears.

"Oh God, I'm sorry, I didnae mean to upset you." He extended his arms, "Come here."

Falling into his embrace, she wept on his shoulder as he rocked her. It felt good. Really good.

When she stopped crying, he looked down at her and said, "You ready to jiggle?"

She sob-laughed.

Taking the log basket, he led her back inside and, with a wry smile, asked, "Shall we go to bed wife?"

Her stomach flipped as he led her to the bedroom where he stood next to the bed and began to strip. She gaped at him wide-eyed. He gave her an encouraging smile, and she copied him and began peeling off some layers. When they were down to t-shirts and underwear, he pulled her onto the bed and lay facing her. Winking at her, he made the bed creak and gave a small moan of pleasure. Her hand shot to her mouth to muffle a snort of amusement. This set Jamie off and he laugh-moaned, his shoulders shaking with mirth.

With a rolling motion of his hand, he encouraged her to play along and she let out a whimper. He laughed and slapped a palm over his mouth which made her snigger. When he bounced the bedsprings noisily, tears streamed down her face and she stifled a squeal.

They jiggled some more, wheezing and panting with quiet laughter. Feigning orgasm, he gave a shudder and gasped. The noise she made set him off and he stuffed a fist into his mouth to stop from howling. Grinning like village idiots, they lay still for a few minutes and stared at one another. Tentatively, he reached a hand towards her and tucked a stray lock of hair behind her ear.

In a low voice laced with irony, he asked, "How was the jiggling for you?"

"No one jiggles better."

They laughed silently.

"Jamie?"

"What?" he mouthed.

"Will you hold me?"

Grinning, he flung back the duvet and they clambered beneath it. He wrapped his arms around her and pulled her close, and she fell asleep cocooned in his embrace.

Jamie worked Saturday mornings, and she woke to find him gone. There was a cold mug of tea on the nightstand and a note saying he'd collect her for the shoot at eleven o'clock.

She spent the morning walking Meg, cleaning the house and grocery shopping. When she heard the Land Rover just before eleven, she settled Meg, grabbed her coat and jumped into the front beside Jamie. He grinned at her and, as they drove the short distance to the big house, they chatted about their morning.

The others were already waiting outside Hourn House in the vehicles. Jamie and Kathryn followed the Colquhouns' khaki Defender, who in turn followed Duncan and Angus in the modern pickup truck.

As ghillie, Duncan was their guide for the day and he led the convoy along a single-track road that wound along the base of Beinn Hourn. As the Defender rumbled and lurched over the rough terrain, Kathryn clung to her seat. Jamie grinned in delight as they bounced through a particularly deep rut.

"Enjoying the ride Mrs Campbell?"

She laughed, knowing he was having fun, thinking he looked more at ease behind the wheel of the Defender than he ever had in a police car.

Duncan led the convoy to a flat piece of ground near to where Jamie said was the start of a stalker's path. Pulling up next to the Colquhouns, Jamie applied the handbrake and killed the engine.

"Welcome to Hell's mountain" said Marcus as Kathryn jumped from the Defender.

Ruth approached wearing a wax jacket, a long skirt and Hunter wellingtons. Casting a censorious eye over Kathryn's jeans, she asked, "Do you shoot? We ought to have asked you before dragging you out here."

Kathryn shook her head. "No, never."

Marcus narrowed his eyes and grumbled, "Oh good grief, don't tell me you're one of those tree-huggin' vegan animal rights nutters?"

"I've never been comfortable with it, if I'm honest" she replied.

Marcus bristled. "Really? Yet you're married to Jamie."

Ruth said, "Leave her alone honey, it's Kathryn's choice."

Kathryn smiled. "I'm more than happy for Jamie to shoot things."

They all laughed, Marcus loudest. Duncan opened the back of his vehicle and handed each of them a rifle and a rucksack, except for Jamie who'd brought his own gun. Jamie took Kathryn's rifle and, while the others attended to their kit, he showed her how to check it was empty, load it, then make it safe.

"Watch out in case she shoots someone accidentally," said Marcus.

"The first aid kit only extends to flesh wounds" muttered Angus, scowling at Kathryn.

Ignoring them, Kathryn watched Jamie as he checked, loaded and cleared both weapons. Once everyone was happy with their kit, Jamie swung his rifle and pack onto his shoulder, and she copied him. He took her hand and gave it a reassuring squeeze.

Ruth gushed, "Oh lordy, you two are so sweet. I've never seen a couple more in love."

Everyone laughed except Duncan who glanced away. Playing to the gallery, Jamie pulled her to him and brushed his lips against her forehead. Her heart leapt into her mouth as she gazed at his mischievous expression.

They followed Duncan on-foot along the stalker's path for several hundred metres. Kathryn's new walking boots began to rub and she could feel blisters forming on her heels. Jamie kept hold of her hand the entire route as they chatted with the Colquhouns, while Duncan and Angus remained silent except for an occasional point and grunt. Jamie indicated wildlife to Kathryn and the group, including a golden eagle soaring in the distance. Their prey today, explained Marcus, was an injured red deer stag. After twenty minutes, they reached a covered ledge which acted as a natural hide with a spectacular view over the valley below.

She whispered to Jamie, "You're really going to shoot Bambi?"

"More like Bambi's grandpa" he replied.

She made a comedy sad face which made him chuckle. Duncan suddenly raised his hand to silence the group and motioned for them to look over to their left, and passed his binoculars to Marcus who focused on where he'd pointed. Jamie followed the line of his sight with his scope and passed his binoculars to Kathryn and through the lenses, she spotted the stag. It was a magnificent beast with enormous antlers. Passing the glasses back to Jamie, she made another face.

He sent her an apologetic smile and whispered, "It won't feel a thing."

In a low voice, Marcus invited Jamie to take the shot and Kathryn suspected it was a test. They all hunkered down and slipped on their ear defenders, and Kathryn held her breath as she watched him ready his rifle and take aim. There was a short pause followed by a powerful crack which reverberated around the glen. The deer collapsed.

"Excellent shot Jamie," exclaimed Marcus peering through his binoculars.

"Aye, nice clean kill," acknowledged Duncan grudgingly.

The group descended and walked over to where the stag lay in the heather. The bullet had hit him square in the chest, and this drew further compliments from the Colquhouns.

Marcus turned to Kathryn and said, "You may not be comfortable with what we do, but we have to ensure a healthy and sustainable population. If we didn't cull the old and weak, we risk losing the herd to starvation due to overgrazing. Isn't that right Jamie?"

Jamie nodded and shot Kathryn an apologetic smile. Kathryn gritted her teeth and resisted the urge to point her rifle at Marcus.

Marcus continued, "And it's important the breeding stock remain true and strong. We don't want anything pissing in our gene pool, do we?" He laughed mirthlessly as she focused on maintaining a neutral expression. While Duncan and Angus tied rope around the beast's antlers, Marcus said, "Shall we let the ladies have some fun? See if Kathryn can shoot straight?"

If you were in my sights, my aim would be true. She said in a saccharine voice, "I'll try not to kill you."

More mirthless laughter. Duncan pointed out the remains of a tree stump in the distance and suggested it'd make a good target. Ruth took aim first and put two clean shots into the stump, and Marcus and Duncan smiled approvingly.

"Right little lady, let's see what you can do," said Marcus.

Kathryn's gut clenched at the thought of making a fool of herself in front of everyone. Reluctantly, she stepped into position and loaded her rifle while Jamie hovered at her side. When she raised the gun, he helped nestle it into her shoulder to minimize the recoil. Standing behind her, he positioned her hands until her eye was aligned down the scope, and talked her through the technique for squeezing off a round. He was very close, his body pressing against hers, and she felt his breath in her hair. His effect on her was distracting and she struggled to focus as her heart thumped in her chest.

He whispered in her ear. "When you're ready, breathe out slowly, hold then squeeze the trigger. Just be ready for the kick." He took a step back while she adjusted her aim. Aware she couldn't hold the weight of the rifle much longer, she pulled the trigger. The weapon thudded painfully into her shoulder and the tree stump exploded. After making it safe, she lowered the gun and slipped off her ear defenders. Jamie rewarded her with a full-blown smile that made her breath hitch. "I'm very impressed Mrs Campbell."

Duncan smiled, and Ruth clapped her hands and squealed, "She's a natural!"

"Next time, I'll expect a stag for the larder," said Marcus.

Or you, thought Kathryn, smiling sweetly.

Angus and Duncan placed the deer on a tarpaulin and dragged it back to where they'd parked. When they neared the vehicles, they stopped and Duncan produced a large knife and set to work field dressing the stag. Kathryn glanced away as he removed the internal organs and a section of windpipe. Marcus explained they needed to do this as soon as possible after killing it, and do it without puncturing the organs.

"See you back at the house" said Ruth cheerfully.

Kathryn felt slightly nauseous as she watched Angus and Duncan heave the carcass into the back of the pickup truck. She climbed into the Defender beside Jamie.

He looked at her and chuckled, "Are you gonna puke?"

Scowling, she replied, "If I do, I'll be sure to hurl in your direction. That was gruesome."

"Guess I'm used to it," he said as he started the engine and rammed it into gear. "But you've got to admit it's more humane than farming. One minute Bambi's skipping about the heather, the next he's on a plate."

"I agree ... but seeing it butchered is something else." She pulled a face.

"Fancy venison for dinner?" he teased.

She slapped his arm playfully. "No, I've vowed to become a tree-huggin' vegan animal rights nutter."

Jamie laughed.

As their convoy wound its way back, he told her about hunting with his father and how venison, trout and salmon had formed their staple diet, and he admitted he used to complain about it.

"You're a good shot. Did your father teach you?"

"Aye, he did." He paused as if counting to ten in his head then said, "but I'd a lot of practice in the army."

She twisted in her seat to look at him. "Guess you've had to kill more than deer?"

Jamie kept his eyes on the road and said nothing.

She whispered. "Sorry if I upset you."

He reached for her hand. "You didn't. I was just lost in thought. I was only a lad when I joined up, too young to realise what it's really about. Next thing I knew, I was in the middle of a war zone full of people trying to kill me and my mates." She squeezed his hand, and he released hers only when he had to change gear. They parked next to the Colquhouns in front of a stone outbuilding at the rear of the main house, and Angus and Duncan pulled up next to them.

When they got out, Marcus strode towards the outhouse saying, "I'll show you where we hang the carcasses."

He heaved open the door to the outbuilding and flicked on a light. The smell hit Kathryn before she saw its source. Two stags hung from chains by their antlers, their rib cages held open by wooden splints to expose the cavity. Blood had dripped into drainage channels cut into the stone floor leaving a congealed mess. She felt nauseous as she watched Angus and Duncan hoist today's kill into place.

"How long do you age them?" asked Jamie.

Duncan replied, "Typically a week but in this temperature, they'll keep longer."

"We'll be tucking into these at Christmas," said Ruth. She took Kathryn's arm and led her out. "I do love roast venison, so much nicer than turkey don't you think?"

Relieved to get out of the game store, Kathryn agreed.

"We must swap recipes," said Ruth.

Kathryn nodded, ignoring the look of amusement on Jamie's face.

On Saturday evenings, the community gathered to eat together and Ruth and Marcus invited the Campbells to join them. Kathryn fretted about what to wear since she didn't own many skirts and only the one long one. Although not something she'd normally wear, she opted for one of the new outfits she'd been given: black jeggings, knee-high black boots and a billowy cobalt blue blouse. She left her hair down, securing the back with a clasp to keep it off her face so it cascaded over her shoulders, and she applied a light touch of makeup. When she emerged from the bathroom, Jamie gave her an approving look.

"Wow Mrs Campbell, you scrub up well."

She turned pink. "Should I wear a skirt? None of the women wear trousers."

He shrugged. "Wear what you're comfortable with."

Knowing he was right and reluctant to cave into social pressure, she announced she was ready and they made their way to the community hall. The main hall was lined with long refectory tables and chairs and a bar and buffet had been set up at the kitchen end. The fragrant smell of food filled her nostrils and her stomach growled. Clasping her hand, Jamie led her towards the bar, and a hush descended as everyone turned to stare. Kathryn felt every eye upon her and a blush crept across her face and neck. She noticed all the women and girls were in long skirts or dresses, in drab colours, and many wore headscarves.

Marcus and Duncan stood next to the bar and she felt almost burned by Duncan's heated gaze. Marcus extended a handshake to Jamie and said to Kathryn, "Goodness Mrs Campbell, you know how to light up a room."

Slipping his arm around her waist, Jamie pulled her to him and laughed, "She certainly does that." Seeming to sense her discomfort, he sent her a look that said, "I've got you."

Duncan continued to gawp at her and his face flushed crimson as he stammered out a greeting. Ruth bustled over and took Marcus's arm. She wore a long plaid dress that made her look even dumpier than usual, and a matching scarf. After greeting Jamie, she gave Kathryn a tight smile as she cast a disapproving gaze over her attire. Jamie's grip tightened.

A scornful smile played on Ruth's lips. "I'm so glad you could join us. Perhaps you'd like to give us a hand in the back Kathryn?"

With a parting smile, she followed Ruth to the kitchen at the rear where several women were busy preparing food.

Sweeping another censorious eye over her, Ruth said, "Maybe you could help Hazel?" She led her to where Hazel stood slicing vegetables.

When Ruth had gone, Kathryn rolled up her sleeves and whispered, "I think I've been banished for being inappropriately dressed."

Hazel laughed. "You look amazing, I wish I'd the courage to wear clothes like that instead of this frumpy thing." She tugged at the brown material of her shapeless dress. "I'm sure my husband would appreciate it too."

"I didn't realise the women here dressed so modestly. I've arrived so ill-prepared."

Hazel glanced around, then in a low voice said, "We never used to, but since Ruth joined us we've become more conservative."

"The men too?" asked Kathryn.

Hazel shook her head, "They wear what they like."

When she said she needed to go on a shopping trip, Hazel offered to lend her some skirts since Mallaig didn't offer much in the way of clothing shops. Kathryn thanked her and they chatted while they chopped salad.

An argument between two women drew their attention. The older woman, who Kathryn recognized as Rebecca from the Christian Wives group, was scolding her daughter Bethany. An embarrassed silence fell over the kitchen as the argument escalated.

Rebecca said, "Do not stray from a righteous path."

Untying her apron, Bethany shouted, "How can you live like this? Open your eyes. You're in here cooking and skivvying while they're out there drinking. How is that fair or righteous? Where in the bible does it say women have to do all the work?"

"Keep your voice down. Your father works very hard, all the men do."

"And you don't? I can't live like this, and I can't bear to watch you tolerate it." She threw down her apron and tore off her headscarf, yelling, "I've had enough," and stalked from the kitchen.

Kathryn and Hazel swapped a raised eyebrow and busied themselves with the chopping. When Rebecca followed her daughter from the kitchen, Hazel said in a low voice, "Think Bethany's finding it hard adjusting back to life here after university."

"What's she studying?"

"Law, she's in her second year."

"Obviously a clever woman."

"She's very smart but it's never sat well with her parents. Neither wanted her to go to university nor had the means to support her. Not until Ruth offered to help."

"That was very generous," said Kathryn.

"Hmm, after witnessing that exchange, Ruth might regret it."

When the food was ready, the women loaded up the buffet and served while the men talked and drank. There was no sign of Bethany, but Kathryn spotted Rebecca in a hushed discussion with her husband who looked furious. She joined Jamie who was sat near the front next to the Colquhouns and Marcus's sons. Down from them sat Dr Vondell and his wife, Hazel and her husband Simon, then others she assumed were senior laity. She noticed the younger estate hands sat at the back of the room with the other singletons.

After Marcus said grace, they tucked into a hearty meal. Kathryn was conscious of the darting sideways glances Duncan continued to shoot her when he thought she wasn't looking, while Angus engaged Jamie in conversation about sheep. Kathryn zoned out of the discussion while she observed patriarchy at play across the community, and wondered what Simone de Beauvoir would have made of it in the 21st century. She caught Cameron, the young estate hand, watching Angus and Jamie and thought about how difficult it must be for him to live in a community with so few women his age.

Marcus cut into her reverie. "What do you think Kathryn? Do panda-eyed sheep make good rugs?"

Kathryn regarded Marcus with a wary expression as everyone stared at her. She said, "I imagine it must be difficult for them without hands."

Jamie spluttered with laughter and Duncan sniggered, while the others gawked at her.

Another social norm flouted, she thought; at this rate they'll be stoning her.

∽

Sunday morning and the church was packed to the rafters. Jamie and Kathryn had arrived with two minutes to spare and they squeezed into a pew at the back. He'd shaved and was wearing a dark suit and tie which Kathryn thought made him look especially handsome. And she wasn't the only one; two teenage girls in the row in front turned and stared until their mother chastised them, and the girls swapped glances and giggled. Kathryn gazed up at him, feeling like a teenager herself caught under his spell. As he took her hand and smiled, she wondered if he was aware of the effect he had upon women. She knew he was self-conscious about his scar but she didn't mind it; it was part of who he was.

Succumbing to social pressure, Kathryn had worn a long navy dress but she'd stopped short of wearing a headscarf. She looked around realising that, apart from the youngest girls, she was the only female with an uncovered head. She also became aware of a hierarchy in the seating, with the Colquhouns at the front, followed by senior laity and families who'd been here longest, with newcomers at the back. She was glad she and Jamie hadn't arrived sooner and mistakenly sat near the front.

Marcus ascended the steps to the pulpit and the room fell silent, save for the babies and children. In a warm, powerful voice, he welcomed everyone and thanked them for coming, then spoke at length about Jean's time with the community and their love and respect for her. After a prayer and a hymn, his voice became stronger as he launched into his sermon. Marcus cast a stern eye over his flock and settled his gaze on Jamie and Kathryn at the back. She felt herself flush crimson as he boomed.

"A man's duty is to care for his wife and family and to submit to God. A woman's duty is to care for her family and to submit to her husband. For that is the natural order of things, and has been since the time of Adam."

Jamie clasped her hand tight as Kathryn attempted to unclench her jaw.

"If God wanted men and women to be the same, he'd have made them that way. Instead, he made women to bear and care for children, and he made men to work and take care of the family. We cannot change what we are, because that is how God made us."

Marcus paused for a few moments to let his words settle, before casting an accusative glance over his flock. His eyes settled on Bethany who was sitting between her mother and father. Kathryn heard Jamie stifle a laugh. But Marcus was only warming up.

"Women are by nature timid and emotional. They need a father and husband to guide them, and the bonds of family and marriage to provide stability. By comparison, men are naturally aggressive and promiscuous. They need the Lord to guide them and a wife to satisfy their carnal needs. Fathers must show their sons how to be a good role model, and run a fair, firm and godly household."

Marcus fixed Kathryn with his gaze and in a raised voice, proclaimed, "Men submit to God, and women submit to their husbands. Accept this truth, for that is what God intended."

Jamie's shoulders were now shaking with silent laughter and she tried to ignore him. As Marcus launched into a rant about how all the ills of modern society were due to the flouting of this divine truth, Kathryn watched the faces of the children and wondered what the effects of years of listening to these destructive words would have on their young minds. As he droned on, she watched as elders laid out trays of bread and large silver goblets on a table at the front.

Marcus announced, "He calls us to share this one bread and this one cup."

After beseeching God to send down his spirit to be upon the bread and wine, he led them in the Lord's Prayer. Kathryn tried to remember the words as it had been many years since she'd attended church. Her grandmother used to take her every Sunday until Kathryn, aged fifteen, simply refused to go. The church, she decided, had no answers and God had no mercy, otherwise he would never have let what happened to her occur. She felt ambivalent towards God and hostile to organised religion.

Marcus descended from the pulpit and stood behind the table. Picking up a slice of white bread, he exclaimed, "Jesus said this is my body which is broken for you. Do this in memory of me." Marcus lifted a goblet. "This is a new covenant sealed by my blood. Whenever you drink it, do this in memory of me."

He then broke off a small piece of bread and popped it into his mouth. The elders passed the trays around the congregation. Marcus raised a goblet. "Blood of Christ, shed for forgiveness of sins." He took a sip and the goblets followed the bread. Kathryn watched as the sheeple - now her and Jamie's term for the congregation - copied what he'd done. When the tray of bread reached them, Kathryn reluctantly took a piece and passed the rest to Jamie.

He whispered in her ear, "What, no wholemeal?"

She stifled a giggle, and took a sip of red wine from the goblet which tasted bitter. With a grimace, she handed it to Jamie who returned a mischievous grin.

After taking a sip, he said in a low voice "Mmm, I'm getting hints of red diesel and boil-in-the-bag cottage pie."

Kathryn snorted out a laugh which caused the family in front to turn and look at her. She covered it with a cough and patted her chest to suggest she'd choked.

Marcus finally gave the blessing and the congregation began to disperse. Jamie and Kathryn lingered at the back until everyone around had left.

With an impish expression, he said, "Right wife, I've got carnal needs it's your duty to satisfy."

Her stomach flipped and, seeing her reaction, Jamie guffawed.

That afternoon, Jamie drove them out of the valley for a couple of miles to a layby and they'd parked up and walked Meg before the heavens had opened. Meg now lay curled up in the back on a blanket while they ate sandwiches. The rain was shelling sideways on the windows of the Defender.

"Mmm, nice filling," said Jamie, "and wholemeal bread. Glad

you're seeing to my wishes wife." He chuckled at the look she shot him.

"That sermon was unbelievable. How can these women bear to sit there and listen to him, never mind let their kids hear it?"

"Aye, even knowing about their beliefs didnae quite prepare me for it."

She twisted in her seat to face him. "Are you religious?"

He shook his head. "Nope. Not been in a church since I was a kid, except in the army when I saw how they used it to legitimise war." He stared pensively through the rain battering against the windscreen. "I'm of the opinion man created God, not the other way around, but I don't have a problem with people who do believe. What about you?"

Avoiding his gaze, she shook her head. "I don't believe in a God that can allow such terrible things to happen to people."

A silence descended, thick and heavy.

When the wind buffeted the vehicle, Jamie said, "Guess we should check in. Christ, we'll be lucky to hear anything above this."

Reaching into his pocket, he retrieved the satellite phone and called Keith's number. She could hear the dial tone and their handler pick up after a couple of rings. She poured Jamie a mug of coffee from the flask as he gave his call sign and spoke to Keith. He relayed his conversation with Jean and told him about her death before she was able to pass on information, and how they'd found nothing in her home or on her body, except for a mysterious reference to St Januarius in Meg's collar. He also explained about the cottage being under surveillance and requested a jammer.

Kathryn heard the long, low whistle Keith emitted and him say, "Certainly sounds like we ain't wasting our time in the back arse of beyond."

After Keith had quizzed Jamie using one of Pia's psychological evaluation surveys, he passed the phone to her. Keith asked how she was and if Jamie was behaving.

"I'm right here," said Jamie.

Shooting him an impish grin, she laughed. "Yes, he's being a very good boy." She told Keith about her suspicions that the cellar was much larger and might house the servers that Fitz suspected were on-site.

Keith told her Fitz was already digging and he hoped to have more information for them next week. After completing Pia's survey with Kathryn, she wound up the call with the assurance they'd speak next week.

As Jamie switched on the engine, he spotted a large bird of prey in the distance and reached for the binoculars.

"I'll be damned," he said, "that's not native to these parts."

Jamie

A routine began to develop where they'd wake in each other's arms, then he would drag himself out of bed and bring Kathryn a mug of tea before going to work. They'd have lunch and dinner together and walk Meg in the evenings so they could talk freely. He enjoyed her company and looked forward to the time they spent together, and he was beginning to realise that as well as being smart and funny, she was also kind and gentle. Seeing the deer shot had upset her and she was fiercely protective of the dog. It upset him to think what had happened to her to make her so fearful of men and so afraid that she'd never once had a relationship.

He also knew how anxious and frustrated she was growing as time passed and they made little progress with the investigation. Until they'd a jammer, the bug in their bedroom meant she couldn't risk using her laptop, and he couldn't get her access to the Society's computer files. For her sake, he urgently needed to find a way.

It was Wednesday morning, three days before Christmas, and Marcus was already in the estate office when Jamie arrived. Sat behind his desk, cup of coffee in hand, he was finishing up a phone call.

"That was Buchanan confirming Jean's death has been referred to the Procurator Fiscal so there'll be a post-mortem and police investigation. He'll be here tomorrow morning to take a statement from Finlay. Why this can't wait until after Christmas, I've no idea."

"I'll let Finlay know," said Jamie.

"How's Kathryn? I hope she's not too upset by recent events. Women aren't strong, they need gentle handling so if there's anything we can do..."

Jamie was beginning to wonder how well Marcus knew his own wife as Ruth didn't strike him as fitting this description.

"She's okay. If anything, I'm worried she'll get bored, so if there's anything you want doing in the office, I'm sure she'd be happy to help. Like you say, women aren't strong so having something to distract her would be good."

Marcus pursed his lips and asked if Kathryn had any experience, and Jamie confirmed she'd worked in an office before they'd got married.

"I'll talk to Ruth. We're going to need to replace Jean; she handled the administration for the holiday bookings and the web site. Kathryn would be part-time, though; a married woman's main responsibility is to her husband."

"I think that's an excellent idea Marcus."

"Good, that's settled then, although I'll run it by Ruth." Laughing, he added, "She likes to think she's in charge around here."

Jamie joined in, amused at the fact he'd convinced Marcus the idea had been his. Marcus disappeared and Jamie went to make a coffee. He overheard voices coming from the main kitchen at the back of the house, and realised Marcus and Ruth were having words. He crept along the corridor and strained to listen.

Ruth said angrily, "I'd rather it was someone we knew, part of the community."

"She is part of the community."

"We know nothing about her."

"Where's the harm Ruth? It's only the holiday admin and you'll need to replace Jean." After a pause he said placatingly, "I know how busy you are my dear with your own work."

"Fine but, in future, ask me first Marcus."

Jamie heard footsteps and he darted into the kitchenette and flicked the kettle on. Marcus spotted him on his way back to the office and said, "I've talked to Ruth and she'll be delighted to have Kathryn's help in the new year."

Jamie thanked him and said he'd let Kathryn know. Back in the office, Marcus stood and looked out the window. Although cold, the sun was shining and there wasn't a cloud in the sky.

"We're winding down here, so why don't you take that lovely lady wife of yours to Mallaig today. I'm sure she's got Christmas shopping to do."

"If you're sure you don't need me?"

"Aye, away and show her the sights, it'll take all of five minutes."

Kathryn

The low winter sun glinted off the Defender as they wove their way along the single-track roads out of the valley. Jamie had suggested bringing Meg and she sat beside them in the front looking every bit as captivated by the scenery as they were.

Kathryn felt like a weight had lifted from her shoulders when he'd told her she'd be starting work in the office, knowing she'd finally be able to make progress with the investigation. If there was anything in those files, she'd find it.

She found music CDs in the glove compartment, and they sang along to the Kings of Leon's *Sex on Fire*, and she teased Jamie about his dreadful singing which only made him holler louder.

He laughed, "I won't judge your cooking and you won't judge my singing, wife."

When they reached the small port of Inverie, they left the Land Rover and took the passenger ferry to Mallaig with Meg in tow. Arriving before lunch, they decided to explore the busy fishing port before meeting with Keith. Jamie offered her his hand and she smiled as she took it, pleased he still wanted to even when not within the community.

They took it in turns to browse in the shops while the other waited outside with Meg. Kathryn found a clothing shop selling long thermal underwear and bought three sets. When Jamie asked what she'd purchased, he did the same using his cover credit card. Jamie said he was going to expense the thermals since they'd both been so cold since arriving in Knoydart and had been wearing multiple layers. After, they found a dog-friendly café and ordered lunch. The café was quiet and they'd the place to themselves until a large gentleman in a tartan cap took a seat nearby.

Over coffee, Jamie regarded her over the rim of his cup. "How you bearing up Mrs Campbell?"

She blew out a breath. "Feels longer than ten days."

"Huh, that bad?"

She leaned in and in a low voice said, "No, not at all, it's just a lot's happened, although we've not made much progress with the reason we're here."

Jamie shrugged. "It'll take time to win their trust. We need to make ourselves useful and inveigle our way in."

"It's time we don't have."

"You working in the office will make all the difference."

"How did you manage it?"

"Told Marcus you were weak and feeble and needed a distraction."

She sent him a killer glare which made him laugh. "I hope you don't really think that."

Smiling, he reached for her hand. "Course not. You're one of the bravest people I've ever met."

A prickle of awareness skated down her spine as his thumb grazed her knuckles. "Do you think we'll be here a while?"

"Expect it'll be at least two months. Does that worry you?"

"The thought of going back to prison is what worries me."

He shook his head, "I won't let that happen Kathryn."

Praying he was right, she said, "But apart from what happened with Jean, I'm enjoying the lifestyle. I thought I'd miss the technology but I haven't. What about you?"

He laughed softly and his eyes sparkled. "Aye, the business with Jean aside, it's been good … but only because you're here." He squeezed her hand.

Kathryn's lower body clenched at the heat in his eyes. "Jamie …

uhm … I meant what I said." She tried to pull her hand from his, but he retained his grip; it felt like a current ran between them.

"So did I. I want to get to know everything there is to know about you baby."

Before she could reply, he rose and went to the counter to pay, and she watched him with a confusing mixture of longing and hopelessness. She knew there was a powerful attraction between them, and the sheer force of it scared her. Was this what her own mother had felt? Was this the reason she couldn't leave her husband, the reason she tolerated his drinking and abuse, the reason she lost her life? This emotion, whatever it was, rendered women vulnerable, and for that reason she wanted none of it. Life was simpler without it and she didn't need it. Did she? But seeing Jamie made her doubt her resolve; she was drawn to him and, in his thrall, she felt utterly powerless.

But even if she did stop fighting it, the situation would only lead to heartache for both of them. She'd spoken the truth; they could never be a proper couple. Although she could endure his contact, a physical relationship was a step too far and the mere thought of it terrified her. Yet endure was not the right word; she could more than tolerate his touch. She liked when he took her hand, she loved waking in his arms, and she couldn't get the kisses they'd shared out her mind. Jamie was in her head. All the time.

With a takeaway coffee for Keith, they left the café and headed to the address near the pier he'd given them.

Spotting Bethany emerge from a door ahead, she pulled Jamie to a halt and pretended to look in a shop window. In a low register she said, "I've just seen Bethany, over to your left, walking towards the ferry. She came out the building with the blue door."

Pointing to the window display, he said, "We'll follow in a minute." After feigning interest in the display, they trailed her to the ferry. Kathryn noticed Jamie didn't look at Bethany directly, using her reflection in the shop windows instead. Taking his mobile phone out, he said, "Hey, stand there, I'll take your picture." As she posed with Meg for a photograph, she realised she'd a clear view of Bethany and the ferry terminal.

When Jamie had taken a picture, they walked back towards the town and she said, "She's on the boat to Inverie."

"When we pass the building she came out of, stop and fuss over Meg so we can take a look at it."

She did as he suggested, making a show of adjusting Meg's collar. The brass plaque on the wall revealed it was a doctor's surgery, the names Dr Andrew O'Neill and Dr Eva McGrath listed on it. They then headed towards Keith's office.

Jamie said, "Hmm, interesting. Why's she come to Mallaig when there's a doctor in the community?"

"Maybe she wanted to see a female GP."

"Aye, you're probably right."

They took the stairs leading to Keith's office. Jamie rang the bell and Keith opened the door, and made a fuss of Meg.

Gawping at him, Jamie said, "Are you some kind of dog whisperer? Anyone else, she'd have your hand off."

Chuckling, Keith, led them into a sparsely furnished room where he'd set up his laptop. Unshaven and dressed casually, Keith looked different to the forbidding MI5 officer they'd previously met.

"Good to see you," he said accepting the coffee, "didn't expect a visit in person so soon. How have things been?" He looked at their held hands and gave them a curious glance.

They chatted about the last few days and then Keith produced a package which he handed to Jamie. "Gift from Fitz. Says a jammer will arouse suspicion so he suggests you put this in the bedroom when you want … uhm … privacy."

Jamie opened the parcel to reveal a digital radio.

"Looks ordinary enough but when it's on, it'll channel only the tuned radio signal to the bug so you'll be able talk freely, use your laptop ... or whatever."

Jamie produced a long flat tin from the pocket of his Barbour jacket and handed it to Keith. "I need a key cut so we can have a closer look at the cellar."

Opening it, Keith examined the imprint Jamie had taken of Duncan's key.

Keith nodded and turned to Kathryn. "Fitz confirmed what you thought, the cellar's much bigger so you may've struck gold." Then turning to Jamie, he said, "Your man Finlay's a mystery, I've been unable to find anything on him, so I need you to check his personnel file again and get a recent photo."

After leaving Keith, they returned to Inverie on the ferry, then found a small supermarket and loaded up the car with provisions, including items Marcus and Hazel had requested. Jumping into the Defender, Jamie looked at his watch and suggested a short detour. He drove a few miles to a white sandy beach and they walked hand-in-hand along it, with Jamie throwing a stick for Meg.

Jamie turned to her. "I reckon Keith thinks we're shagging."

She gawped at him. "You'd better put him right, I don't want either of us getting kicked off this job, me especially."

"We won't, not now we're here."

Kathryn wondered what he meant. Did he think it was alright to have a relationship or just for Keith to suspect it? Knowing it was ridiculous to even contemplate it, she gave it no more thought.

When it was time to head home, she jumped into the Defender beside him. "Thank you, Mr Campbell, I've had a lovely day."

He grinned. "So have I Mrs Campbell."

When they began singing along to Beyonce's *Single Ladies*, Meg threw her head back and howled.

IMMANUEL

"Now faith is the assurance of things hoped for, the conviction of things not seen."

— *HEBREWS 11:1*

Kathryn

The stained-glass windows of the church glowed with pillar candles burning in each arch, and garlands hung between them. A large Christmas tree festooned with silver baubles and fairy lights stood next to the pulpit, and a nativity scene complete with straw and stuffed animals lay beneath the altar. A small choir of children sung carols as Jamie and Kathryn took up their usual seats for the Christmas Eve service.

Simon led the celebrations and after hymns and a prayer, young children enacted the nativity. One of the wise men muddled his lines up after gold was presented, saying "Frank sent this", and there was laughter. When the youngest children dressed as angels filed down the aisle singing *Silent Night*, a glassy-eyed Kathryn put a hand to her chest and oohed along with the rest of the congregation.

Simon gave a touching sermon on the true meaning of Christmas and, at the end, invited everyone to turn to their neighbour and wish them goodwill. After shaking hands with those around them, Jamie turned to Kathryn and their eyes locked. He dipped his head and placed a tender kiss on her lips that made her breath catch. The kiss lingered. When he pulled away, they gazed at one another until the people around them began to leave. Was he just playing his part, she wondered? After, he led her towards the community hall where they'd been invited to dine, and when he squeezed her hand, tendrils of awareness crept up her arm and her pulse raced.

Long refectory tables covered in white linen and decorated with wreaths lined the hall, and they found themselves sitting opposite Simon and Hazel. After shaking hands, Simon poured them each a glass of wine and they chatted about the beautiful service. The hall was filled with the sound of laughter, children and music. Women placed warm plates in front of them laden with slices of venison, and they helped themselves from dishes of potatoes and vegetables. As Kathryn ate, a large hand suddenly pressed down on her shoulder and she flinched. Twisting around, she found Marcus behind her.

"Are you enjoying the stag your husband shot?"

Everyone laughed at her expression and through a mouthful, she mumbled, "Absolutely delicious, in fact I might have seconds" which caused more laughter. Jamie leaned in and kissed her temple and they grinned at each other.

When Marcus had gone, Hazel cast him a dark look and muttered, "He just had to tell you that didn't he?" When Simon shot her a pointed glance, she added, "Well, there was no need."

A silence descended which Jamie broke by topping up their glasses, and they resumed chatting. When the women began to clear the plates, Kathryn offered to help and she found herself in the kitchen scraping and rinsing dishes with Hazel. Once everything was washed and put away, they returned to the men, and families began to gather up their children and go home.

Jamie drained his glass and stood. "Shall we Mrs Campbell?" He offered her his hand.

They waved goodnight to Simon and Hazel and the others around them and spilled from the hall into the frigid night air. Jamie wrapped his arm round Kathryn's shoulder and they walked slowly back to their cottage talking about what a lovely evening it'd been.

Meg greeted them and they took her for a walk down to the edge of the loch. It was a clear night and stars filled the sky. He put his arm around her waist and pulled her into his side as he looked out over the sparkling water. She glanced up at him, at the moonlight reflecting in his eyes. Whether it was the wine or the magic of the evening, she yearned for him to kiss her again. Caught in his gaze, she examined his face; the strong jaw, high cheekbones and arching brows, and she wished she'd the confidence to reach out and guide his lips to hers. They stared at one another for what seemed like an age, until Meg bounded up to them and broke the spell. Chuckling, Jamie smiled and led her home.

Kathryn felt confused.

～

Jamie

He awoke to find her in his arms. Face buried in her hair, he inhaled a lungful of her heady aroma. She stirred slightly and he feigned sleep in the hope she wouldn't wake and move. With his arm slung across her waist and his hip pressed to her bottom, he daydreamed about making love to her languidly on this, Christmas morning.

Last year, after splitting with Emma, he'd got blind drunk and had nursed a hangover through Christmas lunch at his sister's. The year before, when they'd been a couple, he'd spent the holiday at her parents on his best behaviour. This year, his mate Dean would be taking his place beside Emma. He wasn't bitter, not now, time had dulled the pain and lent perspective.

As he raked through the embers of his relationship with Emma, he realised the cracks had begun to show soon after they started living together. They simply didn't get along. They had quarrelled, and this resulted in him drinking and her hurling humiliating invective at him. When it broke down irretrievably, he'd spent even longer hours at work and taken solace in the bottle. He hadn't been the best partner to her; he could see that now and he didn't blame her for leaving but, when she'd left his bed for Dean's, his pride had taken a battering. Yet another reason he was determined not to return to the cyber unit in Glasgow.

This Christmas, cuddling into Kathryn, he was right where he wanted to be. Although they'd never had sex, he felt a strong bond with her that transcended the physical. He longed to spend time with her. In her company he could truly be himself; there was no agenda, no subtext, no guile. She was everything he could possibly hope for in a partner, all wrapped up in a beautiful package. Lying there inhaling her intoxicating scent, he yearned to tug the ribbon and open it.

Ironically though, none of this was real. They weren't a happily married couple, and there'd be no making love amongst the Christmas wrapping paper. And, were he to pursue a relationship with her, not only might he lose the opportunity to carve out a new career in MI5, but he could cause her serious harm. Prior to leaving for Knoydart, Julien had intimated that, should he want it, there'd be a job opportunity waiting for him. For years, it'd been his dream to work for the security services but, coming from his background, he'd never imagined it would be possible. The timing was perfect too since he didn't want to return to Glasgow, especially now Dean had both his promotion and his girl. But his greatest worry was for Kathryn; the stakes were much higher for her. If MI5 suspected a relationship, she could be kicked off this task and put in prison. Despite his feelings for her, he couldn't take that risk; she meant too much to him. He regretted buying her that Christmas gift, but it was too late to do anything about it.

Stifling a groan, he took another potent inhalation, brushed his lips against her temple, swung out of bed and padded towards the bathroom. After a shower and a shave, he emerged to find her frying bacon in the kitchen, the smell of it making his stomach grumble. With a smile, she handed him a mug of tea and wished him merry Christmas. Without thinking, because it seemed a natural response, he dipped his head and kissed her. Startled, she gazed up at him and they swapped a lingering look.

"Smells magic," he said.

"Take a seat and I'll bring it over."

His eyes tracked her every graceful movement as she buttered rolls and filled them, her robe doing little to hide her sensuous curves. He realised how much she hid beneath her clothes.

After breakfast, he eyed her over the rim of his mug and wondered if she'd bought him a present, worried she might feel awkward if she hadn't. Maybe she was thinking the same thing? Taking a chance, he said, "I've something for you, it's upstairs."

She grinned. "I got you a present too but don't get your hopes up." She went to the kitchen and retrieved a gift bag from under the sink.

"Good hiding place," he chuckled.

She followed him up to the bedroom and he switched on the radio which was playing Christmas music. After fishing out a gift bag from the back of the wardrobe, he handed it to her and sat beside her on the bed.

Peering inside, she beamed. "Ooh, lots of presents!"

"One's a joke, at least I hope so."

She unwrapped the first, a large chocolate bar, and smiled. "You chose well, I'll demolish that later." She giggled at the second gift, a book entitled *How to Cook*, and threw the wrapping paper at him.

Catching it, he said, "I'm glad you're laughing."

She appeared to like the woolly pompom hat he'd got her too. Then, holding his breath, he watched as she untied the ribbon on the box and lifted out a grey silk nightdress and matching robe.

She gawped at him. "Oh Jamie, thank you, they're absolutely beautiful." Their eyes locked.

Smiling, he tore his gaze from her and picked up the gift bag she'd given him. He laughed out loud after unwrapping a Beyonce CD.

Shaking his head, he said "Ha ha, you're very funny Mrs Campbell."

"Now I can practice my cooking and you can practice your singing."

After opening the other parcels to reveal a navy cashmere sweater, a woolly hat, and a bottle of Barolo, he whistled his approval.

"I know you like your wine," she said.

"We'll enjoy it with dinner." They gazed at one another and another awkward silence descended. Jamie said, "Thank you for the thoughtful gifts."

"And for yours."

Fighting the urge to lean in and kiss her, he said, "Fancy a walk with Meg? It's a lovely morning."

She smiled. "As soon as she's opened her presents."

Watching her as she smoothed her fingers over her new nightdress, he wondered if he'd possess the self-control not to touch her if she put it on.

My God, what have I done?

Kathryn

It was the best Christmas. Ever.

Childhood memories of the festive period were unhappy ones of her mother and Phil drinking heavily until one or both of them passed out. She'd always prayed it would be him, otherwise he'd come to her room. Then, after her mother had died and she'd gone to live with her gran, Christmas had been a quiet affair consisting of a dull church service and a TV turkey dinner. Last year, the first without her grandmother, she'd missed her terribly and spent the entire day in cyberspace to avoid having to deal with her loneliness.

This year was different. The evening service had been magical enough, but waking on Christmas morning in Jamie's arms had been the best gift of all. And his presents. The silk nightdress was beautiful but it was laced with meaning which only added to her confusion. Did he expect her to wear it tonight and, if she did, what would that signal?

After a long walk with Meg, they spent the afternoon cooking accompanied by a bottle of prosecco and a Christmas playlist. Jamie sang along and made her laugh while he prepared vegetables, a dishtowel draped over his shoulder. As she watched him switch trays around the Aga's ovens, she pondered on the importance food played here. Before, for her, food had been a necessity and she'd lived on tins and microwave meals, but here, it had a binding nature which brought communities, families and couples together for more than mere sustenance.

Along with the Barolo, they indulged in a smoked salmon starter, followed by turkey with all the trimmings. Too full to eat the Christmas pudding she'd bought, they stretched out on the bed, put on the radio, fired up her laptop and binge-watched on Netflix.

Later, as the credits rolled on-screen, she yawned.

"Tired?" he asked.

She caught his gaze. "Yes, but it's been a lovely day."

They looked at each other for the longest time. As she wrestled with whether to put on the nightdress or not, Jamie reached for her hand.

"Kathryn, I want you to have beautiful things but you're right what you said, you cannae afford to get kicked off this job but I swear if you wear that nightdress, I'm gonnae end up doing something that could risk it." He brought her hand to his mouth and kissed it. "Keep it for someone special."

She angled her face away, torn between wanting to tell him that he was her special someone and fearing what it might lead to. Despite her mixture of disappointment and relief, he'd confirmed what she'd suspected: he really did want her. And his words had cut her enough to know her treacherous body wanted him too.

Tears pricked at her eyes knowing that if she reached out to him, he'd sweep her away together with all of his reservations, and part of her wanted to take the risk. No one would ever know if their relationship was real or part of their cover, and MI5 were unlikely to extract them after their investment in the task. No, her doubts were nothing to do with MI5 finding out, and everything to do with whether or not she could ever give him all of her.

Cupping her chin, he whispered, "I'm saying this because I care about you."

Grabbing her flannel pyjamas, she went to the bathroom to change. When she returned to the bedroom, Jamie was asleep.

She slipped into bed, careful not to disturb him, and studied his handsome profile in the dimness. Resisting the urge to wake him with a kiss, she thought about what he might do if she were to wear the nightdress. Feeling torn, she bit her bottom lip in confusion.

But there was something else gnawing at her. Since arriving in Knoydart, she'd given considerable thought to Pandora's betrayal and Scotty's precarious situation, and she'd finally come to a decision. She couldn't let it go unpunished, and she knew Scotty would want vengeance too. He must be scared out of his wits, and Lord only knew where he'd vanished to with the Feds on his tail. However, she was forbidden from having contact with Grey Nemesis and, since her arrest, had been too afraid to reach out to any of them. But it was time to contact Scotty now. She had to be careful as MI5 must never find out she was communicating with a fellow hacker, and Scotty must never learn who her new employer was.

Grabbing her laptop, she propped herself up against the pillows and took a deep breath. Although she'd removed all the controls Fitz had placed on her machine, it was still risky. After ensuring Jamie was still asleep, she launched an old mail account she'd not used in a while, and composed a message:

Merry Christmas! I hope this finds you safe and well, wherever you are. It was our mutual friend Anesidora who, like her namesake, transgressed divine law and sold us out. In time, when my circumstances allow, I'll reciprocate. I cut my own deal but not at the expense of my friends and I need you to know that. If you ever need my help, please let me know.

Your friend x

She left the message sitting in the draft folder, hoping Scotty might remember about the dormant account, and Fitz hadn't learned of its existence. She'd deliberately avoided using names, except for *Anesidora*, the ancient Greek name for Pandora.

As Kathryn thought about her new employer and the sporting estate where she now lived, she chuckled at the realisation she was the poacher turned gamekeeper.

Jamie

Jamie ran along the side of the loch accompanied by Meg. After feeding her every morning, the dog was beginning to warm to him and he could approach her without risking life and limb. Barely light, it was still early and he wasn't due in work for another hour. Ignoring the horizontal rain, he hoped the cold and the exercise would quell his frustration and purge the thoughts racing through his mind.

Several days had passed since Christmas and he'd run each morning. He'd learned years ago that it helped him focus, deal with stress and improved his mood. Since 'nightgown gate', it felt as if an invisible barrier had formed between them and, although they continued to be affectionate in public, privately Kathryn seemed more guarded and he'd been careful not to blur the boundaries. Their saggy mattress didn't help and they still woke in each other's arms but he'd tried not to linger and indulge his fantasies.

And, as much as this growing distance between them saddened him, it wasn't the only source of his inner turmoil. On Christmas night, he'd realised she'd been every bit as torn as him. So, instead of clarifying things between them as he'd intended, his words had only muddied the waters. Now he couldn't shake the fact she'd been as tempted, and that knowledge was not something he could ignore, despite the risks. Sure, keeping things platonic was the sensible thing to do but it wasn't what either of them desired; of that he was certain. And, if he was being completely honest with himself, a relationship was what he'd wanted from the start, since their first evening together in the Royal Oak.

After pushing himself through the pain barrier, he stopped and caught his breath, gulping frigid air into his lungs. Meg ran back and stared at him as if to say 'c'mon, what are you waiting for?'

Bent double, hands braced on his thighs, he panted, "Meg, what am I gonnae do about Mrs Campbell? This is killing me."

Meg angled her head and returned his gaze.

Jamie had reached a crossroads.

～

He showered, ate a quick breakfast and left for work before Kathryn got up. After dealing with a pest control company, the morning passed slowly. There was no sign of Marcus and Jamie was grateful for the solitude as it gave him more time to dwell on the Kathryn issue. He rehearsed in his head what he wanted to say to her, arguing for and against all the reasons they should embark upon a relationship, and then dismissed each scenario for fear of her reaction.

The phone cut into his reverie. It was Sergeant Buchanan sounding none too pleased because Finlay had failed to turn up before Christmas to give a statement, and this was now holding up his report to the Procurator Fiscal. After assuring him he'd chase Finlay, Jamie grabbed his jacket and made his way over to the converted stable block shared by some of the single lads. As he approached, he spotted Angus coming out of the communal door and they exchanged a nod. Jamie took the stairs and rapped on the door to the apartment that Finlay shared with Cameron. Cameron opened the door ruffling his mop of fair hair, and shot Jamie a guilty look.

"Where's Finlay?" said Jamie.

"Gone up the top field with Duncan to check on the sheep."

"Tell him I want to see him as soon as he's back."

Cameron nodded. "Everything OK boss?"

"Shouldn't you be helping with the fencing?"

"Aye boss, just on my way."

Chancing bastards, thought Jamie, as he returned to Hourn House; he'd have to put his boot on the throat of that pair.

Finlay appeared late afternoon and after Jamie had chewed him out for failing to give a statement, Finlay assured him he'd contact Buchanan first thing in the morning.

Kathryn

It was New Year's Eve and the ceilidh band were in full swing playing a first waltz when Kathryn and Jamie arrived at the community hall. She recognised Euan, the accordion player, who was accompanied by two estate hands on guitar and drums, with Simon on keyboard. She knew Hazel would be on vocals later and she looked forward to hearing her sing.

Marcus and Ruth greeted them and handed them each a glass of prosecco. Kathryn had dared to wear a tight-fitting jersey dress that clung to her and Marcus complimented her on her outfit to Ruth's visible annoyance. Aware that Marcus wasn't the only one casting an eye over her curves, Kathryn felt self-conscious amongst the women in their shapeless outfits, uneasy with the attention her new appearance drew from men. When Duncan stared for too long, she felt Jamie snake a possessive arm around her waist. Dressed in a kilt, he looked like a walking advert for the Scottish Tourist Board. Without thinking, she hugged his waist and he pulled her firmly into his side with a grin.

At the end of the waltz, the band asked everyone to take their partners for the Gay Gordons. Taking the glass from her hand, Jamie placed it down with his, and led her onto the dancefloor.

"I warn you, I've two left feet," she said.

"That's compulsory for ceilidh dancing."

After the band reminded the assembled couples of the steps, they began to dance. Jamie, she realised, was an adept lead and, under his direction, she was whirled around the floor. She was surprised at how much she enjoyed the feel of his hand on her waist, and his touch at the base of her spine. Giddy with all the twirling, she found herself clapping and curtseying at the end with all the other women.

She said, "You're a good dancer."

"Shh, don't tell anyone, I've a hard man reputation to maintain."

Marcus appeared and handed Jamie a large glass of scotch, and Kathryn watched as the two men toasted 'Slainte'. Leaving them to talk, she went to find Hazel who was pouring over her music.

Hazel smiled. "You look lovely. Wish I could wear a dress like that."

"I feel like a jezebel."

"Well, you shouldn't. It's their problem …. thou shall not covet and all that." Hazel paused then added with a chuckle, "I just overheard Duncan say to Angus you've a body made for sin."

Shocked, Kathryn joined in with her laughter.

Leaving Hazel to fret over her lyrics, she refilled her glass with prosecco, and watched from the side as couples danced a slow foxtrot. As the men led the women, making subtle adjustments and corrections to guide them, it struck Kathryn how much this reflected the traditional gender roles in the community. She also noticed how few unmarried women there were, and the number of single men, including Duncan and Angus, who watched from the side-lines.

The band announced the Dashing White Sergeant and Jamie appeared at her side with another tumbler of Scotch. After backing it, he tugged her onto the dancefloor.

"We need another person" he said, "ask Hazel."

Kathryn dragged a reluctant Hazel onto the floor. The three of them held hands, Jamie between the women, facing Angus, Bethany and Cameron. Laughing, they danced until they were dripping with perspiration and exhausted. Being man in the middle, Jamie was dizzy by the end, and almost lost his footing. Marcus handed him another tumbler of whisky and they chatted with the Colquhouns until Jamie pulled her up for the Canadian Barn dance.

The band took a break while the buffet was served. Although the sausage rolls helped soak up some of the alcohol, Kathryn felt tipsy. After a few more dances and a lot more alcohol, her head was swimming and she went in search of water. Hazel sang some haunting Gaelic songs, and Kathryn felt emotional as she listened to her beautiful, melodious voice. Bathed in the warmth and laughter of the community, Kathryn realised how fond she'd grown of this place and its odd inhabitants. She was beginning to understand why people chose to settle here. For the first time in her life, she felt a sense of belonging, even if she could never accept some of their beliefs. There was a reassuring feeling of security in the routines and religious practices that governed the community's life, and she could appreciate its attraction.

Jamie put an end to her wool-gathering by pulling her up for the last waltz and she clung to him for support in case she toppled over, although he wasn't in a much better state. As the music ended, he held her firmly and fixed her with his gaze. Dipping his head, he pressed a kiss to her lips. Startled, she stiffened, but when he gripped her tighter, she melted into his embrace as the connection deepened. When the band announced it was almost midnight and time to toast in the new year, he broke away, the heat in his gaze leaving her in no doubt he wanted more.

Reeling from the kiss and confused by her emotions, she ambled over to where drinks had been laid out. A line of red wine bottles caught her eye, their grey and red labels depicting a priest holding aloft a goblet. The wine was called Saint Januarius.

She collected two glasses of prosecco, but before she could say anything to Jamie, Hazel gave the countdown and an enormous cheer went up on the last stroke of midnight. Wishing her a happy new year, Jamie reached for Kathryn and kissed her again, more hungrily. Giggling, she felt him lurch in her arms and she realised how drunk they were. After exchanging greetings with others, Kathryn went to wash her face with cold water in an attempt to sober up. When she returned to the hall, he was talking to Angus, another tumbler of whisky in his hand.

The band played Auld Lang Syne and everyone joined in a circle to dance and sing. As the last bars played out and a final cheer went up, he turned to her with glassy eyes and slurred, "I've a confession."

She watched in bemusement as he staggered away, clambered onto the stage and grabbed the microphone. He tapped it, the sound reverberating around the hall. Into it, he said "It's time I told you the truth..."

Kathryn ran towards him, and as she mounted the steps, he said, "My wife..." With an unsteady hand, he pointed to Kathryn who shot him a panicked look. "I really love my wife."

She snatched the microphone from his hand as everyone whooped and cheered, and led him off the stage. Marcus clapped him on the back as she guided Jamie towards the exit, while people smiled and laughed and wished them good night. After fetching their coats and helping him into his, they stepped out into the freezing night air.

Once they were some distance away, Jamie stopped and swayed, using her hand to anchor himself. "It's true Kathryn."

"Jesus Jamie, you nearly gave me a heart attack, I didn't know what you were going to say."

He grinned at her goofily. "You're the most beautiful woman on the planet. Can I kiss you again?"

Laughing, she hooked his arm. "C'mon Mr Campbell, time to get you home."

She led him back to the cottage, zigzagging slowly. The lights from the cottages gleamed prettily in the dark.

Once inside, he slumped into a chair and gazed at her as she untied his shoe laces and removed his coat while Meg watched. Tugging him to his feet, she guided him upstairs.

Jamie sniggered. "Are you taking me to bed? D'you know how much I want to–

"–Jamie, behave, you've had a skinful."

Rocking on his heels, he said "I really do love you."

Then he collapsed face-forward onto the bed and passed out. Kathryn removed as much of his clothing as she could, and rearranged his limbs into the recovery position. She pulled the duvet over him and went downstairs to fill a tumbler of water to leave beside the bed along with a bucket. When she returned in her pyjamas, he was snoring soundly.

She lay beside him and thought about how confused she felt, torn between her growing love and desire for him, and terror at the thought of what this meant. Could she consider a physical relationship with him? She'd never thought it possible before, with either a man or a woman, and she'd always assumed she'd spend her life without a partner.

In vino veritas – in wine, there is truth, she thought. Pondering on her feelings for him, she wondered just how much truth there was in that phrase.

~

Jamie

Jamie awoke with the headache from hell feeling like he'd been drinking battery acid. Sitting up, he winced in the daylight and peered at the clock. It was almost eleven and there was no sign of Kathryn, but she'd left a glass of water and a box of paracetamol on the nightstand. His mouth felt like it was full of cotton wool. He swallowed two tablets and groaned as he recalled the previous evening. Although vague, he remembered all too clearly declaring his love for her. Hearing her downstairs, his gut roiled and he was tempted to feign sleep until he felt ready to face her.

She appeared a few minutes later with a mug of coffee and an amused expression. "How you feeling?"

"Like I've been hit by a truck."

She perched beside him and grinned. "How much do you remember?"

Casting her a contrite look, he said. "Err … enough."

She laughed. "Can you manage some breakfast? A full Scottish fry-up's the best cure for a hangover."

"Sounds magic."

After sipping his coffee, Jamie headed for the shower. When he re-emerged, the smoke alarm was sounding and Meg was barking. He dressed hastily and made his way into the fug-filled kitchen where Kathryn was wafting a dishtowel at the Aga.

"Is the smoke alarm broken?" he asked, examining the bits of the device which lay on the worktop.

"It is now."

Chuckling, he helped her rescue the remains of breakfast and they sat at the table and tucked in.

"Sorry, it's a bit burnt," she said poking a black sausage with her fork.

Through a mouthful he said, "Still delicious and just what I needed."

He felt much better after eating, despite the charcoal content. After washing up and making more coffee, he suggested a walk. They wrapped up warm, attached Meg's lead and headed towards the loch. It was a cold, crisp day and they squinted in the glare of the low winter sun. His head had stopped pounding and he was determined to clear the air between them.

"Uhm, about last night…"

"It's fine Jamie, we were both pretty drunk."

He swallowed hard and stared at her. "I meant what I said." He let his words settle between them. She opened her mouth to speak but no words came out and she closed it again. Raking a hand through his hair, he said, "At least say something Kathryn." When she didn't, he lowered his head and sighed. "Ah, clearly you don't feel the same."

He turned away and she tugged him back. "Jamie…" she choked, her eyes glassy.

"It's fine, forget I said anything."

"It's not that." There was a long pause in which her eyes filled with tears. "I feel the same … but I don't know if I'll ever be able to … uhm … give you what you want."

"Oh baby." He reached for her and enfolded her in his arms. "Just hearing you say that is enough."

She pulled away. "No, it's not enough. It'll never be enough. I'm broken Jamie, damaged. I'll never be able to let a man touch me…"

Crying, she pulled from his grip and ran off towards the cottage, with Meg trotting beside her. Watching her go, he shoved his hands into his pockets and cursed.

Then he went after her.

∽

Kathryn

She threw herself on the bed, curled into a ball and sobbed into the pillow. She knew it was hopeless, they could never be a proper couple no matter how they felt about each other. Knowing this was going to be torture for both of them; it had been easier when they'd been living in denial. She needed to nip this in the bud and quickly, before they both got hurt.

She heard him return and his footsteps on the stairs. He circled the bed and sat beside her. She twisted away.

He whispered, "We are so not done talking about this."

Grabbing a handful of tissues from the box on the nightstand, she wailed, "Yes we are. Now please leave me alone."

Sighing, Jamie rubbed the back of his neck then disappeared

downstairs. Hugging her knees to her chest, she wept long and hard for what could have been, were it not for what had happened to her. Despair threatened to overwhelm her as she realised just how desperately lonely she was and she cried out as great sobs wracked her frame.

After an hour, she sat up and wiped her face, knowing she and Jamie would have to accept the way she was and the fact she could never have a partner. The sooner they completed this assignment and returned home, the easier it would be for both of them. She switched on the radio and pulled her laptop out from beneath the bed.

Since getting access to Duncan's laptop, she'd spent many hours sifting through the information stored on it. He appeared to use the machine only for work and she'd yet to find anything of a personal nature on it. However, buried deep within a folder called Plumbers, she spotted a JPEG file named Harris which she opened. It showed a class photograph entitled *Harris High School 2011*. Fourteen pupils wearing matching navy blazers were assembled in two rows, the girls sitting in the front, their hands clasped in their laps, and the boys standing behind them. She recognised Angus and Simon instantly. Beneath the title was a list of printed names and she spotted Mhairi MacLean's, the girl who'd disappeared. She was pretty with a lovely smile and long blonde tresses that spilled over her shoulders. Angus stood directly behind her.

Also within the Plumbers folder, she discovered an invoice from a company called *EagleTek Surveillance*. She checked the company's web site which was full of covert spy cameras and equipment. It wasn't clear who had placed the order, or what the item described as a 'home security device' was, but it was priced around the high-end camera range. The order date caught her attention, which was shortly before she and Jamie arrived in Knoydart. Was this the spy camera Jamie had found in the office? If it was, it could have been installed before Jean attempted to get the evidence from the office.

She left the file open, and navigated to her dormant mail account which she'd been checking regularly. Appended to her draft was another message from *[IntoDarkness]*

Thanks for reaching out friend. I'm safe and well despite the unplanned sabbatical. I'd prepared for that day, just didn't think I'd see it, and not as the result of that worthless, back-stabbing, attention-whore Anesidora. Still, it's been a good excuse to travel and see the world and I've found a little slice of heaven in the most unlikely place. Given the hell hounds on my tail, I think I'll be here for some time.

Anyway, I wondered if/when you'd be in touch. I knew you hadn't sold me out - you and I go back a long way. I've been watching developments unfold and I'm still LMAO at the deal you cut. Really? And with the Denebian slime devil himself? You've definitely got it harder 'baby', so if you need anything from me, I'm here for you. Just be careful you don't become a red shirt. And as for that retarded, treacherous spunk-bucket Anesidora, an opportunity will present itself. As the old Klingon proverb goes, "Revenge is a dish best served cold."

Live long and prosper x

Kathryn stared at the message and read it again, twice. How did Scotty know about her deal, and with Jamie? And his use of 'baby' suggested he knew quite a lot about their relationship. But how? Not that she was surprised at his skills; he was the only hacker she knew who could rival her and there was no limit to what he could do ... but did that extend to intercepting MI5 communications?

She chuckled at his Star Trek references, picturing Jamie as a 'Denebian slime devil'. She'd no intention of dying a violent death like a red shirt if she could possibly help it, and she shuddered to think what cold dish he intended to serve to Pandora.

Thank God in heaven Scotty was on her side.

Jamie

Jamie sat downstairs with his head in his hands ruminating over their earlier argument and what he intended to say to her once she'd calmed down. There was no point in going to bed yet since he wouldn't sleep with all this running through his mind. In too deep, he was not about to give up now that he knew she felt the same way about him. His mind was made up; he wanted her. He wanted her so badly he couldn't think, couldn't focus. This challenge, however, was off the scale but he was determined to face each and every obstacle she threw at him, knowing she was worth it.

He knew he'd have to tread lightly since he'd be her first lover and the responsibility weighed upon him. Yet, he admitted, the idea of her being virgin-like appealed more than it really ought to. She was unlike any woman he'd ever met – so pure, so innocent – and he wanted to protect her as well as love her.

Thinking back to his failed relationship with Emma, he was hellbent on not repeating the same mistakes. Before this opportunity with MI5, he'd always thought he'd a clear sense of who he was and what he wanted, but thanks to a beautiful cybercriminal and an enchanted Scottish glen, he was a lot less sure. He'd been too ambitious, had worked too many hours, and drank way too much, and he resolved not to make the same errors with Kathryn.

Tomorrow things would change.

Kathryn

When she awoke early next morning, Jamie was already up and about and her stomach knotted at the memory of their argument, if that's what it had been. Knowing she couldn't avoid him forever, she showered and dressed and made her way downstairs.

Avoiding his eye, she slumped at the kitchen table. He'd made breakfast and he handed her a plate of scrambled eggs and toast. She mumbled thanks and poked at the food with her fork. With mugs of tea, he pulled up a seat opposite her and fixed her with his gaze. He hadn't shaved and his eyes were ringed with sleep bruises.

Leaning towards her, he said in a low voice, "We need to talk."

She pushed her plate away. "There's no point."

He pushed the plate back at her. "Please Kathryn."

She huffed out her agreement and nibbled on a slice of toast as he observed her. When she'd finished eating, she took the plate to the sink and began to wash up. He followed her, turned off the taps and steered her towards the door.

"No, we're going to sort this out. Right now."

His expression left her in no doubt as he grabbed his coat and car keys. Meg followed them into the Land Rover and he drove out of the valley. Although dry, it was grey and overcast and the mist seemed to swirl around the car. Gripping Meg for support, her heart thumped in her chest at the thought of the painful conversation they were about to have and the likely consequence of it. How could they go on living together after she rejected him?

"Where are we going?" she asked, burrowing into Meg's fur.

"Away from here."

After a couple of miles, he swung the Defender into a layby and cut the engine. He jumped out, opened the passenger door and, without speaking, led her along a trail up to a covered ledge. As Meg darted about, he turned to face her and blew out a long breath.

"I don't know what this thing is between us but neither of us can go on simply pretending it's not there. Kathryn, all I want is for us to try."

Tears pricked her eyes. "Jamie … you can't even take off your belt without me having a meltdown. How can I ever …?"

"Because you're one of the bravest people I know, and if anyone can do this, it's you. Think about the progress you've made. Christ, we're even sharing a bed … and it's killing me."

She sob-laughed and looked up at him. "Is it?"

He grinned. "Aye, tis the sweetest form of torture known to man, but I've not had a single night terror since." His expression turned serious. "But if you're willing to give it a try, I'll wait as long as it takes." He cupped her chin, "You're worth waiting for."

"And what if I can't?"

"You don't know that until you try. And if it comes to it, we'll seek professional help when all this is over." He waved his hand in the direction of the valley.

"Jamie, I've been in therapy for years."

"Talking about it's one thing, but you've never tried with a partner … with someone who cares about you. I thought maybe if we took baby steps..." He looked at her beseechingly. "Surely worth a try?"

Gazing up at him, she whispered, "I'll try but I can't promise–"

He smothered the rest of her words with a kiss. As the kiss began to spiral into something hungrier, she pulled away.

"If we're going to do this, there are things I need to tell you. Things that happened to me … so you know what you're taking on."

"Nothing you tell me will change how I feel."

She let out a loud sigh. "You'd better sit down. This'll take a while."

Sitting side by side on a rocky outcrop overlooking the foggy valley, Kathryn told him how her stepfather had sexually abused her from the age of nine. Later, aged thirteen, when walking in the woods near her home, he'd brutally raped her while her mother was passed out drunk following a beating. He'd threatened to kill her and her mother if she told anyone. As she described the drinking, domestic violence and abuse, she felt her dark pit of memories yawn, and she yearned to shut them away again.

She told him how, a few months later, Phil had flown into a drunken rage and strangled her mother with his belt, and she described how she'd returned home from school to discover her mother's body. He'd disappeared. The police later caught him and he was serving a life sentence for murder.

Jamie wept with her as she clung to him, and Meg sat at Kathryn's feet, whining.

She explained that, after she'd gone to live with her maternal grandmother, the horror of what she'd endured had never left her. It manifested as a fear of physical contact which made it difficult to make friends and impossible to have a relationship. Her class mates thought she was weird, and she'd bombed out of school with no qualifications. Her GP had referred her to a counsellor but she didn't like him and had failed to respond to treatment. She'd taken up karate at her gran's insistence and, although it had helped boost her confidence, she'd never been able to get close to anyone. When her social worker gave her a laptop for home school, she'd finally found refuge in cyberspace and had hidden in that world ever since. Until Jamie arrested her.

Gazing up at him through wet lashes, she said, "Now you know everything, I'll understand if you change your mind."

Wrapping her in his arms, he nuzzled into her hair. "I'll never change my mind. I know how I feel, and I've never felt like this about anyone." He pulled back and fixed her with his gaze. "I wish I could change the past, but I can't. I want to take care of you Kathryn, and together I believe we can change the future."

Wiping away her tears with his thumbs, he pressed a tender kiss to her lips and she wilted in his arms. When Meg barked at them, they broke apart with a watery smile.

"Think that's our cue to leave," he said. "C'mon baby, let's go home to that future."

He led her back to the car and on the drive home, he kept hold of her hand, only letting go to change gear before clasping it again.

She asked, "When you say baby steps..."

"We'll take it real slow and you'll set the pace." When she said nothing, he added, "And if all you want to do is kiss, then that's okay too."

"Like that would satisfy either of us."

He chuckled. "Just wait til I kiss you properly."

She felt an instant twinge in her core at the prospect, and she pressed her legs together but the vibration of the car didn't help.

"I've been thinking," he said, "about Pia's approach. It was all about repeating the physical stimulus to desensitise and dampen the reaction. I thought we could try that."

"We certainly can't ask her. Jamie, what if they find out? You could lose your job and who knows what'll happen to me?"

"It's none of their business and we'll make damn sure they don't. And how we behave in public is just part of our cover."

"And after?"

Tearing his eyes from the road to glance at her, he said, "Let's worry about that later. We're likely to be here awhile."

He parked the Land Rover in front of their cottage and turned to her. Cupping her chin, he pressed a long lingering kiss to her lips and murmured, "Baby steps okay?"

She nodded. "Baby steps."

As he made to get out, she stopped him, "I forgot to tell you, I discovered what Saint Januarius is. It's the red wine they were serving at Hogmanay."

He gave her a quizzical look. "Wine? Why would Jean write the name of a wine on Meg's tag?"

"I've no idea."

She also told him about the class photograph she'd discovered on Duncan's laptop of Angus, Simon and Mhairi MacLean, and the invoice for what she believed was a spy camera.

Jamie blew out a breath. "If the office was bugged, someone might have been watching when Jean went to fetch the evidence. Considering this, it's doubtful her death was an accident. And it's interesting both Simon and Angus were in the same class as the girl who disappeared."

She nodded. "I'll do more searching later."

"Don't take too long. Tonight, you and I have other business to attend to."

She felt unfamiliar parts of her quiver in anticipation.

ACTS

Kathryn

That evening, while they cooked and ate together, Kathryn struggled to focus knowing what they'd planned for later. The space between them suddenly felt charged so when he suggested they went to bed, she became flustered. Announcing she was going to bathe first, she locked herself in the bathroom and tried to calm her heart rate. Trembling, she emerged half an hour later wearing the silk nightdress and gown.

Jamie lay stretched out on the bed, stripped to his boxers, his fingers laced behind his head. The room was dimly lit and soft music played through the radio. He gasped when he saw her and his heavy-lidded gaze was hungry. She pulled the robe tighter around her shoulders as she approached the bed. Stretching over, he used the robe's soft belt to guide her towards him until they lay facing one another.

"You really have no idea how beautiful you are."

She felt shy beneath his gaze.

He stroked the side of her face. "I'm only going to kiss you." His hand felt like a brand and sent a bolt of lightning straight to her core. Smiling, he said, "If it gets too much, I want you to tap out."

She giggled, "Sounds like you're going to attack me."

"I'm going to make love to you," he murmured.

Her heart rate rocketed as he pressed his mouth to hers. His lips were soft but there was a hint of stubble on his face. With soft sensual kisses and light brushing actions, he coaxed her lips apart and she felt the tip of his tongue touch hers. She opened to him and let him explore her mouth, mimicking his actions. Her head swam with the sensations bombarding her as his tongue curled, twisted and probed. Breathless, she skated her nails over his jaw and through his hair. He deepened the kiss and she was swept up in a whirlwind of desire and she moaned. He pulled her firmly against his solid, sinewy body, and she felt him hard against her hip. Gasping, she flinched and stopped and, sensing her reaction, he pulled away.

"You alright?" he rasped, looking at her with concern.

Biting her lip, she nodded.

He stroked her face and whispered, "Want to stop, baby?"

Grasping at him, she panted, "No."

Their mouths collided.

Jamie

He couldnae believe it when she pulled him in for another kiss. Winding his fingers through her hair, he tilted back her head and swooped in with his tongue. He slanted his lips over hers, giving her it all, and conveyed with his kiss what he'd been too afraid to say for weeks. As he increased the intensity of their connection, she whimpered and combed her fingers through his hair.

I can control this. I can control this.

As the tip of her tongue touched his, the kiss exploded into something carnal and they clawed at one another.

I. Can. Control. This.

"Kathryn" he gasped as he battled the urge to grind against her.

He pulled away panting and they stared at one another for several minutes as they caught their breath.

Exhaling softly, he whispered, "Baby steps."

He wrapped her in his arms and pulled her to him. He loved the soft feel of her skin, and the smell of her vanilla shampoo mixed with her natural scent. Inhaling deeply, he nuzzled into her hair knowing he'd never grow tired of this, even if it was causing him delicious agony in his nether regions. Lying entwined, they kissed and whispered in the dark until she fell asleep.

Sleep evaded Jamie for hours, partly due to his painful arousal but mainly because of their earlier conversation. Although Pia had hinted at it, he'd had no idea of the extent of Kathryn's suffering. Every instinct he now felt was to protect her, coupled with a desire to kill her stepfather. He was surprised she'd turned out as normal, and that she'd agreed to attempt a relationship with him; she really was the bravest person he knew. It was incredible that she trusted anyone, never mind a man, and he felt privileged. No way would he let her down. He knew there'd be challenges ahead but she was courageous and they'd already made gains, so he'd every faith that with time and patience, they'd succeed.

Pulling her sleeping frame closer to him, he kissed her temple and succumbed to sleep.

Kathryn

Next morning, she examined her face in the bathroom mirror. Her lips were deliciously pink and swollen and she smiled at the memory of how feverishly he'd kissed her. He hadn't been joking either; until last night he really hadn't kissed her properly and she'd been surprised at how much she enjoyed it. She'd never had this degree of physical contact before, not consensual anyway, and she was astonished at how much she could bear.

It was thrilling and she was amazed at the intensity of her own body's reaction, craving his touch even when her head hadn't yet caught up. She found his obvious physical response to her at once terrifying and flattering, and she wondered how it would feel to touch him. There.

She yearned to do it all again tonight. Looking at her reflection, she didn't recognise the person staring back.

Who are you and what have you done with Kathryn?

Today, she'd have to focus her attentions on work and the real task in hand.

Until tonight.

As Kathryn walked towards the back of Hourn House, movement inside the door of the church caught her eye and she spotted Simon and Bethany deep in conversation. Bethany was upset, her face streaked with tears, and a worried-looking Simon appeared to be pleading with her. Kathryn froze in her tracks as she observed him reach for Bethany's arm only for her to shrug him off and flee.

Head down, Kathryn hurried towards the big house, only looking up as Bethany ran past her sobbing. Kathryn darted a glance at the church where Simon met her eye, then tore his gaze away, but not quickly enough to hide his expression of guilt.

As Kathryn approached the rear entrance of Hourn House, she wondered what Bethany and Simon had been discussing that had upset her. She brushed the thought aside as she entered the small administration office on the ground floor, where she was greeted by Ruth.

Ruth expressed how delighted she was to have Kathryn's help since they were expecting a busy year with holiday bookings. After Ruth had her settled in front of a PC with a coffee, she gave her a tour of the web site, the phones and the booking system. Kathryn took notes and they worked through a couple of reservation requests together before Ruth announced she was happy for her to continue with the rest on her own. Ruth said she'd pop back in an hour but to call her if she needed help and she handed her a typed sheet with employee phone numbers.

"Marcus hates mobile phones," she said, "but you simply can't run a business without one these days."

After she left, Kathryn ploughed through the backlog of booking requests. As she worked, she examined the office for signs of hidden cameras and bugs but couldn't see anything. Jamie had said he'd pop by and give the place a sweep. As she completed work on the last booking, there was tap at the door and she looked up to find him smiling at her.

Flashing her a mischievous grin, he said, "All on your own?"

He kicked the door shut with his foot, swept her into his arms and stamped his mouth to hers. She threw her arms around his neck and returned his ravenous kiss, all the more delicious for their illicit surroundings. Her heart hammered in her chest as he pressed her against the desk and deepened their connection.

Gasping, she pushed him away and panted, "You'll get me fired on my first day Mr Campbell."

Jamie chuckled, "It's because you're such a temptress Mrs Campbell."

Smiling, she shook her head at him. Her pulse was still racing after that kiss and the promise of more later.

"How's your morning been?" he asked.

She explained what she'd been doing and he scanned the office furtively under the guise of showing interest. When he'd finished examining all the nooks and crannies, he led her to the door and whispered in her ear. "Looks fine, can't see anything."

She grinned. "I'll get to work then."

Pressing her against the back of the door, he kissed her until their breathing became ragged. She could feel the strength in his arms as he pulled her against him, and her response made her head swim. There was a tap on the door and they sprung apart sniggering. Ruth entered and gave them a curious smile.

Flashing a cheeky smile, Jamie said, "Just checking how my wife's getting on."

After he'd gone, Ruth turned to Kathryn, "Oh lordy, I don't think I've ever seen a man so in love with his wife."

A blush spread to Kathryn's neck. She hoped Ruth was right.

That evening, after dinner, they walked hand in hand to the loch with Meg and chatted about their day. Kathryn told him about the scene she'd witnessed between Simon and Bethany, and Jamie said that he'd had Buchanan yelling down the phone at him because Finlay had still not contacted him about giving a statement and Marcus had done little to help.

She said, "You and Keith said there was something fishy about Finlay."

"Aye, well he's on my radar now."

She explained she'd been able to ferret around the society's internal network, but it was so secure, it was suspicious.

"Won't you be able to hack in?"

She arched an eyebrow and, in a voice laced with sarcasm, said, "Puh-lease, have faith."

Jamie chuckled and touched his nose to hers. "Why did I ever doubt you?" He placed a kiss on her lips and she responded. The kiss escalated.

Giggling, she said, "Do you want to know what I found or not? I'm sure this is dereliction of duty."

Pulling her back, he murmured, "Hmm, in a minute…" He nibbled along her jaw line to the sensitive spot behind her ear before returning to her mouth. Winding a hand around her hair, he angled her head and plundered her mouth with his tongue. She let out a low moan of desire and raked her hands through his hair.

Meg bounded at Jamie's leg and began to tug on the bottom of his jeans, and they sprang apart laughing.

"Jesus Meg" he said, as he tried to shoo her away.

Front paws braced, Meg swapped her grip to his other trouser leg, and Jamie hopped about. Kathryn squealed with laughter as she watched the snarling dog pull at him.

"Get off Meg or I swear I'll let Angus shoot you."

Doubled over, holding her sides, she roared with laughter as Meg held on for grim death.

"Don't help or anything…" shrieked Jamie as Meg strained against the fabric with her teeth.

Bracing her hands on her thighs and with tears streaming down her face, she squealed, "Oh God, that's the funniest thing I've ever seen."

Jamie finally wrestled the dog off and clipped her lead on. Cursing, he dragged her over to a fence post and looped the handle of the lead around it.

"Right, where were we?" he grumbled, grabbing Kathryn and kissing her again as the dog strained to get to him.

When he finally broke away, he cast Meg a sly look and growled, "Better get used to it dug, we're going to be doing a lot of this." Chuckling, he looped one arm around her waist and grabbed the dog with the other as they walked along the shoreline. "Now you can tell me what you found."

Buried within the accounting files, she explained, were a series of invoices for a company called DDE Ltd. for work carried out on the cellar. This was on top of work done by another firm who'd installed the wine racks.

"DDE stands for data and digital environments. They fit out server rooms and the Ehrlich Society has spent thousands. As well as biometric security, it's equipped with an automatic cooling and fire suppression system."

Jamie whistled. "So, we've found the servers."

"It's state of the art, which begs the question 'what the hell are they using it for?'"

He gazed down at her. "Guess we won't know until we get inside. How are we going to do that? The door's steel, no way I can jemmy it open and there's no lock to pick."

"The keypad grants access based on a pin number or fingerprint."

"Have I got to lift Marcus's fingerprints off of a surface?"

She laughed "You've been watching too many *Mission Impossible* movies Mr Campbell. The key to hacking is to target the weakest point.

Usually that's people but I don't think that's going to work, they're pretty clued-up on security."

"So, what's the next weakest point?"

"I'll try obvious stuff like plugging dates of birth into the keypad but I doubt they're stupid enough to have used them. And I'll drop a rogue USB."

"A what?"

"It's a common trick. If someone finds a USB stick lying around, the first thing they do is plug it in to see what's on it, and if they do, I'll be able to inject malware into the machine to gather the information I need."

"And if that fails?"

"Then I'll need to crack the keypad."

Jamie grinned. "Go on, I love listening to your filthy tech talk."

She rewarded him with a full-blown smile. "Filthy tech talk. Really?"

Eyes sparkling, he said in a low voice, "Mmm, you're very sexy when you're in Moniker mode."

"Just how filthy do you want me to get?"

"Really disgusting."

She trailed a fingernail down his cheek. "Well in that case, inside that keypad is a Trusted Execution Environment which is like a vault for storing and processing security sensitive apps and data."

He dipped his head and nibbled her ear.

She continued, "Although it's really secure, nothing's ever a hundred percent and it's vulnerable to memory corruption and program logic-related weaknesses."

"Keep talking" he rasped, "the dirtier the better."

She giggled, "I need to look at the software exploitation countermeasures."

He gave a low moan and kissed her neck. "Such as?"

"Address space layout randomization, stack canaries, control-flow integrity, non-executable stack and heap, stack buffers—"

"Oh God, I'm going to come," he mumbled before smothering her filthy tech talk with his mouth.

~

Jamie

After arriving at work early, Jamie made his way over to the old stable block and hammered on Finlay's door. After a few minutes, he heard shuffling and then the sound of a key in the lock. Cameron peered through the gap, yawning.

"Alright boss. What time is it?"

"Early. Where's Finlay?"

"Uhm, dunno, come in."

Cameron opened the door and indicated a room on the left saying it was Finlay's, before he disappeared into the one opposite. Jamie knocked on the door. Silence. He thumped again and entered. Finlay sprang upright in the bed and gawped at him. The room stank of dirty socks and was a mess with clothes and empty beer cans strewn over the floor and furniture. Pictures of nude women adorned the walls, and there was stack of porn mags next to the bed.

Jamie fixed Finlay with a hard glare. "My office at ten. Buchanan will be here to take your statement. Don't be late."

Jamie turned and left, leaving a sleepy Finlay rubbing his eyes. After returning to the estate office, he made coffee and switched on his PC. He slung his jacket over the bookcase to obscure the hidden camera and searched through the personnel records for information about Finlay McClay. Although, he'd looked before, nothing had jumped out at him as odd. Ruth had created the file, presumably after he was hired. Finlay had been employed on the estate for almost a year, he'd supplied a reference from a previous employer, and no warnings or notes had been added to his file. Jamie took photographs of the information with his phone, then moved his jacket to the back of his chair.

At almost ten o'clock, there was still no sign of Finlay and he went outside to look. Spotting the approach of Buchanan's Volvo, he greeted the sergeant, led him to the office and offered him coffee while they awaited Finlay.

Jamie asked, "Has the post-mortem been done yet?"

"Aye, but I'm afraid I'm not at liberty to tell you anything." Buchanan paused then looked at Jamie, "Don't suppose you know anything about this missing girl?"

"What missing girl?"

"Bethany MacLeod. I got a call last night from her parents to say she hadn't come home."

Jamie shook his head, "First I've heard of it."

"When did you last see her?"

"At the Hogmanay party."

"And where were you last night?"

What the fuck? Jamie tried to remain calm and replied, "Home with my wife, same as every night."

Buchanan sighed, "She's probably returned to university early but we need to check." He looked at his watch, "Now where's Finlay?"

Jamie offered to fetch him and suggested Buchanan remained in the office in case he showed. Grabbing the spare keys to the stable block, Jamie marched to Finlay's room. There was no answer and he let himself in, only to find it had been cleared. His clothes were gone along with the pictures and magazines, leaving only bedding, empty beer cans and a lingering smell. Jamie swore, then began to search the room.

After rifling through the nightstand, wardrobe and chest of drawers, all of which were empty, he pulled back the duvet to reveal soiled sheets. Finding nothing under the mattress or bed, he pulled out the nightstand. A bank card had fallen behind it and rested against the skirting board. The name on the card was Jack Irvine. After pocketing it and taking a look round the rest of the apartment, he made his way back to the office to break the news of Finlay's disappearance to Buchanan.

Jamie didn't mention the bank card.

That evening, Kathryn cooked one of the recipes she'd learned at the Christian Wives meetings, chicken and broccoli baked in a rich cream sauce, served with brown rice. They grinned at one another as they ate with teaspoons since Jamie had hidden all the cutlery as a practical joke, and she refused to acknowledge its absence or ask where he'd put it. After polishing off his plate, he raised his teaspoon and asked for seconds.

When Meg looked disappointed at the absence of leftovers, he laughed, "Sorry Meg, that was too delicious to share."

Kathryn smiled and placated Meg with a dog chew. When they'd walked her earlier, Jamie had told her about Finlay's disappearance and he'd given her the bank card. She left him to wash up while she stretched out on the bed with her laptop and searched for information about Jack Irvine.

An hour later, Jamie appeared carrying mugs of tea which he placed on the nightstand, and he stretched out next to her. The curtains were shut and the radio played a music channel.

He leaned over and kissed her cheek. "Any joy?"

Angling her screen towards him, she said, "Take a look."

After seeing what was on-screen, he stared at her. "You hacked into the Police National Computer?"

"Yes, but only to look at Finlay's file."

He chuckled, "Bloody hell Kathryn, you're so brilliant you're actually scary."

She pointed to his record which listed two convictions for indecent assault and one for rape.

Jamie growled, "Christ, he's a bloody rapist. What the fuck's he doing here?"

"Hiding from the police by the looks of things." She flicked to another screen which showed Jack Irvine was wanted for questioning in connection with an attack on a woman in Kent. "What are you going to do?" she asked.

"We cannae tell Buchanan without alerting him to the fact we're UCs, but I'll call Keith to make sure he's picked up. Buchanan can go after him as Finlay. Unless he caught the boat earlier, he's probably halfway to Mallaig by now. Wee bastard." Jamie exhaled loudly. "I hope he's got nothing to do with Bethany's disappearance. That's two missing girls."

"Is that what this is about, what Jean wanted to tell us? But how's this connected to the scientist and the tax fraud?"

He shook his head. "It doesn't add up. Anyway, well done Mrs Campbell, even if you've just broken a dozen laws." He kissed her again.

Giggling she said, "I've something else."

She tapped the keyboard and a bank statement appeared. She said, "It's Finlay's account and, as well as his salary from working here, he's been getting another grand on top for the past few months from this account." She highlighted an entry.

"Any idea who it's from?"

"Angus Colquhoun."

"Angus? Why the hell would Angus pay him extra on his salary? If it was cash, I could understand but you can't hide this from the tax man."

She navigated to a web site featuring a gallery of photographs from a climate change convention that had taken place in London shortly before the pandemic. Front and centre in one shot stood Ruth surrounded by a group of delegates. Kathryn zoomed in to reveal the faces of those stood at the back. Finlay was amongst them.

Jamie emitted a low whistle. "So, Ruth knew Finlay from before."

"That's not all," she said, tapping again.

When Jean's post-mortem report appeared, he shook his head indulgently saying, "I'm not even going to ask…" He read the conclusion which stated that the cause of death was heart failure resulting from hypothermia. "Hmm, so nothing to prove she was murdered."

"No, but it reveals she was suffering from pancreatitis and was receiving treatment through a GP in Mallaig, the same practice we saw Bethany visiting."

"Why would Jean schlep all the way to Mallaig when Vondell's got a clinic here?"

"I don't know but I'm going to have a sniff around Vondell next."

Grinning, Jamie took the laptop and placed it beside the bed. "Later, I've a much better way of passing the time."

Pulling her towards him, he kissed her with passion.

~

Kathryn

Dr Vondell held a clinic three times a week in a room at the back of the community hall. It was mid-afternoon and Kathryn took a seat in the small waiting area which was empty except for a woman with a young child. She asked the woman whether she needed to make an appointment to see the doctor. No, she was told, it was just a case of waiting to be seen.

The woman threw her a questioning look and asked, "Have you been to see Dr Vondell before?"

She said she hadn't and was new to the community. With a half-smile, the woman nodded.

Kathryn had already spent time digging for information on Vondell without much success. He'd had a long career in the army and then as a GP, but he'd never stayed long in any one practice. She'd searched the General Medical Council's records but no official complaints had been lodged against him and he was still on the register as a practising physician.

As part of her identity, Fitz had created fake medical records in her name and she'd emailed Vondell a copy of them, supposedly from her previous GP practice. Her fake email contained a link to insert a trojan onto Vondell's machine that would capture data. However, to her frustration, he hadn't clicked on it despite taking pains to ensure any anti-virus software wouldn't detect and quarantine her payload, which was the reason she was sat here. The woman and child were seen quickly so Kathryn didn't have long to wait until Dr Vondell emerged from his room and called for his next patient.

At the sight of her, Vondell's face lit up and he offered her a limp handshake. "How lovely to see you again my dear."

She followed him into a room furnished with a desk, two chairs and a plinth behind a curtain. As he closed the door, his eyes swept over her. Sitting next to her, he peered at her over the top of his half-moon glasses. "So, what can I do for you today?"

Kathryn explained she needed a repeat prescription for the

combined contraceptive pill that Fitz had included in her records. She asked if he'd received the email from her previous GP and he said he hadn't checked.

"They assured me that they'd sent it," she said, "would you mind checking so I can chase them up?"

He browsed his laptop. "Ah yes, here it is. Excellent, that makes things much easier."

She smiled as he clicked on the attachment. *Got you.*

Vondell asked her to fill out a new patient registration form and as she completed it, she noticed him scrutinizing her, and she glanced up to find him leering at her chest. Flicking his eyes away, he asked if she'd had any pregnancies or miscarriages and she replied that she hadn't.

Brushing his eyes over her again, he asked, "And do you and your husband enjoy regular sexual intercourse?"

She nodded, feeling herself flush crimson.

"And how many times a week would you say you have congress?"

Certain her face was now volcanic red, she looked at her feet and replied, "as often as my husband wishes."

"Any problems in that department?"

"Uhm no."

She passed him the completed form and curled her shoulders in around her.

Staring at her, he said, "I like to give my new patients a full medical examination when they join, it's one of the benefits of being a small practice. We might as well do it now while you're here. Just pop behind the screen and remove your clothes down to your underwear."

Her mouth fell open. "Err, when you say full medical, what do you mean?"

Leaning towards her, he patted her hand. "It's nothing to be afraid of my dear, I'm just going to give you a thorough check up. It's for your own good."

She swallowed. "Uhm, what exactly?"

Indulging her with a smile, he said, "The usual stuff." He counted on his fingers as he said, "Height, weight, blood pressure, breathing, eyes, ears, nose and throat."

A drip of sweat prickled down her spine as she watched him get up and put on a pair of latex gloves. The thought of him touching her made her feel faint.

"Err … is that all?"

Picking up a stainless-steel speculum from a tray, he licked his top lip as he spread its ends apart. She struggled to breathe knowing where he intended to insert it. He turned to her. "For my female patients, I also like to do a breast examination and full internal."

Kathryn leapt up on shaky legs, the chair screeching across the vinyl, and gasped out, "Sorry, I have to go."

She hurried from the room.

Once clear of the community hall, she darted into the shop and closed the door, the bell jangling above her head. Heart still pounding in her chest, she trembled as she fought to get her breathing under control. When she turned, she met Hazel's gaze as she emerged from behind the counter.

"Kathryn, are you okay? You look like you've seen a ghost."

She nodded. "Fine."

"You don't look fine, what's happened?" Hazel took her arm and guided her to the chair behind the counter. "Come sit down before you fall down. Do you need a doctor?"

Kathryn wailed, "No, I've just come from there."

Hazel gave her a knowing look. "Ah, I take it you've met the good doctor Vondell or, as we like to call him, Dr Fondle?"

She nodded. "Met him? I've just ran out his surgery."

"Sorry, I should've warned you. Unless it's an emergency, most of the women here go to the GP in Mallaig."

"No wonder, I only went for a prescription and he wanted to—"

"—let me guess, do a breast exam and internal?" Hazel squeezed her arm. "Best go to Mallaig."

"How does he get away with it? I mean, surely the women must talk to their husbands?"

Hazel shrugged. "He's one of Ruth's pets. She introduced him to the community after he got into bother at his previous practice. The rumour was he was carrying out virginity tests on young women at the request of their husbands to be. He's instrumental in Ruth's vaccination and birth control programmes and, being a doctor and church elder, people respect him. At least you'd the good sense to leave."

Kathryn shuddered.

~

Jamie

That evening, they walked Meg and Kathryn told him about her visit to Vondell and what Hazel had said.

Jamie huffed out his annoyance. "Doctors are like teachers, it's almost impossible to get rid of the bad ones. They just get muppet-shuffled round the country. The GMC only got their act together after Shipman. Before him, hardly any were struck off."

"But my visit was not entirely without success. He clicked on my phishing email and I've access to his patients' medical records."

Jamie gave a bark of laughter. "You're unreal. Anything interesting?"

"Very. Duncan's had mental health problems over the years including episodes of hypermania and psychosis. There's a psychiatric report on his file detailing a delusional phase when he was sectioned and prescribed psychotropic drugs. Vondell's prescribed anti-psychotics in the past but he's recently stopped and switched him to psychological therapies. I don't understand all the details, we need to talk to Pia."

"Good work, I'll call Keith and ask Pia to dig."

"That's not all. Bethany went to see Vondell last summer for a repeat prescription of the contraceptive pill. He refused to prescribe it because she wouldn't submit to a medical examination."

Jamie exhaled loudly. "No bloody wonder. So that begs the question 'who's she sleeping with'?" He looked at Kathryn, "Do you think it could be Simon?"

"I really hope not, for Hazel's sake. But Bethany seemed pretty friendly with Angus and Cameron at the ceilidh."

He pulled her in for a kiss. "I don't want you going near Vondell again." Gazing out over the loch, he said, "So, we've a rapist on the loose, a sex-pest doctor, a psychotic lunatic, someone watching our every move, another missing girl and maybe a murderer. Not to mention the millions being syphoned through this community." He shook his head. "This place, these people … what the hell's going on?"

"Time's getting on, I need into that server room."

"I nearly forgot, I've a gift for you Mrs Campbell."

She laughed and arched a brow, "Mmm, where is it?"

His eyes sparkled with mischief. "In my jeans." He chuckled at her expression, a mixture of desire and confusion, then reached into his pocket and pulled out a memory stick. "Marcus left it in his machine. Any good?"

She examined it. "Ooh, a FIPS stick with an AES 256-bit hardware encryption system."

He nuzzled her neck. "Mmm, I love it when you talk dirty. So, can you crack it?"

"Yes but I'll need time. Won't he miss it?"

"Doubt he'll notice til Monday."

"I need Keith to get me more of the same model so we can put this one back, and I can drop a rogue stick in the cellar."

"I'll call him tonight and we'll go see him on Sunday. I need to pick up the cellar key. So, what are you going to do with this stick? I want all the sordid details."

She giggled as he nibbled her earlobe. "This model has a security flaw. After successful authorisation, it always sends the same character string to the drive, irrespective of the password."

He swirled his tongue around the hollow at the base of her throat and groaned, "More filth please, Moniker."

She laughed. "I'll use a tool for the active password entry program's RAM that'll give me access to all the data on the drive."

"God you're sexy." He silenced her with his mouth.

Kathryn

While Jamie was at work, she spent Saturday morning cracking the encryption on the USB stick he'd found in Marcus's machine. It didn't take her long and she searched the information stored on it, most of which related to Hart Biotech's acquisition of a company called Glenavon Bottling.

According to Glenavon's web site, they were one of the largest contract wine bottlers and distributors in the UK, working with some of the world's leading wine companies. She recognized many of the documents as standard due diligence, having come across similar when she worked as a temp. She sifted through files of financial accounts, technology and intellectual property descriptions, contracts and legal documents.

She couldn't understand why Marcus had this information and what it had to do with the Ehrlich Society. And there was something familiar about the name Glenavon but she couldn't put her finger on it. She wondered if it was connected to St Januarius wine but couldn't find evidence of this in the files.

On Sunday morning, Kathryn's heart sunk as she watched Marcus ascend to the pulpit, then cast his eyes over the congregation, appearing to focus on the women who all wore long shapeless skirts and head scarfs. All except Kathryn. When his eyes fell upon her, she swallowed.

"I will read from 1 Corinthians 11." He paused for effect before addressing his words at Kathryn. "The head of every man is Christ, the head of a wife is her husband, and the head of Christ is God. Every man who prays or prophesies with his head covered dishonours his head, but every wife who prays or prophesies with her head uncovered dishonours her head, since it is the same as if her head were shaven. For if a wife will not cover her head, then she should cut her hair short. But since it is disgraceful for a wife to cut off her hair or shave her head, let her cover her head."

Kathryn's cheeks burned with shame, and Jamie gripped her hand as Marcus continued his tirade. With a glower at Kathryn, he quoted, "that is why a wife ought to have a symbol of authority on her head."

After the service when everyone was shaking hands with Marcus on the way out, Kathryn whispered to Jamie, "I feel like I've just had a dressing down from the headmaster."

"Ignore him, wear what you want."

"Easier said than done."

She huffed out her annoyance as they joined the file from the church knowing she'd have to shake Marcus's hand.

When it was her turn, Marcus gripped her hand, "I hope you found today's lesson instructive Mrs Campbell."

In a saccharine voice, she said, "Yes, your sermons never cease to fascinate me Marcus."

Ruth sidled up to Kathryn, took her elbow and smiled. "I do hope we'll see you at Christian Wives this week. Rachael's going to be teaching sewing and I've some pretty material that'd make a lovely head scarf."

Kathryn forced her lips into a smile and thanked her. Once she and Jamie were out of earshot, she cursed.

With an impish grin, he wound his woollen scarf over his head and, affecting the accent of a Southern Belle, said, "Lordy lordy Mrs Campbell, I do declare y'all are a disgrace."

She chased him home, hooting with laughter.

After church, they drove to Inverie and took the ferry crossing to Mallaig. They brought Meg with them and she sat at Kathryn's feet during the crossing.

When Jamie knocked on the door of Keith's office, Kathryn let go of his hand. He glanced at her in surprise and she whispered, "I don't want him suspecting anything."

Frowning, he grabbed her hand and muttered, "It'll look more suspicious if we suddenly don't."

She suppressed a smile at the fact he was so affectionate, always wanting to hold her hand or touch her, but she was concerned Keith would mention it to Julien or Pia. Keith opened the door and greeted them. The scruff on his face had grown into a beard and the back of his hair reached the top of his fisherman's jumper. He could have passed for one of the locals who'd come to sell his catch. Glancing down at their clasped hands, he looked from one to the other and gave Jamie a wry smile.

She huffed, "Keith, we're supposed to be married."

Keith gave a wicked chuckle. "I couldnae care less if you're at it like Duracell bunnies on Viagra, how else are you supposed to pass the time up here in the back arse of nowhere."

Kathryn felt herself flush and Jamie guffawed.

While Keith made coffee, they scanned the long wall opposite the windows where he'd pinned photographs and details of members of the community, based on their information. Keith had added 'missing?' to Bethany's picture and said he was taking a closer look at the backgrounds of everyone connected to her. He also explained they'd a liaison officer making sure Buchanan was doing his job properly.

Keith said, "We're monitoring all communications in and out of Knoydart but there's no trace of her. She doesn't have a mobile phone and she's not used her bank card. Guess we'll have a better idea if she fails to show up for the start of term."

Jamie asked, "Any sign of Finlay yet?"

"Nope, not a peep but as soon as he surfaces, we'll collar him. I spoke to the detective leading the inquiry in Kent and he's definitely their man. Right nasty attack it was too."

Keith handed them each a mug and they took a seat. Frowning, he looked from one to the other and said, "Pia's very concerned because Vondell appears to have stopped prescribing drugs Duncan needs to keep his episodes of psychosis under control. She said he's not cured, he's in remission, but without the meds he may become delusional again."

Kathryn asked, "Even with the other therapies?"

"Yes, the way she explained it is he could be living in some sort of parallel universe."

"Great, so we've an armed nut job," said Jamie.

Keith said, "Fitz has done some digging on the work DDE did on the cellar and sent the specifications." He handed her a large envelope. "Cellar keys and USB sticks are inside too."

After scanning the information, Kathryn said, "Wow, that's some server room."

"Aye. We'll get someone out to install a camera so you can see who's coming and going from the cellar."

Kathryn asked how they were going to do that undetected.

Keith grinned. "Your husband gave us the idea. A local firm do electrical safety testing for the holiday rentals, so Jamie's going to ask them to take a look at the dodgy light in the corridor. One of the electricians will be ours."

"The light isn't dodgy though," she said.

Jamie laughed. "It will be."

Keith's expression flicked to one of concern as he looked at Kathryn. "Julien's asked me to remind you that the clock is ticking."

After leaving Keith, they found a bar in town he'd recommended and asked if they could bring Meg inside. The landlord greeted them warmly and went to fetch a bowl of water for the dog. Furnished simply with an assortment of wooden tables and chairs, it was spotlessly clean and they chose a table in the corner by the window. The lunchtime rush, had there been one, had dispersed and they were the only customers until a large man in a tartan cap sat down at a neighbouring table. Meg sat at their feet as they ate while Jamie fed her morsels, and Kathryn teased him for being a soft touch.

"Meg's got used to you," she said.

"Aye, because I feed her."

"Or maybe females just fall at your feet. I've seen the way they look at you Jamie."

He touched his hand to his scar, "Not for the reason you think."

Reaching over, she gently traced the line of the scar with her fingertips, "It's all part of who you are."

Smiling, he reached for her hand and kissed it. "You've a few admirers of your own Mrs Campbell, Duncan being one of them."

Kathryn grimaced. "Are you jealous Mr Campbell?"

He eyed her. "I don't share."

After a long pause, she asked, "Mind if I ask what happened with you and Emma?"

He blew out a long breath, stared out the window and then back at her. "Not much to tell to be honest. It was fine for a while, then it wasn't. I started working long hours to avoid coming home and when I was home, I was drinking too much. In the end, she left me for my mate Dean. Can't say I blame her, but it caused friction in the office. Emma and I worked on the Murder Investigation Team together so I transferred to the cyber unit."

"Is that why you agreed to take this job?"

"That and Dean getting promoted even though I was the one that collared you." He squeezed her hand and mouthed, "Sorry."

"I'm sorry Jamie, it can't have been easy. And for what it's worth, I like living with you."

He smiled, "And I like being married to you."

Her heart thumped in her chest at his words.

Her week at work dragged, but the nights … the nights more than made up for it.

A routine had been established whereby they'd retire early so they could kiss and caress, and each night Jamie would go a tiny step further. Sometimes, she'd balk and pull away, but usually she was keen to try again and push the boundaries of what she could tolerate before panic set in. When she recognized the signs, she tried to accept the anxiety and not fight it and, together, they were learning the triggers: if he rolled on top of her, if his hand strayed, or he ground against her. Gradually, the baby steps grew longer and the method began to produce results.

With the physical intimacy, an emotional one developed too, and she shared with Jamie things she'd never told another soul. She'd never let anyone get so close, nor placed such trust in another person, and she enjoyed the thrill of this almost as much as the kissing and touching. He continued to surprise her, for beneath the tough demeanour, he was a very different person. At home, he was thoughtful and considerate; in bed, patient and tender, and he never pressured her into doing anything she was uncomfortable with.

Tonight, after feverish tongue kissing, he trailed kisses along her jaw line to the sensitive spot behind her ear. After nibbling the lobe, he carpeted her neck with light kisses then worked his way along her collar bone. He swirled his tongue around the base of her throat before descending. As he unfastened the top button of her pyjamas, he glanced up at her as if seeking permission, before undoing the rest. When her top gaped open, she felt exposed but the heat in his gaze quelled the urge to cover herself.

Gazing at her with awe, he whispered, "You're so beautiful, so perfect."

He slipped a hand to her breast and when she didn't stop him, he followed with his mouth. Suddenly unable to breathe and with her heart pounding, she tapped and he sprung off her. Apologising, he soothed her until her breathing returned to normal.

"Don't be sorry" she panted, "you're being a bloody saint."

Touching his forehead to hers, he chuckled. "Saint Jamie, patron of the sexually frustrated, martyred after his relics exploded."

She joined in with his laughter. "Isn't this torture for you?"

He regarded her. "If this is torture, I'll gladly take it every day of my life to do this with you." Then he arched a mischievous eyebrow and laughed. "But you're doing great baby, I mean we just made it to second base."

That earned him a pillow in the face.

VALLEY OF THE SHADOW OF DEATH

"Even though I walk through the valley of the shadow of death, I fear no evil, for You are with me; Your rod and Your staff, they comfort me."

— *PSALM 23:4*

Kathryn

"Fornication!" shouted Marcus thumping his fist on the lectern.

He cast a wild eye over his flock and settled his gaze on Angus who shifted uncomfortably in his pew.

Leaning into Jamie, Kathryn whispered, "Here we go."

It was Sunday morning and they'd taken up their usual seats in the back corner of the church. Bowing to social pressure, Kathryn wore a long skirt and silk headscarf. When Jamie had raised an eyebrow as she tied it into place, she'd hissed, "Not a word," which made him laugh.

They knew Marcus would be preaching today as he and Simon alternated, and they'd been expecting a lively sermon. Marcus was not about to disappoint, especially since gossip was rife after Bethany had been found in Edinburgh safe and well. And pregnant. Her distraught

196 | HELL'S GLEN

parents had visited her but she had refused to say who the father was or to return to the community.

During the hymn, the Sunday school teachers led the children out into the back room and, now that the school term had begun, the older children had left. Jamie flashed her a sideways grin and took her hand.

Marcus continued, "Beware temptations of the flesh for they will land you in hell!" He ran his beady eyes slowly over the men of the congregation. "And they will wreck your marriage. But fear not, for God has given us four safeguards." He thrust a finger towards the heavens. "Number one – beware of her fleshly beauty. Proverbs tells us 'Lust not after her beauty in thine heart...'" He directed his gaze at Duncan whose ears turned pink. "But her end is bitter as wormwood, sharp as a two-edged sword."

Keeping his eyes front, Jamie interlaced Kathryn's fingers in his.

"Avoid her path" bellowed Marcus "for she is a harlot and subtle of heart. Give in to her temptations and in just a moment of time, you can lose everything of value."

Clasping Kathryn's hand in both of his, Jamie placed it in his lap. Hyperaware of its proximity to his groin, she swallowed as she thought about what they'd been doing together in the bedroom.

Marcus screamed, "Beware her lustful eyes ..." Flecks of spittle sprayed from his mouth. "... for she can take thee with her eyelids."

Glad to be out of the spit-zone, Kathryn huffed out her annoyance. Jamie ran his thumb over her wrist, sending pulses of electricity up her arm. She squeezed his fingers as she unclenched her jaw.

Marcus's voice rose higher, "Beware her flattering tongue for there is poison. Her house is the way to hell, going down to the chambers of death." More spittle.

He pressed a finger into Kathryn's palm and started circling round it. Her breath hitched and he pressed more firmly. As Marcus droned on about the temptations of telephone sex, her body reacted to his touch and she exhaled a long breath. Jamie chuckled quietly as he increased the pace and pressure of his finger.

Gripping the edges of the pulpit, his knuckles white, Marcus peered over manically. "Finally, beware the fatal touch, for it can be deadly." When his eyes landed on her, Kathryn felt herself flush crimson. "In Corinthians, we are reminded that 'it is good for a man not to touch a woman.'" His eyes bored into Duncan's. "For what starts with a touch may end with a tomb."

As he looked away, Jamie raised her hand to his mouth and, with an impish grin, brushed his lips over her knuckles.

Marcus reached a crescendo. "As a woman is bound by the bonds of chastity not to desire any other man, so let the husband be bound by the same law, since God has joined together the husband and the wife in the union of one body."

Jamie's eyes locked with Kathryn's and, in that moment, she knew she was forever and irrevocably bound to Jamie. He was her one.

Before Marcus descended from the pulpit, he said, "Before we sing our last hymn, I have an announcement about this year's Spiritual Seminar."

Kathryn knew about the seminar; recently it was all anyone in the community had talked about. Every year, the Ehrlich Society played host to a group of similar-minded church leaders from across the globe for a week of spiritual guidance and reflection. Much of the office work she'd been doing in the last few weeks was in regard to the logistics of accommodating and catering for their visitors.

Marcus smiled down on his flock. "I'm delighted to announce that a special guest will be joining us this year." He paused for dramatic effect, "Elijah Hart. Elijah is Ruth's brother and one of our church's founding fathers, so we are overjoyed to have him be a part of this year's seminar on the theme of stewardship." Raising his hands, Marcus beamed. "Now let us sing."

As they rose, Jamie and Kathryn swapped a look of excitement.

After church, they returned to the cottage to change, collect Meg and the lunch Kathryn had prepared earlier. They bundled everything into the Land Rover and Jamie drove to the start of the stalker's path at the foot of the glen. They walked for a time until they found a suitable picnic spot and laid out a tartan rug on the heather. As they ate, they sat side-by-side looking out over the valley with Meg at Jamie's feet hoping for titbits. Although it was icy cold, the sky was pastel blue and the gentle breeze brought the sound of church bells.

Jamie said, "Elijah's visit should buy us more time. No way will they extract us before he arrives."

"I hope so since we're no closer to figuring out what's going on."

"Although Bethany's been found, we don't know who the baby's father is, and Mhairi's disappearance is still a mystery. Simon and Angus are connected to both girls. They were in Mhairi's class, and could have been in a relationship with Bethany. If Angus is the father and Finlay found out, that'd explain the payments."

"You think Finlay's blackmailing Angus?" asked Kathryn.

"Aye, but I'm not sure why."

Staring pensively into the distance, she said, "I feel sorry for Bethany. Hazel said her father's threatened to shoot whoever's responsible unless he marries her."

"What if he's already married?" said Jamie.

"Or she doesn't want to marry him? Plenty women raise kids on their own."

"It's hard enough with two parents," he said, feeding Meg a crust.

She darted a glance at him, "Sounds like you've experience. Have you got some children tucked away I don't know about?"

Jamie laughed. "None I'm aware of, but I've a niece and lovely as she is, I know how hard my sister's found it and she's married to a guy who shares the load." He turned to look at her, "You ever thought about kids?"

She paused. "Can't say I have … I mean, I never even imagined having a partner."

He took her hand. "Sorry, that was a stupid question."

Gazing at him, she said, "It wasn't, and I suppose anything's possible."

Slipping an arm around her, he kissed her and whispered, "Everything's possible."

Overwhelmed by the direction the discussion had taken and the possibilities unfurling before her, she steered the conversation to safer ground. "I wonder if she'll keep the baby? It'll be difficult to finish her degree, at least for a while, and I don't see the Colquhouns continuing their financial support."

"Doubt she'll opt for the alternative. She's been brought up to believe abortion is a mortal sin."

"Poor girl. Vondell's partly to blame, refusing to prescribe her contraceptives."

Jamie picked up the binoculars and scanned the terrain. "It wouldn't surprise me if Ruth turns this to her advantage. Then she'll have more people beholden to her, Bethany being one of them." Passing her the binoculars, he pointed. "Look, over there."

She saw an enormous stag and several does off in the distance and they watched them for a while.

"Who knew Hell's Glen was so beautiful," she remarked putting the binoculars aside.

He took them and watched a large bird of prey soaring in the distance. "Bizarre," he said, "I'm sure that's a bald eagle. I didn't expect to see one here, they must have introduced them."

He passed her the glasses again, and she watched it soar away.

"Mmm, these are really good" said Jamie through a mouthful of pork pie. "Did you make these?"

"Hey, don't sound so surprised, I learned at Christian Wives."

He shot her a mischievous grin. "Christ almighty, you've gone native!"

Laughing, she gave him a playful thump on the shoulder and, like a grinning predator, he pounced on her and kissed her. She lay back on the rug giggling under him, complaining that he tasted of pork pie. As he possessed her with his mouth, she felt him trace the length of her hip with his fingers and come to rest behind her knee. Pulling her leg up, he placed it behind his own and rolled on top of her, and she moaned in pleasure as their tongues duelled. Meg began barking. They tried ignoring her until she shoved her nose into Jamie's ear and he broke from the kiss laughing. Kathryn gazed up at him and their eyes locked, aware his groin was still pressed firmly against hers. Wide-eyed, she exhaled slowly.

He shifted, "Want me to move?"

"No," she said tethering him with her legs.

Burying her hands deep in his hair, she pulled him in for another kiss and they dry humped until Meg put a stop to it. Cursing, Jamie swotted at the dog like a fly which made Kathryn laugh.

"Bloody dug, I'll shoot her myself." Then, gazing down at her, he said, "I cannae wait til later."

Heart hammering in her chest, she whispered, "The quicker you phone Keith, the quicker we can get home."

Grinning, he sprang up, grabbed the satellite phone from the bag and called their handler. As he updated him about Elijah's visit, Kathryn scanned the valley through the binoculars for the deer. A light glinting on the opposite side of the valley caught her eye and she trained the glasses on it, only to see the back of a figure disappear from view. With only a glimpse of dark clothing and khaki, she couldn't tell who it was or whether the person was male or female.

Jamie passed her the phone and she asked Keith to hold for a second while she pointed to where she'd seen someone. Jamie scanned the area as she talked to Keith and, by the time she'd wound up the call, he had the ordinance survey map out.

He said, "I couldn't see anyone but according to this, there's a bothy over there so it could be a hillwalker."

"At this time of year? They must be hardcore."

"I might take a closer look later this week."

They packed up the picnic and walked back to the Land Rover chatting about what to cook together for dinner.

Later that evening, she sat up, burst into tears and turned away from him.

Jamie scooted across the bed and wrapped his arms around her shoulders. He soothed, "Baby, it's okay."

She wept into his chest, "It's not okay, there's something wrong with me. You can't come near me without me freaking out."

He held her, "Kathryn, it's just gonnae take time. We're going to have set backs, it's how we deal with them that's important. Tonight, was just too much, too soon."

"But I didn't panic earlier when you were on top of me."

He wiped her tears and fixed her with an azure stare. "You're being hard on your yourself. You're doing brilliantly, think how far we've come."

"But Jamie, how are we ever going to be a proper couple if I can't bear to let you near me?" Tears filled her eyes again.

Hugging her to him, he whispered, "Slowly baby, that's how. Now come here and give me a cuddle."

He pressed a tender kiss to her lips, then wrapped her in his arms.

Their setback in the bedroom loomed large over the next few nights and Jamie seemed reluctant to push her further than he'd mischievously termed 'second base'. In the end, help came from a most unexpected source.

On Wednesday, Kathryn was stocking up on groceries at the shop, and Hazel asked if she was going to the Christian Wives meeting the following day.

Kathryn shook her head. "I've really enjoyed the cooking but I'll skip the marital obligations session."

"Oh goodness, you don't want to miss it," said Hazel, "Rachael gives this talk every year and, trust me, you'll want to be there."

"Really?" She pointed to the notice board where the meetings were listed and read aloud, "Building a stronger, healthier Christian marriage?"

Hazel's eyes glinted with mirth. "Please come along, you'll enjoy it."

Kathryn had to admit she enjoyed Christian Wives as it had given her an opportunity to make friends and find out about the women's lives here. And, unwilling to disappoint Hazel of whom she was fond, Kathryn agreed, wondering what the dowdy Rachael could possibly teach her about the obligations of marriage.

The following afternoon Kathryn made her way to the community hall which was packed with the married women of the Society. The excitement was almost palpable and Kathryn wondered what they were expecting to hear that had them in such a febrile mood.

Hazel waved at her from near the front. She'd saved a seat and as Kathryn shuffled up the row of chairs to join her, she was greeted by the other wives who were laughing and giggling like schoolgirls. Rachael stood at the front behind a table. In her early fifties, she was short and plump with long silver-flecked brown hair. Modestly dressed in a long navy dress with matching headscarf, she epitomised their idea of a good Christian wife.

Once everyone was seated, Rachael asked for the main door at the back of the hall to be closed. Casting her eye over her audience, she smiled and the room fell silent.

In a loud, clear voice she said, "The covenant of marriage between a husband and wife reflects the nature of Christ's love for His Church. We believe marriage to be the lifelong union between one man and one woman, and divorce and remarriage to be wrong."

Kathryn stifled a yawn as she listened to Rachael drone on about the institution of marriage. Then her ears pricked up.

"Biblical marriage includes having sex within such a relationship, and sex is not simply for procreation. When a husband and wife become one flesh, it serves as a symbol of the union between Christ and His Church. Marital sex is therefore an obligation, so if your husband wants physical intimacy, you must see to his needs. Likewise, if you want it, insist he fulfils his duty to you."

Oh, here we go, more of the submit to your husband nonsense, she thought. And it was even worse hearing this doctrine expounded by the wives. Kathryn watched as Rachael reached under the table and pulled out a large plastic box.

Opening the lid, she said, "So today ladies, I'm going to talk to you about—" She reached into the box and placed on the table an enormous rubber dildo. "—giving and receiving sexual pleasure."

The hall erupted in shrieks of laughter as Kathryn looked on in horror.

"Told you, you wouldn't want to miss it" grinned Hazel. Then, seeing Kathryn's expression, she added, "Hey, you okay?"

Looking at the wobbling sex toy, she forced a smile. "Sure, I just wasn't expecting … that."

Rachael and her helper handed each woman a similar dildo which caused further squealing as they waved them around and compared them to their husband's penis. A packet of anti-bacterial wipes was also passed round with which to clean them. Biting her bottom lip, Kathryn examined the enormous flesh-coloured dildo and wondered how much pain it would inflict if forced inside her.

Rachael switched on the overhead projector and a picture of an erect penis with appended information labels appeared on the screen above her head. "First, we'll discuss handwork, then oral sex." When the laughter died down, she said, "After you've practised the techniques, I guarantee you'll never have to worry about your husband straying. The secret to a happy marriage, after all, is to keep his belly full and his balls empty."

More shrieks of laughter.

Hazel sniggered. "Now you know why her husband always has a smile on his face."

Rachael continued. "Then after we've mastered his pleasure, we'll discuss yours." The screen showed a labelled diagram of female genitalia. "Given that most men can't find their own backsides with both hands and a map, we need to teach them how to push our buttons." Rachael pointed to the screen. "So, the last part today will be spent discussing female sexual pleasure and techniques you can explore with your husband."

Kathryn and Hazel exchanged a look, threw back their heads and laughed.

That evening, Jamie and Kathryn lay in bed facing one another, stripped to their underwear. He gazed at her and whispered, "How was your meeting today? It's all the married guys would talk about."

"Really? What did they say?"

"Just that every time Rachael gives her talk, they've great sex." His eyes sparkled with mirth. "So, Mrs Campbell, did you learn anything useful?"

She chuckled. "Oh my God did I learn something! I was expecting a lecture on morals and missionary position." She described what they'd covered, and he hooted with laughter.

He teased, "Well if you want more practice, I won't complain."

She swallowed hard and looked at him uncertainly. "The whole thing made me uncomfortable to be honest and just reminded me of how little I know."

"You're doing great. Bet you never thought we'd be doing this."

She bit her bottom lip and looked down at his boxer shorts. Then, with a slow smile that built, she slid her hand down his body and, to his delight, practised what she'd learned.

After, he murmured, "Wow, you really were paying attention in class."

Then he kissed her with a passion that sucked the breath from both of them.

Jamie

On Friday afternoon Jamie went in search of the bothy, taking advantage of the lull in his workload after the electrical company had completed their testing. MI5's man had made himself known to him and, under the guise of fixing an overhead light in the corridor leading to the cellar, he'd installed a pinhole camera which Kathryn could monitor using software.

Jamie drove as close to the bothy as the rough track allowed and hiked the rest of the way. It had begun to sleet and he pulled the collar of his Barbour jacket up against the cold, grateful he'd brought hat and gloves. After about a mile, the bothy came into view. Set at the foot of a steep rocky hill beside a narrow mountain stream, the squat stone-built cottage appeared to hunker into the landscape. He looked up at the sky where snow clouds had begun to gather, and knew he'd need to be quick.

He'd enjoyed the hike despite the atrocious weather. Until Knoydart, he'd been like an overwound spring, unable to switch off and relax without the aid of alcohol. He realised he'd suffered in silence for too long and that he should've opened up years ago about the mental health issues that'd plagued him since leaving the army. However, with Kathryn, he could drop the tough guy act and talk about how he was feeling, without fear of judgement. Despite the circumstances and creeping paranoia, he was gradually unwinding and making progress with her help and support.

He also admitted he was rediscovering the joy he'd once felt for the countryside. He missed this life. Nostalgia overwhelmed him as he thought about growing up in the Highlands, and the times he'd spent stalking with his father on the estate. Every weekend and holiday during the spring and summer months, he'd earned pocket money helping on the shoots. After his father's suicide, his mother had taken him to live on a very different kind of sporting estate in Glasgow; one where the local thugs gave you a head-start before kicking your head in. He'd hated living there and had joined up as soon as he was old enough.

All was quiet as he approached the bothy. He walked around the outside and peered into the woodstore at the rear, and through the square panes in the window. Seemingly empty, he knocked anyway before opening the wooden door which whined on its hinges. Being an emergency shelter free for anyone to use, he expected it to be basic but this was better equipped than most, with an old blackened stove heater set inside a modest fireplace. Surrounding the fireplace were four wooden chairs, and along the back wall, a raised wooden plinth provided a sleeping area supplemented by a metal bunkbed along the adjacent wall. Next to the window was a wooden table laden with pans, kettles and an eclectic mix of plates and mugs. There was a plastic water container for collecting water from the stream, and rope draped across the ceiling for drying clothes. Jamie knew from the estate office records that the Mountain Bothy Association maintained the place and, although basic, it was weatherproof.

He opened the stove heater and looked inside. Bothy etiquette dictated you left the place as you found it which usually meant tidy, with dry kindling for the next occupants; however, the stove was full of ash and empty beer cans and tins were strewn across the flagstone floor. Examining them, he reckoned from the smell they'd been opened in the last few days which tallied with Kathryn's sighting of someone nearby. He stacked the rubbish in the woodshed, and made a note to have one of the estate hands dispose of it and restock the place with kindling. Closing the door behind him, he scouted the surrounding area before he began retracing his steps back to the Land Rover.

As he left the relative shelter of the valley, sleet spattered his face and he increased his pace. Approaching the rocky outcrop at the foot of the glen, he paused to pull down his woollen hat.

Gunfire cracked through the valley and the drystone wall beside him exploded.

∼

Kathryn

Kathryn looked at the kitchen clock and wondered where Jamie was. It wasn't like him to be late, especially when he knew she was making one of his favourite meals, steaks with pepper sauce. She put the parmentier potatoes and vegetables into the warming oven, and the uncooked steaks out of Meg's reach at the back of the Aga, and went upstairs.

After switching on the radio, she retrieved the laptop from her art case. She'd already installed the software needed for monitoring the camera, and a grainy black and white picture appeared on-screen. The images were set to record automatically and she scrolled through the footage to see who'd come and gone from the cellar. Early afternoon, Cameron and Angus had gone inside for a few minutes and emerged carrying a case of wine, but that was all. Since there was still no sign of Jamie, she used Duncan's CCTV cameras to snoop round his house as she still had access to them, but there was no sign of anyone.

It was dark outside and snow was falling heavily. She opened the front door and peered out across the valley towards Hourn House. Lights illuminated several windows but the estate office lay in darkness. Maybe Marcus had suggested a drink, but it was unlike Jamie not to pop over and tell her. For fear of appearing like a nagging wife, she resisted the urge to go searching for him knowing that Marcus and his sons would rib Jamie about it mercilessly. It angered her that she had to sit in the cottage and fret instead.

Tendrils of paranoia wound around her. What if they'd discovered his real identity? What were they doing to him and would they come for her next? But it was her concern for Jamie that terrified her most and brought her feelings for him into sharp relief. She didn't just want him, she needed him.

Pushing aside her worries, she sighed and curled up on the sofa with a book Hazel had lent her entitled *The Population Bomb* by Paul R. Ehrlich, after Kathryn had lent her Simone de Beauvoir's *The Second Sex*. She struggled to focus and skim read instead. According to Ehrlich, worldwide famine would result if humans failed to address environmental issues and limit population growth. Examining the book, she wondered if the name of the author was coincidental.

When an hour passed, she really began to worry.

Jamie

Jamie dived behind the wall, landing hard on his shoulder, as another gunshot exploded overhead sending rock fragments flying. He'd knocked the wind out of himself and he remained flat on his stomach as he caught his breath. Heart pounding, he inched up into a sitting position with his back against the wall. Remembering his training, he could hear Sergeant Major Shinn yelling "Keep your bloody head down Denton."

He looked around. To his right was the path leading to the bothy; to his left, the relative safety of the outcrop. Reckoning the gunman was somewhere on the mountain behind him, he knew he'd have to move or risk being shot at close range, and he cursed himself for not bringing his rifle.

Crouching, he crept along the wall until he came to a gap where it was in disrepair. Steeling himself, he dived into a forward roll across the expanse as another shot smacked into the stonework around him. Swearing obscenities, he darted a glance across the valley but couldn't see anything. He crawled on his elbows, continuing to the point where he'd have to risk running in open ground to reach the safety of the other side of the outcrop. He hunkered down, his back to the wall and knees to his chest, and waited.

And waited.

As daylight faded, sleet turned to snow and, despite the adrenaline pumping through his veins, Jamie shivered against the cold. His trousers were sodden wet and he'd lost the feeling in his fingers and toes. As the visibility decreased, he decided to risk the dash to the outcrop. Hoping his legs wouldn't buckle beneath him, he took a deep breath and darted for the trail. The ground to his right erupted as a shot blasted into it. Running like the hounds of hell were at his heels, he zigzagged to the outcrop and dived behind it as another crack resounded around the valley and a bullet thudded into the grass behind him.

He didn't stop running until he reached the Land Rover. Wrenching open the door, he fired up the engine and floored it home.

Before he'd reached the front door, Kathryn had it open and she launched herself into his arms.

"My God, I was so worried, I thought ..." She pulled away, "you're soaking wet ... and freezing. What the hell happened?"

She pulled him into the warmth of the cottage and closed the door. He locked it behind him, his teeth chattering as he removed his jacket and boots. Handing him a throw, she guided him into the chair in front of the stove heater and asked what had happened. He was too cold to speak and indicated he needed a moment. After adding more wood, she went to the kitchen and made him hot chocolate.

"You need to get out of these wet things," she said handing him the steaming mug.

Gripping it with two hands, he took a sip and shivered, "I'll drink this first."

She went upstairs and he heard her run a bath. He was still shaking as she helped him up to the bathroom and out of his wet outer clothes. She'd added several capfuls of bath foam and the scented bubbles reached the rim of the tub.

"I'll let you do the rest" she said, turning to go.

He caught her arm. "Join me, then we can talk." Then, chuckling at the expression of horror on her face, he added, "I won't peek, honest."

After a pause, she gave him a hesitant nod. "You get the tap end. I'll be back in a few minutes."

Watching her go, he said, "Deal."

He let out a grateful sigh as he lowered himself into the soothing warm water. His muscles ceased shivering and he began to relax. Exhaling slowly, he gazed up at the ceiling and thought about what had just happened and who'd tried to kill him. On the drive home, he'd looked to see who was home and which cottages had lights on but it'd been impossible to tell. Paranoia licked at him as he wondered if someone in the community had discovered they were UCs.

He could hear Kathryn in the kitchen then in their bedroom, and after a few minutes she tapped on the bathroom door and popped her head round. Wrapped in a bath robe and with her hair tied up, she approached him, a shy expression on her face.

Smiling up at her, he covered his eyes. "Promise not to look."

He heard the robe drop to the floor before she stepped quickly into the bath and crouched. Keeping his eyes shut, he shuffled so his limbs bracketed hers. Her slender legs were silky smooth and he was grateful the bubbles concealed his immediate arousal.

Once she'd submerged, she said, "You can open your eyes now."

He opened one, making her laugh and she flicked suds at him. He reached for her and latched his mouth to hers.

Through hungry kisses, she mumbled "Tell me what happened."

"In a minute, I need some mouth-to-mouth resuscitation first."

She giggled and he stifled the sound with his kiss. Eventually, she broke away insisting he talked to her.

When he explained about the shooting, her mouth flew open and she put a hand to her chest. "My God Jamie, you could've been killed."

"I wasn't and I'm fine. I'll report it tomorrow and let Keith know."

She whispered, "I couldn't bear for anything to happen to you."

He stroked her face. "I feel the same about you. But I'm okay. Probably just some numpty who couldnae tell a deer from a human."

Looking as unconvinced as he felt, she said, "I know you don't believe that. Who do you think it was?"

"My money's on Finlay, but it could be someone else."

Reaching for her again, he kissed her, holding the nape of her neck as he angled his mouth and deepened the connection. He groaned out his pleasure as he felt her hand skate down his body.

When he reciprocated, she didn't stop him.

Jamie awoke next morning with a fever, sore throat and pounding headache. He'd intended going for a run with Meg before work but opted for two paracetamol and a walk instead. Taking the satellite phone, he called Keith who sounded as rough as himself.

"You're early" said Keith, "what's up?"

"Someone tried to bloody shoot me, that's what's up."

After telling him about the ambush, Keith asked Jamie to send coordinates of where he thought the gunman had been hiding, and said he'd send a team out that morning to see if they could find bullet casings or anything that'd identify him. Jamie suggested they might be able to lift prints from the rubbish in the woodstore.

Keith asked, "You thinking what I'm thinking?"

"Aye, that our friendly neighbourhood rapist is holed up in the area."

"Explains why he's not surfaced. Delay phoning Buchanan for a few hours, just to give me some time."

"Doubt Buchanan will get round to doing anything quickly."

Keith said, "Hmm, it's not every day he deals with attempted murder." There was a pause on the line then he added, "You okay?"

"Aye, fine, just feel like shit, think it's flu."

"Okay, but from now on I don't want you or Kathryn wandering on the estate on your own if you can help it, and if you do, take your rifle."

Jamie cut the call and whistled for Meg. As he trudged back to the cottage, he realised he was more worried about the effect the flu was going to have on his love life than anything else. He yearned to be back in bed with her, to see the look of sheer pleasure and surprise on her face again when he made her body sing. He'd been delighted at seeing her in the throes of ecstasy for the first time but it was tinged with sadness that she'd had to wait so long to experience it. He wanted to help her make up for lost time and enjoy every pleasure on offer, and he felt grateful he was the one she'd entrusted to do this. Keen to capitalise on the progress they'd made, he was concerned they'd regress if he succumbed to flu.

Kathryn was already dressed and downstairs when he returned, and she handed him a brew and scolded him for not staying in bed.

"I'll be fine once the paracetamol kick in. Anyway, why are you up, you don't have work?"

"I wanted to make you breakfast."

He kissed her cheek and whispered, "We need more wood, want to give me a hand?"

She followed him out to the woodstore where he updated her on his call with Keith, warning her not to stray from the community on her walks with Meg.

"We've a nutter on the loose and if it's Finlay, I definitely don't want you anywhere near him."

Jamie dragged himself into the office equipped with painkillers and tissues and made more tea to sooth his throat. It was gone noon by the time he called Buchanan to tell him about the shooting. He played it down, wanting to give Keith time to investigate the area, and knowing he couldn't reveal to Buchanan his suspicions that it was a rapist on the loose.

The sergeant took the bait, "Probably a myopic hunter. We'd one a few years ago who shot a cow thinking it was a stag."

Jamie finished the call just as Marcus appeared, and he told him about the incident at the bothy and the fact Buchanan would be out to take a statement. Marcus raised his eyebrows and asked exactly when it'd happened and why Jamie had been out there. Jamie explained that Kathryn had spotted a figure on Sunday when they were out a walk with Meg.

Marcus's brow furrowed. "I'll let Angus and Duncan know, and I'll warn the others this evening that they shouldn't venture near there until Buchanan gets to the bottom of it." Marcus sighed loudly, "This is the last thing we need with Elijah's visit coming up."

Jamie sneezed and blew his nose.

Marcus turned to him. "You look like death warmed up son, get home so your good lady wife can take care of you."

Feeling rotten, he didn't bother to argue and instead trudged home to his good lady wife.

~

Kathryn

Jamie spent the rest of the day in bed and Kathryn waited until he was asleep before retrieving her art case and switching on her laptop. She ran through her plan a final time, mobilising the courage she'd need.

Fake it until you become it.

She left Jamie a note in case he woke and wondered where she was, and then she made her way over to Hourn House. It was seven o'clock, and she knew the community would be eating together, which ought to give her ample time to get a better look at the cellar and keypad. She'd finished coding software on the USB stick which would give her access to any machine someone was daft enough to plug it into.

Her heart thumped against her ribs as she slipped through the rear entrance and along the corridor leading to the cellar. She strained to listen for noise but it was silent. She unlocked the cellar and closed the door behind her before switching on the light. Before getting started, she pulled out the sketchpad from her case and made a quick drawing. All was silent, except for her pounding heartbeat. She tiptoed to the refrigerator door at the end and pressed her ear against it.

She examined the keypad and took pictures of it with her phone. It appeared to be a standard biometric door entry system with a built-in keypad and fingerprint reader on the outside, and a main controller inside the secure area. She tried the manufacturer's default entry and maintenance codes, then a list of the Colquhoun's dates of birth without success. She tried lazy codes such as 1234 and the like, also to no avail. Realising she'd have to crack it the hard way, she packed up her equipment and placed the rogue USB stick in front of the door.

A noise behind her made her spin round and her heart skipped a beat. At the entrance stood the great hulking frame of Duncan. Glaring at her.

She screamed.

He approached her, raising his hands placatingly. "Sorry, I didn't mean to frighten you. What are you doing down here?" His voice was surprisingly calm and friendly as he appraised her, his piercing blue eyes boring into her. He tore them away long enough to look at the art case, then back at her.

Pulse racing, she gasped out, "Sorry, the door was unlocked and I peeked in." Beaming at him, she pointed up, "This place has the most amazing roof, I've never seen anything like it. I just had to sketch it." She opened up her case and pulled out her drawing of the vaulted ceiling and handed it to him.

His gaze swept over her before he glanced at her sketch. Smiling, he said, "You're a very talented lady."

He passed her the drawing back, his fingers brushing against hers. Standing close, his eyes scanned her face, and she could read the lust in his gaze. Kathryn's heart thrummed against her ribcage and she struggled to breath, hoping her face didn't betray the lie.

Swallowing hard, she said, "I'd better go, Jamie will be wondering where I am."

His eyes remained fixed on her. "Heard he has flu."

"Yes, he's sleeping."

"Want to join us? There's plenty food left."

Thanking him, she declined saying she ought to return to her husband. She moved to his right and he stepped in front of her. She swallowed hard and looked up at him, her legs feeling like they might buckle at any moment.

Placing a hand on her arm he said in a low voice, "Anytime you want to finish your sketch, I'm happy to let you back in."

Smiling, she left, running home on shaky legs as relief flooded through her.

On Sunday morning Kathryn left Jamie to sleep while she went to church. Tired after a restless night, not helped by Jamie snoring like a truffling hog, she'd hoped to hear Simon preach but Hazel said he'd also caught the lurgy. She'd considered returning home but too many people had noticed her so she parked herself in the usual pew. As she removed her coat and adjusted her head scarf, she noticed Duncan watching her from the front. Returning a brief smile, she busied herself finding the first hymn they'd be singing. To her surprise, she enjoyed the singing and found it lifted her spirits.

Marcus began his sermon calmly, reading from I Romans about the wrath of abandonment, which he explained was what happens when a nation turns its back on Holy Scripture. He outlined the sequence of events, quoting from verse 24.

"He gives them over to the lust of their hearts to impurity, sexual sin, the dishonouring of their bodies among them. When God abandons a society, it becomes pornographic and obsessed with sex, fornication, adultery, every kind of sexual behaviour." Marcus searched for Kathryn amongst the congregation and pointedly added, "We've already seen this happen with the sexual revolution."

She felt her face flush and wished Jamie were with her.

Next, he described the second stage in God's abandonment. "God gave them over to degrading passions ... their women exchanged the natural function for that which is unnatural, in the same way also the men abandoned the natural function of the woman and burned in their desire toward one another, men with men committing indecent acts and receiving the due penalty." He went on to explain that the penalty was the disease called AIDS which God had unleashed on the world for homosexual behaviour.

Determined not to react to his words, Kathryn stared straight ahead, refusing to meet anyone's eye as Marcus continued to describe the third stage.

"God gave them over to a depraved mind so that life becomes filled with unrighteousness, wickedness, greed, evil, envy and murder, including the large-scale murder of millions of unborn children." He thumped the bible. "You shall not lie with a male as one lies with a female; it is an abomination."

As he continued his passionate pro-life, anti-homosexual rant, Kathryn became increasingly angry. Casting her eyes over the congregation, she wondered who amongst them was feeling branded by his hate-filled words and how they must feel since there was the likelihood that several would identify as LGBT.

Marcus let his words settle over his flock before directing his gaze at Kathryn again. Thumping his fist again, he shouted, "Marriage is the only form of partnership approved by God for sexual relations. Anything else is incompatible with His will as revealed in Scripture, and sodomites will burn in the eternal fires of hell."

Unable to listen to any more, she felt like flouncing out but, along with the other sheeple, she sang her praises to an unforgiving deity then lined up and thanked Marcus for his dose of spite and bile. After inquiring after Jamie's health, Marcus held her hand and asked if she'd found the sermon informative, while Ruth, Duncan and Angus observed with interest.

Forcing a smile, she said, "Thank you, it was very informative … not that I agreed with a single word you said." She dared herself to hold his gaze while Ruth gasped her annoyance and Duncan and Angus gawped.

Tightening his grip, Marcus returned a tight smile. There was no absolution in his eyes when he said, "The bible's very clear that the unrighteous will not inherit the kingdom of God."

Smiling sweetly, she pulled her hand from his grip and said, "It's called a bi-ble for a reason, not a straight-ble."

Leaving the Colquhouns to gawk, she walked away laughing under her breath.

~

Jamie

Jamie had spent most of the weekend in bed with aches, pains and shivers, while Kathryn brought him warming concoctions of honey and lemon, gallons of tea, and bowls of homemade soup. Being cared for was a novel experience as he'd lived on his own in recent years, except when with Emma, but the relationship had deteriorated so rapidly they'd never looked after one another.

As an adult, he'd never needed another person. Sure, it'd been fun to have a girlfriend around for companionship and sex and he'd been fond of Emma to the point he'd wondered if she was the one. When they'd been together, he'd thought of her but unless she'd been right in front of him, he realised in retrospect he hadn't. His relationship with Kathryn was different; she was in his thoughts all the time, whether there or not. It wasn't just a case of wanting her; he damn well needed her and the thought bloody terrified him.

By Sunday evening, he was feeling better and she ran him a bath which helped ease the muscle cramps. As he stretched his limbs beneath the foam there was a tap on the door and she asked if she could come in.

"Joining me again?" he asked, laughing at the blush that spread across her face and neck.

"I need to tell you something but you've got to promise not to be angry."

"Oh God, what've you hacked?"

Perching on the side of the tub, she told him about her encounter with Duncan in the cellar, and he tried not to let his annoyance show on his face.

Taking her hand, he fixed her with his gaze, "Please don't do anything like that again without discussing it with me first. You could've put yourself and the operation in danger."

She sent him a contrite nod. "I'm just frustrated about my lack of progress, and to make things worse I called Keith this afternoon and he insists we hang tight and do nothing until Elijah Hart arrives."

"I thought that'd be the case. They'll want us here for his visit." He laced his fingers through hers and kissed the back of her hand. "So, no more solo missions Mrs Campbell."

She nodded. "Keith said they didn't find anything at the bothy but they'll run prints on the litter."

When she got up to go, he said plaintively, "Not coming in for a replay of Friday?"

Laughing, she flicked suds at him and left.

When he returned to the bedroom, he discovered she'd changed the sheets and restocked the nightstand with tissues, painkillers and a flask of tea. Exhausted, he climbed back under the duvet and shivered. She appeared in the doorway holding a hot water bottle wrapped in a towel which she popped at his feet before climbing in beside him.

"I don't want you catching this," he said as she snuggled into him. He enjoyed the soft warm feeling of her at his side and wished he could smell her scent.

"I won't, it's man flu."

He laughed. "A serious case of it."

"Better stay in bed, God forbid it turns into man-monia."

"Cheeky" he said, swotting her backside playfully. Then he wrapped her in his arms and cuddled into her. "Thank you for looking after me Mrs Campbell."

She looked up at him. "I'm sure you'd do the same for me."

Gazing at her, he whispered, "In sickness and in health."

Their eyes locked and, in that moment, Jamie knew exactly what he wanted.

By Monday, he was much recovered. Too tired to go for a run that morning, he'd accompanied Kathryn to Hourn House and made his way to the estate office where Marcus was already at his desk, coffee in hand. The morning was spent planning the logistics around the Spiritual Seminar and Elijah's visit. Marcus seemed on edge and was sweating over every detail.

Buchanan showed up mid-morning and Marcus left while Jamie made his statement. When the sergeant asked him to take him to the scene, Jamie insisted on taking his rifle and he popped back to the cottage for it. He whistled for Meg and she joined them in the Land Rover.

On the journey to the bothy, Jamie asked Buchanan how long he'd been stationed in the area and if he enjoyed it.

"Almost fifteen years and I've loved every minute of it. Usually, it's lost sheep and the occasional missing hillwalker. Except recently with this place. I mean what the hell's going on?"

Jamie gave a dark chuckle. "You tell me. I've only been here five minutes."

"And it's all kicked off since…"

Jamie shot him a side-ways glance. "What are you insinuating officer?"

Buchanan laughed. "Nothing, relax, I checked you out but trouble does seem to follow you about."

"How long have you known Marcus?" asked Jamie.

"Since he pitched up about ten years ago. He's a good sort and I'm glad he met Ruth. Not sure the community would have lasted much longer without the investment she's brought. She's very generous too. Gave our local mountain rescue team money to buy new equipment, and funded a new roof for the church in Inverie."

When they reached the bothy, Jamie showed him around the area and they climbed to where he thought the gunman may have been hiding, and then to where he'd been shot at. There was no trace of anything and Keith's team had cleared the rubbish from the log store.

Buchanan scratched his head. "Hmm, whoever it is will be long gone but we'll keep an eye out and I'll alert the ferry master at Inverie."

Clutching his rifle, Jamie failed to feel reassured.

~

When he returned home with Meg in the early evening, he was greeted by a delicious smell emanating from the kitchen. There was no sign of Kathryn, and he lifted the lid on the pot bubbling on the Aga and inhaled the aroma, suddenly realising how hungry he was. Feeling her arms slip around his waist, he turned and kissed her.

"Hello hubby."

"Hello wife. Something smells good."

She grinned. "Venison stew. Sit down and I'll dish up."

As he tucked into the delicious stew she'd heaped onto a plate with brown rice, he told her about Buchanan's visit, careful with his words. After a second helping and a homemade flapjack, he suggested a walk.

They wrapped up warm against the cold and he watched with amusement as she stuffed her feet into her boots and gasped in shock. Slipping her hand into her boot to see what the object was, she leapt into the air and shrieked as she produced a vibrating plastic spider. He doubled over laughing, bracing his hands on his thighs as she threw the spider into the corner and Meg ran off with it. Turning to him, she squealed in outrage and pummelled his shoulder making him laugh even more. After he'd placated her with kisses and wrestled the spider from Meg's jaws, they made their way to the edge of the loch where he told her about Ruth splashing the cash.

Jamie said, "Makes we wonder what her game is."

"You think she's trying to keep Buchanan in her pocket?"

"Possibly." Cupping her face, he looked into her eyes. "Fancy an early night Mrs Campbell?"

~

Kathryn

Flu spread round the community and Kathryn eventually succumbed to it, spending the rest of the week in bed with Jamie playing nurse maid. He took good care of her and by Sunday she was feeling well enough to hike to their usual spot on the moors with the satellite phone to have their monthly catchup with Julien, Fitz and Pia. It was a dry clear day and they'd eaten alfresco. He'd also brought the rifle which he placed within easy reach of the picnic rug.

Jamie gave them his progress report and spoke to Pia at length before handing Kathryn the phone. As she talked to Pia, she watched him throw a ball for Meg. Always hyper-aware of when he was nearby, even when preoccupied on the phone, she smiled as she watched him. Pia rattled through the standard psychological wellbeing questionnaire, but this week she'd added more questions.

"How are you and Jamie getting on?"

"Well, we haven't killed each other yet if that's what you mean," *Quite the opposite.*

Jamie approached and gave her a sly smile, his eyes alight with mischief as he listened in.

"And you're not feeling claustrophobic sharing a living space?"

"No, we're cohabiting very nicely." *We're even sharing a bed.*

He wound his arm around her waist and kissed her neck. She stifled a whimper and tried to concentrate on the call.

"Are you managing to maintain enough physical contact to suggest you're married?"

"Enough to be convincing." *Oh my, you've no idea...*

Jamie flicked kisses along her jawline.

"Do you believe either of you are forming an attachment to the other?"

Jamie paused and looked at her impishly. Grinning, she said, "Not at all, we're both careful to maintain a professional working relationship." *We're in over our heads.*

He pressed his lips to hers and pulled her into a passionate kiss. Lips still locked, he took the phone from her hand, cut the call, then proceeded to give her his full attention.

They kissed until Meg began barking at them.

When they returned to the cottage, Jamie offered to cook dinner while she checked the footage from the camera in the cellar corridor. She'd been monitoring it regularly and keeping a spreadsheet of visitors' entry and exit times, and a pattern was beginning to emerge. The Colquhoun family all had access to the cellar but Ruth spent longest there, sometimes several hours each day, with Duncan a close second. And, unlike the others, Ruth and Duncan rarely emerged carrying provisions. Duncan appeared to spend his evenings in the cellar, and Angus and Cameron were occasional visitors but they usually came out with bottles of booze.

When Jamie came to tell her dinner was ready, she turned her screen and showed him the results.

"Interesting," he remarked, "what the hell are they're up to?"

"You don't need a state-of-the-art server room to cook the books."

"No, there's got to be more to it. I mean, we can see how Hart Biotech is dodging its tax obligations through its offshore companies and foreign investments. Elijah won't pay a dime in tax unless he brings the profits into the US."

"But why funnel money through a religious charity and make those types of acquisitions?"

He shrugged, "He trusts family and believes religion legitimizes it? Guess you could argue it's being put to good use in poor countries. But, you're right, there must be better investments than wine producers and distributors. There's got to be something else at play otherwise why would Jean and the scientist be silenced after warning that people's lives were are at stake. It doesn't make sense. We need to dig much deeper and quickly too."

LAMENTATIONS

"Let love be genuine. Abhor what is evil; hold fast to what is good."

— *ROMANS 12:9*

Kathryn

The following week was busy with preparations for the Spiritual Meet, and Kathryn was glad to have something other than cooking and cleaning to occupy her, particularly since they'd been told to tread water until Elijah arrived. The nights however … she'd have been happy for them to last forever. She was astounded by her body's sexual awakening and knew that nothing would ever be the same again; she'd never be the same again. In her mind, there would always be 'before Knoydart' and 'after Knoydart'. And Jamie was right; what had happened to her was in the past, but she'd a real chance of a different future.

Lying in bed on Sunday evening, she found the courage to say what'd been on her mind for a few days.

"I want to try, you know, all the way …."

He whispered, "You sure baby?"

Stomach fluttering and pulse racing, she nodded.

"We'll go slowly, okay?"

He took his time, his touch tender and patient, until she felt ready. She closed her eyes in the hope it'd help her relax. Suddenly, an image exploded in her mind's eye and darkness tugged her back to a wood. A body pressing on her. Gasping for breath. Smell of stale sweat and alcohol. Unable to scream. The pain. So much pain. Flailing beneath him, she screamed and pushed him off violently as she battled to dispel her memories. He sprung up in shock as she twisted and clawed her way off the bed. Grabbing her robe, she covered herself and crouched in the corner shaking. Holding her knees to her chest, she wept.

Jamie approached her gingerly, pawing his hand through his hair. Kneeling beside her, he reached a hand out. "Hey baby, it's okay."

Clutching her sides, she wailed, "It's not okay, it's anything but okay." Shaking and rocking, she sobbed.

Placing a hand on her shoulder, he soothed. "It was just too soon, that's all."

She looked up at him, her eyes full of tears. "There'll never be a right time. You'll never be able to touch me Jamie, and we need to end this now for both our sakes."

Ignoring his hurt blue stare, she shrugged off his hand, got up and darted into the bathroom. As she dressed, there was a tap on the door.

"Kathryn, please come out so we can talk about this."

Sobs wracked her body and she gasped out, "I don't want to talk about it, just leave me alone."

"I know you're upset, but we can fix this."

She wrenched open the door to find him leaning against the jamb in his boxer shorts. "You're not listening. I can't be fixed. I'm broken."

Desperate to escape, she pushed past him and rushed downstairs. After grabbing her jacket and shoving her feet into her boots, she fled from the cottage with Meg following.

Jamie

Jamie cursed as he watched her go from the bedroom window. Furious at himself for pushing her too far, too quickly, he slumped down onto the edge of the bed and held his head in his hands.

"I'm a fuckin' idiot" he muttered.

He tried to make sense of what'd just happened and how, in an instant, her face had flickered from pure pleasure to abject terror. Haunted by the fear he'd seen in her eyes and the knowledge he'd triggered it, he berated himself for not stopping sooner.

But they'd come so close, literally within inches of success, and he was not about to give up. Together, they'd made so much progress and had been so happy, so there was no question in his mind of throwing it all away because of a minor setback. Considering how she'd gone from being untouchable to almost having intercourse in the space of just a few months, this was a mere blip. But given the intensity of her reaction, he understood it might seem insurmountable to her at this moment. Once she'd calmed down, he was confident she'd see it this way but for now, he'd let her blow off steam, knowing she'd return when she was ready and they'd talk it through.

Nope, he would never give up on her and he'd wait as long as it took. He had to. He loved her. Really fuckin' loved her.

Kathryn

Barely able to see through her tears, Kathryn pulled her coat around her against the freezing wind. In her haste to banish the images in her mind, she stumbled towards the loch and stood at the edge of the water. She gulped salt-laden air into her lungs and wept.

She wept for the loss of what might have been, for the hurt she'd caused Jamie, and most of all for herself. She'd been a fool to think she could have a normal relationship. It was true what she'd said; she was broken, she couldn't be fixed. And it was cruel for either of them to go on believing in something that was never going to happen. Better they finished this operation and went their separate ways; Jamie back to his career and her back to … what? What was waiting for her back home?

She'd nothing. No family, no job, not even a cat. Desolation washed over her and she wept some more, great sobs racking her frame.

Meg nudged against her calf and Kathryn crouched down and nuzzled into her fur. "At least I've got you Meg." The dog licked her face. "C'mon" she said, "We can't stay here, we'll freeze to death."

Not yet ready to return home and face Jamie, she trudged towards Hourn House. Meg whimpered as they passed Witsend Cottage but Kathryn pushed on and the dog followed. Too upset to face anyone, she searched for somewhere quiet and her eye settled on Jean's cottage. For weeks something had been germinating in her mind, just out of reach, but as she walked towards the cottage, she finally grasped it. *Glenavon*, the name of the bottling firm on the due diligence documents, was what she'd seen on an invoice in Jean's bureau. She knew the cottage would soon be cleared ahead of guests arriving, and she decided to grab the paperwork for safe-keeping.

Leaving Meg on the porch, she stepped inside Jean's cottage and closed the door. Cloaked in darkness, the interior smelled damp and musty and it was eerily silent until Meg began to bark frantically. She flicked the light switch in the hall. Nothing. Hands outstretched, she fumbled her way into the living room and tried the switch. Again nothing. Apprehension mounted with every step and the hair prickled on the nape of her neck. Ignoring the feeling, she took a deep breath and headed towards the kitchen at the rear. She heard the movement before she felt the hand close over her mouth, muffling her scream.

Dragged backwards into the living room, hands flailing, she tried to grab onto the door frame without success. She was thrown violently to the floor, the force of it knocking the air from her lungs. Then he was on top of her, straddling her, a palm pressed over her mouth and nose. She choked, his weight and his hand making it impossible to breathe. Writhing beneath him, she clawed at his wrist and face, but he only clamped down harder. Unable to get a breath, she fought against the blackness that threatened to engulf her. Her teeth found the flesh of his finger and she bit down hard. The pressure on her mouth released and she sucked in a lungful of air. He punched her hard in the stomach, taking the wind from her, and she groaned in pain.

As she battled to remain conscious, he forced his forearm against her neck and grappled with her clothing. She writhed as he wrenched up her skirt, his hands scraping the outside of her thigh. There was a ripping sound as he tore off her knickers, and she screamed at the realisation of what was about to happen. He pushed down harder on her throat, making her gasp for air. Through the horror, she heard Meg's frenzied barking. As the darkness tugged at her once again, she was transported back to the wood. A body pressing on her ... can't breathe ... can't scream. Pain. Terror gripped her as surely as the hand at her throat. He fumbled with his belt and she fought the urge to freeze. Then, sensing the grip on her neck slacken, she screamed. He hit her in the face hard, the force of it almost making her black out.

He undid his trousers and growled, "I'm gonna teach you a lesson bitch."

It was Finlay's voice.

At the sound of the zipper, she fought down her panic and thrashed beneath him. No, she wouldn't let this happen. Feeling suddenly disconnected from her mind and body, she remembered her training with Paul, and bucked hard. He fell forward onto her, his stale hot breath on her neck. Hooking her arms around one of his, she held it to her then, in one fluid movement, she arched, twisted and flipped herself on top of him. Then she let loose, reigning down blows onto his face and throat as he fought beneath her. He grabbed her hair and she rammed her bottom down into his gut making him drop his hands with a grunt, then went to work again with her fists. As she pummelled him, she let out a primal scream of rage. Even when he fell still, she continued, sobbing as she hit him.

Only when she was certain he was unconscious did she roll off and scramble towards the front door. Gasping for breath, she wrenched it open and bolted. Into Jamie's arms. Clinging to him like a limpet, she climbed his body as he wrapped his arms tightly around her.

"What the hell happened?" he asked, his voice laced with panic.

"Finlay. Attacked me. He's inside" she wailed.

He tried to release her. She gripped him, "No, don't leave me, please don't leave me."

"I've got you, I've got you", he soothed, keeping a grip of her waist as he placed her down. He switched on his phone torch and entered the house tugging her behind him. Her legs felt like jelly and she shook.

"Be careful" she said, swallowing the gorge rising in her throat.

He shone the beam into the living room and swept it around. Finlay had gone.

"He was just there," she gasped.

Gripping his hand tight, she followed him through the house. In the kitchen, the backdoor lay open and a cold draught blasted through.

"He's gone," he said.

Terror rose. "Don't leave me, please."

"I'll take you home." He wrapped her in his arms and she sobbed into his chest. "I'll deal with him later. He braced her shoulders and looked her over. "Are you okay, did he hurt you?"

She nodded. "He hit me, but I'm alright. I'll probably feel it later." She rubbed her cheek where he'd struck her.

Jamie hissed out his anger. "I'll bloody kill him."

Before they left, she grabbed the sheaf of papers from the bureau and stuffed them into her pocket. With an arm round her waist, he supported her as they walked back to their cottage with Meg whining at their feet. She explained what'd happened and how she'd fought to stop him from raping her, and Jamie became more and more furious.

Hazel and Simon ran towards them asking if they were alright after hearing the commotion, and they told them what'd happened. Jamie asked Hazel if she could stay with Kathryn while he searched for Finlay. She agreed and Simon offered to let Marcus know and help with the search, and darted off towards Hourn House.

Back in the warmth of their cottage, Jamie held her. Nuzzling into her hair, he whispered "Stay here, I won't be long."

She gazed up at him through wet lashes. "Let the police deal with him. I don't want you getting in trouble for something he did."

He fixed her with his piercing blue gaze. "No baby, I need to do this." Dipping his head, he placed a tender kiss on her lips.

Taking her hand, he guided her to an armchair and sat her down. "God, you're so pale," he said, pulling a throw over her shoulders. The dog lay at her feet and Jamie ruffled her fur and said, "Look after her Meg."

She caught his hand. "Be careful. I don't know what I'd do if anything happened to you."

Squeezing her fingers, he whispered, "Likewise."

Kathryn and Hazel watched as he retrieved his rifle from the gun store in the pantry and filled his pockets with rounds of bullets and cable ties. Swinging the gun over his shoulder, he said, "Lock the door behind me."

After he'd gone, Hazel offered to make tea and filled the kettle.

Kathryn stood shakily. "I'm going to have a bath first."

She wanted to scrub every inch of her skin raw and erase all trace of Finlay.

Jamie

Jamie couldn't remember ever being so angry. He wanted to murder that wee fucker with his bare hands.

He jumped into the Defender and raced towards the big house where Simon, Marcus and his sons stood, all armed with rifles and wearing anxious expressions.

"Is Kathryn alright?" asked Marcus.

Jamie nodded. "Bit battered and shaken but she's okay. We need to find this bastard though."

Barking orders at Duncan and Angus, Marcus instructed them to search the house and grounds and warn each household. Then, turning to Simon and Jamie, he suggested they search the community hall and church.

Jamie said, "I'll drive out to the bothy in case he's headed there."

With a nod, they were gone and Jamie leapt into the Land Rover and took the road out of the valley. Rain sheeted against the windscreen and he'd to slow the vehicle to glimpse the tarmac. After about a mile, he saw a figure running up ahead, and he accelerated. The shape darted off the road and Jamie swung the car round, illuminating Finlay's wild expression in the headlights.

He stopped the car, grabbed the rifle and leapt out into the rainstorm. Taking aim, he fired a warning shot over Finlay's head, and it took every ounce of his self-control to miss. Finlay veered to his right but continued running, and Jamie shouted for him to stop and put another bullet into the ground by his feet. Finlay spun round to face him, his expression one of terror. Pointing the rifle at him, Jamie barked at him to walk towards the car with his hands raised. He complied, shielding his eyes from the glare of the headlights with one hand.

When he came near, Jamie yelled, "On the ground, face down, arms out at your sides. NOW!"

He kept the rifle trained on him as Finlay lowered himself to his knees.

Over the noise of the wind, Finlay shouted, "I fucked your wife so hard she screamed."

Teeth clenched, Jamie took a cable tie from his pocket and approached him.

Finlay sneered, "She's got a really tight cunt. Not so tight now."

Jamie slammed the butt of the rifle into his face and he fell back into an unconscious heap. Rolling him over, he secured his hands and feet with cable ties, then dragged him like an animal to the Land Rover. Lifting him under his arms, he bundled him into the back and shut the door, before flooring it back to Hourn House.

Spotting Marcus and Simon pacing outside, Jamie flashed the headlights and pulled the vehicle to a screeching halt. He leapt out and shouted that he'd Finlay in the back.

Angus and Duncan appeared and Marcus told them to take Finlay to the estate office. Marcus unlocked the office door and flicked on the lights, and the brothers dragged Finlay into the middle of the floor and laid him out on the carpet. He was beginning to come round and he moaned. As Jamie searched his pockets for weapons, he opened his eyes and looked around.

Focusing on Marcus, he wailed, "Help me, he tried to shoot me."

"You attacked his wife," yelled Marcus.

"No, you've got it wrong, she wanted it, begged me for it."

Jamie grabbed Finlay's jacket under his throat and punched him in the face. He fell back groaning, as Angus and Duncan pulled Jamie off him.

"Enough" shouted Marcus looming over Finlay.

Finlay said, "You've got to believe me, she only cried rape when her husband showed up."

"What were you doing in Jean's cottage and why the hell did you disappear?"

Finlay shot a look at Jamie and said, "He and Buchanan want to pin Jean's death on someone. I wasn't going to stick around and take the blame. I've been sleeping in the cottage. Mrs Campbell knew I was there and it's not the first time she's come to me looking for sex."

Everyone turned to look at Jamie who shouted, "You don't honestly believe him do you? He attacked her. Call Buchanan."

"Calm down Jamie", snapped Marcus, "we've only her word for it."

"WHAT?" roared Jamie, "you honestly think she'd lie about that? I saw the state of her."

Angus muttered, "Aye well, she wouldn't be the first woman to make up such a story. What was she doing alone with him in Jean's cottage at this time of night?"

"She wanted me to fuck her, wanted it rough," said Finlay, his voice laced with desperation.

Duncan tutted his disapproval.

Jamie flailed against Angus' grip and snarled, "I'm gonna fuckin' kill you."

"Enough" yelled Marcus, "whatever the story is, we can sort this out amongst ourselves. The last thing we need is another police investigation before Elijah's visit."

"No way," shouted Jamie, "he tried to rape her. I'm calling the police. He's not getting away with this, and he's got some explaining to do about why he's been hiding from Buchanan since Jean's death."

"Now now, there's no need to get the police involved" said Marcus raising his hands placatingly.

Jamie shouted, "Not an option, either you call them or I will."

Marcus exhaled a long breath and looked at Jamie then at Finlay. "Fine" he conceded, "but Buchanan won't reach us now til tomorrow."

"Then lock him up until then," snapped Jamie. "No way can he be let loose to attack another woman."

Marcus nodded then turned to Angus and Duncan. "Put him in the store cupboard next to the cellar. I'll call Buchanan."

Angus let Jamie go and helped Duncan heave Finlay onto his feet.

Jamie fixed Finlay with the full force of his glare and hissed, "If I see you again, I will shoot you."

~

Kathryn

Kathryn lay in bed trying to get warm. Hazel had brought her a mug of tea and a hot water bottle but she couldn't stop shaking, despite wearing her warmest pyjamas and a sweater. Shivering beneath the duvet, she looked up at the ceiling and thought about what'd happened.

Replaying the assault over in her head, she couldn't believe she'd managed to fight him off. And fought she had; she'd the cuts and bruises to show for it. She hadn't frozen as she'd feared, and she'd managed to defend herself. With sudden clarity, she realised that she'd let her stepfather blight her life, and almost rob her of a real chance of happiness with Jamie. No longer would she let that happen. Her worst nightmare had almost happened and she'd conquered it, so now there was nothing to fear except fear itself. If she could defeat Finlay, she could defeat anything ... including her fear of intercourse. Their failed attempt earlier paled into insignificance in light of the attempted rape. She knew something had changed, something had shifted, as if her world had tilted back onto its proper axis. She wanted Jamie, yearned for him, and desire flared within her.

She heard him return, chat briefly with Hazel, and lock the door after she'd left. He popped his head round the bedroom door, then perched beside her.

Stroking the unbruised side of her face, he said, "Wasn't sure if you'd still be awake."

Sitting up, she asked, "Did you get him? Please tell me you didn't kill him."

"I found him and he's locked up in the big house until the police get here. Once he's in custody, his real identity will be known."

After quizzing him about the details, she flopped back on the pillows. She'd stopped shaking and felt warmer. Taking his hand, she looked up at him through her lashes. "Are you coming to bed? I want to talk about earlier."

When he went to say something, she covered his mouth with her finger. "Please come to bed. I need you to hold me."

He brought her hand to his lips and kissed it. "That I can do."

A few minutes later, he crawled in beside her wearing boxer shorts and a t-shirt, and smelling of toothpaste and deodorant. He wrapped her in his arms and she snuggled into his chest, facing him.

He gazed down at her. "Kathryn, I couldn't bear it if anything happened to you. Tonight's put everything into perspective."

"For me too Jamie. I overreacted earlier."

"Forget about earlier, there's nothing you and I can't fix together in time so let's not rush it."

She held his gaze. "I want to fix it. Right now."

Jamie swallowed. "Baby, you're still in shock and you're hurt—"

"—I'm fine … and I want you." She glided her hand down his body.

He exhaled a long slow breath and stared at her for what seemed like an age as if trying to decide what to do. "You've been through a lot tonight. I can wait."

"I can't." She slipped her hand inside his boxers.

His breath snagged as he dipped his head and brushed his lips against hers. Her heart raced as he kissed her. Tasting toothpaste mingled with Jamie, she felt the strength of his arms around her as he pulled her into his protective embrace. Her head swam as his soft lips coaxed hers apart and he touched his tongue to hers. Then the kiss deepened and exploded way beyond anything their mouths alone could satisfy.

They stripped off quickly, and he covered her with his body, taking his weight on his arms, and kissed her hungrily. Breaking from the kiss, she heard herself beg him.

"Easy tiger", he chuckled.

There was a loud knocking at the front door and Meg began barking. More thumping, then the sound of someone trying the door handle and a shout from outside "Jamie? Jamie, you in there?"

It was Angus. They froze and stared at one another.

"FUUUCKKKKK", he hissed. With a quick kiss, he rolled off her and yelled "Aye, I'll be down in a minute."

Cursing, he wrestled himself back into his underwear. When he'd finished dressing, he leaned down, cupped the unbruised side of her face and kissed her. "To be continued", he mumbled.

She reached for him, not wanting the kiss to end.

Taking her hand, he asked, "Will you be okay here?"

She nodded.

"Lock the door."

After he'd gone, she flopped back onto the pillows and let out a groan of sheer frustration.

Jamie

"Finlay's escaped," said Angus.

Jamie roared, "How the fuck did he get out?"

Angus explained that he'd gone to check on him before turning in for bed only to find the store cupboard door open and Finlay gone. He'd alerted Marcus and Duncan and they'd begun a search but there was no sign of him. They were telling everyone to be on the lookout but they needed help to widen the search.

As they approached Hourn House on foot, Jamie noticed a small party of men gathered outside armed with rifles, and he realised he'd left his own in the back of the Defender.

Marcus greeted him, his hands outstretched, "Don't even ask me how he got out."

Jamie glared at him. "If he attacks someone else, this will be on you."

Marcus turned to the men and shouted orders at them, sending small groups to different parts of the community and surrounding area. After the men had dispersed, Jamie turned to him and said, "I'll head out towards Inverie. My guess is he'll try and catch the first ferry out. Have you notified the police?"

Marcus nodded. "Aye, and take Angus with you."

With a look at Angus, Jamie said, "I'll drive. Wait here."

Jamie sprinted back to the cottage to fetch the Land Rover, and knocked on the door calling for Kathryn to open up. When she appeared, he led her upstairs to the bedroom, put the radio on low and explained to her what was going on.

He said, "Finlay was locked in the store next to the cellar. Can you check the camera feed to see if he's on it?"

Putting her arms around his waist, she nodded. "Please be careful."

He pressed his lips to hers and then rasped, "I'll be as quick as I can."

Reluctantly, he let her go, making her promise to lock the door behind him. He drove over to the big house and collected Angus and they headed out of the valley.

Angus was silent on the journey, his eyes scanning the landscape. The rain had eased off and Jamie was able to see the road better than he had earlier. Half a mile out of the valley, they spotted vehicle lights ahead. Duncan's pickup was parked in a passing place and he was standing at the front of the truck in the glare of the headlamps. Jamie pulled up behind him and he and Angus jumped out and joined Duncan at the front of the vehicle.

Duncan pointed. "He's over there."

Jamie peered into the pool of light cast by the headlights to see a dark shape slumped in the heather. It was Finlay's body, one side of his head blown clean off.

Jamie sat in the kitchen at Hourn House with a mug of tea in his hand, glaring at Duncan.

Angus had agreed to remain in the pickup, close to the body until the police arrived, while Duncan and Jamie returned to the big house to tell Marcus and the others. After the search was called off and the men had returned to their families, they'd gone to the kitchen to warm up next to the Aga.

Jamie had taken photographs with his phone of the body and surrounding area for the police, and he examined them, certain Finlay's injuries were the result of being shot from a few metres away with a rifle.

Marcus sat with his head in his hands. "What a dreadful business. Finlay was no angel but he didn't deserve this. Why would anyone kill him?"

They all turned and looked at Jamie.

"Don't look at me. I'd nothing to do with this."

Duncan muttered, "Last thing you said to Finlay was you'd shoot him, and it's not the first body since you showed up."

Jamie snarled. "Who the fuck let him out? That door's not been forced and his hands and feet weren't bound when he was found."

His question was met with silence. Jamie had had enough and announced he was off to bed. "Let me know when the police arrive," he said, stalking from the kitchen.

Duncan called, "I'm sure you'll be the first person they'll want to speak to."

It was after 4 a.m. by the time Jamie returned to Witsend cottage and woke a sleepy Kathryn. She threw her arms around his neck and he kissed her.

"Come to bed and tell me what's happened," she mumbled.

She tugged him upstairs and he stripped off and climbed in beside her, snuggling into her warmth. While the radio played softly in the background, he told her what'd occurred and the fact Duncan was pointing the finger at him.

She said, "I checked the camera and it was Ruth and Duncan who let Finlay out, the same two who spend hours each day in the cellar."

Jamie's brow furrowed. "Ruth? Why the hell would she let him out? The others I can understand; they believed Finlay's side of the story."

She gawped at him, "WHAT? Did Finlay say I wanted to have sex with him?"

Jamie nodded. "Sorry, I didn't want to tell you. This place ... these people ... it's really fucked up."

"And the invoice in Jean's bureau is for a huge order to bottle the St Januarius wine. I've no idea why they want so much of it though." When Jamie shook his head, she added, "So, what happens now? We can't use the camera footage."

"We wait on the police. Buchanan will be here in the morning then I expect a team will arrive." He stroked her cheek. "It's gonnae get really hard from now on in Kathryn. Duncan wants me out of the way so he can have you, and Marcus wants the whole thing done and dusted before Elijah arrives, so we're gonnae feel the heat. Are you gonnae be okay?"

She bit her bottom lip and nodded. "As long as I'm with you, I'll be fine."

"We cannae reveal who we really are, no matter what happens. It's not how MI5 work; they'll want a clean and tidy extraction without ever revealing they planted operatives into a religious community. If it all goes to rat shit, contact Keith and let him handle it. I don't want you flying solo if you're here on your own."

"You think I will be?"

"The police will want to question me for sure, so promise me you won't take any chances. As long as I know you're safe, I won't care what they do to me."

"Promise." She kissed him then whispered, "You look exhausted."

He chuckled, "I am, but as soon as I've had a kip, I'm going to wake you so we can pick up exactly where we left off earlier."

He kissed her then tucked her in the crook of his arm and fell asleep dreaming about what they were going to do.

Jamie awoke with a start. Someone was thumping on the front door and Meg was barking. He sat up and stared blearily at the clock; it was just after seven and he was knackered. Yawning, he rubbed his eyes and swung his legs out of bed. When Kathryn stirred, he told her to stay in bed, and he went downstairs to find Angus on the doorstep.

He looked as tired as Jamie felt and he'd the beginnings of a black eye.

"Police are here, you're wanted at the big house."

"Tell them I'll be there in ten minutes."

As he went to close the door, Angus put a meaty hand to it and said, "I know you'd nothing to do with this. Finlay was a bad 'un and got his comeuppance, but not everyone sees it like that, so just watch yourself."

Jamie nodded, "Uhm … okay … thanks Angus."

Angus turned and went, and Jamie closed the door wondering what the hell that was about. Kathryn appeared and he told her what he'd said.

She asked, "Who gave him the black eye?"

Jamie shrugged. "No idea but I'm off to find out."

After getting dressed, he came downstairs and she handed him a mug of tea and two slices of toast which he wolved down. Before leaving, he snagged his arm around her and pulled her outside for a kiss.

In a low voice, she told him that she'd examined the invoices from Jean's bureau and many were for wine bottlers and distributors which Hart Biotech had acquired. They agreed it was an odd portfolio for a biotech company.

He whispered, "While I'm gone, stash your art case somewhere safe. Any problems, call Keith."

She nodded that she'd understood, and with a last kiss he was gone.

Buchanan had arrived with another officer, a young police constable called Laura McKenzie and they'd taken up residence in Jamie's office, so it was with some annoyance that Jamie found Buchanan in his chair. Folding his arms, Jamie sat opposite him while McKenzie paced.

Without preamble, Buchanan leaned over the desk and got straight to the point. "So, here we are again Mr Campbell. Another body, and no doubt about the cause of death with this one."

"I told you you'd a gunman on the loose."

"And I believe your last words to the victim were you were going to shoot him?"

"If I'd shot him, it would've been with a clean kill to the heart."

Buchanan glared at him. "Where's your rifle Mr Campbell?"

"In the Land Rover."

Buchanan nodded at McKenzie who disappeared from the room. Sighing loudly, he pulled out his notebook and pen and said, "Right, starting from Sunday evening, tell me what happened."

Jamie exhaled a breath. It was gonnae be a long afternoon.

After an hour of going over what happened, Buchanan repeated the same question, "Why didn't you go straight home on Sunday evening after Finlay was locked in the storeroom?"

He sighed. "As I've already told you, I went to Jean's cottage to look through Finlay's things. He'd been sleeping rough and I wanted to see if he'd a gun since someone tried to shoot me."

Buchanan arched a brow. "You expect me to believe that after your wife had supposedly been attacked?"

"There's no supposedly about it. He tried to rape her but she fought him off." *You'll need to try harder than that to rile me mate, I do this for a living.*

"Why was she alone in Jean's cottage at that time of night?"

"She was walking the dog and heard a noise." *You twat.*

Buchanan got up and paced. "I don't buy it." He loomed over Jamie and said, "Here's what I think. You and Kathryn argued, and she went to meet Finlay for sex and it wasn't the first time either from what I understand. You discovered them, and there was a fight with Finlay. Then you hit your wife and dragged her home. You later went back for Finlay, took him onto the moor and shot him as you'd threatened to do."

Jamie took a deep breath and said calmly, "No, that's not what happened." *But it's probably the conclusion I'd have come to if faced with a similar case.*

He explained it all again.

After more questioning, there was a tap on the door and a man and a woman entered, both dressed in dark suits. They introduced themselves as Detectives Gail Martin and Will Robertson, part of MIT, the Murder Investigation Team based in Inverness. After explaining that they were there to question him, Detective Martin cautioned him.

Jamie suppressed a sigh. Things were getting interesting and he wondered how Kathryn was bearing up. Despite his current situation, he couldn't stop thinking about last night and how close they'd come to finally having sex. Only the thought of it kept him going through the next few hours as Martin and Robertson rolled up their sleeves, cracked their knuckles and got started.

Martin disappeared for half an hour and when she returned it was after three o'clock. She finally got round to what Jamie had been expecting, and explained he was being detained on suspicion of murder and she cautioned him again.

Took you long enough. If I wasn't going to miss Kathryn, I'd enjoy this …

Robertson secured his hands in front of him and led him out to the waiting police car. As he walked across the gravel towards the vehicle, he spotted Duncan who sent him a sly grin.

Bastard.

Kathryn

After Jamie had left that morning, Kathryn collected her art case and took Meg for a walk. It was a cold, crisp, sunny day, and she followed the path from the loch to the start of the foothills and climbed until she could see over the valley. From her vantage point, she spotted Buchanan's Volvo parked outside the big house, along with another she didn't recognise. She pulled out the satellite phone and called Keith with an update.

Wanting to observe what was going on at the house, she retrieved her sketch pad and began to draw while Meg sniffed around. Despite the luminous tranquillity, she couldn't shake off her anxiety about what was going on below, despite Keith's calm assurances. She noticed another black Volvo weave its way into the valley, park beside Buchanan's, and two figures emerge and enter Hourn House.

After an hour, she was cold and packed up her things. She searched the rocks and heather to find a hole large enough in which to conceal the art case. She'd spent time that morning on her laptop backing-up her files onto a USB stick which she concealed in a pocket sewn into the lining of her jacket. Rachael's stitching lessons had come in handy. After stowing the art case and marking its position with rocks, she whistled for Meg and picked her way back down.

As she walked along the edge of the loch, Duncan appeared and greeted her with a shy smile. His gaze swept over her and Meg growled at him.

She crossed her arms. "What's happening at the house?"

"More police have arrived with a scene of crime team."

"Are they still questioning Jamie?"

He nodded. "I'll walk back with you." Then he hesitated and looked at her, his eyes brushing over her. "Uhm .. I just wanted to say that, no matter what happens, you don't have to face this on your own."

She forced her lips into a smile. "Err … okay … thank you Duncan."

He nodded, shoved his hands into his pockets and they walked towards the big house in silence. When they passed Whitsun cottage, she put Meg inside. Buchanan was outside Hourn House with another officer and, as she and Duncan approached, they shot her a hard glare and the sergeant muttered something to his colleague who disappeared inside the house.

Shortly afterwards, the main door opened and a woman appeared with Buchanan's younger colleague. The woman approached Kathryn and asked, "Mrs Campbell, can you come with me please." It wasn't a question.

She led Kathryn to the administration office at the back of the house and questioned her about the previous evening. She knew it was to corroborate Jamie's story, and she was as truthful and helpful as possible, even offering to let them search their cottage. Kathryn was indignant at the suggestion she'd met Finlay willingly or had previous dalliances with him, and furious when Detective Martin implied Jamie had hit her. She cried genuine tears at the thought of what he was enduring, and of being without him. Sticking to her identity and backstory was challenging under the pressure and she was grateful to Keith for being such a bastard during training. She'd be sure to tell him, knowing how much it'd amuse him.

After the detective released her, Kathryn made her way to the front of Hourn House where Duncan and the others were still waiting. She felt her face burn with shame as everyone stared at her. She turned when she heard the main door open and Detective Martin and her colleague appeared, leading Jamie across the driveway in handcuffs. Jamie sent a killer glare to Duncan then spotting her, he gave her a rueful smile and mouthed "okay."

She called his name and made to run towards him, but Duncan grabbed her arms and pulled her into his. She covered her mouth and her eyes filled with tears as Jamie was ushered into one of the cars and it pulled away.

When the car disappeared from sight, Kathryn ran towards the cottage. As she approached, she heard Meg's frenetic barking. She called to the dog who came bounding towards her. An officer stationed at the door prevented her from entering and she could only stand and watch as police and scene of crime officers came and went. It reminded her of her own arrest.

Hazel appeared and put a gentle hand on her arm. "Kathryn, come to ours this evening."

Her sympathy was too much and Kathryn burst into tears. "He's innocent Hazel."

Hazel wound her arms around her. "I know and they'll soon realise it too, but until then, come stay with us. Meg too." They glanced over to see Duncan walking towards them and Hazel whispered, "You shouldn't be here on your own."

Wiping her tears, Kathryn nodded. "Thank you, I just need some head space then I'll be over." Casting an eye at the cottage, she added, "Hopefully, they'll let me bring my toothbrush."

Hazel smiled and told her she'd expect her soon.

As Duncan approached, she pulled a face only Kathryn could see and in a low voice said, "Didn't take him long," before she walked away. Hazel and Duncan exchanged a brief nod, then Duncan sidled up to Kathryn, and cast a hungry gaze over her.

Tearing his eyes away, he said, "Uhm, is there anything I can do?"

With a tight smile, she shook her head and pulled Meg in the direction of the path, conscious of Duncan watching her every step.

It was almost dark by the time she found the art case and retrieved the satellite phone, and she was grateful for Meg's company. When she heard Keith's voice, it was as though the floodgates had opened and she wept as she explained what'd happened. Keith remained calm, reassuring her Jamie would be looked after, and he told her Julien had already arranged a solicitor who was on her way. He asked Kathryn to ensure she'd backups of the camera footage as it'd help prove Jamie's innocence later.

"Kathryn, he's one of ours, as are you, and we take care of our own. Jamie will be fine and you have my word he'll not face any charges. We'll have him out before you can say 'Duracell Bunny on Viagra'." When she sob-laughed, he said, "I'm more worried about you. D'you want me to extract you?"

"No, absolutely not. We're so close, and BALD EAGLE will be here soon."

"Okay, but if you feel unsafe at any point you call me, day or night, so keep the phone safe. Understood?"

"Yes." She hesitated before saying what she wanted to. "Uhm Keith … can you get a message to Jamie to let him know I'm okay and I'll be at Hazel's."

He chuckled. "Yes Mrs Campbell, I'll let your husband know as I'm sure he's every bit as worried about you." After a pause, he added, "Kathryn, just remember they're your targets, not your friends."

She wound up the call and after stowing the phone and the art case in the rocks, she whistled for Meg. As she made her way to Hazel's, she thought about Keith's parting words.

Hazel and Simon's cottage was similar in layout to their own but without Ruth's renovations so, in Kathryn's opinion, had bags more charm. Rich oak cladding lined the walls of the living-room, and the kitchen retained the original hand-built cabinets and white Belfast sink. The living room was filled with over-stuffed couches and several cats which eyed Meg nervously.

Hazel said, "Ruth's been wanting to modernise but so far we've resisted."

"Don't blame you, it's so cosy."

They sat around a small pine table in the kitchen with Meg lying at Kathryn's feet. Hazel had cooked stew, mashed potatoes and vegetables and the aroma made Kathryn's mouth water. When they were all sat, Simon said grace and then Hazel served while Simon topped up her wine glass.

Raising his glass, he said, "Here's to having Jamie back with us soon."

Kathryn smiled and said, "I'll drink to that."

He tutted, "It's ridiculous and just sheer laziness on the part of the police. Buchanan's an idiot, so let's hope that pair from Inverness know what they're doing."

Kathryn said, "So who do you think killed Finlay?"

Without hesitating, he said, "Duncan, without a doubt."

Hazel shushed him. "You can't go around making accusations like that Simon."

Ignoring her, Simon said, "I've known Angus and Duncan for years, we grew up together. I've never trusted Duncan and I don't trust him now. He's had episodes of mental illness over the years, but recently he's gotten worse. Angus on the other hand ... well, a nicer bloke you won't meet, although he's got his cross to bear." Kathryn noticed Hazel shoot him a warning glance, before he added, "But since Ruth joined the family and Vondell's been treating him ... well, Duncan's off his rocker."

Passing Kathryn a basket of homemade bread, Hazel said, "Ruth and Duncan are thick as thieves."

"But why shoot him? Why not just turn him over to the authorities like Jamie wanted to do?"

"When Finlay attacked you, that was a red rag," said Simon.

Hazel put a hand on Kathryn's wrist. "Duncan wants you and he'll stop at nothing to get you, including framing Jamie for Finlay's murder."

Kathryn gawked at them. "Me?"

Simon nodded. "Hazel's right and it's not the first time. He was obsessed with your predecessor, Karen Patterson. That's why they left. And then there was all that business at high school—" He trailed off when Hazel shot him another warning look.

"What happened at high school?" asked Kathryn.

Simon turned to Hazel. "She needs to know Hazel, needs to understand how unhinged Duncan is and the lengths Marcus will go to protect him." Then he turned to Kathryn and said, "There was a girl in fourth year with me and Angus. Mhairi was her name. Pretty little thing. Duncan was smitten with her, used to follow her around, turn up at her house, that kind of thing. Anyway, she went missing. There was a police investigation, went on for months but they never found her."

"And you think Duncan had something to do with her disappearance?"

"I'm sure of it. I mean he was fixated with her. But Marcus gave him an alibi and then suspicion fell on Angus. Of course, he'd nothing to do with it, but by then there was so much ill-feeling towards the family that Marcus moved them all here."

Hazel said, "We don't know what happened to Mhairi. She could have run away, it's not unusual at that age, but we've seen how obsessed Duncan can get, and he's desperate to find a wife. We reckon he's had you in his sights from the start so, while Jamie's away, you're best here with us."

"Can't Marcus rein him in?" asked Kathryn.

Simon scoffed, "Marcus might think he's head of the household but Ruth's the neck that turns the head, and turn him she does."

Later in Hazel's spare room, Kathryn pulled the covers over her and replayed the day's events over in her mind. Although exhausted, too many thoughts chased through her head to sleep. As the tension ratcheted up, she wondered if she was becoming paranoid. Then she dismissed her worries as justified, remembering the old adage, 'It isn't paranoia if they're really out to get you'.

She thought about Simon's insistence that Duncan had shot Finlay and was implicated in Mhairi's disappearance. Perhaps Simon was right. Or, if Finlay was the father of Bethany's child, could it have been her father who shot him? Angus had a motive too, if Finlay had been blackmailing him.

Gazing up at the ceiling, she thought of Jamie lying in a prison cell and wondered if he was thinking about her too. She missed him so much, not just his tender touches and kisses, but having him nearby. They hadn't spent a night apart since arriving in the community and she found his presence protective and reassuring. She didn't just want him; she needed him as she'd never needed anyone before. Before Knoydart, she'd carved a life for herself in which it was enough to be on her own, and she could pick and choose when to interact with people, preferring virtual contact in cyber space. But now? Things had changed, and she'd changed. How had that happened?

She knew the reason. She loved him.

Jamie

Wearing police-issued clothes, Jamie lay on the hard cot with the scratchy blanket they'd given him. God, he missed their saggy mattress and the feel of Kathryn next to him. He stifled a groan at the thought of what they could be doing and how close they'd come .... he'd give his right bollock to be back in bed with her.

He was worried about her though, especially after seeing Duncan with her. He was a sleekit bastard and you didn't need to be a cop to see it. He'd suspected Duncan of the killing, even before Kathryn told him of the video showing him freeing Finlay. He'd been told the police had proof it was Jamie's rifle that'd been used to kill Finlay. Duncan was even more cunning than he'd realised, since this was the perfect way to get rid of him and – in Duncan's twisted mind – pick up with

Kathryn. Jealousy gnawed at him, and he was surprised at the sheer, raw strength of his emotions. If that bastard as much as looked at his woman … What was he thinking, and what would Kathryn say if she could hear him refer to her as such? She'd turn his nut sack into a mitten. But she was his and his alone.

A drunken confession at Hogmanay wasn't enough; he needed to tell her how he felt. They'd yet to discuss the future and what would happen after Knoydart, and he wanted to, especially with everything coming to a rapid close. But first, he needed to get out of this cell and back to her.

Earlier, after they'd processed him at the police station in Inverness, he'd met his solicitor, a woman called Debra Alexander. He reckoned her to be late forties, maybe early fifties; it was hard to tell with attractive women. Slender with fine features and shoulder-length blonde hair, he'd bet his other bollock that Keith's eyes had popped out his head when she'd pitched up. She was sharp as a tack too, picking holes in everything MIT had on him. Still, she'd have her work cut out refuting the evidence stacked up against him.

Conscious of the fact their time as UCs was rapidly running out, he needed to be free to finish this job, for Kathryn's sake as much as anything else. The thought of her being returned to prison terrified him and he knew he'd do anything to prevent that happening. Christ, if it came to it, he'd break her out himself.

Jamie knew the police could only detain him for twelve hours and then they'd have to request six-hour extensions by applying to the Sheriff, and only up to a total of twenty four. The clock was ticking for them to gather enough evidence with which to charge him, and he hoped things were progressing further up the Security Service food chain to liberate him. He was also aware that when the police rushed through his fingerprint and DNA results, the report would be marked as blocked and the investigating officers would realise they'd stumbled onto something. Even if they applied to find out why, they'd not be told which would raise yet another red flag.

Needing to distract himself from his worries, he gazed up at the ceiling and pondered on the case. Events had happened so rapidly over the last few days, there'd been little time to consolidate what they'd gleaned recently, and there was something niggling in his mind that stubbornly remained out of reach.

He tried to remember everything he'd learned about Hart Biotech and the portfolio of companies Elijah had acquired. He thought about the community and their odd ideas, so out of kilter with modern society. What did Ruth gain from it? Had she married for love? Surely must have, to entice a smart wealthy woman with a successful career to live in what Keith called the 'back arse of nowhere' as the subordinate wife of a lay preacher. And why did she surround herself with people like Vondell and Finlay?

Who had tried to kill him on the moor and was it the same person who killed Finlay? He was certain Duncan had shot Finlay and he'd had the opportunity to switch the rifles to frame him for the crime. Was Angus also involved? He'd been paying off Finlay for something and he was now sporting a black eye. Still jangling after his arrest and with all these questions floating around his mind, he finally fell into a fitful sleep.

He awoke screaming from a night terror.

END OF DAYS

"And now these three remain: faith, hope, and love. But the greatest of these is love."

— *CORINTHIANS 13:13*

Kathryn

Next morning, after thanking Simon and Hazel for their hospitality, Kathryn returned to the cottage with Meg and tidied the worst of the mess left in the wake of the police search. She then retrieved her art case from its hiding place, intending to take it with her. She packed an overnight bag for her and Jamie then, with Meg beside her in the Land Rover, she drove to Inverie. When she disembarked the ferry at Mallaig, Keith was waiting on her and he pulled her in for a bear hug.

On the walk to his office, he told her he'd received a call on the satellite phone the previous evening about an hour after they'd talked, but the caller hadn't spoken or used an agreed call sign.

She gasped, "I didn't call you and I left my case with the phone in it hidden up in the hills."

"Someone found it and used the phone. We'll examine the call history but it was definitely your number. Have you checked your laptop?"

"Not yet but I doubt they'll have cracked it. I layered the security on it. If you get past the first password challenge, it looks like I just use it for Facebook and email. Even the wallpaper's all puppies and kittens."

He guffawed. "Surely it should be bunnies. So, you don't think it's been compromised?"

"Doubt it. They'd need to know what they were doing to crack the encryption and it'd take time. The police couldn't even do it..." She shot him a contrite look.

Shaking his head indulgently, he chuckled, "Aye, I get why he's smitten with you." He unlocked the office and switched the kettle on. "Better make yourself comfy Mrs Campbell as we might be here awhile before they release your husband. Let's just hope the delectable Debra has him out soon."

Several hours later, Jamie left the police station in Inverness. Kathryn launched herself into his arms and he pulled her in for a kiss that left her reeling.

"I've missed you so much," she gasped.

Laughing, he whirled her around. "I missed you too baby. But I'm here now."

He introduced her to his solicitor, Debra, who'd followed him out. Smiling nervously, given their public and passionate reunion, Kathryn thanked her and shook her hand.

Debra smiled. "Don't worry, legal professional privilege prevents me from saying anything."

And to prove the point, Jamie kissed her again.

Kathryn led him over to where Keith was parked and they climbed into the back of the car, while Debra got in beside Keith. Meg dived onto Jamie's lap and licked his face making them laugh, and he'd a battle to get her to settle back in the footwell. Keith gave them a wry smile in the rear-view mirror and asked how he was. The journey back took over two hours and Jamie soon dozed off, only wakening when Keith pulled up in front of Debra's hotel in Mallaig. Yawning, Jamie thanked her, and she wished him luck.

"I'll be here for a few days," Debra said, "just in case."

While Keith walked Debra into the lobby, Jamie kissed Kathryn with an intensity that left them panting for air. When Keith returned, they sprang apart grinning at one another. Keith drove a few miles south to Morar where he was renting a cottage, and he suggested they spend the night there so they could liaise with the rest of the team before returning to the community the following day. Jamie asked him why he'd moved from Mallaig to Morar.

"Mallaig's ball deep in police, SOCOs, lawyers and special forces at the moment. You can't walk along the street without bumping into one. There's an SAS unit training in the hills, I recognised their CO. Then when I saw the silver sands, I had to be there. Wait til you see the place."

Jamie asked, "SAS? Is that a coincidence?"

Keith caught his eye in the mirror, "Nothing Julien does is a coincidence. He's very resourceful."

She and Jamie swapped a worried glance.

When they arrived in Morar, Keith pulled up in front of a traditional white cottage with a breath-taking view over a spectacular white sandy beach.

"Wow" said Kathryn, "I see why you like it."

"Aye it's stunning. Right, why don't you two love birds take the dog a walk while I put the kettle on."

They left Keith and walked hand-in-hand along the beach, and Jamie threw a stick for Meg. When they were out of sight of the cottage, he wrapped his arms around her and kissed her long and deep.

"I was so worried about you," he said, "and I cannae sleep without you next to me."

"Me too, I've thought about you the whole time."

"I wish we'd gone back to Knoydart, I wanted you to myself tonight."

Heart thumping at the prospect, she whispered, "Soon."

~

While Jamie showered and changed into the clothes she'd brought, she showed Keith the camera footage of Ruth and Duncan freeing Finlay from the store room. After encrypting and sending her data to Fitz, they waited for Jamie to reappear.

Kathryn looked around the cottage, spotting a small conservatory off the living room. Peering in, she spotted a half-finished canvas depicting the silver sands. She asked Keith if he'd painted it and he confirmed he had, dismissing it as a hobby to pass the time.

"It's really good, you've quite a talent."

"Thank you. And have you made use of your own materials?"

She laughed, "Yes, but I'm no where near as good as you."

Keith glanced towards the beach and said, "Maybe when this is over, we'll go paint together."

She smiled. "I'd like that."

Jamie joined them, clean shaven, hair damp and swept back. Her heart leapt as she feasted her eyes on his features. She wanted to reach out and touch him, and he gave her a look that said he wanted to do the same. She slipped her hand into his as they joined Keith at the kitchen table. After making coffee, Keith got his laptop and conferenced in Julien, Fitz and Pia.

Without preamble, Julien growled, "This is a complete shit show, and it's the first time we've had to deal with a UC facing a murder charge."

Keith interrupted him. "He was framed Julien, most likely by Duncan who we suspect killed Finlay."

"We need to extract you both, there's no way you can continue."

Kathryn and Jamie both shouted, "No way."

"It's far too dangerous," said Julien, "Need I mention there's a gunman on the loose? And you've no idea the strings we had to pull to free you Jamie, and the flack we're taking for stalling a murder investigation. And until the real killer is caught, the community won't trust you."

Jamie said, "You cannae extract us at this late stage. BALD EAGLE and the delegates will have arrived today and we'll use the seminar as cover to get into the server room. Kathryn reckons she can crack the biometrics."

"We can't risk it," insisted Julien.

Kathryn said, "Julien, please don't remove us. We both know the risks and we'll look out for each other, and we still have the support and trust of some members. We all know there's something much bigger at play here than tax fraud but until we get into that room, we'll never find out what it is."

Jamie added, "One week, that's all we're asking, then you can extract us."

There was a long pause on the other end during which time Keith, Jamie and Kathryn exchanged a look. Then Julien snapped, "One week, then you're out."

They gave a collective exhalation.

The next hour was spent discussing strategy for the remaining time. Kathryn outlined her plans for cracking the biometric keypad, but Fitz had come up with an alternative solution after contacting a technical author who worked for the keypad's manufacturer. She'd furnished them with codes their third-line engineers used to bypass security, and Fitz emailed Kathryn the details.

"It's convoluted" he said, "but we tested it and it works."

After Pia counselled them on coping with anxiety and feelings of paranoia, she repeated her warning about not antagonising Duncan whom she described as unstable. "There's no knowing what state he's in if he's not taking the right medication to control the psychosis. If he's delusional, his mind will be capable of creating an entire world that allows him to deal with the things he would otherwise be unable to bear."

Keith muted them and said, "Heed that warning, do not antagonise him." They nodded.

Pia continued, "And he's not the only one you need to watch out for. From what I've seen and what you've told me, GREY SQUIRREL's a seasoned manipulator who surrounds herself with people who are beholden to her, and she exploits their weaknesses to control them. You can see this behaviour with Finlay, Vondell and her own family. Manipulators have no boundaries and will stop at nothing to get what they want, so be on your guard with her too. And, speaking of Vondell, there's something else that may be relevant. I came across a paper he wrote some months ago on conversion therapy."

Keith asked, "What's conversion therapy?"

"It's any form of treatment or psychotherapy intended to change a person's sexual orientation or gender identity. Vondell's paper outlines his experiments with drugs and psychological treatments to change male homosexuals to heterosexuals. And guess which company are sponsoring the research and manufacturing the drugs?" She paused for effect. "You guessed it, Hart Biotech."

Jamie shook his head. "They're all whacko."

Julien revealed that no prints had been found on the litter from the bothy. Then the discussion moved onto their extraction, which he wanted handled as cleanly as possible, using the prepared script that Kathryn's mother was ill and they had to leave.

After the call finished, Keith got to his feet and rubbed his hands together. "Right, now that's all sorted, I'm off out." When they threw him a curious look, he grinned from ear to ear, "I've a dinner date with the delightful Debra. I don't expect I'll be back before midnight, but I'm sure you two bunnies will find a way to amuse yourselves while I'm gone."

Kathryn felt a delicious clench in her core as she and Jamie gazed at one another. This is it, she thought. While Keith showered and dressed, Kathryn cooked pasta and fed the dog, barely able to focus with her thoughts full of how they'd spend the evening. Jamie appeared to be in a similar dazed state and when he dropped a plate, they exchanged a wry smile. They'd just finished eating when Keith reappeared, smartly dressed, coiffured and smelling of cologne. Snagging his car keys, he wished them a pleasant evening and, with a cheeky wink at Jamie, headed out the door.

The car was barely out the drive when Jamie scooped her up and carried her to the bedroom, making her squeal with laughter. Setting her down next to the bed, he kissed her and she melted into his embrace.

He whispered, "You sure about this?"

"I want to experience everything with you Jamie."

He grinned, his eyes sparkling. "In that case ..." He kissed her so hard she felt her legs might buckle.

Between kisses, they undressed one another until they were down to their underwear.

He gazed at her in wonder. "God, you're so beautiful."

She pulled him onto the bed and he rolled onto his back, flipping her onto his chest so she was facing him.

Laughing, he raised his hands in surrender, "I submit."

She giggled, "I like the sound of that."

And submit to her wishes, he did. Tenderly. Patiently. Skilfully.

Later, spent and breathless and with their bodies still joined, he buried his face in her neck and hair with a long sigh. She clung to him like a limpet whispering his name over and over.

He raised his head and smiled; his brow dotted with sweat. "You alright?" he asked.

Tears filled her eyes and she nodded.

He flashed her a look of concern. "You crying?"

She sniffed, "With joy Jamie. I never thought I'd ever experience this, any of it. I love you so much."

"I love you too baby."

"Can we do it again?" she giggled.

Laughing, he rubbed her nose with his own. "Absolutely, just give me a few minutes." Then he kissed her and wrapped her in his arms until he'd recovered enough strength to do it again.

And again.

Next morning, Keith drove them to Mallaig and they caught the ferry to Inverie and collected the Land Rover. As Jamie drove towards Glen Hourn, she thought about what they'd done for most of the night. He'd been so tender with his touch, unhurried in his attentions, and he'd taken every care to ensure she was relaxed and he was giving her pleasure. Wondering, how many women he'd been with to hone his skills so, she tried to shove her jealousy aside with the knowledge he was now with her. She sensed something had altered between them, and they'd grown even closer. Physically. Emotionally. Spiritually.

He darted a look at her and clasped her hand tighter. "You okay?"

She smiled and burrowed into his arm. "Yes, just nervous about what kind of reception we'll get."

He chuckled, "Hmm, pitchforks and a wicker man I expect. Anyway, who cares, it's only for a week."

She pondered on what might happen to them after the week was up. They'd been so focussed on the present, they'd yet to discuss the future and she wondered if he'd want to continue the relationship. Would he remain in London working for MI5 or return to being a cop in Glasgow? She'd follow him regardless; of that she was sure. If he'd have her. The mere idea of being without him terrified her and she knew she'd need to broach the subject soon. For now, she'd content herself with the thought they'd be back in their own cottage tonight.

They'd no sooner arrived than Ruth bustled in holding a casserole dish which she placed on the Aga. Jamie had been in the woodstore getting logs and he entered the kitchen carrying the basket, Meg at his heels. The dog snarled at Ruth and Kathryn shushed Meg, apologising for her behaviour.

Ruth said, "We're so glad to have you back amongst us. Hopefully we can put this dreadful business behind us and the police will focus on catching the real killer."

"Hopefully," said Jamie, his voice betraying his lack of conviction.

"Elijah's arrived and we were hoping you'd join us this evening for a welcome reception. He's going to make a special announcement."

Jamie turned to Kathryn and smiled. "We wouldn't miss it."

"Excellent. Oh and Marcus says not to bother with work today, there's too much going on over at the house as it is with the seminar." She cast a condemnatory eye around, "and it looks like you've some tidying up in here to do too."

After Ruth left, Kathryn unpacked and Jamie hunted the cottage for more cameras and listening devices. She later found him skimming through Paul Ehrlich's book *The Population Bomb* which Hazel had lent her. It was all about the devastating impact that growing human populations have on the environment. Jamie glanced up then tugged her by the hand into the woodstore. Bracing his hands on her shoulders, he fixed her with a searching gaze.

"Tonight's the night Moniker. You ready?"

She nodded as her stomach hit the floor.

As they entered the packed community hall, a deathly hush descended and everyone turned to stare. Jamie squeezed her hand and propelled her forwards, despite her feet wanting to go in the opposite direction. Her heart thumped in her chest as the community scrutinised them. Did everyone know who and what they really were?

Marcus approached, his hand outstretched, and boomed, "Welcome back Mr and Mrs Campbell, this truly is a celebration tonight."

Jamie shook his hand and Kathryn offered him an embarrassed smile, but she felt grateful to him as the normal hubbub resumed and others approached to greet them. Ruth appeared at his side, accompanied by a man as small and dumpy as herself, his hair in a ponytail. Ruth introduced him as Elijah Hart, her brother, and they shook hands. He'd a warm smile that reached his eyes and he offered polite platitudes about their current situation. Kathryn remembered her grandmother's words about never trusting a man with a ponytail and she wondered what she'd have made of Elijah. Charming and charismatic, he struck her as being every bit as manipulative as his sister.

"Dreadful business" he drawled, "just hope they catch the real culprit soon. Hard to believe such a thing could happen in such a beautiful place."

After chatting about Glen Hourn, Ruth ushered him off to meet others, and Jamie put his arm around Kathryn's waist and guided her to the buffet. Hazel gave them a hug and Simon shook Jamie's hand and fetched them each a drink.

Although glad to get their return to the community out of the way, Kathryn was anxious at the thought of what they needed to do later and only picked at the food. She caught Duncan watching her from a corner of the room. Stood on his own, a glass of what looked like whisky in his hand, his eyes swept over her. Jamie appeared to have noticed, and he wound a possessive arm around her waist, his gaze leaving her in no doubt he was staking his claim. Duncan stalked off towards the kitchens at the rear, wearing a thunderous expression.

Jamie whispered in her ear, "I don't care what Pia said, time's running out and we need to shake the tree."

When Hazel and the women began collecting plates and clearing the buffet, Kathryn offered to help and Jamie released her reluctantly. There was considerable excitement amongst the women at Elijah's presence and they giggled like school girls until Ruth entered the kitchen, when they immediately fell silent. She noticed Ruth didn't roll up her sleeves and help, choosing to direct others instead. Ruth surveyed the kitchen with a critical eye and asked for the bin to be emptied, and Kathryn offered, keen to ingratiate herself. Ruth disappeared and Kathryn tied up the bulging black refuse sack and lugged it to the fire exit at the back of the kitchens where the bins were stored.

The door was ajar and as she approached, she heard an altercation and froze. She recognised Duncan and Ruth's voices, and Duncan sounded furious.

He said, "I've told you what I want and I'm not doing another bloody thing until I get it."

"And you'll get it … but only after Elijah's left. He's already antsy. Any more scandal, suspicion or police and we'll lose him and everything we've worked for. Just a couple more days, and we'll deal with it."

Duncan sighed loudly. "You said that before and look how that turned out."

"This is different, she's different. Once Elijah's gone, I promise I'll help you remove the obstacle."

Kathryn began to backtrack slowly towards the kitchen as Duncan burst through the doors towards her. Smiling, she moved as if she were just approaching. His expression switched from angry to happy in a heartbeat, and he said softly, "Here, let me take that for you."

Reaching down, he lifted the bag, his hand brushing gently against hers. She met his gaze and its intention was clear. He wanted her. Knowing she was playing with fire but conscious they'd only a week left, she was eager to bring everything to a head. Letting her hand linger against Duncan's, she smiled sweetly and thanked him for his help. She saw him swallow hard as she held his gaze.

He said, "I'm glad you've come back to us."

With her hand still pressed against his, she whispered, "I'm glad to be back. I'm happy here and I never want to leave."

"Do you think you and Jamie will remain ... after what's happened?"

Casting her eyes down demurely, she said, "I do as my husband instructs."

His breath caught and she looked up to see desire flare in his eyes. After a pause, he said in a low voice, "We'll have to make sure you stay in that case."

With a shy smile, she returned to the kitchen and let out the breath she'd been holding in. When she entered the hall with the rest of the women, Elijah got up on stage to address the community, and a hush descended. After thanking Marcus and Ruth for hosting this year's Spiritual Seminar and complimenting the team on their hospitality, Elijah began:

"The theme of this year's seminar is stewardship," he said, his eyes searching the crowd till they found Jamie . "I've just had the pleasure of meeting the steward of Glen Hourn and his lovely wife who play such an important role in maintaining this land." Kathryn felt herself blush as everyone turned to stare.

Elijah raised his hands and proclaimed, "God created the world and he created man as its steward, giving him dominion over all things. As Christians, we have a moral obligation to look after it for Him, and all life on it. But with dominion comes responsibility. On this estate, that means making tough choices such as shooting sick animals, or thinning the herd to prevent starvation."

He paused for effect before continuing, his voice gaining in strength, "Similarly, for humans to live in harmony with nature, we need to make tough choices if we are to look after ourselves and the environment."

After a long pause, he continued more loudly. "Put simply, there are too many of us and our population is not sustainable. As a species, we're having a devastating effect on the planet in terms of climate change, and we face extinction unless we act. It's one of the reasons our church advocates birth control and why we run educational programs throughout the world."

He cast his eyes over his audience and boomed, "Let God guide us in this respect for when he created the world, he also created the means for his stewards to protect it. We have all the tools we require. God's own tools."

He let his words settle before adding, "Part of the solution is dialogue and I'd like our community to play its part in this discussion. It is for this reason I am delighted to announce we will be hosting our very first Global Day of Communion in April, when we will invite all Christian communities to share the body and blood of Christ and join us in doing God's work."

There was considerable applause as Elijah stepped down from the stage, and Ruth fawned over him. Marcus took his place and, after thanking him, he invited everyone to pick up an information pack about the Global Day of Communion. He also announced that because of severe weather warnings of a storm heading their way, sadly Elijah and the other delegates would be departing earlier than planned, together with Angus and Doctor Vondell who'd help coordinate the Global Day of Communion from the US.

Kathryn picked up an information pack and caught Angus's eye. He looked anything but pleased. After the applause faded, Marcus announced the bar was open and there was further clapping. Jamie squeezed Kathryn's fingers, the signal that it was time, and her pulse raced. They slipped out quietly and she waited out of sight while Jamie sprinted back to the cottage to collect her art case. A few minutes later, he reappeared and tugged her towards the back of Hourn House. Before entering, they hid at the back of the outbuildings while she checked the camera feed to see if anyone had recently entered the cellar. The recording showed Duncan leave almost two hours ago, but no activity since, and they moved swiftly to the entrance.

Jamie unlocked the door and flicked on the lights, locking it behind them. Heart thumping against her rib cage, Kathryn approached the keypad and retrieved the sheet of instructions Fitz had supplied. She followed the steps, her hands shaking as she pressed the keys. It didn't work. She tried again with the same result and cursed. Jamie hovered at her shoulder.

Squinting at the instructions, he pointed. "Is that a zero or an O?"

"Shit, you're right, how could I make such a picnic error?"

He raised a brow. "Picnic error?"

As she repeated the steps, she muttered, "Problem in chair, not in computer."

The keypad beeped and the door opened into a cavernous room almost as large as the wine cellar.

He switched on the lights to reveal what appeared to be a data centre.

The right-hand wall was lined floor to ceiling with server racks, while a long desk with a number of consoles sat on the left. The room had a suspended celling dotted with air conditioning grills and ducts, and the floor consisted of suspended metal grills. Jamie whistled.

She placed her art case on the desk and retrieved her laptop and cables and, after surveying the server rack, she connected it to one of the machines. While she worked, Jamie examined the room more closely. On the other side of the entry door was a bank of light switches for the cellar and server room, the keypad control unit and a small LCD screen showing a view of the cellar beyond.

He cursed, "Didn't realise there's a camera in the wine cellar. It's lucky we weren't discovered before."

As she monitored the progress of the file download, Jamie opened a door at the opposite end. The room beyond glowed.

"Fuck sake!" he gasped, "Come and see this."

The room was narrow, extending the width of the cellar, and the long back wall was tiled with monitors displaying audio-visual feeds from the cottages. Each screen was labelled with the property name, and in the top left they spotted Whitsun Cottage and a grainy view of their living room. A long desk with a console sat beneath the screens, and Kathryn slumped into the wheeled office chair before her legs gave way.

Gazing up at the monitors, she said, "They're watching everyone, not just us."

"Only the renovated cottages," said Jamie pointing, "Jean's isn't here and I don't see Simon and Hazel's."

She tapped the console and the screen displayed monitoring software which she used to switch the images of Whitsun Cottage between the living room, kitchen and office. They saw Meg asleep in her box next to the Aga. She toggled the images for other properties to show bedrooms and living spaces. Suddenly nauseous, she put a hand to her mouth.

"Jesus!" exclaimed Jamie, who was at the far end of the desk sifting through a pile of photographs.

She wheeled the chair over to him and he placed them in an array on the desk. Her face was on every one; images of her cooking, eating, reading, and an enlarged close-up of her smiling.

He slammed his palm on the desk making her jump. "Christ, he's obsessed with you." Then, seeing her startle, he dipped his head and kissed her. "Sorry, didn't mean to scare you but right now I want to rip his fuckin' head off."

After leaving the monitoring station exactly as they found it, she returned to her laptop to find the download had almost finished. Jamie walked to the door and peered at the screen.

"Shit! We've got company."

She ran to his side to see Angus approach. She held her breath as he hovered outside the door, his face filling the display. Jamie pressed himself against the side of the door, and removed a long Maglite torch from his pocket ready to wield as a baton.

She ran back to her laptop. The download had completed and she removed the cables and packed it into the art case, fumbling in her haste. With a quick glance around the room to ensure nothing was amiss, she nodded she was ready. Angus was still outside peering into the neighbouring fridge, then suddenly he spun round to speak to someone and Cameron appeared.

He approached Angus who looked upset and angled his head away. Kathryn was unable to hear what was being said, but Cameron seemed to be pleading with him, and he reached up and skimmed his fingers along Angus's jawline. The two men gazed at one another, then Angus cupped Cameron's face and brought his lips to his. As the kiss deepened, Kathryn shot Jamie an incredulous look.

He whispered, "Confirms my suspicions."

When they broke apart, she saw Cameron mouth "I love you" and Angus repeat his words. After talking for another few minutes and another tender kiss, Angus nodded his agreement and Cameron smiled. Then she watched as each took several bottles of champagne from the fridge and left.

Jamie and Kathryn exhaled and swapped a look of relief.

~

Jamie

They hurried back to the cottage, spurred on by adrenaline and elation, talking about what they'd witnessed.

Their visit had confirmed his hunch Angus was gay. He'd known Finlay must have had something over him in order to extort money, but until this evening he hadn't been certain. And, thanks to Kathryn, they now had the information they needed before their extraction. Elijah's speech had also triggered an idea about what the Colquhouns and Elijah Hart might be up to, but Jamie immediately dismissed it as ridiculous.

What worried him were the photographs. They'd been taken over several months, suggesting Duncan had been fixated on Kathryn from the start. Seeing them had sparked fury and jealousy in him, and he knew he'd have to work hard not to show his anger to Duncan. He shuddered to think what Duncan might be capable of, and how he might react if he learned she was a UC. She was so beautiful, inside and out, and so vulnerable that the thought of another man touching her made him seethe.

Back inside Whitsun cottage, his desire flared. She was his, only his, and he needed to possess her. He locked the door, placed the art case at his feet, and pulled her in for a dirty, erotic kiss. Grabbing her hair, he tilted her face up and kissed her long and deep, pinning her to the wall with his hips. Right now, he wanted her so bad nothing else fucking mattered.

Then he led her to the bedroom and showed her just how much he wanted her.

Later, while Kathryn reclined on the bed with her laptop sifting through the information she'd downloaded, Jamie took Meg a walk down to the shore. Fingers of mist crept down from the hills and into the valley, lending a profound quiet and eerie atmosphere to the glen.

As he skimmed stones into the water and watched them bounce along the surface, he thought about their lovemaking. It was beyond anything he'd quietly hoped for and he felt humbled by the fact she'd trusted him completely. She was so responsive to his touch and their coupling was imbued with an intensity that astounded him; he'd never experienced anything like it. Whatever this relationship was, it had transcended above and beyond the physical realm. He needed her like he needed the air he breathed. And the thought of losing her scared him witless.

Although he'd told her he loved her, he needed to make it clear he wanted a relationship so they could make plans for the future, and he berated himself for not having mentioned it before. Without the threat of prison looming over her, she'd be free to make choices but would she choose to stay with him? She'd never said as much, never hinted at it. He knew that working for Julien meant him moving to London, although he might find himself posted anywhere. Is that the kind of life she'd want? To be the partner of an absent MI5 officer?

Along with the mist, doubt rolled in.

He brought her a cup of tea and placed it on the nightstand.

"That's an odd choice of reading material" she said, indicating the book he held, the one by Ehrlich that Hazel had lent her. "It's all about the effects of the human population spiralling out of control."

"How you getting on?" he asked peering at her screen.

"It'll take me forever and a day to sift through this and there's no way I can risk sending it over the ether to Fitz. I've only scratched the surface but so far it looks like data modelling on infection rates and deaths, like the graphs and statistics we saw during the pandemic."

"Ruth's research?"

"Looks like she never stopped working for Hart Biotech."

He stretched out beside her and they sipped their tea.

Passing him the information pack, she said, "Elijah's going to spend a fair chunk of his fortune on this Global Day of Communion. Every church and religious organisation will receive a commemorative bible, wine and wafers to celebrate the communion. And for members unable to attend church, he's commissioned a miniature set for distribution to people's homes. It's a huge operation." She glanced over at him, "Do you think this explains the acquisitions and money trail?"

"Partly, but I've a hunch our unholy trinity are up to something else."

She laughed. "Unholy trinity?"

"Aye, Marcus, Ruth and Elijah."

He grabbed a pad of paper and a pencil from her art case and began scribbling. When she asked what he was doing, he said, "A crazy wall." She cocked a curious eyebrow. "D'you never watch police dramas where they have an incident board with all the clues?"

"You really use such a thing? Thought that was for telly."

"Telly's more accurate than you think. We use an incident board and a timeline board. For burglaries, you'd map times and locations to see connections, but for murder, it's more of a crazy wall showing everyone connected to the victim. Plus, we've got access to crime analysts and HOLMES to help us see links and keep track of everything."

"It's not difficult to hack HOLMES, let me know if you want access."

He laughed. "Oh God, why doesn't that surprise me. You crack me up Kathryn." He leant over and kissed her and they resumed their respective tasks in silence.

After several hours and gallons more tea, she rubbed her eyes and yawned as she looked up at their bedroom wall which Jamie had plastered with paper, post-its, pins and string. As she'd trawled the files, she'd given him snippets of information which he'd pinned to his crazy wall.

"You tired baby?"

She smiled. "I'm okay. How's the sleuthing going?"

Sitting beside her, he fixed her with his gaze and said, "I've a theory about what's going on. You'll probably think I'm batshit crazy but it's the only thing that makes any sense."

"I'm listening."

When he told her, she stared at him and said, "It's the craziest theory I've ever heard ... but if you're right ... oh God Jamie, if you're right, millions will die."

Nodding he said, "It'll be the end of days."

REVELATION

"Ask, and it shall be given to you; seek, and ye shall find; knock, and it shall be opened to you."

— *MATTHEW 7:7*

Jamie

Jamie said, "Prove me wrong. I'll go through it again and then you can tell me I'm mad."

She handed him a mug of coffee and a slice of cake. Outside their bedroom window the wind howled, rattling the panes. It was almost five in the morning and they'd been awake all-night sifting through information and formulating theories. He kept coming back to the same one.

Standing in front of his crazy wall, he pointed to Elijah's name. "So, we know Hart Biotech patented a way of storing live vaccines to distribute across the globe, and they've got previous for funnelling it to religious organisations. Ruth was an epidemiologist at the company and an expert in data modelling."

"And Beth Melton, the scientist, who was key to that patent was murdered," she added.

"We know the Ehrlich Society has a vast network of churches and they run vaccination and birth control programmes throughout the world, and that Elijah's been pumping money into this. Meanwhile, here in happy-clappy HQ, Duncan carries out surveillance on the members and he and Ruth spend hours in the cellar."

He took another bite of cake and smacked his lips with approval. "Before she died, Jean pointed us to the wine they'll use for the Global Day of Communion, St Januarius. It's a good name for communion wine … 'Blood of Christ' and all that. It's produced, bottled and distributed by companies owned by Hart Biotech. But Jean discovered something sinister between Hart Biotech and the Society, and that's the reason she was silenced. She didn't know the office was bugged, and I believe Duncan saw her when she went to collect the evidence, and he told Ruth. We can't know for sure but my guess is either Duncan or Finlay took her onto the moor and left her to die."

"Poor Jean," said Kathryn, "so she was murdered."

"Then there's Finlay, another of Ruth's pets whom she met in London. He appears in Knoydart not long after her mother-in-law is found dead in suspicious circumstances. He's wanted for a rape and assumes a new identity, presumably with Ruth's knowledge. So why bring a convicted rapist into the community? I think she offered him sanctuary in return for doing her dirty work, and I wouldn't be surprised if she had him murder her mother-in-law. The coroner's report hinted at foul play but there was insufficient evidence."

She asked, "Why would she have her mother-in-law killed?"

"God only knows," he said, turning back to the crazy wall. "Anyway, Finlay comes here to work, discovers Angus is gay and blackmails him. Angus pays to shut him up because if it was known he was homosexual, he'd be thrown to the lions. Maybe Duncan finds out or Marcus learns of it. Either way, Angus gets a beating and finds himself being sent to Florida, presumably for conversion therapy."

"I actually feel sorry for Angus," she said, "Lord knows what Vondell will do to him."

Jamie nodded. "Vondell is another of Ruth's pets and he's indebted to her for giving him the position here. He's heavily involved in the birth control and vaccination programs."

"And we know he's stopped Duncan's meds, meaning he's likely delusional again."

"When we pitch up, Duncan takes a shine to you and wants me out of the way. Duncan had the means, motive and opportunity to kill Finlay and, in doing so, protect his brother and get his paws on you." He sent her an apologetic smile, took a gulp of coffee and continued, "I reckon Duncan shot Finlay and framed me for it, and it was Duncan who tried to shoot me at the bothy because, in his mind, he believes he can have you for himself."

Pointing to a leaflet on the crazy wall, he continued, "Amidst all this, is the Global Day of Communion. Our unholy trinity are religious zealots and climate change evangelists and, in Marcus and Ruth's case, they both lost loved ones to Covid-19. We also know Ruth has been modelling the effects of a new pandemic."

Kathryn said, "For another SARS virus."

He turned to look at her. "I believe it's a pandemic based on a virus Hart Biotech have, and possibly already have a vaccine for, hence the dead scientist. They plan to distribute it using communion wine containing the live virus, targeting an elderly church-going population. That's why Elijah has had to acquire the infrastructure and supply chain to bottle and deliver the payload, and why they're involving their huge network of churches."

She nodded. "And as Ruth's modelling shows, by infecting hundreds of thousands on the same day, in every continent, it'll spread faster than Covid and kill many more millions before governments can react." Pointing to her laptop, she said, "I also found results for a clinical trial for a variant that's lethal to the over-seventies but without the debilitating long-Covid symptoms in the younger population. It looks like Vondell and Ruth have been testing this in parts of the developing world under the guise of a vaccination programme."

Jamie said, "This is the tool Elijah hinted at in his spiel about stewardship. To do God's work, they want a massive population cull of the old and weak. Less people means less pressure on the environment." He turned to look at her, "Please tell me I'm crazy."

"It's not you who's crazy, it's them. All of them."

Jamie looked out of the window and scrubbed a hand over his

unshaven face. "Storm's getting up. We've got what we came for and it's time to leave. I'll call Keith, I won't be long. Pack some essentials, we'll go right away before the road closes and the ferries stop."

Grabbing his jacket and the satellite phone, he whistled for Meg and stepped out into the howling gale. He pulled up his collar and hurried towards the loch. After a few metres, he took out the phone and dialled Keith. Meg began barking and growling and he turned to see what had her agitated.

A sharp crack of gunfire and he was thrown backwards with the force of the blast. He landed hard, knocking the wind out of him. He gulped for breath as the pain in his left shoulder hit him, and he clutched at it as he rolled on the ground in agony. Lifting his hand away, he found it drenched in blood, and he pressed on the wound to stem the bleeding, crying out with the pain. Through the gloom, a figure approached and he looked up to see Duncan looming over him with a rifle pointed at his head.

He felt himself dragged and lifted. Pain ripped through him and blackness crept in at the edges of his vision. Then the darkness claimed him.

His return to consciousness was accompanied by the sound of clanking chains and a dazzling white light. He opened his eyes, squinting against the glare, and tried to focus. He was on the floor of the game store, hands bound behind his back, the pain in his shoulder excruciating. Dizzy and nauseous, he felt like he'd been stabbed and the blade twisted and left in. Gasping for breath against the fabric covering his mouth, he twisted his head towards the sound to find Duncan standing over him, tying chains around his feet and lower legs.

Duncan stood and grabbed a length of chain attached to a pulley. As he hauled on it, Jamie felt his legs being lifted, then his hips and body. His torso rose, his head dangling inches from the floor, and he screamed in pain. Kicking and writhing in agony, he saw his blood dripping into a drainage channel cut into the stone floor.

Duncan crouched in front of him and gave a dark chuckle as they locked eyes. "Seems an apt end. In a couple of hours, you'll have bled out and I'll have married your wife. I wanted you to know that before you die."

Kicking, Jamie screamed into the gag as Duncan walked away. Blackness licked at the edges of his vision as the horror of his words registered.

Duncan plunged the game store into darkness as Jamie succumbed to blackness.

~

Kathryn

Kathryn dashed around the cottage throwing essentials into a bag. Her art case with the laptop was already packed and sitting by the front door. She snagged the photograph of her and Jamie at the Eiffel tower as a memento, deciding Paris would be their first holiday as a couple. As she popped a tin of dog food in the bag for Meg, she heard the crack of gunfire reverberate around the glen and she froze. Jamie had no rifle, the police had taken it, so she knew it wasn't his.

Her hand shot to her mouth and she cried his name.

Grabbing her hat and jacket, she stepped out into a storm. She ran along the edge of the shore calling for him. The sound died on her lips as the wind whisked it away and the inky black water, whipped up by the storm, crashed against the pebbles. It had begun to snow and large flakes clouded her vision.

With no sign of either Jamie or Meg, she paced frantically wondering where he could possibly be. She headed back towards the cottages in the hope she'd missed him and he was already home. As she stumbled over the gorse, Meg came bounding up to her and barked frenetically.

A meaty hand covered her mouth and muffled her scream, and she was lifted clean off her feet. She bucked and kicked as she was carried towards a light in the tree line. Meg snarled and barked at her feet, spinning in circles. Panic engulfed her and she felt faint as she gulped for breath against the fingers covering her mouth and nostrils.

A low voice said, "Hush Kathryn, I won't hurt you."

It was Duncan's voice and she squealed and writhed as he lugged her towards his house, its great glass panels illuminated above her. As he pulled her into the entrance, she kicked at the door which bounced back on its hinges.

"Enough now" said Duncan, hoisting her along the hall towards the rear.

He half-lifted, half dragged her into a small bedroom in which a large iron bedframe stood. Short lengths of blue rope hung from each of the posts. As he manhandled her onto the mattress, he pinned her with his weight until she was as helpless as a butterfly nailed to a board. He removed his hand from her mouth and she screamed and kicked. He stretched over, grabbed her wrist and secured it to the far post with the rope. As he tied her other hand, she dipped her head and bit him. Hard. He flinched and pulled away, then pinning her hips down, he secured her ankles until she was splayed out on the bed.

"You're a lively one," he chuckled.

Bucking and writhing, she swore at him as he loomed over her.

He gave her an indulgent smile. "Calm yourself Kathryn, I won't harm you." He perched beside her and stroked her face as she tried to bite him again. "In fact, I intend to take good care of you."

His calm tone and words terrified her, and she yelled, "What've you done with Jamie, where is he?"

"Forget Jamie, your future's with me now."

"Duncan, untie me right now and take me to Jamie!" Tears pooled in her eyes and she blinked them back.

Sifting his fingers through her hair, he said, "You said you were happy here and never wanted to leave. You can be happy here with me. I'm doing this for you; for us."

"Duncan, Jamie's my husband and I demand you take me to him, RIGHT NOW!"

"Jamie's dead Kathryn."

His words were like cold fire running down her spine. She screamed and thrashed. "No, you're lying, where is he, what have you done to him?"

He trailed his hand over her breast and down her outer thigh, making her writhe. "We'll be married and you'll stay here with me and bear my children. Once we're wed and I've put a baby inside you, then I'll untie you."

She began to sob, "I want Jamie. Take me to him."

He slid his hand beneath her skirt and up her inside leg as she tried to twist away. She jerked and screamed.

In a low voice, he said, "I won't touch you until we're married."

"Never going to happen, now get your fuckin' hands off me."

Duncan tutted. "You'll soon learn your place and how to behave properly when you're mine." He rubbed her through the fabric of her underwear and she cried. "It's all arranged Kathryn and in time you'll realise it's for the best." Then he stood and moved away, and she followed him helplessly with her eyes to see Simon in a chair in the corner of the room. Bound and gagged.

She and Simon locked eyes, swapping looks of terror as Duncan approached him. Bending down, he untied his gag and said, "You'll marry us now."

"I'll do nothing of the kind. This is lunacy. Untie both of us."

Duncan slammed a fist into his gut and Simon folded with a grunt. Duncan grabbed a handful of his hair and hissed, "Marry us preacher or I'll shoot you."

Shaking his head, Simon gasped out, "You'll have to kill me."

Duncan stood and grabbed his rifle which lent against the door jamb.

Kathryn screamed, "No, I'll do it, I'll do it, don't kill him." She turned to Simon and pleaded, "Just do it Simon, marry us." She shook her head beseechingly at Simon and mouthed "please."

"I can't Kathryn. I'm a man of God and I will not do this in His name."

Duncan slammed the butt of the rifle into Simon's jaw with a sickening thud and blood poured from his mouth.

He glared at Duncan and spat, "Do what you like but I won't marry you. You need a doctor not a priest."

Through her tears, Kathryn watched as Duncan raised his rifle and took aim at Simon. Unable to watch the unfolding horror, she closed her eyes and sent a prayer to God. A shot cracked through the air, making her ears ring, and she screamed and twisted her head away.

A thud from the corner, a soft hand on her face and a woman's voice. "It's okay Kathryn, it's over now."

She opened her eyes to find Hazel leaning over her, untying her wrists. Raising her head, she saw Duncan's body slumped in a heap, blood spattering the wall, and Hazel's rifle propped against the bed. After she loosened her bindings, Kathryn sat up and hugged her, tears streaming down her face.

Hazel soothed, "Go find Jamie, I'll get help."

Kathryn fled from the house on jelly legs into the storm, her breathing torn and weak as she stumbled through the dark. Meg darted into view, barked sharply and turned. She followed the dog who ran to the row of outbuildings near the big house, then paced and yelped in front of the game store. Using both hands, she wrenched open the door and fumbled for the light switch. The strip lighting flickered and illuminated a scene from hell that knocked the breath from her.

With a cry, she flew towards Jamie, and touched his face. Deathly pale, and streaked with blood, he didn't stir. Meg licked at him as Kathryn pulled the chain, slowly lowering him to the ground. She crouched beside him and cradled his head in her arms. Rocking him, she wept, great sobs racking her body.

As she held him, he opened his eyes and whispered, "Kathryn."

Through floods of tears, she blubbed "Oh thank God, you're alive."

As she undid his bindings, a noise behind drew her attention and she twisted round to see Marcus and Ruth stood in the doorway. There was a rifle in Marcus's hand.

"Good God above, what's happened?" said Marcus, as Ruth crouched beside Kathryn and examined Jamie's wound.

Kathryn said, "He's been shot, he needs a doctor."

Marcus asked, "Who shot him?"

Kathryn shook her head, "No idea, I just found him." She noticed Marcus and Ruth exchange a look. The soundproofing in Duncan's house probably meant they hadn't heard the shot above the noise of the storm, and didn't know he was dead.

Ruth said, "Vondell left with Elijah but there's a retired surgeon at Inverie."

"Aye, if we hurry, we'll get through before it's impassable," said Marcus surveying the covering of snow on the ground.

Kathryn looked from one to the other, trusting neither. But what choice did she have? There was no one else and if she left Jamie here, he'd die for sure. He was ashen and drenched in blood, the stone floor awash with it. "Help me get him into the car," she said.

Marcus passed the rifle to Ruth, scooped his hand under Jamie's waist and lifted him. Jamie groaned and swayed as he struggled to his feet. Kathryn ducked under his good shoulder and supported him as Marcus helped him to the Defender. Ruth opened the back door and Marcus jumped in, dragged Jamie into the rear of the vehicle and laid him on the floor. Kathryn leapt in beside him, along with Meg, as the Colquhouns climbed into the front. Marcus took the wheel and gunned the engine and the Defender lurched over the rough trail away from Hourn House.

Cradling Jamie's head in her lap, she stroked his face as he grimaced up at her. She said, "Hang in there, we'll get you to a doctor."

A tear ran down Jamie's face as he whispered, "I love you baby."

Fighting back sobs, she blubbed, "I love you too. Please don't leave me."

He'd passed out.

"Is there a first aid kit?" she asked.

Marcus reached into the glove compartment and passed her a green box with a white cross on it.

Ruth shot Marcus a look and then, with a mirthless laugh, turned to Kathryn and said, "Honey, there's no point. Did you really think you were going to walk away from this?"

Ignoring the pit of fear in her stomach, Kathryn fought to remain calm and pulled wadding from the first aid kit and pressed it onto Jamie's shoulder. Blood seeped through in seconds and she grabbed more and held it firmly in place. His pallor reminded her of the colour of Jean's body. Kathryn battled against the tears that threatened to overwhelm her. For his sake, when he needed her most, she needed to become strong like Moniker.

Fake it until you become it.

With a venomous smile, Ruth said, "You should have accepted Duncan's offer, you could have been happy with him."

She hissed, "I'd rather die with Jamie."

"You'll get your wish dear. Tell us, who are you really?"

"Kathryn Campbell, wife of Jamie Campbell, your estate manager."

Ruth shook her head in disbelief. "I think not. Duncan told me what he found in your art case."

The Defender skidded and Marcus battled with the wheel to keep it on the road. The snow was falling heavily and they could see only a few feet in front.

"At least tell me why," said Kathryn.

"Oh honey, you know why. We're doing God's work and sometimes in doing so, good people get killed."

"You really believe that killing millions of people, including many in your own congregation, is God's work?"

Ruth twisted to meet her eye. "Of course, I do. As a species, we can't go on like this, it's unsustainable. We need to thin the herd and a virus is God's way of calling the old and weak unto Him so the young may thrive. But we humans interfered with His work, and governments made the wrong choices during the pandemic. They vaccinated the elderly and those in care homes first when these people should have been sacrificed to protect the young. We can't let that happen again."

Marcus said, "It's like deer, you have to cull the population or you put the entire herd at risk."

Kathryn turned to Ruth and asked, "Is this all because your son died?"

Ruth's eyes hardened, her expression so hostile it sent a shiver down Kathryn's spine. Ruth bit out, "I believe my son's sacrifice was God's way of guiding me to fulfil this duty. It wasn't Covid that took him from me. He had cancer but had the hospital not been so overwhelmed treating patients who'd have died anyway, he'd have got the life-saving operation he needed. The bible's very clear about our life span being three score years and ten."

"Is that why you had Finlay kill your mother-in-law?"

Ruth gave a dark chuckle. "Ah, I see you've done your homework.

Of course. I couldn't possibly stand back and watch that horrible old woman get her vaccine while my husband and son lay cold in their graves. If you'd a child, you'd understand."

"Christ, you're a pair of sickos!"

Marcus slammed on the brakes and the vehicle skidded to a halt. "This is far enough."

Unease curled around her, thick and heavy, as she realised this was the end of the road for her and Jamie. Heart thumping in her chest and tears flowing down her cheeks, she kissed Jamie as Marcus wrenched open the back door and pulled her from it. She kicked and punched him and he threw her to the ground before grabbing Jamie by the collar and heaving him out. Meg nipped at his ankles and he kicked her.

Mercifully, thought Kathryn, Jamie couldn't feel a thing. She watched helplessly as Marcus hooked his arms under Jamie's, dragged him several metres beyond the verge and laid him out in the snow. Ruth passed Marcus the rifle then, before climbing back into the truck, she said to him, "Be quick about it dear."

Marcus waved the rifle at Kathryn and forced her to stand beside Jamie's inert body.

"You don't need to do this Marcus," she pleaded. "It's not too late. Ruth's twisted you into believing this is God's work but deep down you know it's a mortal sin. Don't risk your soul to eternal damnation."

Looking her in the eye, he snarled. "On your knees."

She sank down and reached for Jamie's hand. Pulse thrumming in her ears, she closed her eyes as he raised the rifle, and she beseeched God to save them.

Marcus hesitated then growled, "Damn it, fall to the ground."

As Kathryn fell face forward into the snow, Marcus let off two rounds which thunked harmlessly into the ground to her right. Afraid to move and with her heart racing, she heard the car door slam and the vehicle turn and speed off.

After a moment, shaking, she crawled to Jamie's unconscious body. Cradling his head, she searched for a pulse at his neck. Barely able to feel with her freezing hands, she felt a weak beat beneath her fingertips. The snow began to coat their hair and clothes and she knew if she didn't find shelter soon, they'd die of hypothermia. That's if he didn't bleed to death first. Glancing round, she saw nothing that offered protection; they were in the middle of the moor without a rock or a mound for cover.

Using both arms, she scooped snow towards her to form a low wall around them. Wet and heavy, the snow formed easily into shape and she rolled it into a ball, as if making a snow man. She repeated this until she'd several large balls arranged in a horseshoe-shape around Jamie, with a gap at his feet. Packing the edges with more snow, she formed a shield around him and as much of a roof as possible. Before crawling in beside him, she looked around. There were no lights, only the sound of the howling wind as it whipped at her hair.

Shivering uncontrollably now, she fell to her knees, pressed her palms together and prayed. "Please God, help us. Save Jamie, and I promise I will open my heart to you." The wind blew her tears away along with her prayer.

Exhausted and drowsy, she slipped in beside him and covered Jamie with as much of her body as she could. She was barely conscious as Meg lay down on Jamie's other side and whined.

As the blizzard roared overhead, Kathryn passed out.

EXODUS

"And above all things have fervent love for one another, for love will cover a multitude of sins."

— *1 PETER 4:8*

Jamie

Beeping. Voices. Footsteps on vinyl. Smell of disinfectant. Dull throb of pain.

Jamie opened his eyes, blinking in the glare of the overhead light. He looked at the needles, tubes and sensors stuck on him, and the flickering monitors around him. His mouth felt as though it was full of wire wool and he swallowed painfully. He turned his head and Kathryn's beautiful face focused into view. She sat in a chair next to the bed with her nose in a book, and he tried saying her name but only managed a grunting noise.

She sprang up and stood beside him. Touching his hand, she said, "Oh Jamie, I thought I'd lost you."

He chuckled then winced. "I'm not going anywhere baby," he rasped.

"You in pain? Want me to fetch a nurse?"

Knowing morphine would knock him out, he said, "Just water."

He drank in her features as he sipped from the beaker she held to his lips. After a few mouthfuls, he lay back. "Where am I, and what happened?"

"Private clinic in Fort William. You've been here two days. They've pumped you full of painkillers. How d'you feel?"

He grimaced, "Wonderful. How did I get here?"

Perching carefully beside him, she took his hand in hers. "How much do you remember?"

He thought for a few moments. "Hmm, remember Duncan shooting me and hanging me up like a turkey. Nothing after."

She told him about Duncan's abduction of her, Hazel's rescue, and Marcus and Ruth dumping them on the moor to die. Fury coursed through him as she described Duncan's plan to marry her and hold her captive, and Ruth's warped reasoning behind their plot to kill millions.

She said, "Marcus intended to shoot us but, in the end, he couldn't do it."

"How d'you get us off the moor?"

She shook her head. "It's bizarre but it turns out someone hacked a US military satellite and a drone, then sent images of what was happening to Keith and the team in London with our coordinates and a message about preventing another Glencoe massacre. Julien had them scramble an RAF helicopter from Lossiemouth."

He gawped at her. "Bloody hell, and I don't remember any of it. Who was the hacker?"

"Pandora. Julien said the Yanks went ballistic and arrested her. She's facing a lengthy sentence."

He raised an incredulous eyebrow, "You think it was her, the same one who betrayed you?"

Holding his gaze, she said, "All the evidence points to her."

Jamie laughed then grunted in pain. "Not what I asked. C'mon, fess up Moniker, who was it really?" When she didn't respond, he added softly, "I won't say anything … after all we owe them our lives."

"Scotty."

"Your mate who disappeared into thin air?"

She nodded. "Turns out he's been hiding in Scotland and keeping tabs on me. That's what the bird of prey was we kept seeing, it was one of his drones."

"And the Colquhouns?"

"I regained consciousness on the journey back to Fort William and told the officer onboard about the plot. At first, he didn't believe me, thought I was delirious until he got Keith on the line. Keith called in that SAS unit who were training nearby for a 'hard stop' and they stormed the place. The Feds have Elijah and Vondell in custody and have seized Hart Biotech's assets."

"Wow" he said, flinching in pain.

"That's not all. Angus didn't get on the plane. He and Cameron ran off together. He's in custody but Julien reckons he'll not do time now that he's singing like a canary. Angus told us Duncan was the one who dumped Jean on the moor to die, and who shot Finlay. And Mhairi's alive. She hated life in Lewis and was terrified of Duncan, so she ran away. Fitz found her. She's married and lives in France."

"That's a great result."

"Everyone's pleased about it. Julien's outside pacing up and down the corridor, desperate to speak to you. He doesn't know you're conscious."

Jamie grimaced, "Think I'll have that morphine now baby, the bastard can wait."

Smiling, she pressed a gentle kiss to his lips. "Coming right up."

He whispered, "I love you," and she repeated his words back.

Jamie spent the next few days in hospital, with Kathryn refusing to leave his side until the nursing staff kicked her out each evening. Julien had arranged for her to stay in a serviced apartment nearby while MI5 carried out a full debrief. Jamie knew that, once he'd recovered his strength, they'd want to interview him too.

He asked about Meg and she told him that one of the helicopter crew had taken pity on her and put her onboard after she'd refused to leave their side. She'd smuggled her into the apartment and was intending taking the dog home with her. He wondered whether she meant back to her grandmother's house in Glasgow, and cursed himself for not talking to her earlier about their future plans.

After a week, he felt well enough to walk around the hospital room although his shoulder was still painful. He was stood gazing out of the window over Fort William when Kathryn appeared.

"It's good to see you up and about," she said, stretching up to kiss him.

He lay on the bed propped up on pillows, surprised at how tired he felt after such little exertion, and she plopped into the armchair beside him.

"I have some news," she said, excitement in her tone.

He listened as she told him about the job offer from Fitz, and his heart sank. It was everything she'd dreamed about; a well-paid civil service job using her skills, and the chance to study part-time for a degree in cybersecurity, all paid for by the British Government.

But not if she was in a relationship with a fellow MI5 officer, even one in a different division. Jamie knew the rules; they'd been lectured about them plenty, before and during the operation in Knoydart, and there were no exceptions.

In the eighties and nineties, Special Branch as it was known then had been plagued by scandals involving undercover operators. As well as committing crimes, UCs had been in sexual relationships with targets, and some had fathered children whom they'd later abandoned. The resulting media storm meant they'd had to clean up their act and the current rules and regulations were the result. Now, the mere sniff of any impropriety would result in disciplinary action and possible dismissal. If it were known that he and Kathryn were in a relationship, there'd be no career in MI5 for either of them.

As he listened to her gabble about the work she'd be doing with Fitz and his team, despair wrung itself around his gut. She beamed as she described the university course, and he shoved a hand through his hair.

"Hey are you okay?" she asked, "are you in pain?"

He shook his head, hoping his face didn't betray his mounting disappointment. She took his hand and he looked at her as she talked about the future, unaware this spelled the end of his own career in MI5.

"Jamie, say something please."

He forced his lips into a smile. "I'm really pleased for you, it's everything you ever wanted, and you deserve it."

Her brow furrowed. "What's wrong? You're acting strange."

"Nothing, just worn-out baby."

After kissing him goodbye, she left him to rest. As soon as she was gone, he picked up the phone and called Julien.

∼

Kathryn

Julien phoned the following morning to give Kathryn the news. She refused to believe what he was telling her. As soon as she'd hung up, she finished dressing and hurried to the hospital to find Jamie sitting up in bed reading a newspaper. He smiled as she entered.

Hands on hips, she stood at the foot of the bed and said, "Julien's just told me you've quit. Is it true?"

Putting aside the newspaper, he shot her a contrite look and reached for her hand. "Yes, it's true."

Her mouth fell open as she perched beside him. "Why Jamie?" There was desperation in her voice.

He gave her a half smile. "Because I want you to have this opportunity but if they know we're a couple, they won't offer you the job." She went to say something and he silenced her with a look, "the only thing I care about is you. I don't care where I work as long as I'm with you."

"Oh Jamie, I feel like such a fool for not realising what Fitz's offer meant. I'm not taking it if it means you can't work for Julien. I know how much you want this. It was your dream, not mine."

"No, I can't do that to you Kathryn. You deserve this chance, and I'd be selfish to rob you of it."

She gulped at him. "And I can't rob you of yours. I'm not taking it."

"And you'll regret it a few years down the line and end up resenting me."

Clutching his hand, she looked at him through wet lashes. "No, you don't get it, do you? I want you to be happy." She whispered, "I love you."

"Oh baby, I love you too and that's why I've quit." Cupping her face, he said, "I want you to have everything."

"I feel terrible that you have to give up your career though."

He laughed. "Hardly, I'll apply to the Met, and you'll be the best cybersecurity officer in the service." He took a deep breath and fixed her with his piercing azure gaze. "There's something else I want to ask you."

She stared at him, confused.

He stroked his thumb down her cheek and looked into her eyes. "Oh hell, I wanted to do this properly, but I can't wait any longer. It's killing me not knowing what the future holds." He paused then said, "Will you marry me?"

She put a hand to her chest and opened her mouth to speak but no words came out.

"I love you and I want you to be my wife, Kathryn. I miss waking up with you in my arms, I miss that you're not there by my side, and I don't want to spend another day without you."

Swallowing the lump in her throat, she whispered, "Yes Jamie, I will marry you."

Beaming, he kissed her. When it turned into something hungrier, they broke apart panting. Risking the wrath of the nurses, she snuggled into the bed beside him.

She'd never felt so happy.

Jamie

It was several days until he was discharged from hospital with boxes of painkillers and an exercise plan from the physiotherapist. After saying goodbye to the nursing staff, they walked the short distance to the apartment where Meg gave him warm welcoming licks.

Placing his bag down in the entrance hall, she asked if he wanted coffee. Feeling the anticipation he'd been carrying around all morning about to explode, he grabbed her hand and chuckled, "Where's the bedroom?"

She grinned in surprise. "But your shoulder?"

He drew her to him, "I don't need my shoulder for what I've in mind."

Ignoring the forlorn look Meg gave them, he pulled her into the bedroom and closed the door, their bodies a tangle of mouths, tongues and hands.

After, they lay on their side and gazed at one another for a long time. He loved her so much and couldn't wait to make her his wife.

Stroking her face, he asked, "When do you want to get married?"

"Is tomorrow too soon?"

He chuckled. "So eager, but it'll take a few weeks to get a licence. Where d'you want to tie the knot? I thought you might want to do it in style."

She looked at him hesitantly. "If I said I wanted to get married in church would you think I'd gone crazy?"

"No, if that's what you want. But I thought you and God weren't on speaking terms."

"We weren't until I got down on my knees and begged her to spare your life with the promise I'd listen in future. I think I should uphold my end of the bargain."

Jamie smirked, "You gonnae promise to obey?"

She narrowed her eyes at him. "I've not gone that native."

Laughing, he pressed a tender kiss to her lips. "Then we'll marry in church. I'll even come with you on Sundays. If the sermons are half as entertaining as Marcus's, I'll enjoy your reaction."

Mimicking Marcus, she said, "Fornication!"

Jamie nuzzled into her. "Mmm, talking of which …"

∿

He awoke next morning and reached for her, flinching at the pain in his shoulder. When he found she was gone, he sat up in a panic. Had he dreamt last night? Realising he was in the apartment and hearing sounds from the kitchen, he slumped back on the pillows with a relieved sigh.

Gazing up at the ceiling, he smiled as he thought about their lovemaking the previous night. It just got better and better. He loved the bones of her and yearned to touch her again, and just as he was about to get up and drag her back to bed, she appeared in the doorway carrying a tray with two mugs and a box of painkillers. She smiled at him as she placed it on the nightstand. Reaching for the soft belt on her dressing gown, he pulled her to him. She tumbled onto the mattress squealing as he rolled on top of her and kissed her hard.

Feeling something hard at his hip, he reached down and pulled a sheaf of papers from the pocket of her gown.

"What's this?" he asked, looking at the document entitled *MI5 Covert Intelligence and Undercover Regulations.*

"So … I've been doing some reading," she said.

They sat up, propped against the pillows, and she passed him his coffee and tablets.

Pointing at the document, she said, "I've been through every line of this, and the contract of employment, and there are plenty of rules forbidding colleagues from having a relationship but I can't find a single one about spouses."

He arched a brow. "So, there's nothing they can do if we're married?"

She grinned. "Not the way it's worded. I reckon the possibility never occurred to whoever wrote these; probably some fusty old Etonian. So, there's no need for you to resign, or for me not to take the job with Fitz. We'll be married by the time we start in six weeks."

Laughing, he said, "Daresay it'll raise a few eyebrows." He placed down their coffee cups, threw the document aside and grabbed her. "You're very clever Ms Sinclair."

She giggled as he opened her robe and carpeted her with kisses. "It's Mrs Denton to you."

He glanced up at her. "Jesus, you have gone native! You want to change your name?"

"Too right, I want to make damn sure every female in Christendom knows you belong to me."

"You have nothing to fear Mrs Denton, I am yours and yours alone."

∾

Kathryn

They were married four weeks later on a wet Saturday afternoon at the church close to Kathryn's grandmother's home in Glasgow. It was a small affair with Jamie's sister, her husband as best man, and their daughter as flower girl. Jamie wore his kilt for the occasion, and Kathryn a simple white dress.

She liked Jamie's family and his niece Heather was every bit as adorable as he'd described. His sister had agreed to look after Meg for the week so, after the wedding breakfast, Jamie and Kathryn said their goodbyes and headed off on honeymoon.

They travelled in Jamie's recently purchased silver Land Rover Defender. "Something old enough you can't hack", he'd joked. They spent their wedding night in the Royal Scotsman hotel in Glasgow where they'd first shared a bed together.

Jamie had arranged the rest of the honeymoon as a surprise and refused to say where they were going, only that she should pack for a week and bring her passport.

Next morning, when he took the motorway cut off for the airport, she asked, "So where are you taking me Mr Denton?"

"That, Mrs Denton, is top secret and eyes-only."

She arched a challenging brow. "If you don't tell me I'll sing Beyonce songs at the top of my voice until you do."

Raising his hands briefly in mock surrender, he chuckled, "Okay, okay, we're off to Paris. It's time we replaced that fake photograph with a real one."

She squealed, "How romantic."

"There's lots to see, I hope you've brought comfy shoes."

Leaning over, she pressed a kiss to his cheek. "I'm not sure I'll be doing much sightseeing. I have years and years of jiggling to make up for husband."

He laughed. "Then the sooner we get there wife, the sooner we can make a start on that."

EPILOGUE

— EXODUS 21:24

Kathryn

5 months later, Glasgow

She wanted to see the fear in his eyes when she did it.

Kathryn had returned to her grandmother's house for a couple of days to finalise its sale. She was staying in Jamie's bachelor pad, as she still thought of it, in the heart of Glasgow's merchant city which they'd decided to keep as an investment.

They'd settled into their new life in the south east of England, renting a quaint cottage in Buckinghamshire on the edge of a village surrounded by farmland. They walked Meg there most evenings after work, although the dog accompanied Kathryn into the office in London. Meg took her duties as head of security at MI5's Operation Centre seriously, but was otherwise content to lie at Kathryn's feet.

Following his appointment to A Branch at Julien's behest, Jamie had been desk-bound while his shoulder mended and he recovered from plastic surgery on his scar. The Welfare department had approached him and offered to cover his medical costs, which they justified on the basis the scar made him too distinctive as a surveillance operator. After a consultation with a top Harley Street surgeon, he'd gone under the knife and, although his face and painful skin graft were still healing, Jamie was delighted with the result.

Kathryn was not looking forward to his first deployment away from her, but at least she had her work and part-time study to occupy her. Fitz was shaping up to be a good boss, and she was enjoying getting to know the others on the team.

Their marriage had certainly raised a few eyebrows, but it had also resulted in a change to the rules to permit partners to work together, and they'd learned that both Julien and Pia had supported this.

However, there was one last loose end Kathryn wanted to tie up before she continued her new life, but it was not something she wanted Jamie to know about. She felt guilty about keeping it from him as they'd no secrets from one another, but she decided it was in both their interests that he never learn of it. In any case, this was a job for Moniker, not Kathryn.

She'd learned of her step-father Phil's early release from prison a few months ago through the Victim Notification Scheme; a perfunctory letter that punched a hole in her gut. Compassionate grounds it said, due to a serious and life-shortening heart condition. *Bless*.

MI5's Vetting team had called her in to discuss his release; there was little they didn't know about their employees but Kathryn was determined they would never find out what she'd planned. She'd learned enough about their surveillance techniques to ensure she wasn't caught. Since his release, she'd been keeping tabs on him as the Scottish Prison Service put more thought into the security of their establishments than around their servers. She'd tracked him to a halfway house in a Glasgow suburb. She wondered if the neighbours knew they'd murderers and rapists living on their doorstep. Perhaps a small job for Grey Nemesis, not that she'd anything to do with the group now she was one of Her Majesty's civil servants, although she and Scotty kept in regular contact.

Phil had recently left this accommodation for a bedsit in the south side of the city. Worryingly though, she discovered he'd been cultivating a relationship with a divorcee who had a nine-year-old daughter. After eavesdropping on their messages and phone calls, it was clear Phil was grooming the woman to get access to her child, and he was about to move into the family home. It was this that prompted her actions today.

Phil had been assigned a social worker called Kate Anderson who, after a quick browse of her case files, was a busy one. Finding a suitable location was more difficult but, after a scout of the area, Kathryn settled for a café a couple of streets from the bedsit. Shabby with sticky banquette seating and greasy menus, it had no CCTV and few customers. She spoofed Kate's email address and sent him an invite to meet her there at 11 o'clock when she knew it'd be quiet.

She trailed Phil from the bedsit to the cafe, feeling calmer than anticipated. Keeping her grey hoody over her face, she sat in a booth on the opposite side of the café so she could watch without being obvious. After paying for a latte, she pulled out her laptop from her backpack and went to work. She'd spent the previous evening testing the protocol to ensure everything worked, so now it was just a case of waiting for her opportunity.

Phil ordered a fried breakfast then buried his nose in the Sun newspaper. He still looked much the same, just older and heavier but with the same mean eyes, and she wondered if he'd recognise her so easily. She'd soon find out.

She glanced at the time, knowing she still had a few hours before she met Jamie. He was driving up from London with Meg. Keith and Debra had invited them to stay in Morar, where Keith had bought the cottage by the beach he'd rented, ahead of his imminent retirement. She couldn't wait to be reunited with Jamie since it was the first time they'd been apart since he'd been in hospital after his operation. She hoped he'd remembered to pack her art case.

While she waited for her moment, she switched her screen to display the article in the Guardian newspaper which Jamie had sent her a link to. Entitled *Creating Heaven after Hell's Glen*, it featured an interview with Hazel and Simon McNab who'd given an interview about their plans to set up a new religious community on the Isle of

Lewis. Their ambition was to create an equal, inclusive and diverse Christian culture in which men and women had an equal say in the running of the church and their daily lives. There was a quote from Hazel stating that, despite the dreadful scandal which had finished the Ehrlich Society and their tenure in Knoydart, God had sent them an angel who'd guided them as to what should replace the Society.

The café began to empty leaving only Phil and her remaining, and the waitress had disappeared through to the kitchen at the rear. Flicking back to the shell running on her computer, she took a deep breath, lowered her hood and stared straight at Phil. His jaw dropped as a flicker of recognition crossed his face. Holding his gaze, she tapped a key. Seconds passed and he flinched and clutched a hand to his chest. His flicker of recognition changed to one of fear.

Calmly, she stood and said, "That's for Mum."

She took a last sip of coffee, gathered her things and left the café to the sound of smashing crockery.

It never ceased to amaze Moniker what people thought was a good idea to connect to the internet. But you'd think a surgeon might have the sense to change the default password on a pacemaker.

Fake it until you become it.

— THE END —

A NOTE TO THE READER

Dear Reader,

I hope you enjoyed reading *Hell's Glen* as much as I enjoyed writing it. I welcome feedback from my readers, and I read each and every one of your reviews. So, if it's not too much trouble, please leave me a review on Amazon or at Goodreads.

Love,

HJ x

ACKNOWLEDGMENTS

I want to thank my family for putting up with me while I wrote this novel since my mind, like the unfortunate Duncan's, often existed in a parallel universe of my own making during this time. My memories of this world are fond ones though and, although you'll find Loch Hourn bordering the Knoydart Peninsula, Hell's Glen is a figment of my imagination.

They say it takes a village to raise a child; well, it also takes a village to write a book and I've a number of good friends and neighbours to thank: Declan for your cybersecurity expertise; Gail for sharing your knowledge and experience after a long career as a detective; Corrine and Helen for listening to me jaw on about my book during our dog walks. I also want to thank all my wonderful beta readers and tutors at Edinburgh Napier University.

As a technical writer who's worked in cybersecurity for over 30 years, I've come across many amusing and interesting hacks, some of which I include in Hell's Glen (yes, the sex toy hacks are real!). If you'd like to find out more, see Ken Munro Hardware Hacking - DVRs and Dildos on YouTube. For more about the world of undercover policing and MI5, I recommend Undercover: The True Story of Britain's Secret Police by Paul Lewis and Rob Evans, and I Spy and Soldier Spy by Tom Marcus (I couldn't put them down).

Printed in Great Britain
by Amazon

82868886R00181